PRAISE FOR M. L. BUCHMAN

Top 10 Romance of 2012, 2015, and 2016.

— BOOKLIST: THE NIGHT IS MINE, HOT POINT, HEART
STRIKE

One of our favorite authors.

— RT BOOK REVIEWS

Buchman has catapulted his way to the top tier of my favorite authors.

— FRESH FICTION

A favorite author of mine. I'll read anything that carries his name, no questions asked. Meet your new favorite author!

— THE SASSY BOOKSTER, FLASH OF FIRE

M.L. Buchman is guaranteed to get me lost in a good story.

— THE READING CAFE, WAY OF THE WARRIOR: NSDQ

I love Buchman's writing. His vivid descriptions bring everything to life in an unforgettable way.

— PURE JONEL, HOT POINT

THE COMPLETE WHERE DREAMS - VOL 2 OF 2

A SEATTLE ROMANCE

M. L. BUCHMAN

Buchman Bookworks

CONTENTS

Other works by M. L. Buchman:

The Night Stalkers
MAIN FLIGHT
The Night Is Mine
I Own the Dawn
Wait Until Dark
Take Over at Midnight
Light Up the Night
Bring On the Dusk
By Break of Day
WHITE HOUSE HOLIDAY
Daniel's Christmas
Frank's Independence Day
Peter's Christmas
Zachary's Christmas
Roy's Independence Day
Damien's Christmas
AND THE NAVY
Christmas at Steel Beach
Christmas at Peleliu Cove
5E
Target of the Heart
Target Lock on Love
Target of Mine

Firehawks
MAIN FLIGHT
Pure Heat
Full Blaze
Hot Point
Flash of Fire
Wild Fire
SMOKEJUMPERS
Wildfire at Dawn
Wildfire at Larch Creek
Wildfire on the Skagit

Delta Force
Target Engaged
Heart Strike
Wild Justice

Where Dreams
Where Dreams are Born
Where Dreams Reside
Where Dreams Are of Christmas
Where Dreams Unfold
Where Dreams Are Written

Eagle Cove
Return to Eagle Cove
Recipe for Eagle Cove
Longing for Eagle Cove
Keepsake for Eagle Cove

Henderson's Ranch
Nathan's Big Sky

Love Abroad
Heart of the Cotswolds: England

Dead Chef Thrillers
Swap Out!
One Chef!
Two Chef!

Deities Anonymous
Cookbook from Hell: Reheated
Saviors 101

SF/F Titles
The Nara Reaction
Monk's Maze
the Me and Elsie Chronicles

Strategies for Success (NF)
Managing Your Inner Artist/Writer
Estate Planning for Authors

To my Lady Fair:
My thanks for the calendar,
And the journeys we shared
to explore the settings of this tale.
And to my sister:
A tintypist.
Who taught me the love of photography
in the darkroom we shared as teens.

WHERE DREAMS UNFOLD

CHAPTER 1

*P*errin Williams hung up the dress bags and collapsed onto the tattered gray sofa in her design studio. Exhaustion still rippled through her in familiar waves. She felt both the dull ache and the immense satisfaction that typically coursed through her after an exceptionally long bout of clothing design, her favorite form of play.

The gentle light of the warm late-April-in-Seattle morning filled her boutique and design studio with a soft glow that made her want to just sprawl here and giggle madly. Somehow, against all odds, her life had brought her to work and create in this wonderful, safe space.

This time the exhaustion had been earned at the wedding of one of her two best friends. "Jo" Thompson had married Angelo Parrano at an event of grand proportions in the heart of the Pike Place Market.

Many of the Seattle elite had attended. More than a few had commissioned dresses from Perrin's Glorious Garb. Which elicited another giggle that might have been a chortle of self-satisfaction.

No one around yet to tell her if her tired brain had tipped over the edge to gloating, so she let herself revel in the wonder of it all.

To see her designs flashing among the wedding crowd had filled her heart in a way that had left her speechless more than once last night. Because it was a Market wedding, after all, Jo was the new director of the Pike Place Market, the finest street musicians had added their music—including some great dancing music from the rolling-piano guy. The food was perhaps the finest Maximilien's had ever made. Perrin had put a giant sign on the kitchen door, "Angelo not allowed past this point." The groom, one of Seattle's most highly-acclaimed chefs, had it coming. Everyone, including Perrin, had made sure he was reminded of that sign often throughout the night.

The bride and groom had looked so beautiful dancing beneath the moonlight. They swayed together out on the patio overlooking Elliott Bay, a backdrop of scooting ferries and the brilliant glow of the ice-capped Olympic Mountains beyond. The couple had looked so in love. So happy.

Perrin shot to her feet and paced around the studio. She'd gone past tired and tipped right over into hyperactively awake. At some point soon she'd crash for a day or two, but not yet.

She unzipped the first bag. Jo's dress of shimmering pale blue cascaded forth. She'd have it cleaned and properly boxed before Jo and Angelo returned from a week in Hawaii. Neither of them had ever been there, and a week was all either of them could afford to be away at the moment. April was perfect weather in both Seattle and the resort on Kauai's eastern shore, especially known for relentlessly pampering its guests.

Perrin pulled Jo's dress in front of her and posed before the tall antique tri-fold mirror of beveled glass and dark oak. She turned on the lights, the early morning sun didn't reach into this corner of her studio. The pale blue had complimented Jo's Alaskan-dark complexion and flowing black hair. There had been no need for the dress to accent the curves, Jo's body had provided those perfectly.

Perrin tilted her head critically, and then had to roll it around a bit to loosen the crick from a serious lack of sleep. The dress wouldn't do at all on her own pale skin and slender frame. She hung it on the "to be cleaned" rack.

From the second bag she pulled out the bridesmaid dresses that she and Cassidy Knowles had worn. They had been as softly gold as the bride's dress had been softly blue. The gold had picked up high-lights in the best man's suit that Perrin had dressed on Russell.

She'd also accented the mother-of-the-bride's dress with just a bit of the soft gold as well, which had made the photographs really pop. Russell had shared a few tips with her that only a professional fashion photographer would know. Seeing Eloise giving away her previously estranged daughter had brought tears to everyone's eyes.

Perrin sighed and hung the other dresses beside the wedding gown. Cassidy and Russell. Jo and Angelo. That left only Perrin without a man anywhere on the horizon. Part of her didn't want one.

"Avert!"

It was like some order from a space-captain's chair, "Evasive maneuver delta." "Avert!" It always made her smile, and because it was such a silly and simple thought it usually did track her away from thinking of her life prior to meeting Cassidy and Jo in college.

She didn't want a man because of the nightmare example of her family, but she also desperately did want one. One like Cassidy or Jo had found. The rough edges of Russell, the sensitivity of Angelo. And as long as she was making a list…

A knock on her door had her checking herself in the mirror: a simple light wool skirt appropriate for fall and a bright spring shirt topped with a summery sheer batik scarf. She was missing a season. Which one? Oh, winter. She really was tired, something to do with not having slept except for occasional catnaps in the last four or five days.

"Wilson. Please tell me this is one of your crazy jokes." Except the Director of the Emerald City Opera was not given to jokes, at least not practical ones. Bill Cullen glared at the display window of the fashion designer's storefront that Wilson had led him to. The stuff in the window was cute, urban. He guessed it would draw a woman passing by into the shop, just as well as a dozen other places that he seemed to pass every day. They cropped up, more dreams than solid basis in either business acumen or common sense. Then they went away and someone else moved in the next day with their hopes and dreams clutched tight.

He turned away and studied the neighborhood.

Wilson Jervis had dragged him into the heart of the Belltown area to meet a designer. The old brick building did nothing to inspire his confidence. After Pioneer Square, this was one of the oldest portions of downtown Seattle, just north of the business core. Most of the area had been rebuilt, turned into condos and ad-agency-slick small business fronts. She was on a block that had somehow been bypassed by the neighborhood's recent rejuvenation and gentrification.

Its age showed in many ways, darkened brickwork, cracks in the sidewalk. An abandoned tattoo parlor across the street with a "Half-off for Two" sign that might have once lured customers, but was now superseded by the "Out of Business" sign across the glass. Next to it, a small bike shop looked to be doing okay. Belltown wasn't dangerous the way Pioneer Square had been before its restoration, this part of it was just old.

"My wife found her. Trust me," was all the reassurance the rotund icon of the Seattle theater scene offered. He'd been leading the Opera with a confident and mostly unquestioned hand for decades. He'd taken a small company on the verge of insolvency and turned it into one of the five largest opera houses in the U.S., and one of the most respected in the world.

All that still didn't make Bill trust Wilson about this. They were mounting a new opera and it was up to Bill as stage manager to see that it happened perfectly, or at least on schedule and near budget. It was his job to make sure that every piece from set design to costumes to lighting came together by opening night, only six weeks away. What they were doing in Belltown, too early on a Monday morning, was beyond him. Well, not totally beyond him.

Carlotta Gianelli had thrown one of her world-famous tantrums and stalked out yesterday to fly back to Milan and now they needed a costume designer who could perform a six-month miracle in only six weeks. Gianelli had burned up over four months and achieved nothing except some sketches that no one liked or could interpret.

He glared back at the shop as Wilson knocked again.

The glass door bore bold-colored lettering so close to graffiti that he could barely read it. Except he could. The "P" and "G" were actually oversized, ornate letters in the Victorian style. Perrin's Glorious Garb, the second two words attached to the same "G" were actually artful slashes that he recognized as a variety of fashion styles ranging over the last fifty years, somehow done so that they made a unified whole. What he'd almost dismissed as tacky was actually a deeply nuanced understanding of design.

He peered into the window. The shop was dark, but a light shone in back. He spotted a waif coming through the store toward them, silhouetted by the light behind and pulling on a hat despite the warm day.

"We're not open yet," she called through the glass but was already unlocking the door.

She was dressed like some teenager that had been thrown bodily into a closet and crawled forth wearing whatever she fell against. She wore a form-fitting silk turtleneck of new-grass green, an unlikely mauve skirt that evoked autumn swirled in pleats about her calves, and a filmy batik scarf the red-orange of a summer sunset that looked as if it had attempted to throttle her. All mismatched and crazy, the unlikely ensemble somehow looked good on her in a way he didn't care enough about to attempt to fathom. She'd topped it off with a knitwear winter hat with earflaps and a ridiculous pom-pom pulled down over pale-blond hair that brushed her narrow shoulders.

Wilson introduced them and talked his way into the shop as easily as he'd talked Bill away from the San Francisco Opera four years before.

Adira's death had made Bill a single dad at thirty-three years old. His need to escape "their" city and the needs of their two children had been the biggest factor by far. But Wilson had not played that card. Instead, he'd offered a new and interesting job in a different city, leaving it to be Bill's own realization that such a change was exactly what he needed to do for both himself and his kids. Tricky s.o.b. To this day he still didn't know quite how that had happened.

Bill followed Wilson into the shop, letting the Director deal with the sloppily dressed clerk. The shop had been set up like a 1950s diner, all chromed metal and red leatherette. Mannequins sat in booths in a quirky mash-up of eras. A '20s flapper cozied up with a '50s greaser and a '40s housewife. Yet that wasn't what they were. The housewife's wide, white collar wasn't on the housewife dress, it was on the flapper's, and it distinctly accented the cleavage. The greaser actually sported the classic lines of a '20s linen suit, but sewn in denim and flannel.

He could hear the girl bubbling away at Wilson about something. Sounded like a chickadee mixed up with one of those small singing birds. Disconnected flighty bits that, even if gathered together, wouldn't really communicate much.

The next booth included Victorian brocade set in a modern blazer, and a gown design that would be formal enough for an opera opening night yet remained racy enough for the hottest club. Even studying the piece didn't reveal how the two distinct messages had been combined in a single garment.

He glanced over at the shop girl, wondering when the owner was coming in.

This girl was all arms and legs and nerves. Her slender build was only emphasized by her height. Fingers flashed out to emphasize points, her gestures were twice life size. She made a grand sweeping gesture which suggested she might be a dancer as well.

She had rolled out a short rack which bore a set of dresses, wedding and two bridesmaids, and was showing them to Wilson as he slouched next to a particularly voluptuous mannequin in a Wall Street business suit. Cutting a suit to a full-figured woman was hard, and she'd made the outfit pop; that it was in hot '50s poodle-pink wool only made it more so. Then he focused on the wedding and brides-maid dresses. Exceptionally fine work, yet wholly inappropriate for the stage, as it was a masterpiece of subtlety. He'd bet that the clerk would look good in the gold one.

The Director had really lost it this time. All of these clothes were studies of craftsmanship and nuance. But they weren't costumes, especially not ones that would play to the vast three-thousand seat expanse of the ECO Opera House at Seattle Center.

"Where's the designer?"

"Why?" The woman pulled down her winter cap as if to shield herself.

"We're here to see her for reasons that wholly escape me." Up close the girl wasn't so much of a girl. She was a woman, long and sleek. Her hair a long, thick, pale blond that looked too substantial for so elegant a neck. She looked him nearly in the eye despite, he checked, bare feet.

The hat of garish orange wool, with ridiculous ear flaps, had been pulled down almost far enough to hide her eyes, but they shone brilliant blue past pale lashes.

"Why?" Her voice was soft.

"Why what?"

"Why do the reasons escape you?" There was a real "duh" tone to her voice as if he were the one being exceedingly dense and not the other way around.

"Wilson wants to hire her and I want to tell the woman to her face that there's no way in hell I'll work with her."

She regarded him with those bright blues for so long that he had to fight to not look away. There was a mind behind those eyes. And a force of personality all out of balance with the crazed attire and flighty first, second, and third impression.

"Boy, it's going to really suck being you."

"Why?"

"Because Director Wilson Jervis of the Emerald City Opera has just offered me the contract to design the costumes for *Ascension,* your next opera. And because it sounds like fun, I," she turned briefly to Wilson, "thank you Mr. Jervis, yes" then she turned back to him, "have as of this moment decided to accept. Perrin Williams at your service."

She held out a hand and shook his numb fingers strongly when he held them out in shock like a trained puppy.

She was right, it was going to really suck being him.

"WILSON, you can't do this! What are her credentials? What productions has she designed for?"

Wilson lounged back in one of the booths next to the hot poodle-pink business suit. He propped his feet on the opposite seat next to a mannequin sheathed in a dress of tiny mirrors, like a human disco ball. As Wilson landed his feet there, it shimmered. Rather than the expected heaviness, it was a light fabric that moved easily, catching and changing light. Every breath the wearer took would be dramatic and impossible to look away from.

"Ask her yourself, Bill. She's standing right in front of you. This rude chap is Bill Cullen our Stage Manager. Getting the show up is his responsibility. Picking the right people is mine."

Bill turned to look down at her. Except, it still wasn't down. It was across. And she was no longer on the verge of disappearing into her hat. Now she was very present, watching him. He couldn't quite tell, but she almost looked amused.

"Sorry if I was rude, but—"

"No, Mr. Cullen. I've never designed an opera. I've never even been to one."

All he could do was gasp. He held out his hands to Wilson and the damn man just did one of those seraphic smiles of his. The same smile he'd confronted Bill with four years before when he stole him from San Francisco for the Emerald City Opera.

"Further, Mr. Cullen. I have designed for no movies, plays, dramas in the park, or poetry readings. Though I have attended all of those."

Bill reined himself in. He could hear the disdain in her voice, carefully tempered to slap him back with his own attitude. She'd have made a fine dramatic actress, no use to him on an opera stage, but still a precisely balanced performance.

"Then..." he took a deep breath and felt not the least bit better, no matter how much his daughter insisted it would help him. She'd also told him to try using "please" once in a while. "Then, please, tell me why you think you can do this."

"Would you prefer a list of prior creative works, a sworn deposition, or a demonstration?" She was definitely mocking him.

"A demonstration? What are you talking about?"

"This way." She turned and walked away as if he was just expected to follow along.

He looked at Wilson who simply worked his way back to his feet and moseyed along behind her. Bill cursed under his breath and brought up the rear. She led them through the dimly lit shop and through what had once been the doors to the kitchen.

The shadows were deep here. The only light source was the morning sun, reflected off the tattoo parlor across the street and shining in through the front window and the cook's window.

The mannequins in front of the stove looked so real that he thought they were alive for a moment. Dramatic designer coats indicated this was where the outerwear must be sold. One was an apparently typical black leather coat except for massive red buttons as big around as his palm. There was something odd about the cut, but he couldn't tell in the dim light. The other wore the cape that clearly went with the mirrored gown. It would swirl and flutter and draw every eye until the moment it was removed to reveal the mirrored spectacle form-fit to a woman's body.

There was a theme here. Bill didn't have it until he was following the other two into the walk-in freezer lined with shoes and accessories, and then through another swinging door into the design space beyond.

The common theme was that this woman designed for people who wanted to be noticed. Every single piece of clothing was an absolute attention grabber. On the right woman, they'd be irresistible.

Again, Bill imagined the golden bridesmaid dress on the woman who was now waiting by her cutting table. That would be a vision to behold.

"Tell me about your opera."

Bill looked around the room. He'd been in near enough a hundred of costume design studios over the years. From this woman he'd expected chaos and disarray. Instead, it was one of the neatest and most organized spaces he'd ever seen.

The cutting table was large and immaculate, topped with a green self-healing cutting mat marked in standard one-inch squares with thin yellow lines. Two top-of-the-line sewing machines, a long-arm embroidery machine, and a five-thread serger were lined up along the back window. He almost missed an old Singer Featherweight sitting to one side on a small oak desk with the black, curlicued, wrought-iron base. Not only did it appear well cared for, it was the only one that hadn't been tidied up, as if it were the latest used.

He turned and was confronted by a wall of fabric neatly stored in cubicle shelves that ranged floor to ceiling down the long wall. What-ever else this woman might be, she was serious about her work space.

Bill kicked free a stool from under the edge of the cutting table and sat down next to Wilson, across the table from the designer.

"Well, it is an entirely new opera, not just a new mount."

He saw her confused expression. Great. Time to get remedial. They didn't have time for this. But when he looked at Wilson, the man merely cocked his head in her direction and he was left with no choice but to continue.

"Operas are typically done one of two ways. A packaged opera is one that has been previously designed. We pull everything from storage: sets, costumes, props, and so on. Or we rent someone else's. Sometimes we'll mix it up; rent a set from Houston, but use San Francisco's costumes. All we have to do then is adjust, fit, and perhaps replicate a couple pieces that are too worn or too drastically the wrong size. Then there's a new mount. All new sets and costumes. That's expensive and takes a lot of planning."

"But you said this one was more than that." She had remained standing and he had to look up at her. He wasn't complaining. Despite her incoherent taste in clothing, she was fine-featured and very nice to look at. When was the last time he'd really looked at a woman? There had to be someone in the four years since Adira's death, but he couldn't think of one at the moment.

"Yes. A new opera is a new mount with many additional nightmares because no one has ever staged this opera before. We will be the first to present the work which has been in development for over two years. We will be making a statement that will enter the repertoire of dozens of opera companies—or that disappears quietly taking several million dollars of investment with it. Now you see why you aren't acceptable. You make nice clothes, but that is a whole different matter from costuming a new and successful opera."

PERRIN WASN'T REALLY LISTENING. Wasn't even worrying about the gauntlet she had cast at his feet of a "demonstration" whatever she'd meant by that. She was too tired to make much sense of what Bill Cullen was actually saying.

All she knew was that the page on the sketchpad she'd dropped before her on the cutting table was still blank. A square white hole in a sea of green cutting mat. She started looking around the table for a Yellow Submarine and then stopped herself. Not tired enough to hallucinate…yet.

She didn't care that he kept saying she wasn't qualified, that kind of statement only ever made her that much more determined. Too many years of proving her parents wrong about her, that lesson was deeply ingrained. Up until now repeating himself appeared to make him happy so she'd let him do it. But she needed more.

"You still have told me nothing about your opera. An opera must have a setting, a place, a feel, a story, or it would just be noise. Clothes are the same. Without the story, they are just coverings."

"Yes, Bill. Do get on with it."

Perrin liked Wilson Jervis. He was a generation, or even two older than she was, but he had an easy-going manner that was totally belied by his well-known success. She'd never been inside the Opera House, except once to hear an Indigo Girls concert during the Bumbershoot music festival. But Perrin had been commissioned to make enough opening-night-of-the-opera gowns to know of him and what he'd achieved.

And wasn't part of Jo's new job being on the opera board? Or maybe it was Cassidy. One of her two best friends… Or maybe both? Again, brain cells too tired to remember or care.

Bill Cullen she hadn't quite figured out yet. He studied her through narrowed eyes, wary and suspicious. He was like Jeffrey, a bulldog she once knew—all rough and grumpy. She wondered if he also had a mushy heart beneath that bristly exterior, or if he was irascible to the core.

He was certainly far prettier than Jeffrey. Bill Cullen stood six feet tall. He wasn't all shoulders like her friend Russell, not that there was any fat on him. He was simply built of a squarer stock. His dark brown hair and disdainful expression, combined with his strong features, lent itself to two different avenues of expression.

She flipped open her pencil set and selected a simple gray to start with.

He began describing a dark adventure. Part Jules Verne and part Hobbit, evil staff of power. He talked about it being quite different in character from Wagner's "Ring Cycle" which meant nothing to her. Somewhere in his explanation he mentioned a tragic love story. It was his voice that caught her attention. It was a good voice, expressive, clearly practiced at storytelling. She let herself simply enjoy the tones and emotions he wove.

Perrin sketched two side-by-side figures. One stern and foreboding, one the romantic hero. She began adding color and lines to both, letting his deep voice and evocative words wrap about her as she sketched. To the left, grays, browns, boots, and towering shoulders… high collar. To the right, purples and blues of royalty and inner majesty, thin lines of white to promise hope. The valiant savior riding to the rescue. But the trim was in darkest red to suggest that heart's blood would be shed despite the nobility. The white hope quite in vain.

Her hand ached by the time she pulled back enough to again be aware of her surroundings. Dozens of colored pencils were scattered about the table. The room was silent. The cramp in her hand told her she'd drawn for twenty, perhaps thirty minutes without interruption.

As she flexed her fingers, she inspected the drawing before her. The same man, twice presented. The Dark Overlord, and the forsaken nobleman doomed before his time to a tragic end. They would work well at a distance. The overemphasized shapes of one and the powerful colors of the other. She would never make street clothes like these, far too depressing. She wanted clothes that made people smile, or want to get married in. But designing to embody an individual's power itself was intriguing.

She practically yelped when she became aware of the two large men flanking her. She'd forgotten they were there.

Bill Cullen was leaning in, studying her drawing intently.

Wilson Jervis smiled at her broadly after little more than a glance.

"Ooo, she's seen right through you, Bill Cullen. You absolutely nailed him, Ms. Williams. We'll have a contract for your review by tomorrow."

Perrin turned back to see Mr. Cullen's reaction. He was no longer studying the sketch. He was studying her, from mere inches away. She could practically see the thoughts churning in his head. His dark brown eyes, the way two vertical lines appeared on his brow when he was concentrating, the unexpected laugh lines around his eyes and mouth, as if he did that a lot... She knew she would be able to draw his face from memory.

"But can you execute your vision?" His voice was still rough.

She waved a hand to indicate the room they were standing in.

"Actually, Bill," Jervis stopped the man. "Her contract is to design. Any costumes she actually constructs earns a bonus but is not required by the contract."

Cullen's expression slowly shifted to one of chagrin though he didn't look away.

"Tomorrow. Nine a.m. At the—"

"Tomorrow at nine a.m.," Perrin interrupted him. "I will still be asleep. I've been awake for four days for one of my best friend's weddings. I might be up by noon. Maybe." She knew that she couldn't let him have control. He struck her as the sort of man that once he had control, he'd never let it go.

"Would tomorrow at two in the afternoon be satisfactory?" His growl didn't sound all that different from Jeffrey the bulldog's. She couldn't decide whether to be deeply peeved at his tone, or amused at how cute he was at being all male and growly.

"That... " she almost said it was fine, but changed her course just to push him and see what he would do. "Would be far more likely than nine a.m. Do people get up at nine a.m.?"

"I have kids. My day starts at six." He nodded curtly and the two men showed themselves out.

Perrin felt a surge of disappointment that she didn't understand. She hung onto the edge of the cutting table, weaving with exhaustion while she tried to figure out the source of it.

Kids. Bill Cullen had children and was married. She hadn't noticed a ring, but she was so tired she could easily have missed it. Some men didn't wear them, but she didn't like men who did that.

Perrin dreamed of a man who was so glad to be with her that he'd want to wear a ring so that he could brag about her. He would need to feel the connection between them even when they were apart.

And she wanted the same for herself.

She'd seen her two best friends find it. But she also knew that such dreams would never be reality for Perrin Williams. With her past, why was she the one who ended up being the romantic among her group of friends?

That still didn't explain the disappointment. Perrin had long ago learned to chase down her emotions until she understood them. When she was younger, her acute reactions and reckless actions had been sources of grave personal danger. The ride down that path had only been averted by meeting Cassidy Knowles and Jo Thompson on the first day of college, and a million very careful steps since.

That was it. She'd taken a step without being aware of it; a step she took far too often with men, her great weakness. Because while she knew it would never come, she still wanted the dream of true love.

That feeling of let-down could be traced back to the fact that Perrin had liked Bill Cullen despite his irascible self.

But he was married. He'd also scoffed at the only thing she did well, had ever done well, which didn't earn him a lot of points. She gazed back down at her drawings. The dark and the tragic stood side by side. Wilson Jervis had been right. She had captured Bill Cullen.

Without being aware of it, she'd drawn both men with his features and build. And the two images… The Dark Overlord who had so carefully inspected each of her designs, appreciated them, yet deemed her unworthy. Him she'd been far too aware of from the moment he entered her shop. And the Tragic Prince who only showed through when Bill Cullen wasn't so busy being himself.

She took up the lead pencil and clarified a few of the details on his face. The way his hair shaded his eyes: not with its length, but with its rich darkness. The least bit of curl that she hoped his wife appreciated toying with.

Then she began sketching a third image. The face was less clear…a woman's face? A woman's body. Yes. Tall. In her mind's eye, the clothing became clearer.

CHAPTER 2

*Two-thirty. **Damn the woman!*** Five more minutes and Bill was going to Jervis and make sure he didn't send the contract to this damned woman. He'd tear it up himself if he had to.

It wasn't like the day had been off to a good start to begin with. The kids had been in rare form, Tamara showed all the signs of having read a book until the middle of the night. She was lethargic, grumpy, and had snapped at Jaspar. He in turn had added salt to his sister's cereal when she wasn't looking. Bill actually had to snap at them before they pummeled each other, or even worse, messed up their school clothes ten minutes before he had to drop them off.

Then he'd spent the morning finding out that the costumes weren't his only problem. The set designer had been timely, thorough, and innovative in his scenic design. He'd also shown absolutely no concept of what it would cost to build, to move about the stage, or store between productions. Then his lead scenic painter had broken her wrist... Bill ground his teeth and tried to beat down his e-mail that had decided today was the day everything should be labeled urgent.

At two-thirty-three, past the limit of his patience, Bill went to hunt down Wilson to fire this Williams woman before she signed any damned contract. His office was empty.

The old office building had been built into a hillside, with rooftop parking and a flight of stairs descending to the top story where the main offices were. They were a labyrinth of white-painted concrete rooms chopped up with open-plan cubicles. It had once been a moving company's storage facility. The towering storage racks had been removed and the tall ceiling lowered with dropped T-bar and acoustic tiles. The result had been a nice enough office environment with inexplicably long flights of stairs between the tall stories. Rising from the industrial-gray carpet, the walls were magnificent with large production photos of every opera performed over the last forty years by Emerald City Opera.

Timothy, the Production Manager, had seen Wilson about an hour earlier. No one since, not Marci, Consuela, or Chloe. Where had the damn man wandered off to? Bill swung by the front desk where Nia reigned as the eyes and ears of the organization.

As he was asking, he felt someone come in through the front doors. He turned around part way to see if it was Wilson or his missing designer, then forgot how to breathe when he saw the apparition entering the small lobby from the stairs.

The woman who had walked in wasn't the costume designer, but she was an incredible sight to behold.

He heard Nia gasp behind him, but he couldn't turn to gauge her reaction. He couldn't even gauge his own. He'd been slapped by a gestalt vision that his brain was now having to unravel.

Amazingly, it was Perrin Williams—yet it couldn't be.

In place of the crazy-clothed blond waif, he now faced a towering woman of power and majesty. Her hair was the darkest, purest black, except for a stripe of her original coloring. A pale-blond stripe started at her right temple in a three-inch wide band and disappeared behind her head in a sloping spiral. It reappeared on the other side, just meeting the tips of her hair at her left shoulder.

From there, in fabric, the white stripe was picked up and continued its downward swirl across her gown, widening as it went.

The dark purples and blues of her second drawing from yesterday had been incorporated. The thin white stripe of hope on her "tragic noble" was now a blazing banner. The white transitioned, by an exceptional job of hand-dying, into a gold of true glory. If he remembered correctly, every place that had been blood red in her drawing of the Prince had been turned golden in this dress.

She was hope embodied. But its message didn't stop there.

The left shoulder extended to a tall collar encasing her neck right up under her chin and down to the clavicle. But the right shoulder was bare, a line of flesh was exposed down her ribs and that opening too extended around the side reappearing at the far hip.

A thigh-high side slit revealed even more skin in long legs of startling perfection. Every muscle enhanced and accented by the knee-tall, high-heel boots of the dark destroyer sketch. In the boots she was an inch or so taller than he was.

It was a dramatic statement that would play as well from the back of the house as it did from ten feet away. She was joy and hope and immense power all wound together.

And beauty. Gods, she was incredible. Her slender frame had been shifted from waif to sleek by the design. Every womanly shape and curve was accented until her gender struck such a hard slap in the face that it left him reeling.

"Well, I guess that worked." She sounded very pleased with herself.

Bill blinked hard. "Huh? What worked?"

She twirled on one foot proving that the look was as powerful from behind as it was from the front, and at the same time totally destroying the persona. The swirl of her hair and girlish laugh matched the crazed designer of yesterday.

"The look on your face. It so totally worked." She did a little stomping victory dance in her high-heel boots.

He heard a laugh beside him and turned to see Nia nodding in agreement.

"What worked?" He knew he was repeating himself like a child, and not a very smart one. He couldn't help himself, as he turned once more to admire the woman before him. She was breathtaking.

BILL CULLEN really was so cute. Perrin knew she had the ability to shock. But to make a married man turn into a gibbering idiot, that was a new one. Well, not really. But she did thoroughly enjoy doing it.

Had the last thirty hours of frenetic work been worth it? She was now so tired that her body had gone past aching and numb right into zombie. Zombie girl. Her body so disconnected it could wander off on its own and she'd never notice. She giggled at the image.

"What?" Bill Cullen was still being monosyllabic, she'd really gotten him good. "What's so funny?"

"Wow! Back up to polysyllabic, Bill. Well done, you! Gonna go for three syllables together anytime soon?"

That brought the Dark Overlord scowl back.

She decided that made him fair game. "Me. As a zombie, you know, green-and-ghoul makeup, singing opera in a killer dress. It has real possibilities."

She started dancing, Madonna-style bends and hair swoops, and began singing a KT Tunstall song that she didn't really know the words to, so she made them up as she went which was okay because sometimes she wondered if KT did just that. On the third dip and whirl she was so lightheaded that she almost collapsed. She stopped and had to brace herself to remain upright while her head spun.

Her palm landed in the middle of Bill's chest. He didn't waver, the man was solid as if built from the rock of the Earth's very core. She could feel the hard muscle through his thin shirt. She'd always been a fan of hard muscle.

"Are you okay?" His deep voice rumbled in his chest and tickled its way up her arm.

"Solicitous? Are there no ends to the wonders of Bill Cullen?"

The receptionist actually snorted with laughter.

Perrin shot her a smile, but she couldn't stand up on her own just yet. Her head still whirled viciously.

"I'll try once more. Are you okay? Do you need to sit down for a moment? Can I get you some coffee?"

"Coffee? Shit no. If I'm like this normally, can you imagine me on caffeine? So not a pretty sight. I need sleep and food, in that order." Feeling a little steadier, she managed to stand on her own, brushing his shirt smooth as she did so. Nice chest. She wanted to pet it, but it belonged to another woman so she stopped herself.

"How about we go to my office? We can talk over the schedule and then tour the scene shop so you can see the sets, to let you see the tone of the production."

"Uh, as long as we can sit down real soon. It's been so long since I slept that I'm starting to hallucinate tiny conga lines of opera-singing mice swirling about my ankles." She might have slept an hour or two last night, she usually managed at least that—even when a design bit her hard. If she had, she didn't remember it. This design had been ripped out from somewhere deep.

Bill offered his arm. She steadied herself with a hand on his elbow, the only thing that made her steady enough to walk. As he led her back through the offices, a ripple of whispers ran ahead of them and gawkers were soon lining the aisle. Bill was mumbling something about ticket sales department, production design, education…indicating one cluster of cubicles that looked exactly like the last.

A guy walking along carrying a computer monitor actually ran into a wall while looking at her.

By that time she was able to make some sense of the whispers. "The Empress!" said with a touch of awe that she found quite cheery. That was all that sustained her until she reached Bill's office.

It was a smallish space that had a window looking down over an old section of the warehouse district that now housed a Taco Del Mar fast food restaurant and an Asian furniture importer, despite the ancient paint on brick that declared it as "Johnson Expeditors 1914."

The office walls had drawings done by children. There were several framed photos of Bill with two kids, but she couldn't seem to make her eyes focus on them well enough to even pick out gender or age. Then she spotted the couch along the side wall. The last thing she remembered was planting her face into one of the cushions.

"HELLO, Ms. Thompson, my name is Bill Cullen. I'm with Emerald City Opera and we met last week at a board meeting. Do you by any chance know a woman named Perrin Williams?"

He felt stupid for calling one of Seattle's movers and shakers with such a dumb question, but it was all he could think to do. He'd had to shake Perrin fairly hard to rouse her at all. When he'd asked who he should call, she mumbled, "Cassidy or Jo." At least that's what he thought she'd said before collapsing back onto his office sofa.

There were two women he'd met recently at a Friends of the Opera board meeting, where he'd gone to give a presentation about the new production. One of them had been Cassidy Knowles, a leading wine entrepreneur. And Jo Thompson who had replaced the powerhouse Renée Linden and appeared to be no less formidable. He couldn't imagine the association a small-time fashion designer would have with these two, but the names were unique enough that he decided to give it a try.

"Actually it's Jo Parrano now, but yes, I know her. Is she okay?"

"I'm not sure. She collapsed on my office sofa and fell asleep."

He heard a long-suffering sigh over the phone. "She does that. My recommendation is to make sure she's comfortable, then throw a blanket over her."

"But she's in my office," Bill once again felt as if he were being dumb. And like he was whining, which was even more embarrassing. He took a breath and tried to calm down. "I don't quite know what to do with her."

"Welcome to the club, Mr. Cullen. Well, I'm in Hawaii on my honeymoon and I think Cassidy is in France for a vintner's conference. We closed the restaurant and gave the staff a week off, no idea where they will have scattered to. If she still hasn't slept since before the wedding, she'll be down until sometime tomorrow morning. My best advice is to just let her sleep." The woman spoke as if this were somehow normal behavior.

"But in my office?" It hardly seemed appropriate, or convenient.

"Oh, you can work. Nothing much on the planet will wake her. And she'll wake very hungry, so having some food around would be a kindness. She eats anything. Sorry I can't be more helpful."

"Uh, I guess she's okay as long as I don't need to rush her to the hospital or back to the mothership or something."

Jo Thompson had the decency to laugh. "That latter option wouldn't surprise any of us even a little bit. Is she okay there? I could try to rally some troops…"

Her voice was very tentative.

"No. I'll take care of it from here. Congratulations and thanks." He hung up the phone wondering what in hell he'd just signed up for. Well, one thing was for damn sure, he couldn't just leave her there like that. For one thing, his hormones would kill him looking at her in that amazing dress for hour after hour.

He picked up the phone and buzzed downstairs. Then he sat back to wait and allowed himself just a moment to admire the revelation of such exceptional beauty of the woman who wore that amazing dress.

Jaspar and Tamara arrived about the same time that Jerimy, the head of the Costume Shop, arrived from the floor below. The kids ran in and gave him huge, after-school hugs. Whatever else he was messing up, he was doing this right…mostly. Tamara was drifting away and he had no idea what to do about it. She still hugged him when she wasn't really thinking about it. Other times it was suffered, and recently she'd avoided his hug a few times. As a single dad, she often left him with his moorings cut loose and no channel markers on where to go from there.

Jaspar was just gone ten, a cocky, know-it-all, splendid fifth grader. Dark-haired like his dad, but with his mother's wide eyes. Tamara was a sophisticated thirteen-year old acting like she was in high school rather than tolerating the last months of middle school, and who thankfully hadn't yet decided her dad was a crime against nature. She looked so like a young version of her dead mother—a thick mane of dark red hair, and pale, pale skin—that she broke his heart every day, though he would never let it show.

They waved hello to Jerimy and turned for their usual after-school-debrief hangout of the couch, then stumbled to a halt.

"Who's she?" Jaspar tipped his head sideways to study Perrin sort of right side up. "Is she real or a mannequin?"

"She's breathing, dummy." Tamara tipped her head so like her brother that Bill had to cover his mouth to not laugh at them.

He shared a smile with Jerimy over the kid's heads.

"Wild dress," Tamara's voice was filled with a bit of wonder.

"Yeah," how in the hell was he supposed to explain this one? He almost went with spaceship alien as being the most plausible. No, he'd better go for the simple truth, that was bizarre enough on the credibility scale. Jerimy was leaning comfortably against the door frame enjoying the whole scene.

Tamara brushed Perrin's crazy hair back from her face. "I like her hair."

"Don't get any ideas, kiddo. No crazy dye jobs."

Tamara squinched her eyes shut and stuck her tongue out at him. He did the same right back. A good moment. When had he started hoarding those?

"She's our new costume designer, but I think she was awake for five days straight or something."

"She okay?" Jaspar was whispering. They all were.

"I called a friend of hers who assures me that she just needs to sleep. Jerimy, I'm going to take the kids out for some ice cream," there was a small round of quiet cheers. "Before they start their homework," a chorus of less soft boos.

He stood up and grabbed Jaspar around the waist and held him upside down until he was giggling. Been a long while since he'd been able to do that with Tamara. Probably since Adira's death when Tamara had decided she had to become the lady of the household. Hell of a burden for a then nine-year old girl. He and Tamara had both grown up a lot that year. Jaspar had been six, too young to do more than be in shock.

"Ms. Williams," he figured remaining formal in front of his kids was a good thing. "She was modeling a costume design for me when she fell asleep. Jerimy, I was hoping that you could gather some more comfortable clothes, arrange for a discreet change, and then toss a blanket on her. I'm assured that she will be almost impossible to wake for some time yet."

Jerimy nodded. "I'll go gather some supplies, and help." He tickled Jaspar's belly button where being held upside down had made his shirt pull out of his pants. Jaspar squirmed and giggled harder as Jerimy left.

"She's beautiful," Tamara was still studying the sleeping Perrin Williams.

"She's even prettier when she's awake."

His daughter eyed him with a far too thoughtful look.

He shook his head, a clear "no way!" Tamara had alternated over the years between trying to matchmake him, and assuming that he no longer loved Tamara's mother if he even glanced at a woman walking down the street.

Well, she didn't need to worry. This woman was nuts. Not no way. Not no how.

He herded the kids out of there before there were more questions.

But Bill could still feel the outline of where Perrin's palm had rested over his heart. The touch of the Empress, a great curse or a great blessing in the new opera's story. Always unknown, but always powerful.

CHAPTER 3

errin woke slowly. She always enjoyed the crawl back from her "hibernations" as Cassidy had dubbed them. She didn't do it often, but when a design really grabbed her, like Jo's wedding dress, or that outfit for the opera, she just had to chase it until it was done and purged from her system.

She became aware of voices as she languished beneath the warm blankets.

A deep voice rumbling that she recognized easily. Mr. Bill Cullen. He had such a great voice, a far-off thunderstorm brushing soft sounds across an otherwise peaceful summer evening.

A higher voice, still male, but with a definite swish to it. "This is amazing work, Bill. I've been doing costumes since I was a teen, and I can barely tell how she did it. And the hand dyeing here from the white to gold, it's just magnificent. That's a technique that I'd like to learn."

She opened her eyes and looked through the brush of hair that had slid over her face. Black. When had her hair gone black? Last she remembered it was blond.

Oh, the costume. What had people called it? "The Empress." She liked the sound of that.

Peeking through her hair, she could see two men closely inspecting the costume where it hung by itself on a rack. One was showing the inside of the seams to the other. The second one was Bill Cullen, in his classic, arms-crossed Overlord pose that made her smile.

Further inspection revealed that she was on an office couch and it felt as if she'd been here quite some time. But she'd arrived wearing the dress. She was fairly sure of that. So, she lifted the blanket. A black Emerald City Opera t-shirt, with a lemon-yellow stylized ECO logo over one breast. She brushed her legs together under the blanket. Sweats and bare feet.

Then the last of her came awake and she smelled sugar. That got her upright. Bill and the other man whirled to look at her, but all she cared about was the large cheese Danish that had been placed on the low table in front of the couch she'd apparently slept on.

"Good morning."

"Uh, hi!" she mumbled around a mouthful. "Morning, huh? How long… Never mind. Overnight. You have milk or tea or something?"

Bill moved to a small fridge and pulled out a carton of chocolate milk. "After school treat for Jaspar. Tamara is now above that, so I also have ginger ale."

"How old are they? Milk's fine." She took it from him, and knocked back half a carton to clear the Danish so that she could speak properly.

"Ten and the oldest thirteen there ever was."

She hoped not, for the kid's sake.

By thirteen the world had held no more illusions for Perrin at all.

"And you give her ginger ale? You'd get way more dad-points if you stocked in some caffeine-free diet Coke or Pepsi. Trust me on that."

He opened his mouth, clearly to say something about knowing his own kids well enough. So, she cut him off by holding out a hand to the other man.

"Hi, I'm Perrin."

"Jerimy. I'm the manager of the costume department for ECO, I hope you don't mind that I changed you yesterday. You were really out of it, honey." Jerimy was a trim man with a shock of bottle-red hair moussed up into a chaotic hairstyle that suited his blue eyes and narrow features. He wore a very tailored white shirt and black pants with lines that narrowed the hips, and good shoes. He looked sharp, standing hipshot like a runway model.

Bill was wearing jeans and an open white shirt from some off-the-rack store, Sears probably. Bought at the same time he was buying a reciprocating drill or a forty-two tooth screwdriver or somesuch.

"Was he here?" She nodded toward Bill and took another bite of the Danish. Weird combo with a swirl of chocolate milk, but okay.

His jaw dropped to protest his innocence. He must really be gone on his wife to have passed up on the opportunity to see her mostly naked. The bra had been built into the dress after all. Not that Perrin really needed one very often; the one and only advantage to never really growing breasts. Well, that and she could get away with wearing almost any high fashion design.

"Just me and Patsy, she's straight and I'm so not, so your secrets are perfectly safe with both of us," Jerimy offered her a broad wink. She liked him, and not just because he appreciated her dress.

She eyed it critically as she continued to chew.

"The Empress?"

"Yes. You really captured her," Bill turned once more to the dress.

"Wow! You actually paid me a compliment there, Mr. Cullen. You may want to go easy on that. Making my head spin. You, uh, told me about the Empress?"

Bill looked up at the ceiling in exasperation. Well, what did he expect? She'd been asleep on her feet during their visit to her shop—even before she'd started this dress.

"It just sort of came together from the other two designs I drew." Perrin remembered Bill rambling on at some length about the opera's story, but she couldn't remember a word. This design had simply been a natural extension of the story about the first two male characters. Maybe the tone of Bill's deep voice as he'd described the character was in there somewhere, but she couldn't pick it out.

The dress' lines were good, the balance of sex and power.

"Is the Empress good or evil?"

"No one is sure. Even at the opera's end, she is still enigmatic. The powerful unknown."

Perrin cocked her head trying to see the color and tone without wholly discounting shape and line.

"I think it needs a blood-red lining then, to balance the hope of the gold."

Jerimy caught his breath and she knew it was right.

But it had come out well for not knowing anything about the story. She remembered Bill's eyes going dark with heat as he'd first looked at her in the Opera's lobby.

Yes, the dress had come out very well.

JERIMY HAD SPREAD out Carlotta Gianelli's watercolors along the Costume Shop table. They really had quite an amazing setup here. He'd given her the full tour.

"A really major production can have three hundred costumes, which is easily over a thousand pieces not counting shoes and accessories. And sometimes we have two casts for the leads, that means building some costumes twice, in two different sizes."

There was a sewing area that had a dozen machines. Perrin's studio had one four-by-eight foot cutting table. The opera had two matted tables, eight feet wide by twenty-four long. A dozen people could work at each table, though only a half dozen people were in the entire room at the moment.

They had a vented paint booth where red shoes were repainted as blue, fabrics were sprayed with texturing, and papier-mâché headdresses were magically transformed into golden crowns, bishop miters, and magician hats. There were boxes and boxes of shoes simply labeled: Men's 9, Women's 8, Child's 6. Each was a treasure chest filled with shoes, boots, sandals, platforms, and more of almost every imaginable type.

What had surprised Perrin about the costumes themselves was the way they were constructed. Only rarely were they of the fine-finished construction she was used to.

"We only do that for the most special pieces," Jerimy had informed her. "And we never manage anything as spectacular as the one you built." The more typical costumes were well-built, but with massive six-inch seam allowances. They must be uncomfortable for the singers but allowed for the costume to be adjusted to different-sized singers without rebuilding them each time. Take out a couple seams, fit, and restitch.

"The typical costume will last through twenty or more productions, each of perhaps a dozen performances. They're used for a dozen years or more at ten or twenty different opera houses. So, we try to make the costumes as adjustable as possible."

Perrin looked down at Carlotta's drawings. They were little more than blurs of colors. They were cohesive in their color palette. The lines were dramatic. But they didn't relate. It was like a runway collection that really didn't work. Each piece would be fine, but it wasn't a whole story.

Perrin hadn't really understood that until she started doing weddings. For years she'd made couples' clothing, that told a story of two people. But a wedding told the story of the main couple, with their friends supplementing that, and family the next layer beyond that. All of them designed and built to focus back on the couple.

Bill Cullen wandered in, probably to check up on them. She ignored him, as well as she could. He was way too attractive to be allowed out in public. Not rugged like Russell or ever so handsome like his best friend Angelo. Bill Cullen's face was striking because it was rich with character and his emotions brushed so close beneath the surface.

She did her best to ignore his presence and spoke to the head of the costume department.

"There's only one story here, Jerimy."

"What do you mean?" He and Bill came up to stand to either side of her. She'd definitely have to make sure that didn't keep happening with Bill, it only made her body all too aware of things it couldn't have.

She rearranged Carlotta's drawings, at least getting the story's hierarchy correct. Empress and Overlord side by side, Prince and his court below, separated for the good, the evil, and the overly-neutral drabness of the townspeople.

"Damn!" Jerimy cursed. "I didn't even see that. So that's how they're supposed to go together?"

"I didn't see it either," Bill commented. "But you said it only told one story, what's the other one?"

"Other two. Maybe three, but I have to think about that. This," she waved a hand at them, "is the story of the opera. Or at least one part of it." Then she pointed at the dress now hanging behind them.

"That is the story of the individual, of what she is inside. Each must add together to explain where they came from before the opera and where they're going after."

Bill did his arms-crossed thing. Maybe that was how he always stood when he was thinking.

Jerimy returned, as he had a dozen times, to inspect the costume closely as if the answer was somehow in the material itself rather than the design. Perrin recognized that blind spot, she had suffered from it for years, too fascinated by the construction to step back and see how it went together with the surrounding context.

"The other story is the audience?" Bill barely whispered.

Perrin twisted to look at him, she'd never expected Bill Cullen to understand. So few people saw that. From somewhere deep inside, a laugh of sheer delight bubbled forth.

PERRIN'S joyous laugh rocked Bill back on his heels. The smile that lit her face made him feel ten feet tall, as did the approving hand resting lightly on his arm. It was ridiculous to feel so gratified about being right, but Perrin made it easy.

"Yes! Exactly! High fashion design is about who we are, but even more about how we wish to be perceived. So few people see that. Jo in her powersuits, Cassidy in her ever so tasteful black, Jerimy sharp and snappy, and you… " her giggle was absolutely ridiculous.

"What? Finish it."

She pushed him around like one of Jerimy's dress forms on wheels until she stood behind him. Then she pulled at his shirt collar. "JC Penny. Well, I was close."

He turned back to try and explain about finding a minute to grab a shirt while riding herd on a ten-year-old who kept trying to sell his need for hundred-dollar sneakers, and a sullen thirteen-year-old who kept trying on clothes, and hating all of them right along with her body that was maturing far too fast for his fatherly vision of her.

Before he could speak, he heard the kids pounding down the stairs. He always let Nia know where he'd be about the time the school bus dropped the kids off. For the four years since Wilson had convinced him to move to Seattle, they'd practically grown up at the Opera's offices; everyone knew to keep an eye out for them. Most days, he could just work another hour or two while they did their homework, then they'd all go home together. He often did paperwork in the evening or after they went to bed, but it all worked.

They plummeted into the Costume Shop. Jaspar came right up for a hug, but Tamara pulled up short when she spotted Perrin. Her assessing gaze snapped his attention to just how close the designer was standing to him. He took a step away from Perrin and toward Tammy, but she detoured wide and moved to the design table.

"Are these yours?" Tammy looked down at Carlotta's drawings.

Perrin turned her attention as fully on his daughter as it had been on him the moment before.

"First tell me if you like them, truthfully, then I'll tell you."

TAMMY DIDN'T LOOK up from the drawings spread across the table. She didn't like them, and they probably were this lady's work or her dad wouldn't be acting so weird around her.

Last night before they left, he'd been all fussy, making sure he left a big note with his cell number in case she called. Even tucking in her blanket as if it was normal for people to sleep on his office couch. Even at home he'd been saying, "Ms. Williams this" and "Ms. Williams that."

So, Tammy delivered her verdict, which actually wasn't that biased.

"Major yawn."

"Jerimy!" Perrin cried out, startling all of them, causing Tammy to take a quick step back in case she'd upset her. The woman was waving her arm like a pirate captain from the quarterdeck. "The young lady has spoken! This calls for the rubbish bin!"

Jerimy swung one out from under the bench.

"Do it, girl!" Ms. Williams cried loudly enough for her voice to echo about the large space and draw everyone's attention from the other parts of the Costume Shop.

Tammy picked up the plainest drawing. She glanced up at the woman, but still couldn't detect one way or the other what she thought. When Tammy looked at her dad, he shrugged.

Tammy dropped the drawing carefully into the trash can and looked again for everyone's reaction. She'd been around the opera enough to know the value of an artist's work as well as their temperament about it. The time when Jasp was four and had drawn green flowers around someone's set drawing had almost gotten him murdered.

Dad opened his mouth. She could see he was about to tell her it was okay, when the lady poked her hard enough on the shoulder to make her turn away from him. The woman put her fists on her hips, glared down at Tammy, and blew out a huff of air that would have stirred her bangs if she'd had any. Instead she had that black hair with the blond stripe that was even prettier now that she was awake.

Here it comes. Figures. Another crazy adult saying it was okay one minute and gearing up to chew you out the nex—

"Where did you learn how to do that?" The lady didn't wait for an answer. Instead she pointed at Jasp without even turning. "You! Boy! What's your name?"

"Jaspar," he didn't quite stammer in his surprise at suddenly being the center of attention.

"Jaspar, show this girl how you throw out an ugly drawing."

With only a brief backward glance at Dad for reassurance, he took up a drawing, crumpled it a little. Then he glanced at Tammy. She grinned back at him, he was gonna show Ms. Williams but good.

Jasp made a whole spectacle of crushing it into the smallest, wrinkliest ball he could, then ran back a couple paces and shot it into the trash like a basketball.

Tammy could see her dad. Jasp might not get it, but she knew. Each of those paintings represented untold hours of painstaking coaxing and wheedling to get "Carlotta Nightmare," as Jasp had dubbed her, to produce them. They were also the only designs they had, and there were less than six weeks to production.

Last night Dad had been groaning, in between worrying about Ms. Williams, about how the publicity shots were supposed to be this week and there were no costumes yet and—

"Better," the lady told Jasp.

He checked in with Tammy, but she could only twitch a shoulder in a shrug. She didn't know how to read Ms. Williams yet.

"Better, but still lame. Now, watch carefully."

Tammy had to figure out what was going on. Even without the fancy dress, she was very tall and very pretty.

Tammy liked the black hair that matched the opera t-shirt. And she wouldn't mind trying to have a blond swirl in her hair. It pointed like an arrow to the bright yellow ECO logo over her breast. The t-shirt clung to her frame. Tammy glanced at Dad through the fall of her own long hair so that he wouldn't notice her attention. He was staring hard at the woman, which Tammy didn't like much.

The lady handed her and Jasp another drawing and took one herself. So slowly that it was almost painful, she tore it in half: the paper making a long, drawn-out cry of protest. The half-dozen costumers doing touch-up work on the clothes for the present opera rushed over to see what was happening. They stopped and stared, with their jaws down.

She glanced to Dad for permission, but Ms. Williams called them back to attention like they were both still in third grade.

"You have to just do it!"

Jasp raised one eyebrow in question then waited to see what she'd do. Tammy set her jaw and tore it with the same agonizing slowness, Jasp joining her part way through.

Then Ms. Williams overlapped her two pieces and tore them the other way, a little faster.

Tammy and Jasp did the same. Then faster and faster they all tore their paintings and tore them and tore them until they were little more than large confetti.

With a fistful of torn paper, she sent Jasp the tiniest head nod toward Dad. He was sharp and chucked his into the air right over Dad's head. Dad ducked and cringed beneath the shower of bits of paper. At the last second, Tammy changed her target and launched her own fistful of paper over the woman's head who burst out with a wild laugh and threw hers right back, saving a few to sprinkle over Jasp.

———

BILL WATCHED in amazement as three of Carlotta Nightmare's drawings fluttered about them in tiny pieces. He tried to think of something to say, but couldn't as Jaspar scraped up a fistful that had fallen on the table and launched them right at Bill's face where they burst apart into a colorful flurry just inches away.

Perrin dove for another watercolor and began tearing madly. The kids joined in. In the midst of the mayhem that ensued, Perrin very solemnly handed one painting to him.

It was harder than he expected, making that first tear. It was the Overlord, at least he thought it was, it was hard to tell on Carlotta's work and she'd certainly been above explaining her "Art" to anyone who couldn't simply "intuit" it themselves. The second tear was easier, then the third.

In moments, he too was showering bits of paper over his kids' heads.

After the last drawing was destroyed, and Jerimy had the honor of stuffing the last fistful down the back of Jaspar's shirt, they all set in to clean up. Bill saw Perrin take Tammy a little to one side. He moved as unobtrusively as he could to collect some confetti that was closer to them, so that he could overhear.

"That," Perrin pointed at the floor. "So not me." Then she turned Tammy to face the Empress' dress.

"That," Perrin nodded as if reassuring herself. Though he could hear the doubt in her voice as if she didn't believe in her own power.

"That is me."

It was absolutely her. So powerful that she actually unnerved him a bit. And now she'd made friends with his children.

That he was far less sure about.

CHAPTER 4

Perrin would have liked to have someone to call. But with Jo's wedding over and the week-long closure of the restaurant, everyone was gone. Even Maria had taken the opportunity to go on a belated honeymoon with her Hogan. They were taking some extra time and had rented a sailboat for two weeks to cruise along the Amalfi coast of Italy.

She wasn't even sure why she wanted someone around at this moment. She was fine on her own for days at a time. Especially when a challenging design tackled her. It wasn't that she wanted to talk to one of her friends about anything in particular. Perrin just wanted to be around them for a time.

They were her sanity benchmark. She sometimes needed reminding, even now at thirty, that she was okay—a good person and not some product of her childhood. That people liked her who weren't merely looking at how to use her.

So, she sat by herself at Cutters Crabhouse, just her untouched iced tea, some focaccia, and her sketchbook. It was mid-afternoon. Through the towering windows the Seattle waterfront lay spread out below her. Pike Place Market, a close bustle of tourists and hundreds of cool little shops perched on the cliff edge. Out of sight on Post

Alley, Angelo's Tuscan Hearth Ristorante with its "Closed for Honeymoon" sign on the door. Below, the long piers of the waterfront reached out into Elliott Bay. The sun glittered off the water and the snowy Olympic Mountains loomed high in the west on the far side of Puget Sound.

This was as close as she could be to her absent friends. This is where they usually gathered, in Cutter's upscale bar. All dressed to the limit, shimmering together around a too small, wood-and-steel table, perched on high-leather stools, and teasing waiters far and wide. This time, instead of too much alcohol and too many appetizers and laughing until her sides ached, she sat by herself and ordered a cup of chowder and half of a hot pastrami on rye.

It was still a bit early for the after-work crowd, so the bar was uncharacteristically quiet. It would be hopping in a couple hours, but for the moment there was mostly just her, a few stray tourists, and the wait staff.

At the Opera, after they'd all finished the cleanup and the kids were tucked into handy cubicles outside his office, chipping away at their homework, Bill had told her the opera's plot again. He also gave her a script.

"No," he corrected her. "It's a libretto not a script, everything is sung." Even in *The Sound of Music* Julie Andrews didn't sing everything. Singing meant the clothing needed to provide room to breathe even more than room to move.

He'd shown her photos of the lead singers. The Empress was okay, the lead tenor singing the Tragic Prince was a big guy. The Dark Overlord, a rare true bass singer, even bigger. Now she understood some of Jerimy's comments on construction. These were people who made their livings with their chest and gut muscles. Making the proportions balance out would take some doing.

"There was a great tenor," Jerimy had informed her. "Whose chest grew so massive and his legs so out of shape that it actually ended his career when he could no longer stand through a whole performance." She'd stepped through a door into a whole other world.

She'd read the libretto, doodled a little, but she still didn't have any ideas flowing. Perrin wasn't worried, yet. She was supposed to go see the final performance of the current production of *Turandot* this weekend. Bill had assured her it would have a happy ending. Cassidy would be back by then. She'd agreed by e-mail to go with Perrin and Russell had begged to not be forced to go, so that should be fun. A mini girls' night out.

Tomorrow, she'd see the sets and the first rehearsal of *Ascension*, opening in just over five weeks. That's what she was counting on. The libretto gave her plot, but it still told her so little of the world and the people involved.

She doodled quick images of the three designs she'd already done as thumbnails across the top of the page as a reference.

The chowder and sandwich arrived. She ignored the waiter's mild flirt and paid attention to the smells of the sandwich, rich pastrami and tangy sauerkraut. The first taste didn't disappoint in the slightest. She tried to savor it as Cassidy would savor a wine—the interaction of the caraway-seed rye bread and stone ground mustard—but instead found herself just chewing it. Food kept her body running. So many of her friends were foodies that some appreciation had rubbed off on her, but eating alone didn't make it fun enough to be worth the effort.

There was a benefit to ignoring the waiter and paying some attention to food that she usually saw as merely sustenance. If she did those things with the front of her mind, she didn't pay too much attention to her sketching, shutting out that inner editor. She'd continued to idly doodle more ideas to go with the first three as she ate.

Powerful colors, but simpler.

Less complex than Prince and Empress.

More hopeful, brighter lights. But understated.

Costumes to match the character rather than enhance them. To let the person show through without declaring the role outright, avoiding the dynamism of a chosen mantle that so overshadowed what nature had provided. That choice to cloak one's self was so adult. Use the greens and golds of nature. The simplicity of youth.

Youth.

The children. There they were, smiling at her from her sketchpad, clothed like the parental Overlord and Empress. But they didn't have their older brother Prince's tragedy imprinted yet on either them or their costumes.

She paged open the libretto and inspected the cast of characters. There was a younger daughter, a child soprano. But no little boy. Well, they could just go ahead and add a non-singing boy-child role who could follow after his older sister.

That actually gave her drawings for one whole side of the cast, the Empress' lineage. But what of the other side of the house, the marriage-sworn Princess and the Tragic Prince's True Love? Before tomorrow's rehearsal, she could start building the prototypes for the children's costumes.

Jerimy had assured her that they could build whatever she drew, or create patterns from anything she'd sewn. Though he had seemed less sure about the Empress' outfit. But she always finished her design concept while doing the construction. That was her creative process. She'd have to build all of the major pieces at least once herself.

Models. Jaspar and Tammy. Maybe Bill would let her borrow his kids as models. That would really help. She hadn't done children's clothing since her own first efforts, and those had been to hide, blend in, be invisible. Back when—

"Perrin!"

Perrin startled from her dark thoughts and almost dumped her cup of untouched chowder over her now-cold sandwich.

"Josh! Come here, cutey. Give your Perrin a hug!" Josh Harper was so handsome. Totally safe, but fun and funny. Tall, with wavy, light brown hair and an easy smile.

He gave her a big hug that she let herself be lost in for just a moment that washed away the last of her uncomfortable memories.

"How are you, my love?" he teased her.

"Still pining away. Waiting for you to throw over that woman you're married to."

"Yes, I know. If only I didn't love her so much. Alas, we're never meant to be." He gestured for permission then took the seat across from her.

"I could take out a contract on her. I do know some really scary guys. Ones who would, like, do anything for me. Maybe, I dunno, Russell."

"Oh, now I'm really scared." Josh wasn't in town very often, but he, Russell, and Angelo had become good friends at first meeting. It didn't hurt that Josh was a senior food-and-wine critic for *Gourmet Week* magazine and had consistently raved about Angelo's restaurant both in print and on-line.

"But what are you doing sitting alone, my love? Why is there no suitor begging at your feet? And where the heck is everybody? 'Restaurant Closed for Honeymoon.' It was my fifth anniversary, so I couldn't make it to Jo and Angelo's wedding. I went by to pay my respects and it's closed. You have to tell me everything!"

Perrin, glad for a friend, closed her pad and pulled her lunch in front of her while Josh ordered. Then she settled in and filled him in on all the details of Jo's wedding, especially teasing him about the great food he'd missed.

BILL COULDN'T BELIEVE he was doing this. He had a thousand things to get done and here he was playing Seattle tour guide to a tenor and his supermodel girlfriend. They'd flown in together for tomorrow's first rehearsal of *Ascension*.

This was Wilson's kind of job, but he was rubbing shoulders with some of the high-rolling donors at the Seattle Men's Club.

Jerimy had dropped the kids off with Bill's sister for a couple hours, god bless Lucy, and he'd been dragged out on the town. He and Lucy had issues that made it hard to be in the same room together, but none of them were about his kids.

In her soft French accent, the towering blond model, several inches taller than Perrin, had suggested this Cutters Crabhouse place and he'd been thankful. He knew the whereabouts of every IHOP, Mitzel's, and pizza house in all of Seattle. In-crowd bars and upscale waterfront restaurants, not so much.

This place was near the Pike Place Market and oozed urban professional without actually flaunting it in your face like so many modern bars. It was all chrome and high tables with tall leather stools. Waiters in black pants and white shirts scooted about looking immensely sharp, unhurried, and efficient all at once. A wall of windows looked out toward the Seattle waterfront and the Market. Actually, if he ever again in his life found time to have a date, this would be a nice place to bring her.

"Perrin!" The model cried out while they stood in the entry debating between the bar and the restaurant.

There couldn't be two women in Seattle named Perrin.

Sure enough, he spotted the woman at the far side of the bar making grand and ridiculous gestures as if reenacting the Greek battle at Troy for an audience of hundreds instead of the one man who sat with her.

Bill couldn't believe Perrin was here. But her hair, hanked back into a ponytail, revealed the swirling blond stripe that proved her identity even at this distance. She still wore the black opera t-shirt, now partly covered by a knit vest of a rather electric blue.

She was sitting by the window, practically huddled together with some far-too-handsome man. Bill and Carlo di Stefano dutifully followed in the model's wake, who was so cliché that her waist-length blond hair actually floated along behind her. In moments, the two women were embracing like long lost sisters.

"Melanie," Perrin responded in full, bubbling flight. Again, the madcap waif revealed herself in full airhead-blond mode.

Assuming she really was blond with dark-dyed hair, rather than dark-haired with a blond stripe or….

"You've never met Josh, I don't think. I'd introduce you, but he's married and he's mine if his wife ever leaves him because it is sure he'll never leave her. He doesn't even waver when I throw myself at him."

The model towered over the seated man, fists on hips. She glared down at Josh. "You would deny my friend Perrin? What sort of a cad are you, *monsieur?*"

"A happily married one, I'm afraid." He smiled easily up at the long blond.

"Pity, or I might try to steal you from her. You are so very pretty," the model sighed, then leaned down and kissed him cheerfully on both cheeks.

"He is awfully pretty, isn't he?" Perrin agreed.

Bill wondered if all women were mad in this day and age. He was so out of touch with "the scene" now. Not that he'd ever really been in touch. He'd met Adira during senior year of college and that had been it for him. She'd been his quiet center, the diametric opposite of Ms. Perrin Williams in every way.

Introductions were made and they moved to a larger table. He ended up sitting farthest from Perrin, clearly she was a favorite. What he found interesting was he felt a bit put out by how the seating wound up. He hadn't been jealous of Josh Harper when he'd first spotted them so obviously enjoying each other's company.

Had he?

Gods above, maybe he was the one who was going mad.

No, he was simply bothered by the fact that she was sitting there chatting with someone over lunch when she should be back in her shop working on the new designs. Though she had her libretto and sketchpad with her, closed, he noted with some chagrin. He did his best to not grind his teeth while finding something to chat about with Carlo while his model girlfriend ignored both of them.

The problem was that while Carlo could sing beautifully in several languages, he spoke only German and Italian fluently. Bill's German was almost as bad as Carlo's English and his other languages were nonexistent beyond what was needed to manage opera schedules and stage directions.

Here he was in an urban watering hole, which was slowly filling with the young and beautiful of Seattle. And all he really wanted was to go fetch the kids and bribe their happiness with take-out pizza.

One of these days he was going to have to kill Wilson Jervis. At least sitting kitty-corner from Perrin, he was able to watch her, for he couldn't seem to look away.

Perrin could feel Bill Cullen's attention without turning to look. Why did his attention so affect her that she *couldn't* turn in his direction?

She'd also overheard his stumbling attempts to talk with Carlo. She wanted to tease him about it. See if she could goad him into a blustering defense about how he hadn't followed her here because he'd fallen in love with her while she slept on his office couch.

She also wanted to find out more about him and his family. He was so sweet with the kids. Perrin couldn't imagine what that was like. Cassidy's dad had been a good guy even if he didn't speak much, letting Perrin come and stay during college vacations so that she never had to go home. Jo's dad had been a sullen fisherman who lived on his boat or in a bar. Not a drunk, just an every-night regular until the day he'd died. Her own dad... She wouldn't think of him.

Jaspar clearly worshipped his dad, and Tammy, once she'd loosened up about being too careful, had leaned against him happily while she'd reached up to stuff confetti down the back of his shirt.

"So, Perrin. I will be needing a terribly sexy dress." Melanie was laying it on a little thick, sliding her hands down her sleek form, perhaps for the benefit of the others.

A quick wink showed that Perrin was absolutely right.

"I will be coming to the opening night of Carlo's opera. I must be the most beautiful woman on opening night so that Carlo will not be able sing without thinking of me. I must have another of your dresses."

"Did you know I'm designing the costumes for the opera?"

"No? *C'est vrai? Très bon!*"

"Yes! And the best part?"

"*Oui?*"

"It's making Bill absolutely nuts!"

Melanie and Perrin both turned to look at him. He turned from one face to the other, then he blushed.

"Ooo," Melanie rested a hand over Perrin's and whispered after Josh had started a conversation with him. "This one, he likes you."

Perrin looked back at Bill's profile a little more closely. "No… I don't think so. Besides, he's married. You should see his kids. They're wonderful. So alive. So un… " She'd almost said undamaged.

Melanie squeezed her hand. They had recognized that in each other at their very first meeting, a common bond even Jo and Cassidy didn't understand more than intellectually.

"So uninhibited," she corrected. Then she glanced once more down the table at Bill. If she was being objective, she'd say that Melanie was right. That he did like her.

But that made no sense.

BILL TRIED to sort out his own feelings, but wasn't having much luck. He'd expected to spend the afternoon trapped in a yawning chasm of boredom as wide as the world, instead he was intrigued despite his better judgment. Perrin, so overdramatic when talking to Josh or teasing Carlo in broken Italian, was a different woman when talking to the supermodel. With Melanie, Perrin was calm, close, intimate. Her smile warm rather than madcap. Her gestures fluid and graceful rather than flamboyant and occasionally hazardous to those seated nearby.

When at last the party broke up in late afternoon, he figured his duties for the Opera and Wilson were well paid. Melanie had certainly enjoyed herself, which appeared to be enough to keep Carlo happy. They were within walking distance of their hotel and headed off with many hugs between the two women.

Melanie and Perrin were a little daunting to watch actually. Melanie was several inches taller, but they almost could have been sisters. Rather than having that emaciated look that so many models did, they were both simply slender, healthy-looking women of truly exceptional beauty. They were certainly easy enough together to be related.

Josh was headed to Kirkland to review some waterfront restaurant that had just been opened by a two-star Michelin chef. He'd given back his stars, closed his major New York restaurant, and moved west to open a small bistro in the upscale suburb.

Bill watched as Perrin stepped out into the afternoon light and raised her arms as if she were a goddess greeting the setting sun and the glistening waterfront. She strolled toward the waterfront to walk through the city park that lay between Cutters and the Pike Place Market.

It was a beautiful spring evening, the breeze cool, but the air warm. Other people gathered in the park, sitting on benches and staring out at the ferries and container ships working their way through Seattle's harbor. Nothing brought out the people of this city quite like a sunny day.

Bill didn't stop moving long enough to enjoy the view very often anymore. But the view here was stunning, in more ways than one. When Perrin saw that he'd accompanied her, she turned to him.

"I'd like to borrow your kids."

"What? No!" The last thing Bill wanted was his kids under this woman's influence. Or getting more attached to her. They'd already started asking him questions this afternoon once she'd left.

Jaspar liked her, dubbing her as "cool." His current "retro-word." Bill had just introduced the kids to Travolta in *Grease*. There was more going on than "cool" though. The little twerp was always hunting for a new mother to marry his dad. For a while his choice had been Nia at the front desk, then his fifth-grade teacher, and now Perrin was on the verge of replacing Olivia Newton-John. Jaspar didn't quite understand that Olivia Newton-John, while still a fine-looking woman, was in her sixties now and his dad wasn't. Jaspar's only measure? Being older than his big sister, which meant you were old... just like his dad. Great!

Tammy had been just the opposite, though making the same assumptions. His pointing out that he'd met her on Monday and this was only Wednesday did nothing to appease his daughter's suspicions. A teenager who was in and out of crushes almost weekly wouldn't understand that actual, adult relationships didn't happen overnight.

"Why can't I borrow them?" Perrin asked as she arrived at the thick brass railing that overlooked the waterfront. "I promise I'll give them back."

"What do you want them for?" He moved up beside her, giving that anonymous nod that Seattleites always traded with strangers to the guy just a few feet farther along.

Perrin flipped open the sketchbook and pointed to a drawing. Three thumbnails across the top and then the two larger drawings of children. His children!

"Having them as models would really help." Perrin had drawn Jaspar and Tammy in costumes.

She'd captured Jaspar with his wide-eyed wonder at the world. His costume vibrated with that energy as if always reaching for the next thing. He looked caught on the verge of his favorite question: "Why?" He'd gone through the "Why" phase when he was four, just like every other child on the planet, but now he'd circled back around to it, and this time really wanted to know rather than just being assured that there was indeed order to the universe.

Tammy was different. Perrin had caught her on the edge of becoming a woman, but less ready than she thought she was. In ways Bill couldn't sort out, Perrin had captured both her surety and the slight fracturing that occurred from being overeager to grow up. He glanced around to see if anyone else was watching this shocking exposure of his children's true characters, but everyone was interested in their own world, not his. The cool breeze sent a chill up his spine. Who was this woman? Had she been researching his kids somehow? No, she was just…what? A psychic? A…

"There's no boy character in the opera," Bill retreated to the known. He had to, to cover just how perfectly this enigmatic woman had captured his children, as if she'd known them their whole lives.

She waved the libretto at him, "Hello. Not stupid. So add one who doesn't sing. Jaspar would love the role."

"Little twerp would," Bill had to admit with a smile that he hadn't intended. "But his sister would be some kind of pissed if he got to wear a cool costume on stage and she didn't."

"Is the girl's part cast yet?"

Bill tried to think through the cast list. The major singers had all been cast a year ahead for scheduling reasons, and the standing Emerald City Opera Chorus would fill all of the villager and guard roles as well as most of the courtiers. Those with half-solo contracts could fill the Chief of Guard and Missionary roles. But a couple of the middle characters weren't yet cast. That included the child. Children?

"Tammy doesn't sing, except with her guitar."

"So teach her! She only has seven lines and three of them are only one word long."

Bill looked up from the drawing to study Perrin. The sun was almost directly behind her, making her face hard to see. As if she were deeply inscrutable, mysterious, so powerful that she wore the sun as a halo.

She couldn't have had time to read the libretto more than once since she'd left the Costume Shop this afternoon, there simply wasn't time. And the child's lines were spread out. Odd thing to tally on a single reading, unless she'd somehow tallied everything. To avoid feeling totally humbled by the shining Empress, he'd let that one go unremarked.

The light breeze that always ghosted along the Seattle waterfront on even the calmest days made her hair, now out of its ponytail, dance on her shoulders. The brightest blue eyes he'd ever seen argued that the blond stripe, or something near to it was her proper hair color, though the dyed-black look was a nice contrast to her pale skin. It also accented her strong cheekbones.

She'd added a fleece jacket. It was strange in a way that took him a moment to identify.

"Black t-shirt, blue knit vest, REI jacket. You look almost... " He bit his tongue to avoid saying it.

"Almost human." A wicked glint came into her eyes.

"Uh, I was going to say normal."

"Normal compared to what?"

Bill grinned at her, "I think this would be a good time for me to be in a different conversation."

She grinned and leaned against the rail but stayed facing him.

He couldn't help noticing that the guy a little further down the rail was admiring the view, and not the one of the waterfront. He turned away when Bill glared at him.

"Okay, Mr. Cullen. What conversation would you like to be in? Shall I go get one of those first-date conversation deck of cards for you? I'm sure I saw some in one of the game stalls in the Market." She waved a fine-fingered hand over her shoulder indicating Pike Place Market behind her.

"You're amazing!" He didn't know where that came from, but she was. Intelligent, funny, wild... amazing.

After a long pause, she slowly stood up straight, took her sketch pad back from him, and, closing it, slid it beside the libretto. Pulling her jacket closed against a sudden gust, he could feel a type of shield forming around her, like on the Starship *Enterprise.*

"I think I should be going."

It was only then, like he'd been caught in a time warp while watching her change, that he realized that he didn't want her to go. Not at all.

"Why?"

She began moving off.

"No, wait."

She stopped.

"Why?"

For a long moment she stood still, rigid, then turned to face him. There was no sign of the wild blond, or the powerful Empress. Instead, in their place, stood the waif with the saddest eyes he'd ever seen.

"The likes of you aren't for the likes of me, Mr. Cullen. You should go home to your wife and children, I'm sure they're missing you."

"Wait!" he called before she could turn away once more. "Just wait."

So she did. Standing there all alone, the lost girl fighting off a shiver on a warm sunny day, her jacket still clutched closed across her chest. The wind still toyed with the tips of her hair.

"I'm not married." Where the hell had that come from? He wanted to work with Perrin, not bed her.

She eyed him skeptically.

"She died four years ago. A drunk hit her with a car. Broad daylight in a crosswalk." God Almighty! Why was he ripping his guts out in front of this woman? It almost killed his heart all over again to say the words out loud.

The change was instantaneous. Sympathy poured out of her as her hand shifted from holding her jacket closed to holding her palm over her heart.

"I'm so sorry. And I was teasing you about— You must hate me."

"No." Bill closed his eyes, not knowing what he was feeling. "No, I don't hate you. It's just hard sometimes."

Perrin took a step closer and rested a hand on his arm. "You're such a good father."

"What? What makes you say that?" He screwed up more days than he didn't. His daughter was drifting away and he didn't know why or how to bring her back. He didn't spend enough time with Jaspar. They were both growing up so damn fast that he—

"Because it's hard for you. If it wasn't, it would mean you didn't care. Trust me, I know." For a moment longer, the sad-eyed girl patted his arm. Then she began brushing at his shoulders, as if dusting him off.

"What? What are you doing?"

She dusted harder, squinting her eyes as if it were hard work. She moved around him until she was practically pounding him on the back.

He tried to turn to face her, but she shoved against his shoulder to keep him in place and continued her way around him. Passers-by were eyeing them strangely. When she arrived once more in front of him, she brushed her hand lightly a few times over his heart.

"There."

"There what?"

"There," Perrin now stood quite close before him, those sad eyes brightening. "You can now leave all that 'bad father' crap behind, I brushed it off you."

Bill could feel his jaw slacken, but clamped it shut before he looked even dumber than he felt. But he couldn't help looking down to see what now lay at his feet. Nothing but the gray concrete of the walkway.

"You think it's as simple as that?" What kind of a ditzy—

"Of course!" Perrin chirped merrily. "Wait. It didn't work? What's wrong with you?" She moved even closer and lifted up on his eyebrows and inspected one eye and then the other, her fingers cool on his brow. "That's strange."

"What?" He was having trouble breathing she was so near. Her eyes were an incredibly pure blue. And the way she smelled. He'd expected perfume or at least an exotic-scented soap. Instead she just smelled immensely, deliciously female.

"I have a terrible diagnosis for you, Mr. Cullen. Are you ready for it?"

This should be good. He nodded with only a little hesitation.

"You're human. I can't just brush that off you. Not even the Empress can do that." Then she grew solemn. "If it were so easy, Bill, we'd all be so much happier, wouldn't we? I'll see you at rehearsal tomorrow. And I'm expecting you and your children in my shop tomorrow evening for dinner. I'll get the pizza."

His light touch on her arm stopped her from turning. Toe to toe he let himself enjoy the sensation of being so close to her.

"I think, Ms. Perrin Williams, that you may well be the most startling person I've ever met."

"I'll take that as a compliment."

"You should, I think… Yes. You should." He really was a lost cause. He couldn't even pay a beautiful and kind woman a decent compliment without screwing it up.

She rested a hand on his cheek. Then she leaned forward and rested her cheek against his.

An electric shock rippled through him, like a static discharge on a doorknob, but without the pain. A sense of simple wonder coursed down through him. The small pleasure of being touched by an attractive woman for the first time since Adira. That's all it was.

Perrin pulled back, but didn't remove her hand from his other cheek. She studied him carefully from just inches away. Then she leaned in and kissed him.

Bill forgot to breathe, or think, or anything. He simply marveled at the sweet tenderness of her lips on his. He leaned into it: the warmth, the sensation, the trust. He didn't know which overwhelmed him the most, but there was no question that "overwhelm" was the operative word here.

Whether the kiss lasted a second or a handful of minutes, he'd never know. He just knew that when Perrin once again moved back, she'd left a taste of her behind. A taste that he couldn't compare to anyone. Not to Adira, not to his first-ever kiss. This was wholly Perrin Williams. Whoever in the world that might be.

"Well," she whispered from a bare inch away, "that was certainly interesting."

"You sound like the Empress, but you look like the wacky designer."

"I'll try switching that." She composed a serious expression that he wasn't buying for an instant. "We gonna have ta try that kiss again some day soon. Because if that was real… Holy Shit, Batman!"

At least she now *sounded* like the wacky designer. But she looked like the empress. As to the kiss?

"Oh yeah!" Most definitely had to try that again. "Real soon."

CHAPTER 5

*P*errin *sat in the* rehearsal space on the upper level of the Seattle Opera House about a mile from the Emerald City Opera's offices. It was a beautiful space, nearly the same size as the main stage without all the extra space off to the back of the stage and the sides that Bill told her were called wings. The rehearsal space was actually on the top floor of the building, off the side of the upstairs lobby behind an unmarked door. Decorated in a soft beige, it had been turned golden by the tall windows at one end letting in the Seattle sunshine. A shining black grand piano replaced the orchestra.

"This is just our first sing-through," Bill had informed her. "We need to start getting the cast comfortable with the new music. If this were a repertoire opera, they would arrive three weeks before the opening rather than six and we'd move right into staging."

Perrin sat between Wilson Jervis and Melanie in a row of folding chairs along one wall. The principal singers sat in a circle in the middle of the stage, along with the orchestra conductor, the director, Bill, and the Chorus Master who would sing all of the minor roles for now.

Bill had greeted her briefly, barely offering a smile, back in his bustling Overlord role. Perrin could be okay with that. One kiss didn't change the world. She wouldn't even try to count how many men she'd been in and out of love with over the years. Not as many as Jo and Cassidy thought by a long shot, Perrin enjoyed giving them a good story and something to worry about, but more than she'd care to admit.

Some part of her was irritated at Bill's apparent lack of ongoing interest. That kiss had certainly rocked her charts. The Tragic Prince, all his hopes and desires and needs had been wrapped up in that kiss. That she was the woman who had drawn that out of Bill Cullen ranked as a startling concept.

That she had lost herself in that kiss, losing track of where she was and who she was, and simply been present in that moment was an even greater surprise. The one thing Perrin never was? Out of control. Deep inside, she had a very rigid grip on who she was and what she would do.

But for a kiss like Bill's, perhaps losing a bit of her control wasn't a bad thing.

The more she watched Bill as he organized the rehearsal, the less put out she felt about his simple greeting.

Everyone came to him with questions. He had two assistants who constantly brought him questions, some about *Ascension*, some about the *Turandot* closing this weekend. Singers took cajoling. The writer—the librettist she'd been corrected—and the composer were both there because it was a new opera. The former, a thin young man who practically shimmered with nerves and the latter a staunch woman who apparently thought lyrics were a waste of time and should be changed to fit her music or better yet, removed entirely so that they didn't interfere with her creation. Clearly they were not on speaking terms and Bill had to handle all communication between them.

All of this took Bill's attention. As she watched him, she began to see quite how good he was at what he did. The conductor had heavily marked his score with questions, but Bill had found a way for the composer to work with him rather than slugging him as she seemed more prone to do. The singers actually cared what order they sat in around the circled chairs. One man was so big that a sturdier chair had to be found.

When Renata Donatello made her entrance, the room had gone quiet as all attention shifted to her. Renata had taken one look at the Empress' dress and insisted on wearing it to the rehearsal. Perrin and Jerimy had made some quick alterations this morning, thankfully ones that didn't require rebuilding the whole costume, then added the red lining. The compliments that swirled about the room upon Renata's grand entrance left Perrin feeling a little giddy.

"That is the dress I want," Melanie leaned in to whisper. "I want to be powerful like that. That's how every woman wants to feel. You have such incredible skills, my friend."

Now Perrin was having trouble breathing. To have one of New York's most successful models say such things... Perrin could only marvel at what it took to actually feel a stamp of approval, as if what she'd done for over a decade didn't count until this moment.

Two years ago, she'd still been struggling on her own. Now she had practically abandoned the front of the shop, adding a manager and an assistant, and was spending most of her time designing and building. Not that she was complaining, that's what she loved best, it was just surprising.

And to have a woman who was constantly clothed in the finest designer labels insist on having one of her dresses... It made Perrin feel oddly capable and suddenly twice as uncertain, as if she were faking being a designer as hard as she was faking being even close to normal.

Melanie had a point though. While the Empress' dress wouldn't be quite right for her, something closely related would work. Melanie was too sensual a woman for the austere look of the Empress. The punch of power would look good on her, but she needed something other. Perrin flipped to a fresh page on her pad and began sketching a few ideas while Bill organized the singers.

Perrin became focused on the design, building layer upon layer of detail for the dress she'd design for Melanie until she realized that a rush of sound was carrying her forward. She looked up startled to see the singers already well into the first act.

Opera had never been part of her repertoire. She preferred a good band for dancing and didn't really care what era. Blue Scholars, The Band Perry, and The Black Keys shared her playlists with Maroon 5, Madonna, and Styx. Nothing had prepared her for the powerful wall of sound that the opera singers produced with just their voices.

It was in Italian, which didn't help her much, but it didn't matter. Renata was not ordering around Carlo; instead the Empress was crashing a mandate down upon the Prince's head. When the barrel-chested deep bass of Geoffrey Palliser joined the fray, the room practically shook with the Overlord's derision. The Prince's soaring tenor fought for freedom, but found little space between the wall of the Empress' power and the bulldozer of the Overlord's driving rhythms.

It was so completely different from anything she'd heard before it was hard to make sense of it. Even the symphonies that Jo and Cassidy had occasionally dragged her to were no comparison. These weren't instruments, these were people. They weren't hurling music at each other, but rather it was a battle of pure emotion expressed through singing.

The sound swept her along. The mezzo-soprano Princess, her lower-voiced, contralto Maid-servant Confessor, and the high-coloratura True Love vied for the Prince's attention. The audience's hopes and fears would swing back and forth between them. Whichever one triumphed, it would reshape the future of the kingdom, perhaps alter the fabric of the very world.

The final five-voiced chord of Act I crashed Perrin back into her seat and the dim world of reality. It took her a moment to reorient herself in the rehearsal studio space. Several of the singers were talking about the roles, but Carlo and Geoffrey, apparently old friends, were catching up on the latest Italy versus England soccer rivalries.

"What do you think?" Bill was squatting before her chair and looking at her with the kind smile she'd been missing earlier.

"I think I'm in love!" Perrin could still feel the sound of the music vibrating through her.

"Not with Carlo, I hope. I might get jealous."

Perrin placed a finger on the center of his forehead and pushed until he fell back on his butt.

"Wow! This is so cool!" Tammy had taken up her brother's adjective.

Jaspar, on the other hand, had only one comment to make about Perrin's shop, "Ugh! Girl clothes." And then he'd immediately put on his best bored look, one that Bill knew all too well. Though his son did stop to admire his reflection from the dress made of little mirrors. Bill convinced himself that the mannequin's chest was simply the largest expanse for Jaspar to observe himself in and that Bill shouldn't read anything deeper into it. When Jaspar started making faces at himself, Bill felt better. A little.

Tammy took her time. She'd spent enough afternoons down in the Costume Shop with Jerimy that she actually inspected how some of the clothes were made. She "just happened" to pass close to him at one point during her inspection to ask him a question.

"Are these really good, Dad?"

"Yeah," he acknowledged just as Perrin came over from chatting volubly with a customer now departing in a brand-new blue silk jacket that was clearly a custom fit. "Really good."

Tammy nodded and wandered off while Bill inspected the vision headed his way.

Perrin wore a blazer of green and yellow that made her look like nothing so much as a leprechaun. She even sported a bright green hat, shaped like that of a racy secret agent, slanting forward and left, partly covering one eye. When she approached, he saw that she still wore the opera t-shirt beneath the blazer. It made for a deep pseudo-cleavage of black that reached to her sternum, without being the least bit indecent. No one should look good in such an outfit, but she certainly did.

She greeted the kids and then leaned close enough that only he would hear. "I thought about not wearing the t-shirt just to make you crazy." And then in the same breath but a louder voice, "Come on, kids. Let me show you something cool I just made for someone getting married in a couple weeks."

The kids followed her happily enough.

Bill tried, but couldn't. She'd riveted him right to the floor with the image of her in nothing but that deeply plunging blazer.

"PIZZA AS PROMISED!" Tammy followed Ms. Williams as she led them like a girl scout troop into the back room carrying the just-delivered boxes.

Jasp had offered Ms. Williams an "okay I guess" on the new wedding clothes she'd showed them. Then he'd rolled his eyes at Tammy in long-suffering pain. Dad had taught them good manners, but he and Tammy both knew Jasp's pretending to have any interest at all was complete baloney.

"She's pretty," Jasp offered up just in case Ms. Williams had caught his eye roll.

Tammy couldn't look away from the female mannequin, all dressed up for her wedding. It was like the dress in the photo on Dad's bedside table. Well, not really, but it was enough to remind her of what it had felt like to have a mother and how much she missed her every day.

Her dad was acting all weird when he finally joined them in the back room. And Ms. Williams was looking awfully pleased with herself. Then she set the pizza boxes on the big table. They hadn't even spoken together, never mind anything else. Tammy had made sure to stay close to Ms. Williams, just to be sure. But she must have missed something that was going on.

"I ordered two pizzas. Half a pepperoni for Jaspar, because all boys like pepperoni. Half a combo with extra meat for your dad because he probably eats too much of what the kids want and not enough of what he wants." The boys dug right in.

She turned to Tamara, "I got us half veggie and half Hawaiian. How'd I do, Tamara?"

"Everyone calls me Tammy."

Ms. Williams took a slice of the veggie and looked at her over it. "I don't know. I think I'll stick with your full name, it sort of fits you better. You're no longer a little girl."

"Only Mom ever called me Tamara, Ms. Williams."

Ms. Williams didn't look embarrassed, or apologize like other adults Tammy pushed back against.

"Your call. But it sounds like your mom was a smart lady. I'm Perrin by the way. I have no idea who that Ms. Williams person is." She actually shuddered which made it kind of funny.

"Tamara is okay, I guess." Then she looked away. She needed to think about Perrin being all human and normal. She didn't talk down to her at all, which was weird for an adult. It could be a setup, but it didn't feel like one.

Jasp and Dad had each taken huge bites. They were grinning at each other like idiots as they both hooted out cooling breaths over too-hot pizza.

"Well, you certainly nailed those two lame-os."

Tammy took a small bite of her pizza, Hawaiian was her absolute favorite, then figured out how to tell if the woman was being fake-nice to a child. She kept her voice low, so that the lame-os wouldn't hear.

"Have you kissed him yet?"

Perrin looked at her carefully, but didn't stop chewing on her pizza. If she was really shocked, she didn't show it.

She sat on one of the stools and waited for Tammy to climb up on one as well. They were closer to the same height that way.

"Once. And I wonder just how pissed your dad will be that I told you that."

Tammy had only had conversations like this once or twice with her girlfriends, and half the time she lied and she bet her friends did too.

She'd also bet that Perrin had just told her the truth.

"You kissed any boys yet?"

Tammy shot a quick look over at her dad, but he wasn't paying attention. She could feel the heat rushing to her cheeks and did her best to hide it with another bite of pizza, but her stomach was suddenly all twisty.

"A few," she tried to shrug it off, and wondered why she'd just told this woman who'd kissed her dad the truth. "Still don't know what the big deal is."

"When it's the right boy, trust me it will be."

Tammy looked up into those blue eyes. Perrin was talking about kissing as if it was the most normal thing on the planet. As if it wasn't a matter of social standing, or social media hell if you kissed the wrong boy. She tried to find a response, but she couldn't. Perrin was just watching her.

"And until it is a big deal... " Perrin leaned in and whispered. "So not worth the rest of it."

Tammy hadn't thought of it that way. She thought about the boys who wanted to grab, some of them were already asking if she was still a virgin, she knew three girls in her class who for sure weren't. But they were kinda slutty.

But what if she simply said she was waiting until it was a big deal? It just might work. It would sure avoid a lot of hassles.

Maybe Perrin knew what she was talking about.

BILL WATCHED PERRIN WORK. He worried about exposing the kids to her, but he shouldn't be. He'd also "exposed" them to every woman at the opera, both the full-timers and the artists who came in on a freelance contract for just one opera then moved on. Several had made him offers and he'd been tempted more than once, at least for a couple nights of no-strings sex. But he'd never figured out how to actually date with the kids around. They knew his schedule as intimately as he did. Aunt Lucy's on show nights and the occasional crisis at the opera, but nothing else. Evenings were their family-together time.

So, why was he worried about Perrin?

He'd watched her with his kids and she was great. Better than Nia or Jerimy or a half-dozen of the others at the opera? Maybe, maybe not. But they appeared comfortable around her.

Jaspar thought it was all just a lark. He'd giggled when Perrin had measured him, though she'd let Bill do the in-seam measurement while the two girls tactfully were busy down at the other end of the room. He'd eaten so much pizza that Bill was afraid he'd be sick, but instead he finally settled at one end of the worktable with a book of Kipling's *Captains Courageous* that he had to read for school.

Tammy was a different matter. There was something between her and Perrin, something that he hadn't seen happen. It was like two matadors dancing about a ring with no bull present. Testing each other cautiously yet on the same side. Tammy had followed Perrin around and watched everything she was doing, asking a lot of technical questions along the way. Bill had no idea she'd picked up so much from Jerimy and the others in costuming.

Perrin slowed down enough to show her what she was doing, but wouldn't let her sew. "No, not the machines. These aren't like home sewing machines. Maybe I can teach you some other time if it's okay with your dad."

When Tammy had complained, Perrin hadn't turned for Bill's support. She stepped right up to the plate, much like a good parent would.

"You can try the Singer Featherweight some other day."

Tammy's, "Oh man! That's so lame!" groan only elicited a smile from Perrin.

"That's my first sewing machine. I bought it for myself with my own money and taught myself to sew on it. Good clothing isn't about cool machines. It starts here," she tapped Tammy's chest over her heart. "Later it goes here," she tapped Tammy's head. "Figuring out how to build it, that's the easy part."

Easy part. Bill remembered Jerimy's comment about the construction of the Empress' costume, that even seeing the finished gown he wasn't sure how it had been done.

Perrin had pre-built both of the children's costumes she'd shown him yesterday. Just yesterday? Didn't the woman ever sleep?

Now she trimmed, pinned, and seamed with an easy assuredness in her own skills. No sign of the sad waif. And with shedding the leprechaun blazer, she'd also shed most of the eccentric crazy-girl.

In the wake of their departure they'd left a very pleasant woman with a crazy hair dye-job. And a very competent one.

It took less than an hour for both costumes to come together. He was shooed to the far end of the studio and forced to sit with his back to them for the final fitting. He'd seen the clothes all evening on the worktable, he didn't know what the big deal was. But by then she had both kids on her side, and Tammy gave him one of her, "Don't be a dork!" looks. He finally complied.

For lack of anything better to do, he began reading the Kipling. He'd forgotten the story. Two young boys, one arrogant and lost at sea, another raised on a Gloucester fishing vessel working the Grand Banks. And how the boys grew into men. He really wasn't ready for Jaspar to be doing that, not anytime soon. No more than he was ready for Tammy to grow into a woman which was happening much faster. She—

"Okay," he jumped when Perrin spoke close beside him.

He started to turn, but she stopped him with a quick hand on his cheek, exactly where she'd placed it yesterday as they kissed. They shared a look that proved he wasn't the only one who'd been thinking far too much about that moment.

"Close your eyes." He did, though reluctantly. It was the first excuse he'd found to be this close to her all day. She took his hands and guided him to his feet and back down the workroom. He squeezed her hands in his, an unobtrusive enough gesture. She stumbled. Using their shared grip, he had to steady her as she continued to lead him. He liked having that effect on her.

"Okay, are you ready?"

He nodded.

She let go then gave him permission to open his eyes.

There Jaspar stood, not merely as he'd been drawn. He'd become the youthful promise unfulfilled by the Tragic Prince. He was still so pure, hope for the future brimming over with energy and life. The contrast on stage would be shocking when the boy entered in Act II Scene II. The Prince would be abruptly diminished in the audience's eyes, because here, embodied in Bill's ten-year-old child, was everything the Prince had been given as a birthright but been unable to attain.

And then a young woman stepped from behind the screen. Her dark mane of red hair swept up off her shoulders. Her dark eyes watching him with a frankness and a knowledge that no child could possess. There was a tragedy about her, as if she understood her elder brother's failure where the younger did not.

The clothes revealed nothing beyond her sweet shoulders, nothing except the promise of everything she was to become. It would be she who survived the ultimate tragedy. She who carried on to become the next Empress. This was not some young girl, this was a young woman, a woman just born from the child she'd been and discovering her own power.

"Tamara?" he managed only a whisper. He hadn't called her by her given name since the day the woman who had given it to her died. But this was no young Tammy.

Her smile bloomed.

His children hooted, "Oh, we got you, Dad. We got you so bad." And the two operatic figures dissolved back into his children as they threw themselves into his arms.

All Bill could manage was to hold them both tight and kiss them atop their heads.

When at last he looked up to thank her, he saw that Perrin had left the room.

CHAPTER 6

" __W__ *hy did you leave?* Where did you go?" Bill had finally chased Perrin back to her lair in the store. It had taken three days, but he'd done it.

She'd done more than leave for the few minutes after she'd transformed his children into operatic wonders, perhaps to do some busywork in the front of her shop. In the days since then she'd become invisible. Arriving at rehearsals mere minutes before they started, departing immediately after they ended.

She'd delivered the children's costumes to Jerimy. The photographer had been thrilled and photographed them with Renata the Empress for the publicity campaign. Perrin hadn't shown up for the photo shoot.

And the opera had gone crazy. Okay, no crazier than usual, but he'd been unable to get a single minute to track Perrin down in three days.

Carlo's girlfriend Melanie had gone to Paris for a fashion shoot. Carlo, while not dumb enough to begrudge her career, was now impossibly prickly about everything that wasn't absolutely perfect.

Lord spare Bill from opera-sized egos. Geoffrey Palliser threw a fit about not yet having a costume so he couldn't be on the advertise-

69

ment. Pointing out that his contract had forbidden the use of his image on precisely such promotions did little to mollify him.

Voice lessons with Tammy had taken another chunk out of his afternoons, though under the Chorus Master's guidance she was coming along wonderfully, showing some real aptitude for the small role. Jaspar wasn't interested in the singing, but did listen carefully when the director provided stage directions.

Twice Bill had come by Perrin's shop only to find it closed and dark. She clearly wasn't a morning person.

It was now early evening on Friday. The last of the light was bleeding out of the Seattle sky. The scent of early flowers in small planters outside her shop hovered on the still air. Jaspar was at a friend's and Tammy was at the library for some schoolwork. With his single stolen hour, he'd walked into Perrin's Glorious Garb and barely nodded at the clerk before breezing into the kitchen space and through the accessories display in the old freezer and into the design studio.

Perrin had flinched when he walked in. So, he'd sat down quietly across the cutting table and waited for her to settle before repeating his question.

"Why did you leave?"

She began fiddling with the drawings spread across the table. The only light in the room was the worklight directed at the table's surface. She was little more than shape and form, though her hands were caught by the light. Just a glance revealed the drawings of the rest of the cast, but he forced his attention off them knowing if they went down that path, they might lose track of the present one. He'd promised to pick up Tammy in an hour. It was all the time he had to fix whatever this was.

His eyes were adjusting enough to see that Perrin wore a form-fitting silken turtleneck as black as her hair, and wool slacks almost as blond as the stripe that still remained in her hair. Simple, chic, and a real pleasure to look at.

"Why are you avoiding me?"

"It looked like a great family moment. I didn't want to… " She wouldn't face him.

"Didn't want to what?" Bill wanted to lump this in with his usual job of coaxing along crazy artists, but it didn't feel that way. The dozen drawings spread across the cutting table proved that whatever she needed to create her art, it wasn't coaxing. She'd done them impossibly fast. And if they were even half as good as the first ones, they'd be the finest costumes Emerald City had put on stage in years.

She stood and began gathering them up. "Let's just say that it wasn't my place to intrude and leave it at that."

He stood up and circled the table. When he reached for her hands, she pulled them back.

"Please don't," the sad-eyed girl was back, clutching her drawings as if they were all that anchored her.

He let his hands fall to his sides. "Did I do something wrong? One of the kids?"

"God no!" That snapped her attention to his face. "They're wonderful! And you're so good with them. I didn't belong. It was your moment. So I left."

"A moment you created."

"I didn't belong. That should be enough for you," she insisted, then moved over to the next table and slipped the drawings into a portfolio. She held the closed case out as a barrier between them. "Since you're here, you can take these to Jerimy."

"Don't you need them to build from?"

"No, they're in my head once I draw them. But it doesn't matter, I was only hired as a designer. There are just a couple designs missing. I'll send those over as soon as I figure them out."

"But you built the first three, I thought you'd want to do the other major costumes. And you know that your contract has a clause paying you more if you do so. I also thought you'd want to maintain the quality of—"

"Here!" She slammed the portfolio flat against his chest so that he had to grab. "You've have them. Now just go!"

She turned her back on him and retreated into the darkness, making it only two or three steps before she ground to a halt.

Idiot! Bill shouted at himself. There was something far bigger going on here than any lousy set of drawings. He'd been so slow to see it, that he'd probably just made bad matters worse. He set the portfolio on the table and moved up behind her.

He placed his hands on her upper arms.

She shrugged him off angrily.

He did it again and held on this time. When she didn't protest anymore, he turned her slowly clockwise so that the blond stripe climbed upward across her hair as she came to face him.

"Why can't you accept that you didn't want me there?" she asked as soon as he had her fully turned.

"But I did."

"You idiot!" She shoved him hard in the center of his chest, forcing him to stumble back a step. He regained his balance just before he ran into a clothing rack. He'd expected to find her weeping, instead he was facing the Empress brought to life.

Perrin stormed several paces away from him until she was blocked by her sewing machines. Then she stalked back toward him, stopping close in front of him in the narrow aisle between the cutting table and a wall of fabric folded onto shelves.

"Those kids!" she jabbed a finger in the direction of the changing corner where the kids had been. "They're precious. You can't have them imprinting on me. You can't let them. Please, Bill, for their own safety, you can't let them. That's why I walked away. So that you don't connect them to me."

"Are you so awful?" He said it as a joke. It was totally ludicrous for her to think so.

NORMALLY PERRIN DIDN'T GIVE a damn what a guy thought, let him get screwed up by being around her. But she'd never been with a single dad. There'd never been so much at stake.

She clamped down on her lips so hard they hurt and then nodded once. Fiercely. Yes, she was that awful.

Bill laughed.

The goddamn man laughed at her.

She pounded the side of her fist against his chest, which did nothing but bounce off.

"You are far and away the least hazardous woman I've ever run into. Whack-a-doodle! Oh yeah! Hazardous, not a chance."

"I'm fucking toxic!" she shouted in his face.

Any man with the least common sense would turn tail and run, glad to be shut of her. She'd been through this enough times to know for a fact that even this little bit of the truth worked to drive men away. She also knew that she truly was toxic. Her past was a poison that ran through her whole life and eventually killed every relationship she'd ever attempted. She was just being preemptive this time, for the kids' sake. She couldn't risk contaminating them with her past.

"Get the hell out and leave me alone!" she yelled again, the pain raking at her throat as she tried once more to drive him off.

"Perrin!" He got right in her face.

"What!?"she shouted back, pissed that it hadn't worked.

He moved forward, forcing her backward into the deeper darkness. *Shit!* She'd pushed too hard. If she screamed would anyone hear her? Raquel had stuck her head in just five minutes ago, but Perrin had nodded it was okay to lock up and leave. She'd been so stupid. Now she was all alone and Bill was far stronger that she was.

She stumbled back and fell into a chair. She prepared to fight. Her scissors were almost in reach if she just—

Bill pulled over another chair, set it in front of her, then sat down in it.

He didn't attack.

Just sat there.

Perrin fought for a breath. Her heart beat faster than any rabbit's possibly could. *Was she safe?* All of the old emotions were pounding her adrenaline right past redline, and she'd never been able to do anything about it. Ever.

He reached out and took one of her hands gone suddenly nerveless.

"Crap! You're freezing. And your hands are shaking. What the hell? Are you okay?"

She shook her head, it was all she could manage.

"Wait."

Perrin could see a dawning comprehension in his eyes and knew she'd underestimated him and interpreted it all wrong.

"Wait. You thought I'd… I'd never attack a woman!" His shock appeared genuine.

"Heard that often enough." Then she flung up her free arm, wrapping it over her mouth and clamping her hand on her opposite shoulder. She had to stop whatever she was going to say next.

Now Bill looked truly shocked.

She'd given him the unanswerable. No protestation of innocence could work against such a statement. She freed her other hand from his and pulled her knees up until she could wrap both arms around them and her heels were on the edge of the chair.

"I'm sorry," she mumbled through her knees. "I'm so sorry. You didn't deserve that. I told you I was toxic."

He huffed out a breath. He didn't leave. He didn't shout back. He didn't cock back an arm to hit her. He just huffed out another breath.

"Well," his voice a soft rumble. "I'll buy hurt. I'll buy that there's someone on this earth who would be better off dead for whatever they did to you," he actually sounded pissed on her behalf. Then, impossibly he smiled at her.

She had no idea what to do with a smile. Her childhood taught her to never trust it. Her adulthood merely taught her that the man smiling wanted something, usually sex, and was being nice enough to ask first, even if non-verbally. But Bill's smile made no sense. Especially not with what she'd just accused him of. But he still smiled at her nonetheless.

He crossed his arms over his chest and slouched back in the chair as if just getting comfortable. The worklight behind him making him little more than a silhouette. Not quite giving him a halo.

"But if you want the title of toxic, you're going to have to convince me, because I'm not buying it."

"I'm not telling you my life's story."

"You have something better to do this evening?" He was being Mr. Oh So Amiable.

"No. But I'm still not telling." Though if he kept it up, Perrin might find she wanted to smile again, not something she'd done in the last three days.

"In that case," Bill stared up at the pipes on the ceiling as if contemplating the breadth and width of the broadcloth of the universe. "I'll just have to convince you that you aren't."

"Can't fight reality." She wished to God he could, but not even the Tragic Prince could do that.

"Hey, I work in opera. You can't get much further from reality than that. So, here goes. You ready?"

She nodded. Did this man know what he was doing to her? No one had ever been on her side except Jo and Cassidy. Her two college friends loved her and did their best to protect her from herself, and she'd always bless the heavens for the two of them. But no one ever really tried to understand her. To have a man try to protect her from the impossible… That was new and felt amazing inside.

"My first exhibit should be my kids. But I don't want them in the middle of this any more than you do. So I'll simply just happen to mention that what you've done for them in just the first two days since you met has already changed them, and in a good way. Did you know that Wilson Jervis offered them formal contracts which included Union Scale contributions to their college funds? Do you have any idea how proud that made them to be earning money for the family? How proud that made me? And Tammy is really enjoying her voice lessons."

"You said it was unfair to use them, and it is." Though she loved hearing how they were doing. They'd barely met, yet she'd missed them horribly these last days. It was the closest she'd been to tears in a long time, just hearing about them.

"So, for the official first example, I'll offer Jo Thompson."

That startled her enough to sit up and look at him. "You know Jo?"

"Not really. But I called her on her honeymoon while you were passed out on my couch. That one of the most accomplished and powerful women of Seattle loves you so much speaks volumes. By the end of the call, she was ready to get on a plane with or without her new husband. I take it she knows you well?"

Perrin nodded, "No one better, except Cassidy."

"Who is my second official exhibit. You mentioned she will be coming to the opera with you tomorrow. Yet here you are being miserable and still she's not here with you. As I happen to know she's in France, she also must be very attached to you to attend an opera on the same day she flies halfway around the world."

Perrin had forgotten about the jet-lag when she'd invited Cassidy.

Bill waited for her to accede his point.

"She's the best." This man deserved some truth. "Cassidy saved my life." She managed to say it without getting too choked up.

He took that as a win without asking for details; another point in his favor even if he didn't know it.

"And third, at lunch, I couldn't get near you because Melanie and Josh were just so glad to be in your company."

She hadn't really thought of it that way, they were just good friends. "How does all this make your point?"

Bill laughed again, but it didn't make her angry this time.

He reached out and slowly unclamped her hands from around her knees until he was holding both hands, and her feet slipped back to the floor.

"You tell me. Does that sound like someone who's toxic? Someone who sweeps every person they meet off their feet and they never recover?"

"Maybe not. But… "

"No! Cut that out. It's my round. I won it fair and square and you're not going to spoil it. Hell, I deserve a prize. If I'm stuck being human, you are hereafter going to have to live under the cloud of being 'not toxic.' Can you live with that?"

Perrin managed to smile at him. "Guess I'm stuck with it, aren't I?"

Bill just grinned and stroked his nice warm thumbs on the back of her freezing fingers.

She stood slowly, not releasing his hands. Ever so gently, she lowered herself down until she was sitting in his lap.

"You're right," she acknowledged as she settled into place. "You have to get a prize."

"I wasn't trying to get you to—"

And she kissed him. Softly, just barely rubbing her lips over his.

"And that," she deepened the kiss for a delicious moment before pulling back to finish her sentence, "is exactly why you deserve a prize."

Then she stopped any reply with her lips and tongue.

His hands slid out of hers as she reached up to dig her fingers into the waves of his hair. It was even softer than it looked.

He slid his hands around her, snugging her body more tightly against his. His hands hesitated at her waist.

Perhaps she did know Mr. Too-Decent Bill Cullen better than she thought. Reaching down, she coaxed one of his hands upward. They were good hands, big, strong, and they hadn't hit her, not even when she'd pushed him to the edge. When she shifted it onto her breast and clamped her hand over his to keep it there, he was still so gentle. How could she have ever doubted that in this man?

He buried his face in her neck and just stopped there, one hand on her breast, the other equally still on her waist.

She wrapped her arms around him. And he seemed content to stop there, to just remain there.

"You miss her that much?" she made a guess.

He nodded without raising his head.

"Have you even touched a woman since then?"

He hesitated, then shook his head.

She held him against her and stared at the lit worktable. How had she ever thought anything but the best of him? He was too damn decent for his own good.

"Okay," she didn't know quite what to say, but she knew it was up to her to say it. "Mr. Bill Cullen, you listening?"

He nodded against her neck. He brushed his thumb across her nipple almost absent-mindedly, sending really, really good shivers running down her body.

"Between this non-toxic but whack-a-doodle gal..."

"You heard that," he mumbled into her neck.

"I heard that. Between her and this fallible human guy, we're striking a deal."

"What?" he nuzzled her collarbone and almost stole her breath away.

"There is never a question of right or wrong. Okay?"

He froze, locked in place against her, his hands almost brutally tight on her for just an instant in his shock. Then he eased off, slowly sitting up until they were face to face just inches apart.

"That's what Adira always said. She was the wisest woman I've ever known."

Perrin knew she wasn't wise, but she was smart enough to know when she'd just received the highest compliment of her entire life.

She didn't try to kiss him again. She simply pulled his head back to her shoulder and cradled him there, until a while later when he finally said he had to go and fetch his daughter.

Just inside the darkened doorway from her shop, he did take a few minutes to show her just how much he appreciated her.

After locking the door behind him and watching him drive off, she thought about how much she appreciated him. The aftermath of his final kiss and caress still heated her body deliciously.

CHAPTER 7

"*C**assie!" Perrin sprinted through* the lobby crowd at the final performance of *Turandot*. Cassidy had worn her black turtleneck and the sunset sweater that Perrin had picked out for her so long ago to totally slay her future husband on their first blind date. She'd finished it with a flirty black skirt and the knee-high boots that made her look so fabulous.

Cassidy turned just as Perrin crashed into her. She kissed Cassidy hard on the lips.

"I hope Russell won't be jealous, but I'm just so glad to see you."

Cassidy reeled a bit, but went with the flow as she always did, "Glad to see you too. Wish Jo was here so that we could really make it a night out."

"I know!" Perrin stamped her foot and noticed just how much of the local crowd was grimacing at their PDA, like public display of affection was a crime even in Seattle. So, she raised her voice enough to be clearly heard, "Just like that bitch to run away from us and get married."

The crowd rippled away from them in a slow wave of evening gowns and suits. The mezzanine and two balconies offered prime views of the main floor. Sure enough, when Perrin looked up they were being the center of attention.

She spun in a whirl. She'd been inspired by the leprechaun outfit and made a Marilyn Monroe *The Seven Year Itch* pleated skirt of the flowiest bright yellow-and-green rayon to go with the green-and-yellow blazer, though she'd left the shirt off this time revealing skin down to her solar plexus. She finished the whirl and stumbled into Cassidy.

"Let 'em dream," she whispered. "Bet half the guys here will be fantasizing about us tonight, not knowing we're both totally straight. Think they'd be disappointed if they knew?"

Cassidy offered one of her staid smiles.

"Sorry, you're all jet-lagged. I haven't a brain in my body. You sure you're okay with sitting through an opera?"

"I'm here."

Perrin gave her another hug, this time as if she were fragile, "You can always sleep on my shoulder, you just can't weep there."

Cassidy blinked at her as if finally coming awake while they climbed the sweeping grand staircase up to the mezzanine entry level.

"Uh, Perrin. What did I miss? You seem even more Perrin than usual."

"I met a guy."

"I'm shocked," her tone was drier than one of her wines that she critiqued for a living.

"I met a nice guy." Not the right reaction yet. "A nice guy with kids."

"That's sweet... Wait! You did what?" Cassidy finally caught up with the conversation.

"I know! Shocked the shit out of me too. Oh, I've have to stop saying that in case I run into his kids."

"Here? There are never kids at the opera."

"Oh, I don't know. Maybe we'll get lucky."

Cassidy grabbed her arm and turned her toward the glass and steel rail of the mezzanine level. They leaned on the rail. Down below was the main lobby they'd just climbed up from, still milling with people.

A wall of glass five or six stories high showed the outdoor steel scrims. Huge sheets of a fine mesh filled the gap between the opera hall and the next building over, starting twenty feet in the air and climbing to the very top of the structure. They were lit with a bright flow of dancing colors across the mesh. Like a slow kaleidoscope of spring colors.

"How do they do that?"

Cassidy glanced at it, then back at Perrin. "Magic. Who cares? Now spill. I've only been gone for five days. What in the world is up with you?"

Perrin clamped both hands on the top of the rail and sort of pumped herself back and forth. It was all she could do to control the energy bottled up inside her.

"He's really nice. And so damn decent. You know Hogan?"

Cassidy looked at her in utter exasperation. "Maria's Hogan? The man who married the woman who practically raised my husband? The one we all have dinner with every Tuesday evening? That Hogan?"

"Yeah, that one," she loved that she was making Cassidy totally nuts. That would pay her back for being out of the country when Perrin needed her so badly. "Well, I think he may even be more decent than Hogan."

"Uh," Cassidy stopped as she thought about it. "I'm not sure that's possible."

Perrin slanted her best friend a look.

"Okay, prove it."

For the first time Perrin focused on the three-story tall mobile that hung just out of reach. It was made of extension ladders and measuring tapes. It was filled with hammers, pliers, saws, bits and pieces of all the tools she'd been shown in the scenery shop. And a bunch of stuff that looked electrical.

"That's a pretty crazy mobile, don't you think?"

"Perrin!" Cassidy's voice was practically a she-lion snarl. Maybe it was time to answer. But she couldn't quite resist and answered the question with another question.

"You know how you told me after your first time with Russell that really great sex is even way better with the right man?"

"Yea-ah…" she drew it out cautiously.

"Despite every opportunity and encouragement, last night I may have had the best sex of my life and…"

"And what, Perrin?"

"We never even took our clothes off."

Cassidy blinked at her.

Perrin could hear Cassidy analyzing this news. She had the same look that she did when she was tasting one of her wines, that discerning palate and mind that had made her one of the nation's most successful food-and-wine critics before she quit to form the Washington Wine Cooperative.

Her best friend stared at her for the longest moment and then did exactly what Perrin had been hoping for, praying for, because otherwise she was totally losing her mind and she didn't know if she was ready to be doing that.

Cassidy pulled Perrin into her arms and held her tightly. In her ear she whispered, "Oh, I hope so for your sake, Perrin. I really really do."

"Hey," Perrin pulled back and wiped at her friend's cheek. "You know the rules, no crying or getting drunk unless we're all together."

Cassidy brushed at her eyes and offered a watery smile. "You were right."

"I was? Is that a first?"

"Jo is in such deep shit for running off and getting married on us."

"We mustn't tell her or Maria until they're both back and we can all get together."

"Deal," Cassidy sealed it with a very un-Cassie-like smack on Perrin's lips. Maybe after a year of being happily married she was finally loosening up a bit and cared less about what others thought.

It took some doing, but Perrin found their way backstage after the opera. There was a maze of beautifully carpeted corridors and unmarked doors that led to strange linoleum hallways that seemed to lead nowhere. The soft indirect lighting giving way to harsh fluorescents, which meant they were on the right track. Or that they were hopelessly lost and someone would have to send in a search and rescue team after them.

Racks of clothes lined one side of the white linoleum hallway, and a line of doors along the opposite wall led to small dressing rooms. As they moved along the hall, the costumes became fancier and so did the dressing rooms. She and Cassidy peeked in one that wasn't occupied at the moment. It had a piano in the corner, an upright, in beautiful condition.

"Must be what they use to warm up their voices before they go onstage."

Then the costumes ended, and a line of cramped offices appeared along the right-hand wall.

"Hey," Cassidy pointed at a sign on an open door. "You said Bill was the Stage Manager."

Perrin grabbed her hand and dragged her in. "Let's go peek."

It was big enough for a desk, three chairs, and a long whiteboard which was covered in incomprehensible hieroglyphics. "LR#1 blwn gel fresh #4. Cortisol III.2 4st. Strk-7a call," and dozens of other notations that must mean something to Bill, because they certainly meant nothing to her.

"His desk is awfully neat. Do we trust a man who has such a neat desk?" Cassidy leaned forward to look at a small framed photograph.

"I wish I'd brought some really red lipstick. I need to leave a really blatant lip print here somewhere."

"Perrin," Cassidy's tone brought her up short.

"What?"

Cassidy pointed to the picture of two giggling children.

"That's Jaspar and Tamara. What does that have to do with lipstic —Oh crap! This is so hard, Cass. I don't know if I can do this." Of course his kids would be as likely to be here as at the Opera offices. Finding a red-lipstick print from their dad's girlfriend would be way worse than inappropriate. It would be— "I'm such an idiot. I'm just gonna screw this up so bad. Cass, you have to tell me what to do. You're the smart one."

"Actually, it was Jo who was valedictorian at college. And personally I think that you got that 'C' in PE just so that Jo would get the honor instead of you. Remember, I saw your GRE scores in case you went to grad school and I know neither of us came close to matching yours. How did you arrange to get a 'C' in a field hockey PE class anyway?"

"Remember Ms. Kennelly?"

"Stick-in-the-Mud Kennelly? Sure."

"I made a pass at her. She was totally freaked. But after that she didn't dare flunk me the last semester Senior year, despite my never attending another class. Probably too afraid I'd wind up back in one of her classes. It worked great, but don't tell Jo."

Cassidy crossed her heart like the true friend she was.

Perrin heard a voice rumbling out in corridor, placating one person while handing out instructions to another. And his voice sounded as if he'd just finished ripping someone a new one.

"That's him," she tried not to go all weak in the knees.

"PERRIN! YOU MADE IT!" Bill wanted to devour her, she looked glorious and delectable. That same blazer as the other night, but without the t-shirt made him want to drag her down to the floor and pick up where good manners had stopped him last night. Had he even slept last night? Yet he felt energized rather than exhausted.

He spotted the second woman just in time. Bill slammed a brake on his libido and held out a hand to shake Perrin's as if they were just two professionals.

She looked down at his hand, then rolled her eyes at the other woman, "What did I tell you about him?"

"You were right. He's too damned decent."

Perrin stepped into his arms and kissed him long and deeply

enough to completely scorch any of his body's responses that hadn't already gone ballistic over the outfit.

Then she stepped back, "I, uh, may have already told her about us. Bill Cullen, this is Cassidy Knowles, my best friend in the whole world."

"I know her, you just distracted me. We sort of met at the last board meeting, Ms. Knowles. You're the one who saved Perrin's life."

Cassidy startled and turned to face Perrin even before Bill could shake her hand.

Perrin shrugged, "That's all I told him." But she appeared very interested in the tiling of the floor.

Then Cassidy turned back and took his hand, shaking it carefully.

"What did I just miss?"

Cassidy inspected him closely. "You had best be worth it, Mister Cullen. To the best of my knowledge, you are only the fourth person on the planet to know that."

"Fifth," Perrin offered without looking up. "I told Melanie a while ago. She kind of already knew. Forgot to tell you she was here this week, dating an opera singer, but she's gone again. Back in five weeks for opening night."

Again some inexplicable exchange occurred silently.

At length Cassidy turned to face him once more. She was perhaps five-eight, a good four inches shorter than he was. And very trim, though with fuller curves than Perrin. But he was left with no doubt that the woman before him, having somehow saved Perrin's life once, would do absolutely anything she felt necessary to do so again.

CHAPTER 8

*P*errin had the drawings spread down the entire length of her workbench. She'd had to get them back from Jerimy, because the last of the designs were being stubborn. She just couldn't see them.

The heavy colors and threads of hope and failure in the lineage of the Overlord and the Empress. The vile reds and blacks of the court Magister and his cohorts in the clergy. The opera had set them as almost pure evil, bent on the destruction of the royal lineage and replacing them with their own line. The Magister would bring about the ultimate downfall of the Tragic Prince. His snare would fail to catch Tamara as the young Empress-to-be.

But the arranged-marriage Princess, and the Prince's one True Love were eluding her. These were the two women who tore the Tragic Prince in two directions, ultimately allowing the Magister's untimely blade to make his end.

Once she had the Princess, then the Maid Confessor and Queen Mother should follow easily enough. But at the moment, nothing about any of the four of them was being easy. Nothing!

She'd tried most of her tricks. Sketching, painting, pulling pieces randomly out of the scrap bag and stitching them together on the embroidery machine until something came of it.

And not a decent idea.

"Perrin," Raquel stuck her head in. "You have a visitor."

She almost cried out in relief. A customer needing a special dress, or a friend, she didn't care. She knew it couldn't be Bill, he had one opera coming down and meetings about getting the set construction for *Ascension* back on schedule. He said he'd be frantic all week.

"Hi, Perrin," Tamara peeked around from behind Raquel.

"Hey, you! Come here!" Without thinking Perrin had thrown her arms wide.

Tamara eyed them for a moment, then came forward and accepted the hug. Perrin kept it brief, as she would if just meeting some friend on the street. Bill hadn't been kidding, the girl was so self-conscious of every nuance of being thirteen. Of course, Perrin was also the woman who'd kissed her dad.

"So, did your dad drop you off?" She wanted to ask where he was, why hadn't he at least come in to say hello, how was he. He'd been so busy that she actually hadn't seen him since the night she and Cassidy had attended *Turandot.* They'd barely traded late night texts after the kids were in bed. But she thought it better not to ask. It was best to appear completely neutral on the topic of her dad.

"No, he didn't," a little hesitant. Then in a rush to block Perrin's next question, "I was hoping you could show me more about design and sewing. I really want to—"

Perrin held up a hand to cut her off. She too had once been a teenage girl. Her life had been nothing like Tamara's, but she knew the tones of voice that had and hadn't gotten her out of trouble. The first part was a clear lie, even if the rest of it sounded true enough.

Keep it light, she told herself.

"Wow, girl! You just told a whopper, didn't you?"

Tamara blanched but struggled on valiantly. "No. I really wanted to learn how you made those costumes. I don't get how you..." Her voice petered out as it became clear that Perrin wasn't buying the distraction for a second.

Before she could make further excuses, Perrin held up her hand.

Tamara wisely closed her mouth.

"Okay, first you sit and listen to the world according to Perrin. Then you get two choices."

She didn't look happy about it, but she climbed up on the stool across the cutting table, dropping her school pack on the floor.

"Your dad doesn't know you're here." She didn't make it a question.

"Gretchen's."

"And when he shows up and you aren't at Gretchen's, how much trouble will you have found?"

Tamara shrunk down in her seat. "Lots. Seriously grounded at least."

"Girl, he's going to put one of those house-arrest GPS ankle bracelets on you and never let you out of his sight again. He loves you so much that he'll probably end up in jail for punching anyone who gets in his way while he's trying to find you."

"No way... " Suddenly she didn't look so self-assured.

"Way!" Perrin informed her. "That's assuming he doesn't have a heart attack from worrying himself sick about you first. Lost, maybe missing in the Big Bad City."

"I'm old enough to get around Seattle on my own if I want to. Besides, he's always at work. What does he care about—"

"You have no idea how much he cares. His whole world revolves around raising you two. He's so afraid he's going to screw up, that's probably what makes him screw up half the time."

Tamara appeared to be mulling that one over seriously.

"So, time for your two choices," Perrin informed her.

"Am I going to like either one of them?"

"Not a chance."

It took some negotiation, before they ended up with a compromise. Perrin would call to break the ice, then hand it off to Tamara.

She dialed Bill's cell and put it on speaker phone. Only after she did so, did she think that maybe dialing his number from memory hadn't been the best choice. Thankfully, Tamara appeared too miserable to notice. With each ring, Tamara cringed down further on the stool.

"Hi Perrin. I have to be quick. I'm sorry, but I'm really busy right now. Gods but I miss you."

Tamara heard that one loud and clear. Her head shot up and she faced Perrin rather than continuing to study the chips in her nail polish.

"Uh, Bill. I think I may have just screwed up. I have you on speakerphone."

There was a pause, "Who else is there?"

Perrin nodded to Tamara to go ahead. She had to repeat the gesture to get some action.

"Uh, hi Dad."

"What?!" His voice roared out of the phone and echoed about Perrin's design space. If his daughter had needed any proof of what Perrin had told her, his tone said it all. She positively cowered, in shame rather than fear, Perrin was glad to see.

"Bill," Perrin cut him off. "Before you lay in, I've already done a good job of making her feel like a total shit. She understands what she did wrong. How about giving her a one-time 'Get Out of Jail Free' card?"

There was a long silence. So long that Tamara started cringing again.

"Is she okay there with you? I could probably find someone to come and—" His voice was tight, but he was holding onto control. Barely.

"She's fine with me, Bill. I won't let her out of my sight. You have Jaspar?"

"Yeah. The little thug just shook me down for a buck for the soda machine but I'll bet he's getting a candy bar instead."

Tamara nodded her agreement.

"His sister agrees, candy it is. Take as long as you need, Bill."

"Thanks, Perrin, you're absolutely wonderf— Aw, crap! Explaining this is another problem I've left in your lap. Tamara, give her a chance.

Sorry about that, gotta run." And he was gone before she could even reach out to cut the connection.

Tamara was eyeing her carefully.

"Look, girl, I got you off the hook this one time. You gonna throw me to the wolves?"

Tamara considered that for a while and then shrugged that maybe, just maybe they had a fair trade.

Perrin could see the next question building, but was not at all ready for it when it finally arrived.

"You going to marry my dad?"

Perrin managed a laugh. "Whoa there! I've only kissed him twice, wait, three times. We're barely dating. We haven't even gone out to dinner together, if you don't count the time you guys were here for pizza."

"Is he good?"

Perrin rested her elbow on the table and her chin on her palm and inspected her interrogator. How did you deal with a kid? A kid who has probably spent the last four years doing her best to be mother to a young boy and a comfort to her own father? Truth, she decided. She hadn't any basis to go on, so she would simply always tell the truth. It was the only option she could think of that had any chance of success.

"I mean, is he like you said, 'the right boy'?" Tamara added another question over Perrin's silence.

"Tamara, honey. You've gotta make a promise to Perrin."

"What?"

"Stop asking such hard questions, please?"

It earned her a tentative smile but no promises. Guess that would have to do.

"Is he good? He's almost as good a kisser as he is a dad, which is pretty incredible. Is he the right boy? I have no idea in the world. The other question I have to ask, 'Am I the right girl?' I can't believe that I am."

Tamara did another of her deep thought things before responding. "I don't know the answer either, but I can kinda see how you might be."

Man oh man. And she'd thought the questions were tough.

"LOOK AT THESE. Maybe you can tell me what's missing." Perrin had enjoyed teaching Tamara through the quiet afternoon, she was an apt student. She quickly understood right and wrong sides of fabric, seam allowances, and pinning. Cutting on the bias had tripped her up, but she was getting a handle on it. She also successfully threaded the Featherweight several times as well as jamming it up once royally.

But the unfinished costume designs had lain there on the cutting table the whole time and beckoned silently. And she was no closer to solving them.

"There's a lineage missing." Perrin had set out blank pages of paper with the role titles on them: Princess (arranged marriage), Maidservant Companion, Queen Mother (of Princess), and True Love (same lineage?). She'd set small snips of different fabric possibilities on each, but they all looked like crap.

Tamara stopped in her efforts to undo the latest snarl she'd made by catching a fold in the machine. Only way to learn stuff like that was do it wrong enough times.

She came over to lean on the table beside Perrin. Close, if not quite rubbing elbows. A good sign that she wasn't too uncomfortable about Perrin and her dad.

For a long time, they looked at the blank pages in silence. Then Tamara turned to face the room. She started doing all of the things that Perrin had done. She'd walked slowly about the room, running her fingers over a red velvet, a blue chiffon, and some black corduroy. Occasionally Tamara's hand hesitated and Perrin noted which fabrics they were, just in case she couldn't come up with any other ideas.

The girl dug through the patches bag under the table for a bit, asked a couple questions about the crazy-patch embroidery Perrin had rammed back into the bag in frustration. Next Tamara would be walking through the whole store and find nothing to help her. And then Perrin would call Bill and admit that he'd been right all along, that she was a clothing designer and not a costume designer. Crap, but she really didn't want to let him down.

Tamara was passing the rack where Perrin hung works in progress, and also some of her own clothes in case the weather changed, or she suddenly felt cold.

She stopped there, and Perrin twisted around to see what she took down.

The electric-blue knit sweater Perrin had worn to lunch last week.

"You getting cold, honey?"

Tamara took it off the hangar and brought it back to the table. She folded it up and set it on the Princess' blank sheet. Stepping back, she tipped her head sideways to inspect it.

Perrin waited for it. Let her eyes drift over the texture and color. The knits were soft, following lines and curves, a sharp contrast to the rest of the highly structured costumes. They'd be able to accentuate or diminish based on how they were knit: ribbed, stockinette, cabled... And the blue. It was close. So close. Not electric-blue, but...

"Jewel tones," she let it out as little more than a sigh. Then she squealed. That was it! That was so it! Knit jewel tones.

She swept Tamara into a hug and then leapt up to waltz about the room with her. Both giggling madly as they went. When they passed her computer, she tapped the play button. Fleetwood Mac *Second Hand News* came roaring out of the speakers. And she did a shimmy that Tamara did a good job of imitating. They'd circled the cutting table twice, even doing an impromptu two-woman conga to totally the wrong rhythm when Tamara shouted something to her.

Perrin leaned down to hear.

"You and Dad will be perfect for each other."

"Why?" she shouted back.

"You both have the same crappy taste in music." Then Tamara did a shimmy-dip-twirl that Perrin did her best to copy as they danced a full circle about the cutting table. Arriving back at the computer, she stopped Stevie Nicks in mid-throaty growl.

"Come on, kid," Perrin grabbed Tamara's hand. "We're getting out of here."

"But Dad thinks I'll be here."

"You own a cell phone?"

She held it up. "But only for emergencies."

"Fine, as soon as we're in the car, you text him. Say, 'Perrin had clothing emergency. I'm with her.' Make sure you put 'Hugs' or a smiley face or something at the end. He did a real hard thing letting you off the hook before. He deserves something nice."

They dashed out the door, Raquel and Kirstin barely having time to wave. They piled into Perrin's mini-van and pulled out onto the streets of Belltown.

Tamara dutifully punched out a text. "Is 'love you' too mushy?"

"For your dad, you can never be too mushy."

She finished the text, with a somewhat evil grin.

"What?"

Tamara looked out the window, watching downtown Seattle unfold and carefully avoiding Perrin's question, but obviously terribly pleased with herself. "Do you always drive so slow?"

Perrin looked down to check as they drove up the Mercer Street ramp and merged onto I-5 northbound, "I'm going the speed limit."

"But like everyone is passing us. Even Dad doesn't go the speed limit."

"Well, first, I have someone else's kid in the car, which is kind of freaking me out. Second, yeah, I usually go the speed limit in self defense. I know how easily I get distracted, so moving slower helps. Now give, or am I going to have to pull over and wrestle you to the ground for your cell phone."

Tamara studied the slowly moving landscape and gave out a long sigh of exasperation at their lack of progress. But her smile hadn't gone away.

"I just included a P.S."

"Sewing machine privileges," Perrin threatened.

"I only said, 'Perrin wants her fourth kiss soon.'" At Perrin's strangled sound the kid just laughed. "Think it got a reaction?"

Perrin just imagined Bill's reaction and hoped he didn't drop her then and there for telling such a thing to his teenage daughter. Then she imagined the look on his face and wished she could be there to see it.

"Where's Tam?" Jaspar had to tug on his dad's sleeve to get his attention. He was sitting in his office and glaring at his phone as if it had just bitten him, like that gerbil did to Tommy Hancock in Mr. Melk's class.

"She's with Ms. Williams today."

The costume lady. Wait. Hadn't she told him she'd be at Gretchen's? She never lied to him. Sometimes she got his help when she needed to tell one, but she'd always told him the truth. Or had she? What was going on all of a sudden?

"When's she getting back? I'm stuck on homew—"

"Not for a while, buddy. Look, I'm jammed up in this meeting for maybe another hour. Then I'll help you. Okay? Can you work on something else until I'm free?"

Jaspar looked at the other men in his dad's office. They had a lot of papers and drawings and notes and stuff spread all over the table. They were all looking at him, waiting for his dad.

He also had his phone out and was looking sorta pissed, like when he was trying not to scream at him or Tam for doing something dumb. He didn't scream except when they'd really earned it, but he had that look.

"Sure, Dad. Whatever."

Jaspar went back to the cubicle across the hall from his dad's office where he usually did his homework. The problem was that he didn't have any other homework except this lame book report on stupid *Captains Courageous.*

Tam usually helped him, even on books she hadn't read. She'd make a game of it, just asking so many dumb questions that eventually he'd figure out what he wanted to say.

Now she was off with the costume lady doing girl clothes stuff. She'd gone all gaga over those dresses at the store. Bor-ring. Though getting to be in the opera was kinda cool. He'd liked that at first, even if the backstage stuff was way cooler, but they never let him work on any of that. Like he was still eight or something.

For some stupid reason he'd thought that being in the opera meant they'd all be spending more time together.

He turned to scowl at the book sitting on his desk. A story about a kid brain dead enough to fall off a ship in the middle of an ocean. Maybe he should have just drowned. Not that any dumb sister would ever notice.

<hr>

BILL STARED BACK at the phone message. The meeting continued around him, but what had been a fascinating snarl of problems to unravel just moments before had turned into a meaningless buzz.

Clothing emergency was cute and funny. He could hear Perrin's voice declaring it like a national crisis or an incoming missile attack. It had made him smile until he scrolled the message enough to see the last line.

P.S. Perrin wants her fourth kiss soon.

His daughter had just told him that a woman, who he'd met less than two weeks before, had told his *teenage* daughter that she'd kissed him three times. And wanted to do it again.

What kind of a game was Perrin Williams playing at?

There was no possible way this could be happening. Perrin was right. Not about being toxic, but about how he should be much more cautious about letting his kids come in contact with her. What if things didn't work out? What if she was a crappy parental figure? Which the present message sure pointed to.

And this sure as hell wasn't his definition of slow. She was bonding faster with his daughter than she was with him. How was he supposed to trust someone who did that?

What if she hurt the kids somehow? Not intentionally. She'd never do that, there wasn't a mean bone in her body.

And it wasn't helping matters in the slightest how much he

couldn't stop thinking about her body. The way she had responded to him for that one stolen hour. It had been incredible, as if every touch not only seared him, but her as well. He'd never responded so strongly in his life, maybe not even to… Damn it! He really had to cut that out. Adira was only diminished by the fading of memories over time. That's all that was happening. Whereas Perrin Williams was so vibrant, so alive, she shone like one of her costumes.

"Everything okay, Bill?"

He looked up at Timothy Winters, the Opera's Production Manager.

"Uh, don't know yet. Give me a sec."

He read the message again.

I'm with her.

He wondered if that was Tammy's voice or Perrin's? Perrin's. She'd been making sure that he knew she was keeping Tammy close and safe, no matter what else was going on. Maybe she was being an okay authority figure after all? She had been the one who made sure Tammy called him within minutes of entering her shop. She'd also made it clear that she'd already straightened his daughter out on lying about where she was. That was actually far above and beyond the call of duty for a girlfriend.

It was only the last line that was pure Tammy. Somehow, Perrin had decided that telling his daughter that they had kissed each other was the best option. Then, instead of any emotional storm Tammy had signed with a *Love you.* That was something he hadn't seen in far too long. Then he understood, Tammy was teasing him about Perrin. Not something she'd do if she was mad or overly shocked.

For a moment, he wondered if Perrin knew about the last line. Bill had to smile. If she didn't, he'd bet that Tammy would find a way to tell her. Kids never missed an opportunity to get back at adults.

Welcome to my world, Perrin Williams.

"What do you think, Bill? Do we have time to get these plates punched or do we need to spend the extra to get them drilled?"

Bill keyed an answer into the phone, hit send, and began juggling the production schedule versus the painting and staging schedules so they could save the money with punching.

———

PERRIN AND TAMARA had ridden in silence for several minutes. Tamara fiddled with the radio but no one had music, all ads at the moment. They were both just killing time to see what Bill Cullen's response would be.

At long last the phone buzzed back and gave a cheerful ping as Perrin was pulling into the steep, narrow parking lot.

"What does he say?"

Tamara looked at it. Then appeared a little puzzled. "He just sent a one-letter response, 'K.' Which is short for 'Okay' when he's in a real hurry. Maybe he didn't read the P.S. part of it."

Or, Perrin could hope, he'd decided that the single response covered both messages in the text. They continued in silence, each thinking their own thoughts until reaching the store.

"What is this place?" Tamara climbed out and glared at the building.

Perrin looked up at the aged two-story, concrete-block building, with peeling taupe-blah paint. To one side was a vacant lot, some old apartments towered over it from behind.

"A knitting store, Tamara."

"But it says, The Weaving Works?"

"Don't you trust anything I tell you?"

Tamara considered, "I guess I trust you."

"Good, the moon is made of green cheese and Justin Bieber has a poster of you on his wall."

"Eww!" But Tamara was smiling as they arrived at the door. "Hey, that's cool."

Knitting in a bright sock yarn wrapped about the door handle.

"There's more of it," Perrin pointed to the bike rack in front of the store. The galvanized steel had been knit over in a succession of the colors of the rainbow. "The Weaving Works" had been boldly knit right into the fabric.

"It's called yarn bombing."

"That is just so cool!"

"You've been hanging out with Jaspar too much. You're using his adjectives."

"He's my kid brother, I don't get a whole lot of choice on who I hang out with. I would have filed a request for a girl, but I was only three when they had the punk. He's mostly okay except for being a boy. Don't tell him I said that."

"Deal." Perrin pulled open the glass-and-steel door. "Welcome to knitting heaven, Tamara."

They toured the whole store together. Racks of every color and type of yarn towered about them. Like a small, labyrinthine bookstore, its shelves stocked to overflowing with heavy yarns for fisherman's sweaters, fine yarns for baby clothes, and feathery "eyelash" yarns for when you just wanted to feel utterly ridiculous.

"Check this out," Tamara called Perrin over to the Jamieson yarns. "The skeins are so small and cute. I just love the colors."

"They're my favorites," Perrin pulled out four different colors. "Come on."

She led Tamara to a small mirror.

"Watch your face as I hold up each color." She started with a blue and Tamara shrugged, then an orange that clashed with her hair and her complexion.

"Eww!"

Then a black.

"That one's good."

The Perrin held up the dark green heather yarn. It played off Tamara's rich-red hair. With her fair skin, it snapped all attention to the girl's dark eyes. The extra softness kept it from being too severe beside her young woman's features.

"Wow…" Tammy offered on a long drawn sigh.

"This doesn't mean all your clothes should be Loden green, but when you want to really knock out some boy, this wouldn't be a bad place to start."

They took the skeins back to the shelves.

"Hey Perrin. Why aren't there any guys here except for that one over there looking bored?"

"Not a lot of male knitters. Funny thing is, there are a lot of cultures where it was traditionally the male who did the knitting. Now, this is just a cozy place for women to hang out. See the big table in the corner with a couple knitters around it? There's almost always someone there to sit and knit with. Or you can bring in hard problems if you get stuck and someone will always help you out. I often think that this is how the world would feel if it was run by women."

"Cozy."

"Exactly. Now, we need the color sets for the four designs we were missing."

"You want me to help you pick colors for clothes that will go onstage?" her voice was wispy and awed.

Perrin figured it was part of that distant-and-impossibly-remote "Dad's world" and Tamara felt as if she were just a kid intruding. Like Tamara, Perrin had been plenty precocious, and that had caused its own set of problems. Well, it wouldn't for this girl. Not if Perrin had anything to say about it.

"You're the one that found the solution to something that's been making me crazy for over a week. You solved it, I'll make sure every knows that. As a matter of fact... " Perrin stepped over to the display of knitting tools and pulled down a massively ridiculous crochet hook that had to be there as a joke, it was two feet long and almost as big around as Perrin's wrist. She rolled it to the label, "Size 50." It wasn't a toy, some project actually required this monster. That was just too crazy. If she could think of what to do with it, she might buy it.

"Kneel, Empress-to-be Tamara Cullen."

"You're kidding."

"Kneel, or I tell your dad that I'm not the only one kissing boys."

"Oh man!" Tamara knelt.

Perrin tapped her lightly on each shoulder with the crochet hook, then thonked her on the head hard enough to elicit an, "Ow!"

"I hereby dub you my official design assistant. Rise oh Tamara of the thank-you-for-saving-my-butt design team."

As she clambered back to her feet, several of the nearby women who had stopped to observe the goings-on offered a round of applause.

Tamara blushed a brilliant red while Perrin waved the hook as if acknowledging her adoring subjects. When the applause had turned to kind laughter and everyone had returned to their shopping, she turned once again to Tamara.

"Now, assistant, let's go choose some colors."

CHAPTER 9

"**G**od. *You should have* seen her, Bill. I wish I could have shared it with you. We had the best time picking out the yarn." Perrin's voice over the phone was almost as breathless as Tammy's had been.

"Wish I could have seen it." He wished it so much it ached. His daughter had come home from her afternoon lit up like she was the queen of the world. Any lingering desire to chew her out for lying to him about going to Gretchen's died when she threw herself into his arms.

"It took her a good half hour at top speed to tell me about all the things the two of you had done. And she can talk awfully fast when she's on a roll."

Bill lay back on the top of his bed covers and stared at the dim ceiling.

"You aren't upset, are you?" Perrin's voice was soft.

"Upset? At what?"

"Well, I mean I know I shouldn't be attaching myself to her, or letting her attach to me, but she's such an amazing kid. And she wants to grow up so badly. Do you remember what that was like?"

Bill remembered joining the high-school theater as a freshman and having his entire life changed when Mary Ann, an awe-inspiring junior, had wandered across the stage carrying some tools to go fix a broken Fresnel lamp. She'd been tall, slender, with dark hair down past the middle of her back. His worldview had altered in that moment. He'd never grown up fast enough to get her attention. Hell, he'd never once been able to tell her how he worshipped her in the two years they did shows together before she graduated and was gone.

"Yeah, I remember what it was like. I just wish it wasn't my girl doing it. And no, I'm not upset. I just wish I could have been there with her… With you. How can I miss you so much? We hardly know each other."

"You could ask me out on a date."

He could, if he could just figure out how to arrange it. *Turandot* was finally down and the set struck and returned to storage. For a while, the weeknights and weekends were his once more. His and his kids.

"Where are you now?"

"Why? Are you asking me out now? I thought your kids were asleep."

"They are. I just wanted to picture where you were, what you were doing. What I really wish is that you were lying on the pillow beside mine." And he did. Against all likelihood, he could picture her here, in the bedroom where no woman had ever been. He wanted to turn and see Perrin beside him. All her chaos, all her uncertainty, all her beauty, and all that magnificence curled up beside him. He could see it so clearly, as if she were—

"I'm in my studio."

"Oh," a dose of reality. He was sprawled on the bed thinking more about sex than any teenage boy, and she was working.

"I'm lying naked on my cutting table, just waiting for a strong man to come and ravage me."

The heat that flashed through his body left him sweating and his pulse racing.

"O-kay. That's an image I going to be glad to be stuck with for a long time."

Perrin giggled, just like a happy teenage girl who was thinking as much about sex as he was.

"How about something simpler?"

"Spoilsport," she made a raspberry sound. "Such a party pooper, you don't even want to come here. Big meanie would rather leave me all alone and unravaged in my little bed."

"Thought you were… " he lowered his voice to make sure it didn't carry down the hall to the kids, "… sprawled naked on your design table waiting desperately for me?"

"Oh no, any strong and willing man would be fine. You just happen to be the one I'm talking to. And I'm not naked, I'm wearing a flannel nightgown. Yes, all alone in my own bed."

"Not how I pictured you." Not at all. He'd thought Perrin would be one to sleep naked, or in one of those oversized t-shirts that always made a woman's legs look so amazing.

"No, Bill Cullen, I've never worn a little black teddy, nor am I planning to anytime soon. Not even for your fantasies. If you're going to ravage me, you'll just have to deal with a woman who wears plain white flannel nightgowns."

"Not even pink?"

"Nope, white."

"JC Penny's?"

"Caught me."

"Actually, that's an image I could definitely work with. And no, Perrin Williams, I don't want to ravage you… " he let the silence drag for several seconds. "I'm desperate to ravage you."

Her voice was soft and dreamy. "You'd better make it soon, Bill Cullen. I don't know how much longer I can stand it if you don't."

"I've have to see you. What are you doing tomorrow?" It so hard to form normal, practical thoughts with her voice whispering into his ear.

"I thought you were going to be with the kids."

"I am. I was thinking we could have a picnic."

"With the kids?" she sounded suddenly cautious and practical. He knew he should be as well.

"They do appear to know you better than I do. Maybe it's time I caught up a bit."

"You're sure?"

Was he? Even though he'd been the one to invite her, Perrin was still giving him an out. Pushing him to do what was right rather than what she knew was their mutual desperation to be with each other. Yet another layer of flighty designer was peeled off to reveal the practical woman inside.

"Some day, Perrin, you're going to have to tell me why you carry your shields so high."

Her echoing silence told him he'd screwed up. Cassidy Knowles had only reinforced Perrin's statement that she wouldn't be sharing her life history. He cursed himself for being eight kinds of dumb. To have been hurt so badly and rise above it, how much strength had that taken? How many conscious choices had she made to be a better person despite her past? He didn't even need to know what her past had been to know what affect it had upon who she was. She had risen triumphant from whatever ashes...

"I don't know if I can, Bill. I truly don't know if I can." Her voice was so small.

"I'm sorry, honey. I'm so sorry. I shouldn't have said that."

Again the interminable silence. *Honey?* He was becoming awfully attached to her. Well, it was no less than the truth, he was.

"Would you still like me on your picnic?" Her voice was even smaller if possible.

"Yes. No equivocation. No doubt. I'm not the fastest guy around, but I eventually get there. I would very much like you to join us."

Another silence.

Then, after the silence had dragged on long enough that he wondered if she was still there, he heard a quiet, "Thank you."

"It's raining!"

"I noticed!" Perrin dove into the back of Bill's car and wound up sitting next to Jaspar.

Bill made a signal to Tamara to move back. He should have thought of it sooner, but it had been her turn to be up front.

Perrin stopped her before she even had her seatbelt undone. "Don't! You'll just get wet and I'll get wetter if we try to trade."

"Some day for a picnic, Dad," Jaspar accused him as if he had personal control of the weather.

"It was sunny this morning," he glanced over his shoulder at her and mouthed a, "Hi!" which Perrin returned. It was so damn good to see her he could hardly stand it.

"I guess we could go to a restaurant," Bill leaned forward to look up at the sky through the windshield and cursed the changeable spring weather.

Jaspar declared his opinion with a loud snoring sound.

"Gotta do better than that, Dad," Tammy joined in on her brother's side. "Perrin did pizza and cool costumes last time. You're gonna have to top that."

"Ouch! Don't I get a break, extra points for being your father who can make you wash dishes every night for a month if he feels like it?"

"Nope!" the kids both roared back at him.

Perrin shot him a grin in the rearview mirror.

"What?"

"How about the backup plan we discussed last night?"

She was definitely smiling, something up her sleeve. They hadn't discussed any backup plan. Oh, she was trying to help him save face in front of the kids, bless her.

"Which one?" he asked, trying to keep up with the game.

"How about the one at CenturyLink Center, on Occidental."

"Oh right. Sure."

She winked at him as he pulled back into traffic and Jaspar started telling her all about his stage role even if the backstage stuff was the part that he found to be really "wicked."

A glance at Tammy told him that, as usual, her dad hadn't deceived her for even a moment.

———

"A DOG SHOW!" Both kids had screamed aloud the instant they saw the sign. Bill had spotted the poster, but they hadn't and he'd kept his mouth shut. Perrin was so brilliant it was hard to fathom.

What finally clued in the kids was a sign running vertically down a street-corner light post. Only when he approached it did he see it had been knit in English Setter white and brown with six-inch tall letters that you wanted to pet they look so fuzzy and friendly.

"Yarn bombing," Tammy informed him when he asked.

"It's cool," he acknowledged.

"Wicked, Dad. According to Jasp, that's the right word today. Get with the program." Tammy smiled and took his hand so that he didn't feel too fuddy-duddy-daddy, one of her phrases.

Once through the door the kids raced off to see everything at once.

Bill tried to keep up, but Perrin grabbed his hand to slow him down.

"You're not going to find a place safer than this for them to get off the leash a bit. So to speak."

He guessed that was true, but it didn't make him any happier. At least they had their cell phones with them if they found any trouble. The Exhibition Center was a tall space. Not enough to feel like outdoors, especially not with all of the steel and concrete structure and numerous pipes running across the ceiling, but enough to give an airy feel to the event.

The vast floor space was clogged with people and dogs. Teacup poodles checked out German Shepherds. Dachshunds greeted anyone who'd listen, and terriers tried to watch everything at once. The animals, all muzzled, were surprisingly well behaved. But it was hard to move without getting wrapped up in a leash or seven.

Off to the right was a vendors' area for everything from vets to dog hair-care products and specialty foods. Most of the booths had a dog sleeping at the owner's feet.

To the left were big courses for agility, speed, and whatever other kinds of competitions happened at a dog show, barricaded off with thigh-high fencing. An Australian shepherd was running the course at the moment. A large ring was also fenced off for the show dogs, presently a collection of wrinkle-skinned Shar-peis in every shade of brown, black, and tan. Toward the back, a surprising distance away, there appeared to be long rows of kennels and grooming stations for the participants.

An indoor dog show in Seattle, who knew.

Perrin had.

"You're an absolute life saver."

"I saw the rain, did a quick Internet search, and this was the best I came up with. I hope it's okay?"

"Okay? It's bloody perfect. Though I'm not taking home a puppy. Not even if all three of you gang up on me. No how. No way."

"Yes sir, Mr. Bill Cullen, sir." She saluted him.

He couldn't help himself. He leaned in and kissed her.

She let him for a long moment, then pushed him gently away. She started them moving forward again, moseying forward though he was oblivious to what was around them. All he could think about was the woman beside him.

"God that felt good."

"It really did, didn't it?" Perrin agreed with him.

"I want to do it again."

"Don't. Tamara's expecting it. But Jaspar won't be. Let it be enough that we're holding hands."

Bill glanced down in surprise. They were. He traced it back in his mind. They had been ever since the entry when she'd stopped him from rushing after the kids. It had felt so natural that he'd thought nothing of it.

"This going slow plan sucks."

She bumped shoulders with him. "This is so not slow. We really need to figure out what's going on between us soon. If there's even a chance for us, or if I'm going to hurt your kids horribly, even unintentionally. I'd rather walk out the door now than hurt them, though it might kill *me* to do so."

"Well, you're the woman three steps ahead of everyone. Any brilliant ideas?"

Perrin went silent at that. They managed two whole aisles of the vendors' area without any ideas between them. Two aisles of things they would never need in their lives. Hand-tooled leather collars fit for a mastiff. A small bookstore with everything from a photobook of the Queen's corgis to how to train your dog for sheep herding.

"They still do that?"

"Apparently."

Buffalo meat dog food. Emu meat dog food. Vegetarian dog food as if the master's predilection made any sense for the pet.

They circulated out by the agility ring so that the kids could spot them more easily. Now it was Golden retrievers racing the course at a dead run, guided by whistles and hand gestures of their trainers. At impossible speeds they were ducking through knee-high pipes, leaping over barriers, and winding through upright stanchions so close together that the dogs looked like eels while passing through.

"Could you get free Tuesday evening? Not the night, but at least the evening?"

"Why? What do you have in mind?"

Perrin shook her head, "Yay or nay, Mr. Cullen. You either can or can't."

"I'll find a way. Actually Lucy, my sister, has been wanting the kids for an overnight. Would a night as well be okay?"

They were so close together that it felt as if their bodies were about to meld, though their only actual point of contact was their clasped hands.

"The night would be wonderful." Perrin almost looked teary, though he'd never seen her cry.

"What is it?"

She shook her head part way, then hesitated, somehow knowing she'd told him too little and it was on the verge of bothering him.

"I just can't get over that you want to be with me. That's all."

"That's all?"

She nodded.

"Woman, you are going to make me totally insane yet."

"Really? Cool!" Her voice had flashed mercurially to bright, chipper, funny.

He scanned the crowd, but didn't see the kids. Eyeing her carefully, he could see the edge of the tease and tried to figure it out, but couldn't.

"Okay, what am I missing?"

"You actually like me enough for me to make you totally insane. That's cool."

"Wicked!" he corrected her. And yep! She had him pegged for sure.

JASPAR SPOTTED THEM. Dad and Ms. Williams sat at a small table with four chairs at one end of the dog obstacle course.

Ms. Williams who Tam kept calling Perrin like they were best friends. Fine, if they didn't want him around, that was just fine.

Though Tam had been cool as they'd gone to visit the dogs. And she'd said she was sorry that the boy in *Captains Courageous* hadn't at least been captured by pirates rather than fishermen, so maybe she was still okay.

But now Dad sat holding hands with the costume lady. That didn't feel right.

"Hey Tam?"

"What?" She was all involved in the dogs racing around the track.

He tipped his head toward the distant table and the grownups. Then he pretended he was more interested in the collie dogs that were coming into the ring so that it wouldn't be like they were both spying if they got caught.

"Bet they've kissed."

His sister was quiet so long that he turned away for a second to look at her. Her shrug said enough for a clear yes.

"Is she trying to marry Dad?"

Again the shrug, different meaning this time. This time Tam didn't know. He turned his attention back to the dogs.

Stuff was changing again and he didn't like this change one bit.

"Do you think we should be worried about the kids yet?" Bill looked at her nervously. He'd been doing his best not to fuss.

Over Bill's shoulder Perrin spotted the kids down at the other end of the ring. Tamara noticed her attention almost immediately, which told her that the girl had been keeping a close eye on Perrin and her dad for some time. Tamara said something to Jaspar, then grabbed her brother, held rapt watching the dogs, and began towing him by the shoulder in their direction.

"Oh," she turned her attention back to Bill. "I can make them appear if you want."

"How?" He narrowed his gaze at her.

"Easy. They're growing kids." The kids had made it about halfway through the crowds. "Ready?"

"Sure. Do your worst, lady."

Perrin closed her eyes and waved her hands over the empty table as if consulting a crystal ball. "Gee, I wonder if anyone's hungry?"

"We are!" the kids shouted from inches behind Bill who practically levitated out of his chair he was so shocked.

He stuck his tongue out at her as he hugged his kids.

"You all go find us lunch. I'll hold the table. I eat anything."

Bill led them away and she sat there.

She felt odd, as if she both was and wasn't Perrin Williams. If she was, it wasn't a version of herself that she recognized.

She knew the driven designer, consumed by the need to create beauty and joy with each of her dresses.

She knew the "cheery loon" who kept both her friends and newly-met strangers on their toes. The one who could never seem to let a straight line lie on the ground untended, unquirked. The one who kept everyone at a safe distance, even those closest to her.

And the woman who drove men away before they could even begin to get close—her she understood less, but knew well. So often Perrin had wondered if that woman was afraid that she'd be tested and found wanting, or was she just plain afraid?

And she remembered the girl, remembered her far too well. The one who took years to learn that waking in terror was not normal. The one who didn't understand for years more that she was the only one who prayed each night to wake up in the morning and learn that she'd been orphaned while she slept.

These were all at least familiar.

The one she didn't know at all sat here ever so quietly. A hundred dogs running about her. And a man who had offered her a glimpse of another world, an impossible fantasy somehow come to life. This new Perrin scared her to death. Because she dared to want.

She could feel her heart start racing until it was in rhythm with the rushing dogs.

Look at you playing Happy Family games.

She couldn't think.

Who do you think you're kidding, you loser!

Couldn't breathe.

Run!

She had to run!

She couldn't stand!

Clawing at the table, she managed to gain her feet. A chair crashed to the floor somewhere behind her. An English Setter glanced her direction and missed a gate.

She turned to push free of the crowd too close around her.

She ran blindly into a man who wrapped his arms around her.

She fought, struggled, would have clawed if she could but the arms tightened around her until she couldn't move.

"Whoa! Perrin. Perrin!"

The nightmare never knew her name. Not that name. It knew a

different one, a name she hadn't used in twelve years. Perrin was her safe name.

Safe name. Safe.

"Perrin!"

She knew that voice. She followed the voice back. Back until she found the face that…

"Oh god, Bill. I'm so sorry." She covered her mouth and searched for the kids.

They were only now returning, heavily laden with trays of food.

She turned away, so they couldn't see her face. "Give me a minute. Just a minute."

He held her just a moment, an infinitely reassuring moment, then kissed her on the forehead and released her.

"Okay, land it there, kids."

She heard a chair scraped upright. A dog bark. The slow return of normalcy about her.

It had been years since she'd lost it like that. Years since she'd lost her firm grip of control. She stepped farther away, hoping to find and leash a few more pieces of herself. Even Jo had never seen that part of her. Only Cassidy. Only her.

"A kiss on her forehead doesn't count as number four, Dad," Tamara teased somewhere behind her.

"Number four what?" Jaspar sounded grumpy.

"So dense," Tamara complained to her dad.

Jaspar made a raspberry sound.

She could feel them waiting for her to join them. A nice, normal family. They had no wife or mother, but were a good, solid family nonetheless.

And they'd all begun to cast her for the missing role… *her!* Perrin Williams! How could they be so wrong? She closed her eyes. Perhaps if she couldn't see them. She focused on the excited panting of the dogs in the nearby ring and the hum of the crowd's conversation. Perhaps if she couldn't hear them. Perhaps then she could walk away.

But she *could* hear them. And when she managed to turn, she could see them; involved in some game for which the prize was someone else's French fry. Thankfully, Bill had seated the kids with their backs to her.

Ten steps. Ten lousy steps and she could rejoin them.

Or she could turn and run.

She looked over her shoulder toward the entrance, the chaotic Seattle weather had now allowed sunshine to light the wet street beyond the glass entry doors, making it glisten. The distant view of daylight painfully bright and real compared to the industrial lighting inside the hall.

Perrin turned back and took the ten steps to the table. They were hard. Maybe the hardest thing she'd ever done. She had to count each one under her breath to make them real, to prove to herself that she was making progress.

But she made it.

She'd soon lost half her French fries to Jaspar, clearly the table's master of the game she didn't bother trying to understand. He may have been targeting her specifically, but that didn't seem likely. Bill ended the game at that point anyway. It didn't matter. She wasn't sure if she could eat much.

Bill's knee pressed hard against Perrin's own as he teased Tamara about her third career choice of the week: opera singer, fashion designer, dog trainer.

Bill's knee. It was all that anchored her in place. But it was enough.

———

BILL FELT her pressing her knee so hard against his. What had just happened? The woman beside him made the lost waif look rational.

"You gotta see them!" His son started towing Bill out of his chair and pointing toward the grooming stations at the back of the dog show.

Once he was on his feet and the table was cleared, Tamara had started leading them. But she drifted back to coax Perrin out of her chair when she didn't follow right away.

Perrin had scared the hell out of him. The stark terror on her face exceeded anything in the awful movies his kids sometimes made him watch, even the ones he wouldn't let them watch. He'd certainly never seen anything like it in real life. For a moment Perrin had been gone and the woman in her place had been terrified for her very life.

Somehow, she'd reached deep and pulled it together. He'd watched her fight some titanic battle while he'd distracted the kids. It had almost killed him to not go to her as she stood so alone in the aisle, facing whatever demons had sent her crashing into him. But he couldn't.

She was also right, they were going to have a talk, and real soon. If there was something he needed to know to protect his kids, she'd have to explain it, shields be damned. Or else they were through.

A glance back showed that Tammy had slipped a hand around Perrin's forearm, for Perrin's hands were plunged deep in her pockets. She'd looked like a ghost of herself. She was slowly recovering, but he could see the brittle layer, the near transparent façade holding her together.

He almost called Tammy away, maybe Perrin had been right about not bonding with the kids.

But he couldn't do it to her. She looked so frail, and that wasn't the woman he knew. That wasn't the woman who had brought his daughter back to him so effortlessly, and had designed those magnificent costumes.

He'd wait and see. He just hoped to god he wouldn't be left with some huge disaster to clean up.

"Here they are," Jaspar practically squealed.

In moments both kids were down on their knees. A beleaguered Cairn terrier looked up that them as eight little puppies walked all over her.

"Aren't they just so cute?" Tammy scooped one up carefully to show him the little brindle-coated pup.

Bill glanced at the owner, a big man relaxing comfortably in a small folding chair, he offered a friendly nod. "Your young 'uns know the way of it." His accent Kentucky or Tennessee, but with an overlay of watching too many episodes of *Game of Thrones*.

"Be ready to adopt in another month. The sire is over to yonder giving his all for Best in Show. Won't get it, but we won't be tellin' him." The man winked to show he was just glad to be here.

Perrin drifted up to Bill. She tentatively reached out and touched him lightly on the hand, asking permission. He wrapped his fingers around hers and she clamped down hard, proving that all of the sewing had made her a very strong woman indeed.

Not releasing his hand, she again glanced for permission, far more tentative than she'd been even half an hour before, then knelt behind the children. For a moment he feared that the life had gone out of her, as if that wild spark of life and fire were gone.

"Your dad swore that we'd never convince him to get a dog," her voice was close to normal. "Not even if we all ganged up on him. What do you think, should we try?"

Okay. So, the spark wasn't gone. She'd simply been asking if she'd screwed it up permanently. Not yet. His antenna were now out, but she was still okay.

He squeezed her hand briefly to let her know they were still okay.

"But no dog," he told the three of them.

He hoped she'd ease up on her grip soon, before his fingers went completely numb.

It took a while to extract the kids, but Bill had made it out with his fingers intact, and no dog. But it had been a close thing on both counts.

In the sunny afternoon, they'd walked along the waterfront, doing all of the touristy things together. They rode the Seattle Great Wheel, the hundred-and-seventy-five foot Ferris wheel standing at the end of one of the piers, their gondola practically scraping against the low scudding clouds at the top of the trip. They poked into Ye Olde Curiosity Shop and made faces at the shrunken head and explored one of the most amazing kitsch collections he'd ever seen.

Jaspar had departed Pirate's Plunder with an eye patch that he could see through, but looked opaque from outside. Tammy found a head scarf that made her look mature and, in pulling back her hair, exposed a younger version of Adira's beautiful neck.

"That green color looks great on you, kid."

Tammy had offered one of her enigmatic smiles.

"Makes you beautiful like your mom."

That earned him the melty-happy expression he'd been hoping for.

It was only as they wandered into the Seattle Aquarium that he noticed Perrin wore an identical scarf.

"You like it? Tamara insisted we had to match."

"What color is your hair? Really?" The scarf did look good on her, mixing the blond and the black into a soft cascade onto her back. He fooled with it a bit, relishing the softness.

"The white-blond is about as close as I've ever let it get. It was originally a gold-blond, but I left that behind long before I was eighteen. First goth black, then just any color that goes with my latest clothing design."

He'd like to see that original color some day. See it grown out, all golden-blond. Maybe in that gold dress he'd seen the first day. But it wasn't his place to tell her how she should look. And he liked the nutty style, it made her uniquely Perrin. But he'd wager that the true blond would be stunning. There must be something behind that eighteen line, all her stories stayed on this side of that line.

And that led him back to his earlier dark thoughts. Who was she, under the woman that she wore like a fine set of clothes? Who was the terrified creature he had glimpsed so briefly? The one who'd thought that he'd… He shoved the thought aside in disgust.

He knew he was falling in love with the first woman. He'd been in love with Adira, knew what that felt like even if they were so different. Adira his quiet anchor and Perrin who made him feel more alive than he ever had other than the first time he'd held his children. It was a shock, but he could recognize it in himself.

The second woman worried him. Worried him badly.

CHAPTER 10

"*Jerimy!" Perrin raced into* the Costume Shop and spotted him by a rack of *Turandot* costumes. He was boxing them for storage, they must be freshly cleaned.

"Perrin!" He shouted back and met her halfway. He gave her a strong and totally unjudgmental hug. She needed that right now. All Sunday and Monday she'd been so worried, fretting at the problem like a sore tooth.

Bill hadn't changed how he treated her despite her panic attack at the dog show, but she'd felt different around him. Having revealed that awful fear inside her, she didn't know how to go back to showing him only the carefree and happy woman she'd worked so hard to stitch together over the years.

Jerimy didn't know any of that and she could just be her old, familiar self with him. He squeezed her hard enough that she had to gasp and giggle. She kissed him on each cheek before they let each other go.

"Do you knit? I need a bunch of knitters. Wait until you see. Where's my portfolio?"

"The one in your hand, beautiful?" he teased.

"Well, no, but it will have to do," she teased back and tossed it down on the table. Then she opened it and pulled out the final four drawings. She set them in a row and stepped back. These had come from somewhere deep. They were actually some of the best drawings she'd ever made, the women on the page practically breathed.

Jerimy didn't gasp, he didn't marvel, he didn't exclaim. He did something far more respectful, he went very still and silent.

When she couldn't stand it anymore, she moved in to point at the yarn samples she'd taped along the side.

"They're all hard jewel tones, but all in soft knit. Even the cables in their cloaks have a softness."

"They're pure light," Bill said from close beside her.

Perrin actually cried out a little to find he'd come up so silently that she hadn't noticed.

They were, pure light. "That's the point. They are not tragic themselves, but are nonetheless caught in the Prince's tragedy. It makes them so much more sympathetic."

"I know these three women in real life. Who's the fourth one?" he pointed at the Queen Mother.

"What are you talking about?" She turned back to inspect the drawings more closely.

Bill leaned forward, extending an arm between her and Jerimy to tap each drawing in turn. So close she could feel him, smell him. Her head whirled at the wonder of him.

"You, Perrin, in two roles, Empress," he pointed to the drawing Jerimy had tacked on a corkboard on the wall, "and the True Love. Jo Thompson is the Princess and Cassidy Knowles her Maid-servant Confidant. I'd have expected that to be the other way around, but what do I know."

Perrin looked at the drawings in surprise, he was absolutely right. Without realizing, she'd used the three of them as models rather than the opera singers she'd met at the rehearsals. Of course, Jo would be the Princess, for she was honor and truth incarnate as well as being typically ever-so reserved. Cassidy's passion was a little closer to the surface though still reserved. She was the deep, quiet bond that strung them together. Bill Cullen wouldn't know that yet about either of her friends.

"Who's the fourth one?"

Perrin looked at the Queen Mother, the quiet bedrock of the world.

"Mama Maria. You'll meet her tonight."

All he offered to that was a soft grunt. He knew her mother was a part of a past she *wouldn't* talk about. He thought it was a choice, but it wasn't. She *couldn't* talk about it; not and retain her control, perhaps not even her sanity. But nor could Perrin explain Mama Maria in just a sentence or two.

"She looks nice enough."

"She's amazing." Perrin had missed her so much. But, she and Hogan came back last night from their honeymoon. Tonight they'd be together again. She needed a subject change for her own sake, and fast. Oh right!

"Knitting!" she practically cried it out, loudly enough for the two men to jolt. "We need knitters, Jerimy. I'm okay, but I'm not good enough to do these, and not quickly. Please, please, please tell me you know some fabulous, gonzo, out-there knitters."

"Pretty lady, do I ever! Patsy. You have a minute?"

A short, voluptuous redhead strolled over from where she'd been overseeing the packing of costumes. Unlike Jerimy, her freckles proved that her red hair was natural, though the lemon-yellow streak over the crown certainly wasn't.

"Patsy is the gonzoest knitter in Seattle. And she's a gang leader, if you can imagine a knitting gang."

Perrin looked down at her. She stood maybe five-three. She wore an opera t-shirt that fit her in a way very differently from Perrin's. She'd redone the collar to have a deep vee that exposed a well-freckled cleavage and a tattoo of a pair of knitting needles, as if her generous breasts were still being knit into reality.

"What have you got?" Her voice was biker drawl as if she led a motorcycle gang rather than a knitting one, whatever that meant. She leaned her elbows on the table and went silent for several minutes.

Perrin almost felt a need to shuffle her feet or something, but Jerimy's smile reassured her, and she waited.

"The Princess' cloak is gonna be the beast."

That's when Perrin understood what was happening, because it was something she did herself. Patsy was structuring the garments in her head, thinking how to execute them, potential problems, what worked and what didn't.

"What if we felted it, to get that structure over the shoulders?"

Perrin nodded, that would work. "As long as you can keep it light enough to get the movement we need on the lower part when she rushes across the stage."

"Maybe felt from the lower point of the shoulder blades and up, then knit onto the back of that structure for the rest of it. Shift these cables here and here as structural elements. Are the colors intarsia? Or do we alternate them like a Fair Isle? It will affect the flow of the cloak."

They reviewed it piece by piece. Perrin was peripherally aware of when Bill drifted off. Jerimy hung close by, but added little. Clearly his assistant would be the master of these costumes.

When they were done, Patsy looked up at her. "Yeah, we got this. I'll get the girls and we can get it done this week. Have to think about the gusseting so that they can be used on different singers."

"That's why I designed in this layer of buttons down the side as a common theme. I thought multiple sets of buttons might work."

Patsy nodded. "I like it. Be better if we could lose them though, wouldn't it?"

Perrin had to smile. It was fun to work with another designer who didn't see any predefined box when they were doing their art. She didn't even have to acknowledge that it would be better and that she'd trust Patsy to go ahead if she found it.

Jerimy hung the last four drawings with the others on the corkboard, completing the primary costumes for the opera. There was still an immense amount of work to be done to execute it, but the designs were all there.

Jerimy made fresh coffee, Perrin took tea, and the three of them pulled up stools in a circle to admire the display.

Perrin had always worked solo, until Cassidy had practically forced Raquel on her. She'd hated giving up the control at first, but over the last two years her tiny one-woman shop had grown past what she could handle. Russell's amazing ads and Jo's sharp marketing advice had expanded Perrin's Glorious Garb past anything she'd ever envisioned. Other than the weekly meeting where they reviewed the books together and Perrin signed all the checks herself, she rarely had to think about the business itself anymore.

Raquel wasn't a designer, but she was a very astute business woman. One who recognized how to take care of all the things Perrin didn't give a single damn about. It had let Perrin handle all of the designs and construction, though she still outsourced some of the work to Georgie in Duvall. At Raquel's insistence, all of the designs in the shop had long since been uniquely her own and it was working. They still occasionally sold items off the rack, but more and more they were moving into custom work. Raquel had shown the numbers to Jo, and Jo had concurred that the direction change was sensible, which was good enough for Perrin.

But she didn't get to often sit with other designers and just talk shop. She could get to like this, just she, Jerimy, and Patsy sitting around together. It felt normal, real, as if she belonged and was accepted. Just the way Bill and the kids made her feel. As if it was normal.

"So, Patsy, what's a knitting gang?"

For once it didn't matter that sitting here quietly was the least normal thing on the planet for any of the incarnations she'd ever invented for Perrin Williams.

CHAPTER 11

*P*errin had stepped out onto the sidewalk and was locking up the shop for the day when Bill pulled up in his car. He climbed out, even though she was clearly ready to go.

He didn't ask. He didn't hesitate.

He swept her up into his arms, drove her back against the door hard enough to knock some of the wind out of her, and kissed her as if they'd been apart for years rather than hours. She locked her arms around his neck and returned the kiss just as ardently.

She let herself become wholly lost in the taste, feel, smell of him. His body responded and, when he went to pull back, she partly wrapped a leg around him to pull him even closer, wishing she'd thought to wear slacks rather than a dress so that she could really get some leverage. Then he leaned into her shamelessly.

Bill was starting to slide a hand under her sweater, and she was on the verge of letting him, when some teenagers in a passing car honked their horn and shouted out encouragement. He pulled back abruptly.

"Uh," he tried to help her straighten her clothes. "Hi."

She leaned in and gave him the gentlest kiss. He really was decent, even when lust was raging through him, he was decent. He was so damn cute.

"Hi, yourself. If you're going to greet me that way every time we meet, you have a winner plan on your hands, Mr. Cullen. Though I don't know what your kids will think."

He leaned his forehead against hers. "Can we, for a single night, pretend that I'm just a normal lust-filled guy who doesn't have two kids?"

"I can. Can you?"

"Probably not. But it's worth a try. For starters, you did say something about a request to be ravaged on a clothing design table. I happen to know that there's one not far from here." He eyed the darkened shop behind her suggestively.

Perrin almost wilted as he cupped his hands behind her and pulled her hips against his once more.

"If you keep doing that, you just might convince me to actually do something that crazy. Though we'd be late for dinner. And we can't do that."

"Dinner. Forget dinner. Order out. Much sex." He sounded like a caveman. A deliciously handsome, well-built, wonderful caveman. Maybe she should clothe him in furs, she did have a partial bolt of faux leopard in the shop.

Perrin kissed him again, locking her arms behind his head and pulling in so hard that her lips hurt before she let him go. He shifted down to nuzzle her neck.

"No. Later. I promise. After dinner." She managed between desperate breaths totally failing at sounding like a lusty cavewoman.

He groaned without raising his head, "You drive a hard bargain, lady."

"Bill."

He slowly lifted his head until he looked at her from a breath away. She kissed him lightly.

"At dinner, you'll meet the most important people in my world. Once you know them, then you'll know me a lot better too. I'm hoping it will let you better judge whether we can still risk being together, you know, what with the kids I'm not supposed to mention and all. Because I'm way past being rational about you."

"Says the woman being all practical." His kiss, so soft, so thorough, actually made her moan. It wasn't something she ever did unintentionally, but Bill drove it from her body. She'd have slid to the ground, if the door weren't against her back and his hands on her waist, because her knees were totally gone.

"After dinner, do we still get to have sex?" His voice was rough with need.

"Oh god, yes!" The need vibrated through her just as it did through him. Even a night of meaningless sex with Bill Cullen would be worth almost any price.

But what if it were meaningful sex?

Perrin set that question aside carefully for the moment, and nudged him gently toward his car.

"Perrin!"

Bill watched from the doorway of a condo near Pike Place Market as a lovely woman in her late forties threw herself at Perrin. Maybe this was the Maria he was supposed to meet. Perrin leaned down and the hug they shared was so tender and so happy, he actually had to look away to give them at least a little privacy.

"Dinner," Perrin had said. She'd failed to mention that the place would be packed solid with people and the air rippling with such amazing scents he seriously considered drooling. He couldn't even begin to make sense of the crowd.

"Hey," a deep voice behind him. "Keep moving forward."

Bill glanced back over his shoulder. The guy behind him was big. A couple of inches taller than Bill and enough shoulders that you wondered how he fit through doorways.

"Wait a sec, who are you?"

Before he could answer, Cassidy Knowles came up the hall behind him. "This is the man that I told you about, Perrin's friend. Bill Cullen, Russell Morgan, my husband."

The guy suddenly loomed taller, his light eyes darkening. "Bill.

Cullen." His voice deepened like a storm gathering over the infinite deep of the ocean.

Before Bill had time to duck for cover, someone was tugging on his sleeve from behind.

"Bill," Perrin's voice.

He turned carefully, keeping an eye on the big guy for as long as he could. He ended up facing the woman Perrin had first greeted.

She glanced over Bill's shoulder at the man Bill could only assume still loomed behind him.

"Oh, cut it out, Russell. There's beer in the kitchen, now be a good boy and behave."

The big guy slipped by a little sheepishly carrying a couple bottles of wine.

Cassidy patted Bill on the shoulder as she passed. "He's harmless, but he means well."

Bill remembered the far more nuanced, but perhaps more dangerous threat this woman had made on Perrin's behalf and restricted himself to a careful nod in reply.

"Hello, I'm Maria," she held out a graceful hand.

"Mama Maria Amelia Avico Parrano Stanford," Perrin corrected her and slid a hand around the smaller woman's waist. Mama Maria could never have spawned the tall, blond beauty that was Perrin, being darkly Italian and full-figured, but they stood as close as Adira and Tammy ever had.

Bill didn't know if he should shake the offered hand, or bow and kiss it. He decided on the latter. It earned him a bright laugh and a quick hug.

"So, Perrin brings home a man for the first time. And she doesn't tell me beforehand. That means that she's really worried." Maria briefly flashed a radiant smile at Perrin. "And my Perrin never worries about men. I look forward to getting to know you Mr. Cullen."

"Bill." He tried to think of something more intelligent to add, but didn't come up with anything.

"She's scary smart," Perrin told him, leaning down to kiss Maria on the temple.

"Just like you."

That earned him Maria's full attention. "You see her?"

"I, uh," Bill scrabbled about to find an answer to the odd phrasing of the question. "I see a brilliant, beautiful, chaotic, loving, wild, confusing-as-hell woman who I can't seem to look away from. If that's what you mean, then yes."

Maria pulled him down to her level using their still-clasped hands and then she kissed him lightly on each cheek.

"Yes," she whispered in his ear. "That's exactly what I mean." Then she stood back up. "Now, go meet everyone," and she gave him a gentle push into the room.

Perrin took his hand and went to lead him forward as the latest arrival greeted "Mama Maria" and began asking about her honeymoon. A quick glance revealed a darkly handsome Mexican man and a beautiful, slim Italian woman, both in their twenties, both sporting wedding rings. They had that newly married look, both smiling so hard their cheeks must be hurting. Even fifteen years later, he still remembered that feeling with Adira. So sharp, so visceral, it took his breath away.

"Uh, hang on," he tugged Perrin to a stop, pulling her sideways slightly out of the fray. "I need a second."

She held his hand and kissed him on the shoulder, then settled. Though he could feel her vibrating with good cheer.

First he looked at the setting. It was stunning. To his left was a long table, already laden with flatware and candles and several cold dishes. The wall behind the table was covered in pictures. Formal portraits and candids, many more of the latter. Though when he leaned in, he saw that even those were magnificent. He recognized a number of the faces as being in this room.

"Russell's work. He's such an amazing artist with his camera, I just try to be as good with my fashions as he is with a lens."

"Russell, the big guy?" At Perrin's nod, all he could do was wonder. More proof that you could never judge someone from the outside; Bill would have guessed stevedore or professional intimidator for a loan shark. Of course, he *was* married to the very elegant and sophisticated

Cassidy Knowles which told another story. One that he'd like to hear someday, though he doubted he'd believe it, they made too odd a couple.

The side wall was mostly books which led to a comfortable-looking seating area near a wall of windows. Beyond the windows spread the Seattle waterfront in all of its sunset glory. The condo was perched at the top of Pike Place Market. The piers that they had explored over the weekend were spread immediately below. Elliott Bay, alive with ferries, sailboats, and a tug-escorted container ship, stretched out into the distance where the Olympic Mountains rose silhouetted against the sunset sky.

"It's magnificent."

"Thanks." A man had also retreated to their safe corner as the crowd in the condo grew. "Hogan Stanford, Maria's husband. Have you met her?"

"Oh yes," Bill spotted her headed into the kitchen. "I've definitely met the Queen Mother."

"Queen Mother. That's good, I like it. Isn't she amazing?" His smile, more serene but no less radiant than the other couples, told Bill exactly who had been on the honeymoon with Maria.

"Nice tan. How was the trip?"

"You a sailor?"

"Not much," Bill looked out at the water and the several sailboats skimming along in the last of the evening breeze. "But I'd like to take the kids out someday."

"Oh, we can definitely arrange that. Make an outing of it. Russell's boat or mine. Then—"

"Did you say, 'kids'?"

Bill found himself shaking hands with Jo Thompson. She stood quite close and was not releasing his hand.

"I did. I have two of them." Jo Thompson made an interesting contrast with the other two friends. Perrin had told him enough to know that the three of them had gone through college together. Perrin might not speak of anything prior to turning eighteen, but she couldn't say enough about the two women she'd met twelve years ago on her very first day of school.

Perrin was the tall, slender blond. Cassidy, the trim, and nicely figured brunette. And Jo Thompson the seriously built, raven-haired, Alaskan beauty. Bill also knew that if he didn't take some control shortly, Jo and Cassidy would steamroller him right back out the door on Perrin's behalf.

"You three," Bill offered a nod to include the approaching Cassidy. He noted with some chagrin that Hogan had wisely abandoned ship. "You must have cut quite a swath through the men."

"You've got no idea!" Perrin offered one of her ridiculous giggles. Suddenly she was in full whack-a-doodle mode. "Jo found this one guy and latched onto him for four years, just so she didn't have to deal with dating. Sneaky, but dull. Cassidy, sheesh, she was so shy that if she hadn't had Jo as a roommate and me across the hall, no guy would have even known she was there. It was all up to poor Perrin to make sure these two had any college stories to tell at all."

Bill watched with interest as the two women reacted to Perrin laying out their sex lives at his feet. No shock, no surprise, and, curiously enough, no anger. The slightly manic Perrin was a wholly accepted fact and still they loved her. Cassidy had even slipped a hand around Perrin's waist from the other side as she continued.

"And no matter how much sex these two are getting from their new husbands, about which they tell poor Perrin depressingly little, they still haven't turned me into an auntie. Now I ask you, Mr. Cullen, is that fair?"

Bill looked at the two women, inspecting them as carefully as he would an opera singer about to tip off the deep end. They were expecting… Well tough! It wasn't what he was thinking, so all sails ahead or whatever sailors said and damn the consequences.

"I'm on your side, Perrin. I think that's really unfair. They should be having much more sex. And not telling us the all the juicy details, where's the fun in that?"

He could feel Perrin do a little dance step hop of glee against his side. Cassidy almost doubled over to hide a sharp snort of laughter.

Jo, who had retained his hand, studied him with those dark, dark eyes of hers before delivering her verdict.

"You just might do, Mr. Cullen. You just might do." Her slow smile lit her face like magic as she shook his hand solidly. He'd thought her pretty enough, but that rare smile transformed her into a great beauty.

When the two women finally moved off, probably to compare notes, Perrin threw herself into his arms.

For a long moment, he didn't care who was watching or what they thought, he just pulled her in and buried his face in Perrin's hair and reveled in the scent of the woman in his arms. He loved feeling her warmth. Holding her joy tight against him.

The dinner itself was a long, wonderful, maddening, incredible experience. At the table, Bill had ended up between Maria and Perrin, apparently a place of quite some privilege. Which raised eyebrows in some parts of the room, but not many.

Thankfully, there were a lot of stories in addition to his own. Maria and Hogan's sail up the Italian coast. Angelo, the handsome Italian chef who had married Jo Thompson, was still working on opening his second restaurant by the Seattle Center. When Bill told him when opening night of *Ascension* was, Angelo immediately decided that was a perfect night for a Grand Opening of his restaurant as well. Maybe he'd even get some before and after opera patrons for dinner.

Russell, rather than continuing to threaten Bill, started talking about some kind of a mutual marketing campaign. While a restaurant was small potatoes compared to a new opera costing upwards of five million dollars to produce, he suggested some interesting possibilities. They made an appointment for the next morning to talk about it further. He'd make sure to vet the guy personally before bothering Wilson or Chloe over in Marketing.

The Mexican man, Manuel, apparently a fine Italian *sous chef,* had taken the glowing Graziella to his family home in Oaxaca for a combined wedding and honeymoon which explained the newlywed smiles.

Angelo declared a reception dinner at his restaurant next Tuesday, rather than dinner at Maria and Hogan's. "And, Manuel, you will not be allowed in the kitchen." Based on Manuel's reserved look, Bill would wager on his finding a way in no matter what his boss said.

Maria and Hogan had married at Christmas, but not wanted to travel until the pastry chef for the new restaurant had been trained and approved by Maria. Apparently the second week of Maria's honeymoon had been even harder on Maria from worry than on poor Ignazio trying to meet her standards all on his own. A round of toasts and many cheers were raised on his behalf, while he did his best to glow at the far end of the table, it mainly looked like a blush from where Bill was sitting.

All that news traveled back and forth over some of the most amazing food Bill had ever eaten. Lasagna, so not microwaved. A mac and cheese made with fresh-made pasta, very aged cheese, and prosciutto. A side of salmon broiled with baby asparagus, venison flank braised with a mushroom-Barolo sauce, so rich it almost killed him. Steamed vegetables tossed in a white wine, lemon, garlic sauce... The plates seemed infinite yet were all consumed. It was capped off with a pear poached in stout beer for dessert. The evening was finished by tiny cups of decaf espresso laced with Frangelico hazelnut liqueur and many heavy sighs of contentment.

"You folks do this every week?"

Maria nodded at him, "Is there anything better than family around a table?"

Bill tried to come up with something, but... "Not a one I can think of, ma'am."

"Tell me more about your children."

"Better than that, if I'm invited next week, I'll bring the kids if they'd be welcome."

"Always!" Maria replied emphatically. "Children are always welcome." She waved a hand at all the new couples seated about the table, "I expect many children to sit at this table for many years to come."

Bill lifted his right hand, where it still held Perrin's left. He liked that they were opposite handed, so that they'd been able to hold hands for much of the meal, even while they ate. He kissed the back of her knuckles. It delighted him that it was so normal it didn't distract her from her conversation further down the table, other than to squeeze his own hand back without turning.

When had he tipped over the edge? What moment had he decided that not only did he want to come back next week, with Perrin, but to offer to bring his children? That was… He could feel the blood draining from his face. Too fast. It was all happening much too fast.

Tammy, who had already been too grown up, was blossoming straight into womanhood from Perrin's influence. And Jaspar was what? He'd practically thrown a five-year-old's tantrum about staying at Lucy's, though he'd been looking forward to it just days before. Bill had looked to Tammy for guidance, but she'd shrugged her shoulders helplessly. He'd tried talking it through, and finally just told him to get over it. He apologized to Lucy when he dropped them off for the horrid mood Jaspar was in. He had no idea—

Maria tapped her tiny espresso cup against his, drawing his attention back to her. "It's hard to know what to do, isn't it, Mr. Cullen? Especially when children are involved."

All he could do was nod.

"I was very careful with men around my son and Russell. But perhaps I was too careful. They turned into such fine boys, that I must have done something right, but Angelo grew with no father. John Morgan, Russell's father and my employer, was a good man but he was no father to Angelo. He had a wife and a son of his own. A thousand times I wonder if I made the right choice."

"He'll make a good father. They're a beautiful couple."

Jo and Angelo had begun to clear the table. When he rose to help, Maria rested her hand lightly on his arm. "Not on your first visit." Others were already rising, apparently based simply on who wasn't deep in conversation at that moment.

He settled back in his chair, not sure if he was comfortable with the continued conversation. How was he supposed to change his mind and say that he couldn't bring his children when she was being so gracious?

"Yes, it's hard to know, Mr. Cullen."

Bill turned to face Maria once more.

"So, it will be our secret. You will bring your children when you are sure and not before."

The relief was stronger than might be seemly, but he couldn't help that.

"Perrin was right, you're scary smart, Maria Stanford. She didn't mention that you are also amazingly kind."

Maria sipped her coffee, leaving him some space to gather his thoughts. Scary smart indeed.

"I don't suppose you'd care to tell me anything about the woman beside me?"

"You mean other than I wish with all my heart that she, of all women I've ever met, had been my daughter?"

That knocked Bill back in his seat. Everyone, except her new husband, called her 'Mama Maria' as if she were mother to them all. Yet from this amazing crowd of people, she had singled out Perrin.

"Really? Why?"

"Yes, really. And because Mama Maria is scary smart, you said so yourself, therefore it must be true. And there is one other thing I would tell you, Bill."

It was the first time she'd used his Christian name, as if he'd finally asked the right question, it had just taken him all evening to find it. She reached out and placed her hand over his heart.

"All the love you have in your heart for your children and your poor departed wife?"

"Yes?"

"Perrin will need that much. She will need so much before she will trust herself. So you will have to trust for her."

"Why can't she trust herself?"

"That's up to her to tell you, if she decides to."

"And if I can't trust her that much?"

"Phfft!" Maria flicked her fingers dismissively. "Your heart already knows or you would never have mentioned bringing your children here. Your mind just don't know it yet, but it's already true. Don't worry, dear boy. You'll get there."

THEY SAT QUIETLY in his car. Bill had pulled up in front of the store, parked the car, and turned out the lights. He made no move to get out, and Perrin waited with him in the dark silence. A lone streetlight was shadowed by the trees leafing out along the sidewalk. A few other cars were parked along the block, but there was little traffic.

"I don't know if I can do this." He kept his hands on the wheel.

Perrin didn't move, suddenly still as a frightened child.

"No, that didn't come out right," he reached out and picked up the hand he'd held most of the night. "There's just so much inside me. It's all so jumbled up that I don't know what to do with it. It's good, Perrin. I swear to god it is, but it's big. So big."

She slowly slipped her other hand over his, trapping his fingers between her hands. Her tension eased, but her silence didn't.

"I… " He looked up at the trees, down the street, over at the out-of-business tattoo parlor. Right back where he'd started. "I don't know what to do with all that's going on inside me."

"Welcome to my world," her voice was soft. "I'm smart enough to know what's going on inside me. But I can never seem to straighten it all out. Like trying to build a costume that keeps falling apart because a key seam was never sewn, but by the time I fix it, another three have unraveled."

He turned to face her. Her face but a pale oval in the dim light.

"Can you be smart for me tonight, Perrin? I honestly don't know what to do with it all."

"Me?" He'd shocked her. Himself a little too.

"Don't see anyone else in the car volunteering."

That roused her laugh.

"I love your laugh so much." The words just came out of him. He did. It was like a thousand stage lights come alive. Her laugh shone into the darkest places and shone pure, bright light.

"You want me, of all the loony people on the planet, to be smart for both of us?"

He could only nod.

"Okay," she huffed out a breath. "Okay, I can try, but understand that you only have yourself to blame if this comes out all stupid."

"Understood. It's a risk I'm willing to take."

She looked away and studied her darkened shop for a long time.

He waited, one hand clamped to the wheel, the other still wrapped so warm between her two hands.

"Okay. Looks as if it's going to come out as a series of questions."

"Like I haven't had enough of those tonight. Talk about the Italian inquisition, it was a tough room."

"Hey, you asked me to take over here."

Bill nodded, "I did. Go for it. I trust you." That snapped her attention back to him. He hadn't expected those words either. Maria's words. But who else would he trust in this situation?

"Me?" her voice was a whisper.

"Yes, I do. You. The scary smart lady sitting here beside me like a blessing. So ask. Please?" He actually begged a little. Everything was so mixed up inside him.

"Okay…" her voice was shaky. She took a deep breath. "Okay. Let's start with a key one. After meeting with everyone, do you still want to be with me?"

"So much it's killing me."

"That's a good answer, Bill. That's a really good answer. I like that answer too. So if that's not the problem, then let me think what's next."

Bill sat in the dark and waited. He had kissed this woman a half dozen times, total. They hadn't had a proper, just-the-two-of-them date yet. His kids were half mad for her. And his own feelings?

"Are you afraid that if we make love, your life will never be the same?"

"Yes." The answer dragged out of him.

"Okay, we're tracking so far."

"Tracking?"

"We're both being scared silly by exactly the same shit."

That reached him. That finally punched through whatever knot had been slowly winding tighter and tighter in his gut all night. It wasn't the answer yet, but it was the first strand, broken rather than merely loosened.

"Keep going. You're doing great, Perrin."

She let go of his hand, "I can't think while we're touching." Then she grabbed it back between hers, "No, not touching you is even worse."

"That's not a question, but yes, I feel the same way."

Perrin smiled over at him.

"Okay, I think this is the final question of the first round."

"Fire away."

"Could we go inside to finish this before I freeze to death?"

"Shit!" Bill scrambled out of the car and hurried around to open her door.

She didn't lead him to her shop as he'd expected, but rather around the corner. She stopped at a door on the side street. A half dozen mailboxes hung along the wall for the various apartments above her shop and the one beyond. Perrin unlocked a door that led to a flight of stairs.

The stairway was hung with a beautiful series of quilts. It was as if he was following a stream through the seasons. Working his way upstream, the first quilt led him from ice winter to red-and-gold fall. The second stream, appearing to flow out of one quilt and into the next, followed the summer colors and included a pool with a bear pawprint and a golden flower. The third quilt started the stream flowing between banks the color of spring, eventually rising to where it flowed out from under blue-white ice, just as it had ended down below.

"Are these yours? The four seasons. They're beautiful."

"I quilt sometimes, not often." They left them behind at the head of the stairs and Perrin led him down a hall that made his eyes water. It had a green ceiling, a zebra stripe wall to one side, a yellow wall to the other with a purple-lettered poem painted on it in tall letters.

He read a few lines, it was a really bad poem.

"These however, are so not me."

Bill considered remarking that was a good thing, but wasn't sure of how good the sound insulation might be. Besides, he remembered the last time Perrin had used those words while standing in a pile of confetti. At least the floors were a rich, if hard worn, hardwood. None of the residents had applied "their art" to improve them.

She led him to the door at the end of the hallway.

Perrin's apartment was neither neat nor messy, it was lived in, but perhaps not very much. Clearly, her life was downstairs in her shop. There were nice coverings on the couch, a television, but no computer. Several fashion magazines. A wall of reference books on types of art: architecture, fiber, painting, sculpture of a dozen varieties, early Japanese, Italian Renaissance. It was all about art forms and they looked well used. This is where she obviously found many of her out-of-the-box ideas. He couldn't decide if it was an incredibly focused collection or astonishingly unfocused. Assuming the former, it was immensely eclectic within its range. She moved into the kitchen while he inspected the books.

"I don't see any on opera."

"They have books on opera art?"

"About a thousand: lighting, costume, sets, you name it. I'll get you a couple."

"Thanks."

A totally mad quilt, clearly done in one of her gonzo frames of mind, filled the wall above the couch with a dozen blocks, each in a different style with different fabrics. Yet the colors tied it together into a cohesive quilt. A wild one, but cohesive.

He found her making tea in a small kitchenette with a table that could seat only two. She still looked cold and he moved to hug her.

"No," she fended him off. "You touch me and we're going to go straight to sex, do not pass go, do not collect two-hundred dollars. And as good as that sounds, it's not what you asked for."

"I was being an idiot. Come here."

She didn't. So he tossed his jacket aside, dropped into one of the chairs, and just enjoyed watching her move about the kitchen fetching mugs and digging out a box of blueberry tea.

"Sorry, I think this is all I have at the moment."

"Kids' favorite. I've learned to like it."

She poured the hot water and sat across from him. "Ready for round two?"

"No. But let's see where we go anyway."

PERRIN LOOKED at Bill over their tea cups and tried to decide just how brave she was feeling. Maria had liked him. She'd liked him a lot. Jo and Cassidy too, which helped, but Maria was the wise one. And she and Bill had talked quietly together through so much of the meal.

She'd done her best to listen to everything, while pretending not to. She'd missed a lot, but had heard Maria admonish Bill that "he already knew about his heart," he just didn't know that he did. There was no way to be sure what they were talking about, but there were things Perrin already knew about herself. Really knew. Even if they were scaring the crap out of her.

Bill waited so patiently. He'd said he trusted her. Trusted her more than himself. No man had ever said such a thing. Well, if he was going to trust her, how could she return less?

All it took was being brave, right? She wasn't very good at brave. She could do it if she hid behind crazy Perrin, because then it was someone else. And it came out as a joke that no one believed. But she couldn't go there with this man. Not when they sat quietly together in the night. Not when she felt the way she did. She'd have to be her more rational self tonight.

"Okay, do you want the scary question first or the hard one?"

"That's a choice?" He brushed a hand through his hair and she wished she had the nerve to do the same, but she didn't dare touch him at the moment. Not for his sake but for her own.

"It is."

"No third choice? Wild sex maybe?"

She shook her head. "As wonderful as that sounds, not yet."

"Shit! Why doesn't this look good? What the hell. Hard one first."

Perrin really didn't know which one was worse, but she wished he hadn't chosen the hard one.

"First, I want you to know that if you want to walk out the door afterward, I won't ever blame you."

She could see that he almost made a joke, then a denial, but finally thought better of it and set aside his tea mug to listen.

Perrin didn't know how to do this one. Maybe like she'd told Tamara about tearing up the drawings, "You gotta just do it." Well, she was about to risk tearing up her life, but she saw no other path.

So she just did it.

Perrin told Bill about a father with a taste for young girls. About a mother with a coke habit she supported by selling her daughter to anyone who came to the trailer. Perrin left nothing out, not skipping one sordid detail of eighteen years of hell that had been her childhood.

She told of her arrival at college, an escape she still wasn't sure how she'd managed, her test scores earning her a full scholarship. And how, after one particularly horrid drug-laden and abusive affair, it was Cassidy who had taken her own meager savings to fly Perrin home with her. They had gone to her father's small vineyard just across Puget Sound on Bainbridge Island.

How Cassidy's father had been kind. Simply kind, expecting nothing in return. She'd never known such a thing was possible. After that, for four years, she'd listened as well as she could to what Jo and Cassidy had told her to do. For four years, she'd slowly left behind a wounded child and invented Perrin Williams. Legally changing her name senior year so that the diploma would bear her "real" name.

She didn't cry as she told Bill of her true past. Tears were still locked away too deep. She'd often laughed until she cried with Jo and Cassidy. Only once since her early childhood, the first time Mama Maria had said she wished Perrin had been her daughter, had she cried for herself.

But Bill cried for her. Tears ran untended down his face. He tried to reach for her, but she pulled back. Not trusting that she could survive the searing power of his touch and not shatter.

"I haven't had a panic attack like the one at the dog show in over five years, but I can't guarantee there won't be another. So here's the hard question, Bill. Can you still trust me around your children? Do you want to risk a woman with that past stepping into the mother-role for your children? Because that's where this might be headed, or we wouldn't be having this conversation."

With a shocking abruptness, Bill stood and whirled away, striding out into the living room.

Perrin closed her eyes, wrapped her arms around her belly to hold herself together, and waited for the final judgment and eternal damnation of the front door slamming shut.

But it didn't happen.

Not even after she waited.

When she dared open her eyes, she could see his back. He stood in the center of her living room facing her couch and the sampler quilt she'd made ages ago to teach herself basic sewing and design skills, her first-ever effort. His arms were crossed so tightly that they were straining the fabric of his shirt.

He didn't move. She waited five minutes, ten. But still he didn't move.

She stood and moved into the kitchen doorway. Almost close enough to touch him. But she couldn't bridge the gap.

"What's the scary one?" His voice was so harsh, so angry. She'd never heard anything like it, but she now knew better than to fear him. He'd never strike her. Whatever his anger, it wasn't directed at her.

She'd made it through the hard one, now she had to face the scary one. The one even more likely to send him running down the hall away from her. She swallowed hard before trying to speak through the fear of losing him.

"I love you."

The words fell into the silence of the room and lay there untended for long enough that her stomach knotted into a hard, snarled ball.

"That's not a question." Then he turned to face her. His face was calm, though his cheeks were still wet. He stepped forward, and reaching out very slowly, brought his hands to her shoulders. If she could have stepped back, she would have. But she was too numb, too afraid. Not even for Cassidy had she let her heart out into the world with her words.

He pulled her in, leaving the decision to stop wholly up to her, but she let him do it until she could lay her cheek on his shoulder and he wrapped his arms around her. She couldn't seem to unlock her own arms from around her midriff, so she simply leaned against him.

Bill rocked her gently, ever so gently. Then he whispered to her.

"Yeah. That's the same one that's scaring the shit out of me too. But it's not a question. I love you, too. It makes no sense that it could happen so fast or so completely, but I do."

Some time later, Bill's slow rocking turned into a slow dance in the middle of her small living room.

Perrin was fairly sure that she was the one who kissed him first, rather than the other way round.

He was definitely the one who swept her up in his arms and proceeded to carry her into the coat closet. She redirected him to the bedroom with giggles for his curses.

Bill set her on the bed, then sat beside her. He brushed his fingertips ever so gently over her cheek.

"Don't!" Her shout was sharp.

"What?" He jerked his hand back as if she'd burned him.

"Don't you dare treat me like I'm fragile. I'm not fragile. Earlier this evening you wanted to ravage me. So ravage me. I won't break!" Perrin was so pissed she wanted to swipe at him.

"Not fragile? Not fragile?!" His voice rose as abruptly as hers had. "Any idiot who thinks you're fragile needs his goddamn head examined. You lived through... through... " he pointed helplessly back toward the kitchen. "... that. You're the goddamn strongest and most amazing woman I've ever met. I'm being gentle because I can't believe what you just told me. *That* you just told me. That you let me in so far. How can you dare to trust me so much? That's what I'm trying to understand. I'm in awe of you, Perrin Williams, not afraid I'm going to break you!"

"Oh." If she'd been gone on him before, she was right off the deep end now. The way he saw her was incredible.

"Oh?" He huffed out a breath. "Is that all you have to say after my whole tirade is, 'Oh'?"

"Best, I have, Mr. Cullen."

"Shit!" he cursed. "Where was I?"

She took his hand and placed it against her cheek. "Right here." Then she closed her eyes and turned her head to rub against his fingertips.

Ever so slowly, he relaxed and began again. He traced the lines of her face. She followed the line of fire as he tested every shape and curve: cheek, chin, eyebrows, lips, and tip of her nose.

She was floating by the time he had moved down her throat. He didn't hasten his investigation of her body in the slightest as he unbuttoned her blouse, released her bra, and teased her breasts until the nipples ached.

When his mouth latched onto her, she hissed at the pleasure so intense it was pain. He knew exactly what to do to drive her upward. No man had ever been so gentle. No man had ever been so intent on giving her pleasure rather than taking his own. She allowed herself to go where he led, to become a conduit of Bill's touch. Each line he drew, each place he tasted built until she was clothed in nothing but the light and heat he spread over her skin as he went.

He rolled her over until she lay on her stomach, and he continued to clothe her in his gentle brushes and kisses. He turned it into a massage. One that started at her feet and built as it flowed up her legs, over her buttocks, driving her deliciously into the bed, and up over her back and shoulders.

Just as he had made her feel clothed in traceries of light, now he stripped her bare with a deep cleansing touch. She didn't remember turning onto her back once again, didn't know when it happened and didn't care. He suckled her until the waves finally burned through her insides, scorching away the last remnants of darkness trapped inside her.

When he laid his lips between her legs, she exploded. She cried out as a tidal wave of pure pleasure rushed over her. No man had ever touched her like this. None had ever sent her to such places, ones she didn't even believe existed.

But now she knew.

They did.

When he went to drive her upward again, she managed to flutter her eyes open. He was still fully clothed.

"That was one hell of a ravage, Mr. Cullen."

"You're magnificent, Ms. Williams."

She managed to sit up, despite her muscles all gone to liquid.

Her fingers weren't working that well with how her nervous system was buzzing, but she managed to unbutton his shirt. His muscles twitched and quivered under her touch.

"That's a very nice chest, Mr. Cullen."

"My wife liked—Aw shit! I'm sorry." He went to turn away.

She stopped him with a kiss. "Bill. I'm not asking you to push your wife out of your heart to let me in. I know she's dead or you wouldn't be here with me. I think it's nice that you loved her so much. It really shows in Jaspar and Tamara, they'd know if it wasn't true."

"But you deserve—"

"Exactly what I'm about to take." With that she pushed him back on the bed. She dug in a drawer for some protection, then she greedily took all he could give. How many times they made love, how many times the waves rolled through each of them, releasing their bodies and clothing their hearts in such glory, Perrin didn't know.

But even as they collapsed onto each other and slid into sleep, Perrin knew that however much she'd had, she wanted more.

ill groggily surfaced. Seven a.m.

Crap! An hour late! He tried to leap into action, but his body totally failed him. Then he remembered where he was. No kids. No lunches to make, no need to double-check they had their homework in their packs.

He rolled over, but there was no one beside him. It was just breaking daylight beyond the lacy curtains. The room he hadn't seen last night was now lit with a soft light. Everything that was utilitarian in the rest of Perrin's apartment, had no place here in her bedroom. Here there were warm colors, soft textures. Rather than a closet, rather than just a closet, one whole wall had been turned into shelves and hanging racks. Here were the clothes, both casual and incredible, worn by both the real Perrin and the wild-girl she presented as a smokescreen to distract others.

But where was she?

Even as he struggled to wake up enough to go find her, the bedroom door swung open. An elegant, burl-wood door harp played a cheerful chord as the door bumped lightly against the dresser.

He'd never seen anything like what came walking into the room. Perrin had said she slept in a flannel nightgown. What she hadn't said was how amazing she looked in one. It was easy to forget how tall she was because she was so slight, but the columnar gown emphasized her length. And her black-and-blond hair stood out even more strongly against the white. The gown was of such fine material, that even the tiny breeze of her forward motion made it wrap and cling against her amazing figure.

And the smile that greeted him wasn't the least bit tentative. There couldn't be any question about how they felt, not after last night. Her smile was as luminous as the morning light. Her fine features, so delicate yet so strong.

"Are you ready for some coffee?"

His brain said, "Yes." But the rest of him had other thoughts. A reaction she clearly noted through the thin layer of the sheet over his bare hips.

"I was hoping that's how you felt." She set the tray on her dresser then moved to sit beside him.

When she reached out a hand to brush his cheek, he used it as leverage to drag her against him, crushing his mouth to hers.

She lay down full length upon him and melted against him until they would be one body if not for the thin flow of soft fabric separating them.

"You," he ran a hand up her magnificent body, "requested a ravage, Ms. Williams. I think it is time you received precisely that."

"Why Mr. Cullen, that sounds like an absolutely brilliant idea."

And he did. For a moment, he considered if he should be gentle, not wanting to scare her. Then he imagined her as the Empress—the great, the powerful, the embodiment of woman. What kind of a lover could make the Empress lose herself? A gentle one would please her, but that wasn't the point of a ravage.

He rolled her onto the bed beside him. When Perrin moved to pull off the nightgown, he brushed her hands away. In some ways this too was her shield, where she wrapped herself into safety. Well, this morning, he'd not violate that, instead he'd honor it as a part of who she was. He rubbed the fabric over her, tasted her through its thickness, drove her with his hands, though never directly touching her, until her body thrashed and she groaned begging for more.

When he could stand it no longer, he rolled her on top of him, slid the nightgown up her legs, and took her beneath the cloak of flannel now spread over both of them.

With her palms against his chest, she rose above him, the most magnificent being he could imagine, and then she drove her hips downward as he arched up into her.

Her head thrown back, her exquisite neck curving ever so perfectly, her body thrumming against his as they both greeted the morning with their shared pleasure and joy.

BILL WAS SHOWERED, dressed, and totally pleased with his morning when Perrin's phone buzzed as they were leaving her apartment. She checked the message and then made a cheer and did a little shimmy dance. Today she wore tailored wool slacks and a cashmere sweater, one of which hugged and the other of which clung.

Bill's first thought was how badly he wanted to drag her straight back into the apartment, but she was skipping ahead of him down the poem and zebra-stripe hallway.

"It's finished!" she called back to him.

"What is?" He had to hustle to keep up with her.

"C'mon slowpoke!" And she was gone.

She stood at the street corner when he caught up with her and there was certainly no need to ask what she was looking at.

A solid maple tree, with its long straight trunk, had been wrapped in yarn. It was the colors that were so electrifying. The upper half was in the conflicted color of the lineage of the Tragic Prince, the lower half, the jewel tones of the Princess and True Love. Over them both, in large, blocky letters that were actually knit into the design was simply the opera's title, *Ascension,* in the dark, forceful colors of the Overlord.

"An *Ascension* yarn bomb? That's cute."

"I had Patsy's yarn gang do it for me."

"It's sweet." Bill brushed a hand down the soft surface.

Perrin the wild girl was looking at him…and grinning like a jackal.

Bill surreptitiously checked the soles of his shoes to see what he had just stepped in, but he had no idea.

hen Bill arrived at the Opera offices, he scraped in only minutes before his planned meeting with Russell.

He only had a moment to look up Russell Morgan online.

Bill tried to get organized, and thought of the shape of Perrin's shoulder.

Russell Morgan had been a world famous fashion photographer until he'd practically disappeared two years ago, closing his New York studio. Bill clicked over to see any images. There were several paparazzi shots of Russell with that supermodel Melanie draped on his arm.

Bill shook his head in wonder, and remembered how it felt as Perrin's strong fingers dug into his hair.

There were photos of Russell's wedding to Cassidy Knowles at a lighthouse. And some very nice ads for Perrin's Glorious Garb, Pike Place Market, and the Washington Wine Cooperative.

Bill was about to scrub at his face to force himself to focus when Nia called him to the front desk.

In the lobby, not only Russell, but also Angelo were chatting happily with Nia. It wasn't quite flirting, both men were decent enough to make sure their wedding rings were on clear display, but everything else about it was flirting.

"There's the man!" Russell's crushing handshake warned Bill that last night's threat before dinner might not have been so idle. Angelo's friendly hug and very solid thump on his back reinforced the message strongly. Angelo was not as tall as Russell, but his shoulders showed he pumped a lot of iron.

The main thing Bill pumped was a lot of paper, and as much patience with work and kids as possible. He was in good shape, Perrin had remarked on it any number of times and places on his body… Gads! But if these two guys wanted to squish him into a little ball and drop him into a garbage can, there was nothing that he could do about it.

He skipped the standard office tour, though he did take them through the halls the long way around so they could see the more recent production photos on the walls.

Russell nodded his head as he looked at them. "Claude's work, nice. Oh, and there you used Enrique. A little dark, but he always is."

At first Bill was trying to remember the directors and designers for those productions. Then he remembered a brief meeting a few shows back as one of his assistant stage managers had reported that she'd be escorting Enrique Rinaldi during a rehearsal to photograph the production. You couldn't have a photographer running around the house during an actual performance.

Bill looked more closely, but the photographer was not noted on the prints, only the production, date, and visible cast members. Russell Morgan was able to recognize the photographer's work as easily as Bill recognized a well-tempered singer versus a lunatic diva, in other words, at a glance.

They went down to the Costume Shop. Jerimy wasn't there, but Patsy pulled out the main clothing racks for *Ascension*.

"Damn!" Russell brushed one costume aside, then another to expose the fronts. "Look, Angelo. Look what she did. Perrin is really incredible. I swear I could take her international tomorrow. I wouldn't do that shit to her, but her designs could walk Paris."

Bill agreed, then realized that this was a leading fashion photographer, he would really know. Without saying a word, Bill pulled out the Empress and hung it in the clear so that it was fully visible.

Angelo let out a long, low whistle of appreciation. "Can you imagine how Perrin would look in that one?"

Bill remembered her arrival. The manic, sleep-deprived, stunning beauty with the blond swirl in her newly black hair, and that dress wrapped around her.

"She was magnificent in it." He lost himself in the memory for a moment, the sheer power she had radiated, like a beacon in the night.

Only belatedly did he become aware that he had the absolute attention of the two men.

"You saw Perrin in that?" Russell's voice was low, dangerous.

"She was amazing. Then she crashed onto my office couch and slept for nineteen hours and twenty-three minutes."

"She does that," Angelo acknowledged cheerily.

"Your couch," Russell's voice went even lower.

"By Bill's dreamy look," Angelo offered up as if he hadn't noticed Russell's tone. "I'd say they used more than the couch after they left dinner last night."

Russell took a step forward, Bill stumbled back into one of the cutting tables.

"He has this ticklish spot," Angelo said perfectly matter-of-factly then poked a single finger into Russell's lower rib cage and began wiggling it.

"Hey!" Russell leapt aside. "Cut that shit out! I'm onto something here."

Angelo went after him again, ducking what looked to be a potentially vicious headlock. "What you're onto is messing with Perrin's love life. And frankly, if there's anyone scarier to mess with than Mama, it has to be Perrin."

Russell found the headlock, just as Angelo nailed the spot making Russell squirm sideways and step back, dragging Angelo with him by his neck.

Sensing trouble, Patsy, Jerimy's assistant, had come up behind them, though Bill had no idea what the little woman could do. She barely came up to Russell's armpit. What she did was deftly slide a clothes hamper behind their knees as they stumbled back another step, and the two men collapsed backward onto the floor in a flurry of scarves, hats, and gloves.

Bill looked up at the ceiling and remembered Cassidy's comment from last night: "Harmless." *Yeah, right.*

After cleaning up, the three of them sat around one of the cutting tables on tall stools. It had taken longer to drag Russell and Angelo clear of the clothing than it had been to get it all back in the hamper.

Patsy went about her business, whistling the old Grateful Dead tune, *Man Smart (Woman Smarter)* which thankfully neither of the other guys appeared to recognize. She had members of her knitting gang coming in to start building the last costumes and she was setting up a big table encircled by comfortable chairs. Someone rolled a large knitting machine off the elevator and Patsy rushed over to help. He hadn't thought the costumes were that numerous to need a knitting machine, but maybe they were. The outfits for the court's entourage characters had to match their leaders after all.

He left her to it and returned his attention to Perrin's self-declared protectors.

"Sorry," Russell shook his head. "Actually no. I'm not a bit sorry, even if Cassidy will kick my ass for interfering. Perrin's fragile. She needs protection more than she will admit or even knows."

Bill considered pointing out that his assessment was quite the opposite, but decided that discretion was the better part of survival.

"While Russell is still blowing steam," Angelo slapped his friend on the back, as if he was choking, hard enough to echo about the room though Russell barely wavered. "Someone care to tell me what the hell am I doing here?"

Bill could only shrug. He'd only expected Russell. And he'd mainly agreed to take the meeting because Perrin thought Russell was such an artist. That he'd dragged one of Seattle's finest restaurateurs along with him, didn't make any sense that he could see.

"It's in that boy's brain," he pointed at Russell, "maybe you can beat it out of him. If not, I'm sure we could call Mama Maria and she'd be glad to come help."

That seemed to work. Russell scraped his hand back through his hair.

"Man, you try to be a little protective of your friends and suddenly everyone's threatening me with Maria."

"Is it working?"

Russell glared at him balefully, "Yeah, I guess it is. Okay, here we go. Your new opera, are you planning any opening night events?"

"We actually have a couple of them. The high rollers, bigger donors, get a very nice catered dinner with entertainment and free passes into the final dress rehearsal. Then there's also the after-opening-night party; that's for the primary cast members and the really major donors."

Russell was nodding. "Have you contracted venues or catering services yet?"

Angelo didn't see it, still looking confused, but Bill heard it loud and clear. He'd play along as a politeness, but didn't expect it to go anywhere.

"Consuela, our head of fundraising, has the bids, but we haven't reviewed or signed anything yet. The first event is a large tent venue for three hundred people on the Seattle Center grounds: heaters, string quartets, arias by various artists, the whole nine yards. The second event is typically an indoor venue, a hundred people, maybe a little more, mostly standing, high-end finger food and a fair amount of champagne."

"He can do that," Russell assured him blithely.

Angelo caught up with the conversation. "Wait! Three hundred? Are you nuts, Russell? Is that buffet or plated?"

"Plated."

Angelo groaned.

"That's individual service for three hundred people of an appetizer, three courses, plus dessert," Bill informed Angelo as if driving in the spike. He was starting to get the rhythm of these two. It was kind of fun to watch.

Angelo's eyes had crossed. "Uh, you have any paper?"

Bill found a sketchpad and pencil in a drawer under the table and slid it across to Angelo who began tinkering and figuring.

"So, Russell."

The man looked at him suspiciously.

"Hogan tells me you have a great sailboat. Any chance of taking my kids out for a sail?"

It was like he'd hit the magic button. Russell brightened as he talked about the fifty-footer he'd refinished and taken up the Inside Passage to Alaska with Cassidy shortly after their marriage. He even had a picture in his wallet, right next to one of a black cat and Cassidy that was absolutely breathtaking.

"Okay, I can do this. I'll have to close the restaurant for the night and hire some extra staff as well. Russell, you're going to be a goddamn busboy for me to pull this off, but I can do it."

"Do what?"

Russell dug into his pocket and pulled out a crumpled printout and shoved it across to Bill.

An advertisement. It was beautiful. It had power and beauty. A picture of the Empress hijacked from one of the posters gave it a real gut punch.

Master chef Parrano's new restaurant, Angelo's Piedmont Hearth, hosting as its Grand Opening, the party to celebrate the World Premier of *Ascension*. It was a breathtaking promotion of both the opera and the restaurant. It splashed a couple pull-quotes of Angelo's Tuscan Hearth, that sounded stunning, including one from Cassidy Knowles.

Bill pointed at the last. "That's kind of an insider review, isn't it? I mean you two obviously went through the same reformatory school, but why are you getting a nice lady like Ms. Knowles wrapped up in your skullduggery."

Russell grinned at him, "Well, when she wrote that review about a meal, I was busy messing up—our first-ever, blind date—, you may be right."

"I still don't know how you ever convinced her to talk to you again," Angelo was shaking his head.

"'Cause I'm just that good, doofus. And way more handsome than you."

"Well, it sure wasn't your brains or good manners as your cat has more of those than you by a long shot."

Bill decided that balance was a good thing, and they'd both been beating up on Russell as an easy target. So, he turned to Angelo.

"But I have to protect our donors. I mean, how do I know your food is any good?" Angelo's reputation was unquestioned. Bill had often wished he had an excuse to eat Angelo's food, as he was sure the donors would be. But being a single dad with two kids didn't really go together with fine dining.

Russell reached across the table to punch Bill on the arm in a friendly fashion while Angelo spluttered then glared at Bill.

"We're booked solid the next two nights, but then I can set up a special. You come to my restaurant. I will show you just how goddamn good I cook."

"Does his English always come apart when he's upset?"

Russell nodded his head sadly. "Maria tried to bring him up right, but he's Italian. There's only so much you can do."

Angelo spit out something in Italian that sounded both melodic and guttural.

"Right back at you, brother," Russell said with some affection.

"Okay, so," Bill had a sudden idea. "If I do *deign* to come and try your restaurant, I'll want to bring a date."

The two men sobered and shared a long glance.

Angelo answered for them, "Perrin is always welcome. Always. No matter *what* she drags in with her."

Bill had the feeling that the last part was added as an afterthought insult, no real heat behind it anymore.

"And my kids."

"Do I hafta?"

Bill tugged on Jaspar's tie. Even using a clip-on, the kid somehow was wearing it crooked.

"Hey, it's a nice restaurant and the girls are probably going to look sharp." Tammy had been consistently going to Perrin's after school when she wasn't needed for a rehearsal. But Perrin had promised him that Tammy wasn't allowed to sew until after her homework was done. He'd been checking up on her homework, as he always did, but Perrin had been as good as her word. Jaspar appeared to be enjoying the exclusive Dad time, even if that often just meant reading a book while Bill worked.

"Girls!" Jaspar scoffed.

"Look here, Jaspar. If I have to wear a tie, so do you."

Jaspar stuck his tongue out at Bill, but moved to the bathroom mirror and adjusted it himself until it was close enough. He'd inherited Bill's curling hair rather than his mother's flowing locks that had gone to Tammy. A quick brush did little to help, especially as he was a past due for a haircut.

Bill was really trying not to be nervous. He'd seen Perrin only briefly as he'd picked up Tammy a few times. A couple late night phone calls did little to slake his desperate desire to see the woman.

To distract himself as they drove to the restaurant, he asked Jaspar to teach him the new Italian words he'd learned. Carlo di Stefano had, once he calmed down from his girlfriend Melanie's departure, sort of adopted Jaspar. Already the kid had more Italian than Bill had picked up over years of dealing with singers. Carlo had wisely started with cat, dog, elephant, and the like. Then he'd moved on to *giovane principe*, "Young Prince," and the other titles in the cast. Now they were ranging off into everyday life vocabulary.

While Bill appreciated it, he also cursed that now he'd have something new he had to keep up with to encourage and support his kid as if he weren't already juggling enough. Next year Jaspar could start a language in sixth grade and Italian was presently the favored option. Spanish Bill could keep up with from living in California and working with Mexican stage hands. French he'd at least have a head start because that had been Tammy's selection. But Italian? And ten years old, headed for sixth grade… Life was moving too fast. It had to slow down at some point, didn't it?

He parked and they walked down to the restaurant where Perrin had said she'd meet them.

"Hey look, there's another one!"

The walk sign on the corner had one of the *Ascension* yarn-bomb banners climbing its pole.

Angelo or Russell… Russell, Bill decided. He was the marketing brains, Angelo was the cook. He must have asked… who? Patsy? Well, that would explain the need for a knitting machine. But it didn't just feel like Patsy and her knitting gang.

It wasn't just some slap up of Perrin's designs, the yarn-bomb itself was a designed piece. Perrin, it had to be. So, Perrin had designed a couple yarn-bombs to promote the opera. That was really decent of her. Definitely above and beyond the scope of the contract. And, like the costumes, the yarn-bomb was quite attractive. A tourist stopped to photograph it with his wife standing beside it smiling.

When they entered Angelo's, Bill was taken back to his life with Adira. In the beginning they could afford one date a month out together. They'd started at the local pub with a brew and a burger. Actually in the very beginning there'd been months where Kentucky Fried Chicken had been a splurge. But over the years they'd slowly climbed up. A good Mexican restaurant, a steak house, a nice little bistro. By the time the kids came along, "date night" had become a monthly tradition. Their last dinner out had been a massive splurge at the Allegro Romano on San Francisco's Russian Hill, just a week before she was killed.

The rich scents of fine Italian food were a slap to the face that momentarily overwhelmed him with all he'd lost. It was too much. Too fresh. Four years of dealing with it, of telling himself the next day would be better, of putting on the good face for the kids, and here it all was as immediate as yesterday and as harsh as forever.

Air. He needed air. He turned back for the door as it swung open. Out of the evening light, a vision came toward him. Perrin had somehow walked the line between dressing for him and for his children. She wore a simple evening gown of bright red. Thin straps curving behind her neck and exposing bare shoulders told him that the dress was probably backless beneath the light shawl that had slipped down to hang by her elbows. All of her sleek form was traced, enhanced by the simple lines of the dress. Elbow-long gloves of the same material only enhanced the image. It covered, but it promised.

During their one night together, he'd done his best to memorize every one of her gentle curves. Her gown invited him to appreciate them anew.

Then he focused on the woman who had arrived holding Perrin's hand.

Woman?!

"Tammy?"

She managed a curtsey then a brilliant smile that she shared with Perrin. Her dress, rather than the knockout statement of bright red, was as dark and dusky as her hair. It followed the lines of Perrin's, obviously the dresses had been designed to complement each other, but it was far more demure. Where Perrin's elegantly revealed, Tammy's dress modestly suggested.

He knew Tammy had a figure, he'd helped her buy her first training bra for crying out loud, an incredibly embarrassing moment for both of them, though he'd done his best not to let on. But without him noticing, she'd started growing into her mother's beautiful figure. The dress followed her lines, which made her pretty rather than enticing. Instead of the bare shoulder-backless look that Perrin wore, it was actually as high-necked as a turtleneck. A simple silver chain an accent to the deep red material that covered her so chastely. And it wasn't merely dressing up a child in a fancy dress, she wore it as a woman would, fully aware of her own impact upon those around her.

"It's the Princess-to-be," he still had trouble equating this growing girl with his own daughter. "Tammy, you're gorgeous."

Her glowing smile and bright giggle did nothing to destroy the image.

He wrapped her into a hug, which she returned more strongly than she had in a couple of years.

He mouthed a, "Thank you" to Perrin over his daughter's head.

Perrin reached out a gloved finger and brushed it along his cheek.

"So," Perrin broke the tableau and looked at Jaspar. "Are you too busy being incredibly handsome or would you be willing to escort me into dinner?"

<hr>

JASPAR TOOK MS. WILLIAMS' hand and led her forward without any hesitation about coming in contact with a "girl." He knew that's what was expected of him tonight. His job was to be the "little grownup gentleman" and do whatever the adults said. He could see how important this was to everyone, except him. He was like a chorus member in an opera; kill him off in Act I and no one really notices whether or not he rejoins the villagers in Act III.

A glance back showed Tammy all dressed up in her girl dress as if she was already an adult, her hand on Dad's arm like they were on a date together. Well, she wasn't fooling him. Jaspar knew for a fact that spiders still creeped her out and she hated most kinds of fish. "Dog food," she called it when Dad wasn't listening.

A pretty lady, dressed in a neat black dress that didn't make her look like she was all on display or all pretending to be grown up, greeted him with a pleasant, "*Ciao.*" It was an Italian restaurant. He'd missed that. Carlo should be here. He'd like it.

"*Ciao,*" Jaspar's reply made her smile like she really meant it. He dug for Carlo's Italian lessons and tried to make complete sentences without stumbling over them too much. "*Quattro per la cena. Il nom...nome? Cullen.*" Then he remembered to add a polite, "*Per favore.*"

Ms. Williams said something that sounded like a compliment, but he didn't care. The waitress's smile grew, "*Bueno sera, Signor Cullen. Benvenuto a Angelo's. Mi chiamo Graziella.*" Her accent was different than Carlo's. It was lighter and fit a girl. Even a grown up one. And she'd spoken slowly enough that he had time to translate "good evening," "welcome," and that her name was Graziella.

Jaspar eyed Ms. Williams without really looking. She was so tall and her hair was still that weird color that had made Tam stop wanting to be around him. The waitress, with her long dark hair and quiet face would be better for Dad than Ms. Williams. And she already spoke Italian and had treated him like an adult.

"You, boy!" Ms. Williams had said when they tore up the drawings. Sure, she'd made it fun, but everyone kept calling him "boy," like a baby. No one was calling Tam "girl" anymore. It was all of a sudden "young woman this" and "young woman that."

The waitress greeted Ms. Williams and Dad like she already knew them, and then led them to their table. She wore a ring, but it had no big diamond. And lots of girls wore rings, it didn't mean they were married.

"You have to be kidding me, Angelo." Bill sipped his espresso and enjoyed the perfect brewing of it. "No one can learn to cook that well in just thirty years. You sure you aren't at least, oh, three hundred and something."

Angelo grinned at Bill's words and sipped his own espresso. He must get a hundred such compliments a day, but still he appeared genuinely pleased.

Angelo had joined them for a few moments after the meal. The kids were polishing off their apple sorbet with caramel glaze sprinkled with pistachios as voraciously as their manners allowed.

Perrin rested one of her gloved hands on Angelo's arm, but turned to Bill. "He is always this magnificent, except if Jo comes to dinner. Then he is too distracted. We almost had to ban her from the restaurant for ruining our food during their courtship."

"Uh, but how did you straighten that out?"

"Easy," Perrin answered for him. "He married her." Her saucy wink told him that while her words had been for the kids, it had actually straightened out before that, probably when Angelo and Jo had become lovers.

Angelo captured Perrin's hand and kissed it. "It's all Perrin's doing. If not for her, my Jo might well have slipped away and my life would have been ruined."

As if Bill needed yet another reason to respect this woman.

Bill thought back over the dinner at Angelo's Hearth. It was the first time they'd all been together, since the pizza night. They'd all been present at rehearsals together several times, but that wasn't the same thing. Tonight they'd had a meal as a family.

Perrin had sat across from Jaspar and beside Tammy. It was a perfect, thoughtful choice. Had she sat across from him, he'd have been too distracted and paid no attention to the kids. Instead, the children had been included throughout the dinner.

She'd made them laugh with stories of the crazy clothing that people had asked her to make. Some of them so fanciful as to be wholly impossible, yet she told each story as if it was absolutely true. By the end he believed every tale, well, except for the one about the representative from the Vulcan Science Academy's Wardrobe Mistress coming to Earth to order fancy party robes for their high council. But the rest of it she made sound at least possible if not wholly believable.

Tammy had talked about sewing her dress, she'd done a lot of it herself, albeit from Perrin's design. Still, it was so beautifully made that it totally floored Bill. "She made me take out the seams an awful lot of times before I made it right." He still couldn't get over the fact that not only was his daughter a teenager, but she looked like one.

Jaspar had worked on his Italian with them, especially when he discovered that Graziella, the beautiful young maître d' who Bill had met only briefly at Maria's dinner, spoke fluent Italian. She kept coming by the table, leaving behind another few words with each passing. And, unless Bill was vastly mistaken, she'd also started Jaspar on his first major crush. Being informed that she was newly married didn't abate his ardor in the slightest. Apparently he saw that as no obstacle in whatever his plans were.

"Hey kids," Angelo looked toward them, "want to see what our kitchen looks like?"

"I bet it has a stove and everything," Tammy offered him with a laugh.

Angelo did his best to look hurt, but didn't succeed very well.

Perrin elbowed her and the two of them, thick as thieves, rose to follow before Angelo could even pretend a decent whimper.

"Where the women lead, we must follow," he told his son, and they followed along behind Angelo.

It was quite the scene. A woman, who might have been Graziella's evil, though equally attractive twin, was hopping up and down on one foot in her impatience. "C'mon, Manuel, if you cooked any slower you'd be as bad as Angelo."

"Ah, Luisa," the Mexican chef at the center of the cook line teased back as he slid across a beautiful plate that must be the braised venison with wild morel sauce that Bill had almost ordered. "Beware, *señora*. You encourage me to follow in the footsteps of the *maestro*."

Luisa growled, dressed the plate with tiny dots of some dark sauce, and turned around with perfect timing to place it in Graziella's hand just as she breezed through the kitchen.

Perrin was leading the kids down the line to meet everyone. Without breaking their amazing flow, they greeted his kids as if this was a normal thing to do, and even described a bit of what they were doing.

Angelo remained beside Bill, off to the side watching the line's progress. He nodded once to himself, clearly satisfied with what he was seeing.

"Maria will be sorry that she missed a chance to meet your children. She starts early and usually leaves before dinner service."

"She works here?"

Angelo eyed him carefully. "With how long you spent talking to my Mama at dinner on Tuesday, I thought you would know everything. She is the best pastry chef you can imagine."

"Uh, I kind of remember that," Bill searched his memory. It was there, but way down the list. "We talked about a lot of things that night."

Angelo nodded down the cook line to where Perrin and the kids were sampling a red sauce, though where they'd fit another bite after that meal, he had no idea.

"I've known Perrin for two years. She's a very positive person, always glad to see you, always great fun to be around."

"But?" Bill could hear it clear as day. However good they were together, their relationship was still fragile. If Perrin's friends decided Bill and his family weren't good for her in some way, it could shatter what little they'd built so far. He knew Perrin sometimes relied on them more than herself in such matters. But that didn't seem right somehow. Maybe she only let them think they did… She still confused him much of the time.

"But," Angelo acknowledged his question. "I always assumed she was happy. But now that I see her overflowing with it around you and your children, I have to wonder about how she truly felt all this time I've known her."

Bill didn't know what to say to that one. From the moment that she'd shattered his pigeon-holing of her, by staggering into the Opera drunk with exhaustion and glowing like the Empress, he'd only ever seen her as joyous.

But happy? And that he and his family made her feel that way was something else again. A part of him worried that some addictive part of her past had become dependent on him for her happiness.

Then he had to remind himself that the Perrin Williams he knew was strong and incredibly smart. Maybe Angelo had known a different Perrin. But the one Bill knew didn't strike him as the sort of person to entrust her emotional well-being to another. Share with them, absolutely. Care about their opinion? She couldn't help it, she wanted everyone around her to be happy too. Depend on them for how she felt? Not a chance.

"Well, if it makes you feel any better, Angelo, she's making me damned happy as well."

Perrin and the kids began heading back from the far end of the cook line, each bearing another serving of the dessert. Even the somewhat fierce Luisa stopped her service to meet the kids.

"Back when Russell and I were first bringing girls home to the kitchen where Mama cooked for Russell's parents, she said something to us that I've always tried to do. 'Follow the quiet voice of joy. Follow it like nothing else matters.' Best damn advice Mama ever gave me. It's why I cook. It's why I'm married to Jo. Might have made the road a little easier if we'd listened to her a bit more often."

"You ended up in an amazing spot, Angelo."

"I did, my friend." His friendly thump on Bill's back was almost as solid as one he'd deliver to Russell. It was an acceptance. A welcoming.

As he returned to the cook line, Angelo kissed Perrin on each cheek, scruffed Jaspar's hair, and bowed so deeply to Tammy that she blushed fiercely.

"Hey, where's my second dessert?" Bill complained as they reached him.

Perrin held out a spoonful of caramel-covered sorbet. "If I have to finish this on my own, I'll die of a pleasure overdose. You have to help me."

He took the bite, and did his best to relish the quiet voice of joy, as the four of them stood to the side watching the busy kitchen and eating their three desserts.

CHAPTER 14

ince the dinner, it had been a great week for Bill. The sets for *Ascension* were almost back on schedule, not quite, but that was normal with only a couple weeks to go until opening night.

The knit costumes, once completed, had totally wowed the cast members and the director. They quickly scheduled an extra photo shoot as soon as all of the primary cast were costumed. It hadn't been hard to convince Wilson Jarvis to foot the additional advertising costs of a last minute poster-and-banner campaign. Even Geoffrey Palliser had decided to amend his contract so that the Overlord could stand beside the shining Empress.

In a moment of inspiration, Bill had tried to contract Russell for the photo shoot. Except it turned out that one didn't just contract Russell Morgan. Even trying to do so really pissed the man off. That's when Bill had learned that not only was Russell rich, but he was also the heir to the Morganson shipping fortune. He only did projects he was interested in. Perrin, bless her, said that she hadn't had to work very hard to talk him down, despite Bill's bungled initial approach.

Perrin and Jerimy's makeup artist, a big Polish man named Mika Kalinski with a heavy accent, massive hands, and remarkably delicate control, had conferred at length on the final looks.

It was too late to hit the national and international press, but the new *Ascension* poster now graced the back of several Seattle buses as well as a couple of I-5 and Aurora Avenue billboards. It was hard to tell if the spike in ticket sales was due to that, or the ever growing yarn-bombs.

Bill had finally asked Perrin once about the yarn-bomb campaign, over a lunch they'd managed to share in his office. She had evaded the question of her involvement by turning the conversation sideways into how creative they were. After that, Bill adopted a "don't ask, don't tell" policy regarding them.

The campaign grew rapidly over the next few days. At first the knit advertising had appeared only on the occasional crosswalk sign and light pole. Now it seemed he couldn't turn a corner without spotting one. The news services picked up the story, then they showed one that impossibly ran across the large bar holding stoplights out over the middle of a busy intersection. That looked dangerous to install and was probably illegal.

That was too much. He pulled Patsy and Jerimy into his office for a meeting.

"Not one of ours," Patsy didn't even take a moment of thought.

"What do you mean?"

"We've only been doing verticals on the big stuff. Also, you said this happened last night. We were busy then doing thirty tree trunks around Green Lake. Every jogger on the three miles of shoreline track this morning saw them. For horizontals it's been mostly bicycle racks. We don't mess with any traffic signs. One of my friends actually went to jail for ten days because she yarn-bombed a Stop sign a couple years back."

"To jail?" That was not the kind of publicity he wanted for the Opera under any circumstances.

"Yeah. She exactly recreated the whole sign in red and white knitting, and then built yellow petals all around the edges. The problem was, it wasn't reflective. Turns out those signs are specially designed to reflect headlights back at the driver. It was really pretty, the arresting cop let her take a picture before cutting it down, but we know better than to mess with any of that."

Bill slumped back in his chair, "So how did it get up there at the corner of Broad and Western?"

Patsy whistled. "Did you get a picture?"

"I didn't have to." He did a quick search on his computer and turned the screen for them to see. It was already on the *Seattle Times* news site.

"Wow. That would be a tough installation, and to not get caught there would be even tougher. They have to have traffic cameras in an intersection that big, but we're clean. It's definitely not one of ours. No tag."

Bill looked at the picture but he didn't even know what he was looking for.

Patsy had him scroll down to another picture in the article until she found a yarn bomb on the courthouse flagpole. She pointed to the bottom, below the last "N" in *Ascension*.

He could just make out a tiny "S#1KG."

"We put that on every single thing we do. That's our gang's marker or tag, Seattle's Number One Knitting Gang. Some people go anonymous, but we felt that was like making book reviews under false names on Amazon, kinda low brow not to take ownership of your own words, or knitting."

"Then how did this happen, Patsy?" Bill scrolled back up to the picture of the street maintenance crew going up in a bucket truck to cut down the yarn-bomb.

Then she smiled. "We're going viral, boss."

And she'd been absolutely right. Over the next week after the release of the posters, magnificently designed by Russell, yarn-bombs began appearing in the oddest places. Bus bumpers, store signs that had nothing to do with the opera. They often wouldn't even say *Ascension* but Perrin's color palette was unmistakable.

The Fremont statue of *Waiting for the Interurban*, of a half dozen people and a dog waiting for a bus, was seriously bombed. People were always dressing up the statues: warm scarves in winter, ridiculous sunglasses when spring finally came to the rainy city. Someone had taken the poster to heart. They'd made costumes for each of the figures, following as many of the details as possible from Russell's poster. Even the child cradled in the woman's arms now wore a fair imitation of Jaspar's costume.

Russell had called and told him to get his and his cast's asses down to the statue for a group photo. By the time Bill had them there, Russell had somehow corralled a half-dozen news services into showing up, including a pair of nationals. The resulting media blitz had been amazing, and cost nothing.

Jaspar and Tammy loved the photo shoot. But they didn't stand together like he would have expected. Even Russell's attempt to coax them together had no effect. They stood on either side of the Empress and Overlord. It worried Bill, but he let it go as too far down his list of things to worry about. The kids always worked everything out.

Reports were coming in from Tacoma, even Portland was getting bombed, but most of it was concentrated in Seattle.

The day he saw one across the steel bumper of a fire truck stationed near his house, he decided that keeping his mouth shut was definitely the better part of discretion. That it was still there days later, smoke-stained, worn in a few places, but left in place by the crew, only spoke more to the popularity of the event.

"It isn't just sales for this opera that are increasing," Wilson Jarvis happily told King 5 News. "The Seattle community's support for this Emerald City Opera production of *Ascension* has also begun translating into a sharp increase in subscription sales for the next season. We're just thankful for this opportunity to be attracting more interest and tourism to our great city. By the time *Ascension* opens two weeks from tonight, we expect to be fully sold out, despite adding two performances. So be sure to get your tickets to *Ascension* soon."

Leave it to Wilson to work the title of the opera into every other sentence.

Bill had to miss the Tuesday dinner because of a rehearsal. It was too bad, he thought the kids would really enjoy it. At least having the kids in the opera saved him from palming them off on Lucy or a baby sitter. Though Tammy was getting so grown up, maybe he could trust her to be the responsible adult when they had to be home alone. He knew there were younger girls than Tammy who made money babysitting, but still it felt too soon for him, if not for her.

He'd asked Perrin to send his apologies to Maria personally. She reminded him that this week was Manuel and Graziella's wedding reception at the restaurant. *Damn!* He'd forgotten and felt awful, but he couldn't get out of it.

After a quick round of begging Marci, he'd managed to bag two of the last tickets to the only Monday night performance when the restaurant would be closed. He'd swiped one of fundraising's best ECO-stationery note cards, thankfully Consuela stocked some without "Thank You" embossed on them in gold foil. Bill wrote a cute note, slipped in the tickets along with an invitation to come backstage after the show, and made Perrin promise to not forget it in her purse.

WHEN JASPAR TRIED to beg off from going sailing, Bill should have seen something bad was coming. He should have, but he didn't.

Perrin felt as if she were floating when she arrived at Cutters Crabhouse. It was Friday evening, a week since her dinner with Bill and the kids. The place was hopping with Seattle's finest, well-dressed for after work mingling, ready to see and be seen.

Perrin even saw two of her own designs, but didn't know the women. That felt odd. Even though Raquel and Kristin were doing a great job of running the store, it still felt odd to be disconnected from the day-to-day contact with customers. Not that she'd have had time even if she had the desire to work the front of store again.

Her life had become a complete blur. She was in a hundred places at once, and needed to be in a thousand. Her emotions were all over the map as well.

Jerimy had insisted on her approval of his and Patsy's teams' renditions of her designs. Those had turned into wonderful discussions of what they'd each seen and liked.

Jerimy had a Master's degree from NYU in Visual Culture: Costume Studies. Who even knew there was such a thing. His deep focus on Western Europe had contrasted nicely with Perrin's lighter-depth self-education across dozens of global clothing design traditions. They discussed the rise of the pleat, the exposed midriff of the historic belly dancer, the urban Japanese woman, and the modern American teen.

Patsy, the queen of modern clothing, often jumped in with surprising variations that she'd seen. Perrin departed each meeting with so many ideas for new designs clogging her brain that she could hardly think.

Patsy tried to keep her up-to-date on the wild success of the yarn bombing. One evening she'd borrowed Tamara and the three of them had gone out with the S#1K Gang. They'd bombed three seats in every Capitol Hill hospital waiting room, covering them with premade slip-covers in the palettes of the Empress, the Prince, and the True Love. It only took a minute for them to crochet the side seams to hold the premade knitting in place.

They'd all worn masks that Patsy had made, modeled on the opera's characters. Security guards had been alerted, nurses had applauded, and people stuck in drab waiting rooms for hours on end had been cheered up.

Afterward, they'd all sat around together and eaten tiny scoops of gelato in a brightly lit little shop. Tammy's eyes had been so wide as she did her best to behave as if she did this every day. Clearly, sitting with six grown women from Patsy's twenty-three to Cornelia's sixty-seven, ranked as one of the coolest things she'd ever done.

"I didn't get that grown-ups could be so much fun!" she'd bubbled as Perrin had driven her home afterward. "I want to grow up to be just like them."

Perrin had laughed, "Which one?"

"All of them at once, but especially you."

That had sobered Perrin instantly. Tamara had made it a simple statement of fact. Perrin could see how the others could be role models, but didn't quite understand how it could apply to her.

She'd talked about it in the kitchen with Bill over more blueberry tea while Tamara took a shower to get ready for bed. Jaspar had apparently sacked out early. They were careful to sit on opposite sides of the dining table in case one of the kids came in.

"Guess he was tired," Bill apologized on his son's behalf, but she missed saying hi to him. She actually hadn't seen much of Jaspar at all since the dinner she'd so enjoyed.

Bill continued, "Don't see how you could miss the role you're already playing in Tammy's life, makes perfect sense to me that she'd respect you."

At her blank look, he'd laughed.

"The girl never stops talking about you. She's actually doing better in school, which she was always good at anyway, because she's staying up late to get ahead the night before. She wants as much time working with you as she can get. She's begging me for a sewing machine for her birthday in a couple months. She's even convinced us all to watch one of those clothing design shows on television. It's a good thing that it's only one night a week, or Jaspar would be having a meltdown. As it is, he does his best to moan and complain whenever they get to a part she really wants to hear. Took him a while to figure out that she'd just rewind to listen again until he shut up."

"He's such a boy, isn't he? So much like you."

"Huh," had been Bill's grunted reply. Even after she'd explained it to him. "Well, we're moving into the Opera House this week, the kid always seems to enjoy that. Wilson even signed up for a special rider on our insurance now to let Jaspar hang out with the crews, as long as there is always a responsible person about. The team leaders have been more than willing to have him as a junior apprentice and gofer."

Perrin wished she could see more of Jaspar, but along with the Opera's growing popularity, Perrin's Glorious Garb was receiving more attention. She and Raquel were already interviewing seamstresses to build the copies of Perrin's designs because she could no longer keep up with the orders. She'd never much liked making the same thing over and over anyway. Yet another small piece of the business to let go of.

One day she'd been going so crazy that she'd actually shown Tamara how to scale a pattern to different measurements for one of her simpler designs. Perrin hadn't been able to find a single fault with her work.

"I'd like to offer Tamara a part-time job," she'd told Bill during one of their nightly phone chats.

When he was done spluttering in surprise she'd explained.

"Minimum wage, maximum ten hours per week. Any time she spends on her own clothes are on her own, but when she'd helping me, I have to pay her. It's only fair."

"What about your time? Twenty seconds ago you were telling me how frantically busy you were."

And she was. "I wouldn't mind. I'll just… "

"You'll just charge my twerp daughter three dollars an hour for any time you spend helping her on her own projects. Any time you spend training her for your projects is your own cost, and no fudging on her behalf, Williams. She keeps a timecard, you make sure it's correct every week. If she learns something about business while she's doing this, it will make it more digestible for me. And she pays for her own materials—"

"No."

"Yes. At cost. Retail."

"Wholesale," she'd countered, caving that far because she knew Bill was the better businessperson of the two of them. All she really cared about was the design, which is why Cassidy and Jo had made her hire Raquel to run the store.

And they'd worked it out. Raquel had drawn up a contract. Tamara and Bill had reviewed it together until Perrin was sure Tamara understood every clause and then she'd executed it, with her dad signing beneath.

———

AND NOW, at the end of the wildest and best week of her life in Seattle, she couldn't wait to sit with her friends. Just as she entered the front door to Cutters she spotted Carlo and Melanie leaving the restaurant. She rushed up to them.

"You're back!" she hugged Melanie in greeting. "Hi Carlo, you're looking very mellow." She offered him a broad wink and the three of them shared a laugh.

"Yes, she last night *arrivata*. Little…" he turned to Melanie and said something quickly in Italian.

Melanie translated in her soft French accent, "We did not much last night sleep. Oh sorry, translating is tricky. We haven't slept much since I arrived." They shared a smile that explained exactly why. "But now he must or Monsieur Director will be very angry with him tomorrow morning when he can't sing a note."

"Perfect!" Perrin kissed Carlo on each cheek then grabbed Melanie's hand. "C'mon, you're my date tonight. Go away, Carlo. Go sleep."

Melanie wished him a good night, kissed him sweetly enough, but Melanie appeared a little too happy for an excuse to join her.

Carlo, bemused, headed off.

"What was that about, Melanie?"

"What was what…" she trailed off and made an eloquent and graceful shrug. "We—"

"No, wait. Don't tell me. You'll just have to repeat it for the others."

"What others?"

Perrin didn't bother to explain but dragged her into the bar. Cassidy, Jo, and Maria were already at a four-top table. They all welcomed Melanie, and Perrin could detect no hesitation between Cassidy and Melanie, even though the one had married the man that the other woman had loved. They soon scared up an extra stool and all crammed around the small table.

"Well, tell us." Perrin jumped in and watched Melanie considering. She liked the supermodel. In addition to loving Russell despite all his rough edges, she'd always been so kind to Perrin about her designs. And there was a shared pain the others would never, thankfully, understand, but had been obvious to both of them soon after meeting each other. While Melanie had faced far less physical abuse, she too had risen from a trailer-trash background and a beyond domineering mother. A past she covered with an unbreakable calm and a soft French accent.

Perrin watched Melanie's shields of caution continue to rise. True, she'd only sat with Jo and Cassidy a couple times and had barely met Mama Maria.

"Okay," Perrin jumped in for her to set her at ease. Funny how a little embarrassment could actually do that sometimes. "Unlike me who is so falling in love but not getting nearly enough sex, Melanie is getting too much sex and not enough romance. How much longer does Carlo have with our Melanie? Will he make it to opening night? Your fans want to know and we want to know now. We promise we won't tell. Right everyone?" Perrin made a criss-cross between her breasts and glared at each of the others until they did as well.

"You're safe now," she told Melanie. "You can trust them." She knew from her own experience with Bill that "safe" and "trust" were very powerful words that perhaps Melanie needed to hear. Mama Maria looked at her with the tiniest widening of her eyes that told Perrin she'd done it exactly right, enough so to surprise even Maria.

Melanie grimaced, then threw up her hands and laughed, a bright musical sound that turned a dozen heads at the nearer tables who were trying not to stare at the supermodel suddenly in their midst.

"Yes. Maybe. Carlo is very nice, but he has…limitations."

"Perhaps he is good for fun, but not worth keeping long term." Cassidy made it a statement of perfect understanding.

Perrin leaned over and kissed her on the shoulder in thanks for making Melanie welcome.

"Yes. I should like to attend opening night, Carlo tells me such wonderful things about the music and the staging and the costumes," she rested one of her elegant hands over Perrin's.

Perrin envied her those hands. Melanie's first jobs had been as a hand model, and they were still one of the best features on the beautiful woman.

"And I am not mercenary, he is charming and fun. But maybe when the curtain comes down on the opera, perhaps so it does on Carlo and Melanie."

They stopped to order drinks and appetizers. Perrin ordered one of her usual Cosmos. Melanie tasted the white wine Cassidy had ordered for the table and, after a soft "oh my" of appreciation, she asked for an empty glass and cheerfully accepted Perrin's judgment of "wimp." Crab cakes, shrimp cocktail, and a big bowl of steamers would get them started. The waitress left behind a plate of Cutter's focaccia bread gloriously drowned in rosemary, garlic, and olive oil.

"So…" Melanie turned to Perrin, clearly not wholly comfortable with being the center of attention, "In love and not enough sex… Was I right about Bill Cullen? He does like you?"

"He told me…" Perrin looked around the table. Well, if Melanie didn't want to be at the center of attention having just joined them for the first time, Perrin knew exactly how to shift the conversation for a good long while. "Bill told me that he loves me."

There were understanding nods around the table. Some softening of looks, but it was something most men said too easily and they all knew that.

"And I believe him."

That knocked back everyone around the table.

Mama Maria reached a hand right across Melanie's lap to grab Perrin's hand.

Perrin took a deep breath to steady herself then met Maria's gaze. They didn't need words. For five long heartbeats they held hands and looked at each other. For five poundings of blood in Perrin's ears, emotions flowed across Maria's face as they must have across her own. Fear and hope, relief and amazement, truth and acceptance, and finally approval. That was all it took. Then Maria's face lit with a smile that could brighten the whole world. With a quick squeeze, she sat back and apologized to Melanie.

Maria placed her hand briefly to her throat, where the gold chain that Perrin had given for her wedding rested every day, often Maria's only jewelry aside from Hogan's wedding band. It had been a gift from the heart and a bond between them. Perrin had to fight hard to keep the tears inside where they belonged at Maria's ultimate sign of hope for a marriage and a future.

The others were still gearing up to question her all about being in love and why she believed him. Perrin wasn't sure if she was up for that, so she went for a much safer topic. She leaned in close and all the others leaned in as well, including Melanie. She glanced around to meet each of their gazes before whispering her subject change.

"Do you have any idea how hard it is to get some decent sex with a single dad? You wouldn't believe how creative we've had to be."

Mama Maria laughed. Of course she'd know what Perrin was doing, but the others all fell for the trap and wanted to know just how creative.

<hr>

THE PROBLEM, Perrin had to admit that night as she crawled into bed alone and watched the ceiling spin slowly, was that even being creative had achieved so little.

She and Bill had found that their best opportunity to see each other at all was having lunch together. On days when he was too busy to even leave the office, she'd at least arrive with sandwiches to share at his desk among the prop layout plans. She'd never thought about the problems of a scepter being carried off one side of the stage, then needed at the head of a staircase on the opposite side two scenes later.

When she could coax him out of the office, they lunched in her apartment. Okay, they had fantastic sex on her bed, her couch, the floor, the kitchen—more than once they hadn't made it past leaning against the closed front door—followed by him bolting down a sandwich on the ten-block drive back to the office.

They had tried finding a moment at the Opera offices, but with the pending production the staff was increasing and there wasn't even a quiet corner. The Opera normally employed a hundred people full-time. But for a new build of a major new opera, there were over four hundred people underfoot everywhere they went.

Then the ballet that had been in residence at the Seattle Opera House after the production of *Turandot* had closed and cleared out. Emerald City Opera descended on the Opera House like a hammer blow. In twenty-four hours the main electrical, pressurized air, and propane systems had been in place. There were parts of the set that would appear to burn during the dramatic second act, giving the Tragic Prince physical scars to match the psychological ones.

Forty-eight more hours and the set was in place. Impossibly, hundreds of pieces of scenery were delivered and assembled. Two trucks constantly worked the loading dock, disgorging great loads from the scene construction shop, that were then rapidly assembled. Another truck was actually parked on an elevator a story below that then delivered it directly to the stage right wing.

The crews who had been setting up in the Emerald City Opera's offices were also preparing for the move across town. The lowest floor of the offices was normally props storage. One end had been taken over by an eight-person props team. They'd even backed up a semi-truck trailer to a loading door which contained a full machine shop where they made anything they didn't already have: swords, lanterns, armor, fake foodstuffs for the grand banquet, including the tables and tablecloths. It was amazing to watch.

The other end of the ground floor was taken by fifteen electricians servicing and calibrating the lighting instruments. Massive coils of cable were stacked on pallets or dumped into bright yellow rolling hampers. Light poles and triangular steel trusses made up of those funny zig-zag metal pipes were loaded onto semi-trailers for the fast approaching move-in day.

This world was a mystery to Perrin. It was also the only place she ran into Jaspar during the whole week. But he looked to be very busy learning how to wire a connector properly, so she didn't disturb him.

On the second floor, the costume department was really humming. The chorus had started coming through for fittings. A dozen seam-stresses were fitting pre-made pieces to measurements cards. And altering the many costumes that didn't work out quite right. A man they planned to use as a village cartman had recently joined a gym and his shoulders no longer matched his card nor fit his intended uniform. A woman was four months pregnant, still able to sing, but her form-fitting gown had to be switched with someone else's less revealing attire.

In the middle of the floor, a temporary makeup department had been set up. There, Mika worked with five other specialists to turn the photographs of the designs he and Perrin had developed into face cards for every single character: base powder Ben Nye BV71, Sandy Rose CR3 cheek rouge, auburn eye pencil blended with… The list went on to define the lip outline which emphasized them at a distance, degree of blending or highlights, aging lines on backs of hands and neck, wigs, prosthetics like latex scars, stage blood to be coordinated with costuming as they'd be laundering it out of the costume after every performance.

A couple of the major roles, the Prince, Princess, and the True Love had several face cards. For Carlo as the Prince sometimes he had a makeup call between two scenes as his look evolved: hope to scars to loss of hope to premature age to destitution and ultimate failure as he dies in the arms of the Princess who loves him. His final aria ending with a demented cry for his murdered True Love.

"So Bill," Perrin asked after they'd stolen a kiss in the office's central freight elevator, "Is it always going to be this difficult for us to have sex?"

"Make love?" He'd brushed a hand down her body that electrified every single nerve ending.

"Oh man. You have to cut that out."

"Cut out this?" he kissed her fiercely for two seconds while groping her wildly. "Or stop telling you that I love you?"

Perrin made sure that her clothes were straight by the time the elevator stopped even if her pulse was thoroughly chaotic.

"Okay," she struggled for a breath then nodded for him to open the heavy steel gates that split horizontally across the middle to raise and lower. Just as he put his hands on the heavy strap to start them moving, she rubbed her palm downward over the front of his pants then whispered in his ear.

"Don't stop doing either one." She shoved the door down so that it clanged open and walked out onto the main office floor, leaving Bill to trail somewhere far behind.

CHAPTER 16

"*Today's a dark day,*" Tammy informed Perrin as she slipped into the back seat of Bill's car. Jasp was being a total pill. Sure it was his turn up front, but he hadn't even offered to move back for Perrin. Perrin had shrugged it off before Dad could dig in.

"What's a 'dark' day?" Perrin had on a nice blouse of pale blue, so plain it was almost a shock. But Tammy was learning. She could see just how well made it was and how perfectly it fit, not clinging, but not loose and sloppy like some generic store thing. It didn't have to be wild like their red dresses to be amazing. That's what she wanted to do, make clothes that made her look that nice. Even Perrin's jeans fit way better than Tammy's despite how long she'd spent poking around the mall's racks to find a pair that fit just right.

"Dark day means the stage is unlit. Everybody gets a day off. So today's pretty much the last time we're gonna see Dad even close to sane for the two weeks until opening night."

"At least you get to see me at rehearsals," he called back as he pulled into traffic.

"Yeah, that's righteous," Tammy replied. It was Jasp's latest word, though it tended to make Dad snort with laughter when they used it.

She wondered if Jasp had figured it wrong. "If you think he's been busy these last couple weeks, just wait. It's cra—"

"That's what I wanna do," Jaspar cut her off. It wasn't his normal kind of cut-off.

Something was wrong and she didn't know what it was. And it wasn't just today. With Jasp she always knew, but not this time.

"I'm gonna do what Dad does. I'm gonna know all about electricity and machine tools and none of that costume crap."

Dad glanced up into the mirror in apology to Perrin, and Tammy could see the look. When had she grown tall enough to see his eyes in the rearview? Very righteous.

But Jasp missed it. He usually caught onto adult stuff faster than she did. Tammy had found she had to figure out things that Jaspar saw right away and blurted out. He was a just a stupid boy in a lot of ways, but he was "people smart."

She hated when he descended into one of his troll moods. It reminded her too much of when Mom died. That had been bad for all of them, Jasp had refused to believe her for weeks that Mom was never coming home again. And Dad had been mostly out of it. She'd learned to anticipate and defuse the troll, but she always knew why Jasp was doing it. Tammy couldn't see this one yet. She'd have to get him aside later.

"I have to worry about the 'costume crap' too," Dad tromped down on him. "Though between Perrin and Jerimy I have to worry less than usual." He looked at Perrin again in the rearview mirror.

Wow! Did Dad have any idea how much he was showing how he felt about Perrin? They were way past fourth kiss. She was losing track of everything. When had that happened?

Jasp just hunched down in the front seat and glared out the window.

PERRIN NOTED that Russell actually looked pleased rather than amused when Jaspar declared his boat, the *Lady Amalthea,* as "righteous."

"I named her for a unicorn who turned briefly into a princess but decided she was better off as a unicorn."

"Smart lady!" Jaspar declared.

While the guys were bonding over the boat, Perrin climbed aboard and gave Tammy a hand to steady her. It was a beautiful Saturday morning and there were a lot of boats headed out from the Shilshole Marina. There was a fresh wind, which meant good sailing, but the weather was warm enough she'd probably only need a light windbreaker once they were under way.

Perrin had always liked the boat, she was like her owner in so many ways. She was just as pretty as Russell was handsome, but she was rough around the edges too. The two of them matched. Russell had spent a year refinishing the 1940s sloop, Russell had taught her that meant one mast not all the way at the very front. But for all her fine finish, she was narrow inside.

"It's called a Pullman style cabin," Russell told the kids on the guided tour before they left dock. They'd all climbed together down the narrow ladder until they were standing well below the waterline. "Like those railroad cars in the old movies where you sleep down one side and walk down the other."

On one side of the off-center aisle down below was a galley, a table for seating four people that could turn into a narrow bed for two, a tiny bathroom that he gave them detailed instructions on how to use, and the boat ended in a double-bed up forward.

Perrin had dug out some good stories about what a motivated girl could do on that particular bed. They shared a look that made Cassidy blush, even if she was smiling brightly. Perrin kissed her on the cheek to make up for it and received a hug in return.

On the other side of the aisle was a narrow bench, long enough to sleep on if you stuck your feet into the space behind the ladder. Russell called it a pilot's berth. "Because it's closest to where the pilot needs to rush in case of an emergency," he pointed at the ladderway back to the cockpit. A tiny wood stove, an awkward bench and a tiny closet completed the way forward.

Cassidy had raided the restaurant to create a massive basket lunch.

Nutcase, Bill's small black cat, was the only other passenger, almost as rough-mannered as her owner, but also sweet to the core. The kids both took to her right away.

Russell lost a lot of ground when he insisted that the two kids had to wear life vests, but made up for it by producing small racing vests that didn't inflate until they were submerged, rather than the big, poofy orange things.

Russell recruited Jaspar and Bill to help him get the boat away from the dock, though Perrin had seen him do it single-handed any number of times when Cassidy was too busy to help. Perrin preferred just being a passenger.

"It's nice to let myself be taken care of sometimes," Cassidy leaned back, seated her sunglasses firmly and smiled up at the warm mid-morning sun. "Nothing better than a spring day in early May."

Perrin made sure that she and Tamara were slathered in sunscreen and both wearing floppy hats, their fair complexions would crisp out on the bright water. She'd only been fooled once. The air felt so fresh and cool when you were gliding over the water. She'd burned red as a lobster on her first trip and had to finish the outing lying on a cool bunk below, being tossed about at the mercy of the waves.

The three of them sat in the cockpit and let the world go by.

Perrin talked about some of the new designs she was working on, including Melanie's dress. Tammy tried so hard to pretend that she could still breathe normally after Perrin told her she'd get to help on the whole dress. Perrin had to hug her so that she wouldn't hyper-ventilate.

Cass understood perfectly and began teasing Tamara about being careful not to become too famous or Cassidy would have to chase her off, because nobody was allowed to compete with Perrin. It forced Tammy to laugh, breathe, and think of something else. Meanwhile the boys coiled lines and unwrapped sails. In moments they were headed out.

Her favorite moment was after the sails were up, but not yet drawing wind. Russell would nudge the tiller aside with his knee, lean down to kill the engine, then wink at his wife as it spluttered to silence. He did it every time. A shared memory Cass had never explained and Perrin didn't want to intrude on. Sort of like the moment she and the kids had torn up those awful paintings. That memory was theirs, not for others.

The boat dug in, suddenly at the wind's call, there was a visceral surge that echoed deep in her body. It was a place of peace, a perfect moment.

Bill dropped down beside her and slid an arm around her waist just as Perrin realized quite how alike this moment was to when she was lying in Bill's arms. Quiet, peaceful, powerful. Centered.

She leaned against him and closed her eyes, letting the motion of the boat just take her where it wanted to go. As long as Bill's arms were around her, she knew she'd be safe.

Tammy saw her chance after lunch.

Jasp had been sticking close by Mr. Morgan, learning all about sailing. He'd obviously geeked out when Mr. Morgan taught him how to steer. She couldn't quite bring herself to call him Russell, even if she felt fine with Cassidy. He was nice enough, but he was so big and imposing and so...male. At last she supposed that's what it was, but whatever, she stuck with using Mr. Morgan.

Tammy wouldn't have minded learning to sail too, but talking with Cassidy and Perrin like grownups, and watching her dad with Perrin was occupying her mind.

She wondered how Perrin would answer the question now about whether she was trying to marry their dad. There was no way to get her alone to ask. She and Dad were suddenly attached at the hip.

But now Jasp had gone forward alone to sit on the front hatch and stare out at the waves. So Tammy left the cockpit and headed up to the bow. The couple of ropes no bigger around than her thumb that ran like a railing along the edge of the deck didn't look like enough to stop anyone. There was a thin netting between the lines that didn't impress her much either. The boat was tipped way over and the water was rushing madly by just inches below the edge of the deck. From the cockpit, it hadn't looked like they were going so fast.

She backed off. The walkway down the other side of where the cabin stuck up through the deck was high out of the water. She tried that side. A glance back showed Cassidy, Dad, and Perrin all laughing together. Mr. Morgan, clearly keeping an eye on everything, nodded easily at her from where he sat at the tiller, clearly telling Tammy that she was right to go along the high side of the cabin. Lesson learned. She decided he was okay and hoped that he wouldn't laugh at her too much for how she had to edge forward on the tilted deck clutching the thigh-high thin rope with both hands.

Earlier, Jasp had been trotting up and down the deck as if it was nothing. She didn't have the feel of this yet. Every time they hit a wave, she was sure they were going over, or at least that she was. Finally she made it, very glad she was wearing the life vest.

She edged up and squatted beside Jasp, "Hey, Troll."

"Go away."

Usually that nickname at least earned a courtesy laugh.

"C'mon, Jasp. Give. What's up with you?"

"With me? Up with me?!" He spun to face her, his skin suffused with deep red, and blotchy as if he'd been on the verge of crying. He hated crying.

"Yeah. With you!" She learned sometimes you had to face his steam with your own steam. "You've been grouchy all day."

"Like you care."

"I do. Honest."

"Yeah. You care, just like Dad does. Only not about me. You two only care about her." He made the pronoun sound awful, like it was acid or evil goo.

"That's not true." Tammy glanced back down the long deck to where Perrin sat curled in Dad's arms. They'd been like that the whole trip. It wasn't true, was it?

"Are you blind?" Jasp hadn't bothered to look back, he was just staring over the bow again, out at the rushing waves, blinking hard at the wind. Wind that was dragging tears straight back from his eyes and into his hair so she hadn't noticed them at first.

"Not blind, troll. She's neat, that's all."

"She's not neat. She's trying to shove us out."

"No!" Tammy protested. "She's not like that."

"Idiot!" he shoved her away and she fell on her butt.

She shoved against his shoulder hard enough to knock him off the hatch. He tumbled down the sloped deck and landed hard against one of the vertical metal things that held up the lifelines every couple feet.

He cried out. Jasp struggled to stand, reached out with a hand to steady himself, but his arm hung funny and it didn't work. The boat dropped down over a wave, making them almost weightless at just the wrong instant. With another cry, Jasp stumbled and fell over the lifeline into the water. His life vest inflated with a loud pop, then he disappeared toward the back.

She screamed.

That's the only part of what happened next that Tammy clearly remembered, her own scream. How it tore at her throat, at her heart. How it hurt her ears and echoed from the sky. She'd already lost her mother and now she screwed up and Jasp was gone. Just like that. Only this time it wasn't some drunk driver who did it. It was her.

Mr. Morgan's shout and dive over the side were a blur. At some point, someone, Perrin maybe, remembered Tammy was alone at the bow and came to get her.

The rest was just images. The boat rocking in the water, no longer moving. A wet Mr. Morgan and a crying and shivering Jasp. Phone call for an ambulance to be at the dock.

And tears. She'd cried herself sick and remembered throwing up somewhere, maybe off the edge of the dock. Someone carrying her. Mr. Morgan? Whoever, they'd still been wet. Her own clothes now clammy down one whole side of her body. She and Perrin in the car, her dad with Jasp already gone.

She knew she'd have nightmares forever of Jasp falling into the water and never coming back.

Just like Mom.

CHAPTER 17

errin knew what she had to do, and hated it. Hated the situation. Hated herself most of all. At least she was used to that part of it.

She sat in the farthest corner of the painfully white hospital waiting room. As far as possible from Jaspar now behind some anonymous curtain in the ER, far from the three yarn-bombed chairs she and Tammy had done together a mere few days ago, and close by the sliding glass doors she'd have to use in a few minutes.

She wanted to run through them now and out into the fading Seattle afternoon. Run and never stop, but there was one thing she had to do first. So she waited, her hands clasped in her lap until all feeling had long since left them, staring straight ahead at a poster about identifying different reactions to different types of bug bites. Normally, it would creep her out, but she was too numb.

It had all gone wrong so fast, that's what she couldn't wrap her head around. One moment she'd been curled against Bill, laughing with Cassidy and Tammy, and the next a screaming Jaspar had gone shooting by the stern. Russell had been in the water so fast he hadn't been ten feet behind the boy. So fast, Perrin didn't even have time to be afraid for him. Cassidy had turned the big boat back to Russell and Jaspar so fast it was a miracle.

But on the drive to the hospital she'd learned that it wasn't an accident, not merely a bad wave and a clumsy ten-year old. Tamara had sobbed out her story, unheeding and unaware of where the axe had fallen. This wasn't just a bump in the road, it was the end of the line. It was going to kill her heart to walk away, but she had to. But first…

Bill staggered out into the waiting room looking haggard. He scanned the weekend crowds, about two-thirds of the chairs were filled, before spotting her and coming over. He dropped into the seat beside her. The dark rings under his eyes showed the awful toll the last few hours had taken on him.

"Well, that was fun."

She couldn't make herself laugh, not even as a kindness.

"Clean break. Bit of a mess because of all the jostling, but they have that sewn back up and the bone reset. They gave him a painkiller, so he's resting easier now. Tammy won't leave him, not even when he yelled at her. Can't figure that one out, he never yells at Tammy like that. First one he goes to when he's hurting, even before me. She just sits there like a ghost, holding onto his foot like she'll never let him go." He scrubbed his hands over his face then offered her a weak smile, "How's your day been?"

"Bill… " her throat closed. How was she supposed to say what she had to say to this poor, exhausted man? A deep breath didn't help, mostly because she couldn't make her diaphragm take one.

Finally catching her mood, he sobered and turned to face her.

"I only stayed to say goodbye… " she didn't even pause for a breath, the only way through was absolute truth to the end… and speed. She had to say it fast or maybe it really would kill her. "The reason they fought is that I'm the problem. I've taken you and Tamara away from Jaspar and he's angry. He's so angry and hurt. He'll be even angrier that you're out here now with me. Your children need you and all I'm doing is driving them away. Don't come after me. I won't talk to you. I won't see you. I owe that to your children."

She stood and walked out the door before he could respond. When she made it through the door, she saw Cassidy and Russell had arrived from putting the boat away. She did the only thing she could think of, she turned in the other direction and ran—it was all that was left for her to do.

RUSSELL CAUGHT Bill around the chest before he was five steps out the door. It was like running into a wall.

"Go!" Russell shouted at Cassidy, who had already taken off after Perrin.

Bill pushed against Russell, but to little effect. Ten, twenty, thirty seconds later, whenever he stopped his futile struggling, it was too late. Perrin, with Cassidy trailing far behind, was long out of sight.

Russell's clasp turned into a friendly arm around the shoulder, with a grip that not even a grizzly bear could break free from. Russell led him back inside.

"Wonder what got into her?" Russell offered it conversationally.

Bill didn't know. Her words had made no sense. His kids were crazy about her. It was because of Perrin they were in the opera production, becoming more involved every day. Tammy couldn't stop talking about her. And Tammy was really smart about people. Her response made Bill trust Perrin all the more. Quirky as she was, the woman daily proved her ability to be a positive role model for his daughter.

So what had happened?

"She couldn't mean what she said, could she?" he asked Russell.

Russell guided him back to the very chairs he and Perrin had been sitting in moments before. The big man opened his mouth to respond but the fear was too big for Bill to give him a chance to speak. The fear just kept stumbling words out of Bill's mouth.

"About never coming back? About never seeing me again? She couldn't mean that?"

Russell's face turned grim, "She said that?"

Bill could only nod.

"Shit," Russell muttered under his breath. "You never know with Perrin. Mama Maria practically adopts her, Cassie worships her, and to me she's flighty and damned stubborn. You wouldn't believe how good that woman is at getting her way."

Bill buried his face in his hands. He understood the stubborn woman, the one who drove herself so hard. She'd done six months of work in the last four weeks, totally charming Tammy and himself in the process. Charming? Dammit! He loved the woman. He even loved her for her pig-headed protection of his children.

"Dad?"

Bill jerked his head up at Tammy's voice.

"He's asking for you. I don't think he wants to see either of us, but he'd rather it was you than me." She looked around, her face still tear-streaked, her eyes almost blood red. "Where's Perrin?"

Behind Tammy, Cassidy came in through the door still breathing hard. She shook her head once, "no."

Bill rose, nodded to Russell and Cassidy, then, wrapping an arm around his daughter's shoulders, they went to see his son.

———

PERRIN WAS SO LOST. She'd zig-zagged through streets, alleys, backyards. No way she could face Cassidy, but Perrin's long legs and the speed she'd learned so many years ago in college field hockey had outdistanced her quickly.

It was her own self she couldn't seem to get away from. She glanced up at a street sign. Yesler and 34th. She forced herself to turn away when she saw the *Ascension* yarn-bomb climbing the crosswalk sign's pole that she'd been leaning against.

She became aware of the traffic sounds, the afternoon cooling into darkness, the pedestrians eying her strangely as she leaned there trying to recover her breath.

She was so totally lost.

And she had nowhere to go. She had no bolt hole, no safe place where none could find her. When had she let go of that? *Stupid!* Where was it now that she finally needed it?

Even now Cassidy would be rallying the troops, Jo and Maria. She knew how relentless they could be, she'd done the same for Jo and Cassidy a couple of times herself.

Now when she needed to be alone, she had nowhere safe. They'd check her store and apartment, thankfully she'd left her cell phone home for the day so she didn't have to feel guilty… guiltier for not answering when they called her.

She couldn't go to a hotel. For a day out with Bill and the kids she'd stuffed her apartment key in one pocket and her driver's license and a twenty-dollar bill in the other. Twenty bucks wouldn't even buy her a bus ticket out of town.

"Shit!" Her curse startled several people she hadn't noticed waiting for the light.

Out of options, all she could do was select the least painful one.

Turning north and west, she started walking slowly back toward downtown.

Mama Maria opened her condo's door even as Perrin stood debating whether or not to knock.

"Oh, I was just headed back out to… " she trailed off as she studied Perrin. Then, with a gentle hand on her shoulder, she guided Perrin inside.

She didn't say a word until she had Perrin seated on the couch by the night-darkened windows, a cable-knit throw blanket around her shoulders, and a big mug of steaming tea she could barely hold against the chills. The warm afternoon had long since gone to a dark, cool evening. Her sleeveless blouse wholly insufficient to protect her.

The front door opened and closed behind her, making her twitch. The tea burned her fingers and spilled on the blanket. Maria didn't embarrass her even more by trying to help. She simply turned to Hogan who had stumbled to a halt at the entry to the living room.

"Yes, Hogan. She's found. Could you let the others know, and then make us dinner, just for the three of us I think. Tell the others that tomorrow is soon enough for questions."

After Hogan nodded silently and headed into the kitchen, already dialing the phone, Maria sat on the couch beside her.

Perrin managed to set down the tea, wiping her fingers on her pant leg before she wrapped the blanket more tightly about her. Then she simply leaned forward and lay her head in Maria's lap. Lying there, she told the story of the day between bouts of shivering, partly from the cold, partly from self-loathing.

She should have seen it. In retrospect, had seen it. Jaspar going to bed early to avoid her when she knew full well he felt bedtime was for "little kids" and was always pushing the limits; her one visit to their house a perfect excuse. Somehow arranging never to sit by her at the opera, not even when his sister did. Perhaps especially not when his sister did.

When they'd first met, the boy had been such a bright and shining light. Somehow she'd missed the change as he shifted toward the Overlord's darkness.

Maria just let her talk, slowly brushing at her hair until she was done. Run dry of all emotion.

"I have to leave, Maria. I can't stay. Not even in Seattle. I would think of them all nearby. Worse, I might see them. I can't do that. I can't."

"You were never dumb, Perrin my girl."

"Except about men."

"You were never dumb," Maria made it such a definitive statement that Perrin couldn't argue. "Perhaps less than sensible at times, but you always knew exactly what you were doing even when you were screwing up."

"I know this time too, Mama Maria. Honest I do."

Maria pushed her upright until they were facing each other. She was silent for the longest time, just looking up at Perrin with those dark eyes that demanded honesty.

"I didn't say that I won't hate leaving, but it's the best for everyone, Maria. You know that."

"Not best for you, my girl."

"I can't put that ahead of what's best for Bill's family. I know I should, but I can't. I care about them too much. It will be okay. I'm used to it being hard."

"And do you think that you'll hurt them less by leaving?"

That one she didn't have an answer to. She'd seen Bill's eyes as she'd said goodbye. He'd been devastated before the words even registered. She was just glad that Russell had stopped him and Cassidy had followed in his stead, because she might not have had the heart to run away from Bill. Tamara would be shattered as well.

"Oh god, Maria," Perrin clasped the blanket more tightly and folded both fists over her aching heart, "anything I do makes it worse." She hung her head.

Maria raised her chin with a gentle hand. "So, we do this one step at a time."

"We?" It was the most heartening word Perrin had ever heard. Because she certainly couldn't do this on her own. "What next step?"

"You already know, sweetheart." Maria pulled her down enough to kiss her on the top of the head, just as she had the day she'd told Perrin she'd wished to have had Perrin as her daughter. "You know, you just wish you didn't."

Perrin thought a moment, then nodded. She knew. It was so hard, but she knew.

BILL COLLAPSED at his dining room table, too exhausted to breathe, way too tired to make a drink or eat any dinner. At least they were all home.

Back at the hospital, on the way back into ER to see Jaspar, Tammy had spilled about what exactly had happened on the bow of the boat and why they'd been fighting to begin with.

Perrin. Of all idiotic, dumb-ass, idiot moves he'd made as a single father, that one took the cake. Perrin had opened a new world for Tammy, giving her a gift of such magnitude that his daughter was growing and changing daily as she scrambled to take it all in. And Perrin had done the same for him, showing him that a part of his heart he had thought forever dead, still existed. Hell, it thrived beneath her shining radiance, her Empress' touch upon his heart proving to be a benediction beyond price.

But he'd missed what was up with Jaspar. Missed how many times Jaspar had come in to ask for help with homework. Because Tammy wasn't around anymore. "Just another hour, buddy." Which had turned into two or three as he worked to keep the opera on track. He'd barely registered when Jaspar had drifted away to the technical crews to get away from him as well.

Crap! There had to be more ways he could screw up as a parent, but he didn't know what they were.

He'd known better than to confront it head-on with Jaspar. It would be too obvious that Tammy had told him and it would just drive them all further apart.

He wished he could ask Perrin, she was so good at these things. But she hadn't answered any of his surreptitious calls made out of earshot of the kids. He didn't know if she ever would again. Russell's statement, about how Perrin always got her way, scared the shit out of him. It wasn't that she was manipulative, but she was tenacious as hell when adhering to what she believed to be right; a trait he appreciated under any other circumstance.

He still hadn't worked up the nerve to call Maria, and now it was probably too late.

He lay his head on the table trying not to think of his son in a drugged sleep with a cast in his bedroom. Or of Tammy, refusing to leave the chair beside Jaspar until she'd fallen asleep against the foot of the bed and Bill practically had to carry her to her own bed.

The buzz of his phone jerked him from his stupor. He fumbled it from his pocket. Just a text. From a number he didn't recognize. He almost deleted it, but decided it couldn't hurt to look.

I'm okay. So sorry.
Tell Tammy not to come tomorrow.
I will call. But not yet.
-P

Bill blinked hard, could feel the burning in his eyes. He wiped at them and his hand came away wet. Who knew he'd be the one in the relationship who cried. He thought he was done with that after Adira's death. All he could think was how hard it must have been for Perrin to send that message after the things she'd said.

And how desperate he was to cling onto even the tiniest thread of hope.

CHAPTER 18

"*Y*ou look *très misérable,* Perrin." Melanie's light greeting did nothing to cheer Perrin. She sat alone in her design studio and wondered why she bothered. A place where she always found joy and inspiration now only felt empty. She kept wanting to glance over her shoulder and see Tamara's intent frown as she concentrated on pinning a seam just right. To hear the girl's laughter at the simple joy of learning something new.

And each of those thoughts was accompanied with the void where Jaspar stood. She didn't know how he looked when upset, happy, sad, mischievous… Perrin had inklings, but they weren't anchored in her heart the way Tamara's were. It wasn't that she loved Tamara better, a grown-up couldn't afford to do that between children, but Perrin certainly knew her better.

"Perrin?"

"Sorry, Melanie. I didn't sleep well last night."

"*Non.* That is not so. You did not sleep at all and your heart, I can see how your heart is hurting. The little girl, she is not here."

Perrin did her best to close the topic. "Only me today. Let me show you the sketches I made for you." She pulled them out of the portfolio and spread her drawings across the cutting table.

Melanie watched her for a long moment and then came around the table. She turned to inspect the sketches, but not before pulling up a stool so close that their hips touched. She wrapped an arm around Perrin's waist and pulled her close as one friend would with another. In that position they went through the design in detail.

Melanie pointed out a line of the hem that she had seen Donatella Versace put on the Paris runway just last week. To avoid being labeled derivative, between them they restructured the lines.

Perrin slowly shifted beneath Melanie's kindness and her shared passion for original fashion. The model's casual, friendly embrace, her deep insights, and her gentle understanding did almost as much as Maria's no-nonsense kindness. Cassidy would have worried and fussed. Jo would have been her typical quiet, steadfast, pillar-strong self at a loss as to how to help and never understanding how much being herself did just that. Melanie simply let Perrin be her own, upset self without comment or judgment.

When they were done, there was a peace between them. The design would be stunning. Not merely analogous to the opera costumes, but uniquely its own statement. Enough so that Perrin knew she'd need to dig Russell out of his cave to make sure he was there to photograph Melanie's arrival at the opening. Which was another thread of her life she'd have to re-tie.

And she'd have to get him to talk with Wilson Jarvis about how to turn the Emerald City Opera opening into a red carpet event that the entertainment news would cover. Yet another future payoff for Seattle and the Emerald City Opera. She had almost a dozen designs that Raquel had sold from the store that would be walking the lobby on opening night, though none were like Melanie's showpiece.

Melanie tried to coax her to go out, to call her friends and make an afternoon of it. It was tempting, she definitely had some fences to mend there. But there was another one, far more important. And just because it was hard, she wouldn't shy away from it this time.

———

JASPAR SAT in his dad's office. Getting the day off from school almost made up for having his arm in a cast. Tomorrow he'd get some good mileage out of it from classmates, even more than having sailed the big boat. 'Course his dad had called the school and gotten all his homework assignments, so it wasn't a totally free ride. And he couldn't do squat downstairs with the crew with his arm in a cast.

Dad had been cool about it all. Clearly Tam had filled him in, but he hadn't gone all parent-fake about it either. He'd made a point of settling Jaspar in the office, rather than out in the cubical he normally used for homework. And the stuff he was doing was neat once Jaspar started paying attention to it. More than once Jaspar had forgotten all about Kipling's story of Kim's adventures in India to listen to what his dad did to make the opera run.

When she got off school, Tam had been so afraid to come up to him that he'd given in way sooner than he planned. She sat on the couch and was all girly, offering to get him a soda, seeing if he wanted help with anything.

When Dad was out of the room he asked her quietly, "Why are you here anyway? Why aren't you with her?" No need to explain who he was talking about, though he hadn't meant it to come out so nasty. Tam looked miserable, right on the verge of tears for like the hundredth time since he'd been hurt.

"Dad said it was better if I didn't," she sniffled hard. "I checked Dad's phone. She sent him a message saying she didn't want me to come."

Man the waterworks really were going. Tam was really, really sad about it. He didn't want that.

"What was the rest of the message?"

She told him.

Jaspar had to think about it a bit. He had a funny feeling that the most important part of the message wasn't the part that Tam cared about. Ms. Williams had said she was sorry. By itself, it might mean she was sorry that Jaspar had broken his arm, but that didn't fit the rest of it. And it didn't fit what a mess Dad was today, like he hadn't slept or anything. Twice he'd seemed to forget what he was holding in his hands. When they'd gone out to lunch together, though it was embarrassing that Dad had to cut up his hamburger so that he could eat it, his dad didn't eat much of his own.

Ms. Williams had said she was sorry and said that she would call, though *not yet.*

Almost every night for the last month he'd heard his dad talking with her. He couldn't make out the words, except once or twice when he'd snuck up outside the bedroom door, but you didn't talk that much to a girl unless you really liked her.

Dad came through the office, said something about Jerimy and the costumes. Did the kids want to go downstairs with him?

Tam, rather than leaping up as she had about costumes even before Ms. Williams first showed up, checked in with him. Jaspar tipped his head a little so she'd know he was fine with it and it was okay if she went.

She double checked, which made him even less angry at her. He did the finger flick for her to get gone, like when he was sick and she was hovering too much. She went, but Jaspar told Dad he was fine, wanted to read his book. What he really wanted to do was think.

He didn't like that everything had changed. And he didn't like that it had happened so fast. Tam was done with middle school next month. When did she get so old? And girl-shaped. Like he didn't even recognize her, though he could see that boys sure did. Even grown-ups would stop to watch her go by. They used to always say, "What a cute kid." Now it was all, "What a beautiful girl." Like she'd changed and left him behind. And those dresses.

Jaspar squirmed around on the couch trying to get more comfortable, but his arm was hurting and it wasn't easy.

Tam had looked even more like an adult in her costume and those dresses she kept making with Ms. Williams. She was good at it too, everyone said so. Maybe it was more than just wearing them. Even before Ms. Williams, she was mostly down with Jerimy and Patsy, like she really cared about that stuff. He'd always been able to find her there when he needed something.

It wasn't like the electricians, or even better sailing that whole big boat with no one but Mr. Morgan paying any real attention to him. But maybe it was what she liked.

Jaspar slowly became aware that there was someone standing at the office door.

Ms. Williams.

"Dad and Tam are downstairs."

She nodded, but didn't move to go to them, just stood there.

"What?" Dad would harass Jaspar about such bad manners, but he wasn't here.

"Can I come in?"

Jaspar shrugged a yes and then wished he hadn't. His arm really hurt.

She didn't just breeze in like she seemed to always... Oh no! She was gonna do one of those serious adult-conversation-with-the-kid things. He really didn't want to deal with one of those right now.

She sat down on one of the chairs and faced him.

He knew he was going to be rude, could feel it building up.

"I really screwed up, didn't I?"

It took Jaspar a moment to figure out what she was talking about. He'd expected her to start with his arm or the book open on his lap or something safe. Even Dad usually did that, pretty much everyone except Tam did that.

"It's not that I like Tamara better than you, I just know her better. I understand girls better than guys. Before your dad, I hadn't met all that many guys that I liked enough to be friends with. Russell and Angelo married my best friends, but even them, it took me a long while. I'm really sorry for how I treated you, even if I didn't mean to."

Jaspar had to blink at her, as if she was turning into a different person without even moving.

"What I brought for you today isn't some lame bribe to try and make it all better. It's for the opera. Anything else, well, I just hope you'll give me a chance to try and figure it out better than I have so far." Then she opened the long bag she'd brought in. First she pulled out a dark cloth, elaborately sewed in the same colors as his costume.

"What's that?"

"It's a sling for you to wear with your costume." She spread it out on the couch beside him where Tam had been sitting. "It will cover the whole cast and just make it look like your character was wounded in sword practice or something."

"But I don't have sword."

She reached into her bag again and pulled out a wooden sword complete with belt and scabbard just like the one Carlo wore as the Prince, only smaller. It had been painted to look so real he had to touch it to make sure it was wood.

"This way you can still go on stage and your character will still make sense."

On stage. He hadn't even thought about how that might be a problem for a kid with a cast. But she'd thought of it and figured out how to fix it.

"Thanks," he tried to think of something more intelligent to say.

She nodded and stood up to leave.

"You gonna wait to see Dad and Tam?"

She shook her head now.

"You're making my dad and my sister really sad."

That stopped her in the door as if he'd just stabbed her with his new sword. He hadn't really meant to.

Ms. Williams took a deep breath before turning to look at him, her hand braced on the doorframe. "I know."

Now Jaspar got why she'd said she was sorry. Why she'd said the rest of the text.

"You know what, Ms. Williams?"

"What?" She didn't let go of the door frame.

"It might be okay if you called Dad tonight."

She was silent for the longest time before she nodded to him and whispered, "Thank you, Jaspar. I don't know if I'm ready, but thanks." And she was gone.

He was still thinking about what it all meant when his dad came back.

"Hey, nice sword. Where did that come from?"

He shrugged and ran his hand down its smooth length.

Tam came in and spotted the sling lying where Perrin had left it beside him on the couch.

"Hey, that's cool. A sling as a part of your costume. It matches perfectly, and the sword explains your injury."

Tam didn't get it, not yet. It always took her a couple extra moments while she thought about and tested a new idea. She was right more often than he was, just slower to make sure of it. Maybe about Ms. Williams she'd been right and he'd been wrong.

Dad figured out where the sword and sling had come from fast enough though. He dropped into a chair as if Jaspar had just hacked his legs out from under him.

CHAPTER 19

Perrin skipped the Tuesday dinner to work on Melanie's dress and the one she'd wear herself to go with it for opening night. Actually, she'd have to make three more. As the costume designer, she'd been given three tickets to opening night, and Carlo had obtained two for Melanie. So between them they'd invited Maria, Jo, and Cassidy. The men had all agreed to pitch in to help Angelo as the restaurant's opening neared and he descended into near total panic. Maria was going to be done with pastries before the performance and would leave the service to the new pastry chef.

Five dresses total. With Melanie's to play off, the designs had come together quickly and easily. The dresses would be very similar in look, though matched to each woman's figure of course. And each would be primarily in a single color from the opera that best highlighted their complexion: Cassidy's black, Jo's sky blue, Maria's red, and Perrin's gold. Melanie would be the montage that each of them complemented. They should all arrive together in a limo. That would create a proper sensation.

Jo and Cassidy hunted her down later that night, coming to the shop and banging on the glass.

They'd tried to make sure everything was okay and ask how could they help. They tried to force food on her from a care package Maria had put together before sending them over. They tried to get her to stop for a moment.

Perrin didn't have time for any of that. In minutes she had them working in the studio; and they cut, pinned, and sewed to her direction. It didn't take long for them all to settle in and work together. They talked and they laughed—it was so normal. Perrin would never know what about and didn't care. All she cared about was how much she loved these women and how much they loved her. She made a point of telling them so several times as they worked.

Then she had one more idea. One she didn't even need to sketch. It was a good idea, but she wasn't ready to work on just yet.

JERIMY'S CALL TO meet with Richard, the lighting designer, brought Perrin to the Opera offices. He also tactfully informed her that Bill would be over at the Opera House overseeing the first staging rehearsal walk-through that afternoon, which she greatly appreciated.

She, Jerimy, and Richard sat at the big cutting table, all of the primary costumes turned face-out on racks in front of them. Jaspar sat quietly off to the side watching. She was starting to understand that about him. Tamara would think something through. Jaspar followed his instincts.

Jasper was an older soul in a way, despite Tamara's mothering of him. His mother's death had made him more like Cassidy. Actually they'd both lost their moms at about the same age. Cassidy had become an adult that day, as had Jaspar. He'd been a bit more buffered by Tamara's care, but Perrin could see the similarity of the effect.

Jerimy turned off the lights in this end of the Costume Shop. Richard had set up a pair of lights about ten feet apart and laid out a dozen different colored gels. The colored transparent sheets fit into steel frames that then slid into slots at the front of the lighting instruments.

"Now we can see what challenges you've set me."

The white light was the closest to what Perrin was used to working with. Fashion runways were brightly lit so that every detail could be seen. There was some coloring, but not much. And most of her designs were designed for wear in daylight, office light, or at some party. Again, all shades of white.

Then he put a pale blue in front of one instrument and a soft pink in the front of the other. It was as if the costumes had jumped into three dimensions.

Jaspar had moved up on Jerimy's other side, "Could you do that again?"

Richard slid the two gels out of the way and then dropped them back in.

"Okay, thanks." With that single demonstration, Perrin could feel Jaspar neatly filing away whole categories of information. Just as Cassidy had during college when she also took classes at the Culinary Institute of America just up the highway. Each new bit of knowledge neatly filed, creating an order to the chaos that surrounded them.

Richard turned on a third light in between the other two, shooting forward from a low stand right in front of them.

"This one is called Bastard Amber, that's its real name."

"But it's pinkish, why do they call it that?" Perrin left Jaspar to ask the questions, though she would have asked the exact same thing.

"Hold your good arm in front of the instrument."

"It's warm," Jaspar commented.

"Right. These instruments throw a lot of heat. Wait until you're onstage with half a hundred instruments on, you'll really heat up. Now watch your skin." He dropped in the gel.

"I don't get it."

"You look more natural," Perrin told him. "Your skin is warmer, more alive, but the costumes look kind of the same."

Richard slid the gel in and out a few times.

In exasperation Jaspar had her trade places with him.

"Her skin is so light, you can really see it," Richard said before dropping the gel back in.

Beyond the bright light, she could see Jaspar nodding. "I couldn't see it so much up close. It's kind of too much for her, isn't it."

"Try some of the others."

Jaspar started holding one after another in front of the lens without putting them in the slot.

"The red makes her look all blotchy, even worse than the fake amber."

When he tried a green filter, Perrin did her best to make frog noises.

"Ick! What's that for?"

Richard laughed, "You usually use it behind people for landscape scenes, underwater like for the Rhinemaidens in Wagner's *Ring,* or even a darker one for dangerous forest."

Jaspar made a couple more changes then declared, "This one makes her look nicest."

"Good eye. That one is a good match for her skin. But now look at the costumes behind her."

"Uh," Jaspar studied them. "It's okay if she's the Princess or the True Love, but it totally sucks if she's the Empress."

"Well, I'm no Empress, so we're all safe there." Perrin turned around to look at the costumes as Jerimy and Richard laughed. "You're right, Jaspar. That's nasty."

They shared a smile.

"You see, Jaspar," Richard began making notes, "there's no perfect lighting. It's a balancing act and compromises."

Mika came in with the makeup cards and they soon passed beyond where Perrin could follow. It was a language as unique as her own about texture and line. It was the language of light, and she could see Jaspar absorbing it just sitting there at Richard's side.

TWO NIGHTS LATER, Perrin almost didn't answer when she saw Bill's number on the phone. She wasn't ready to talk to him yet. There was too much to un-say and too much that couldn't be said yet. Not while everything was so out of order. She wouldn't even know where to start. Well, perhaps he would know.

Finally, steeling her nerves, she answered.

"Hi, Ms. Williams."

"Tamara," she fell back and was thankful for the stool behind her when she landed on it.

"Uh, I have to be quick. I had to use Dad's phone to get your number. You aren't mad at us, are you? At...me?" The girl's voice nearly cracked from the strain.

"Oh god no, Tamara. Never mad at you. Feeling like an idiot six different ways, but never mad."

Tamara sniffled slightly. "That's what Jasp said, but I didn't believe him. Guess I should have. The little troll is always right. Jasp wore the sling and the sword today at rehearsal; it looked great."

"That's good." Perrin knew she was missing something. Jaspar had told Tammy that Perrin wouldn't be mad. Did that mean that maybe Bill wasn't...

"We don't have rehearsal tomorrow night. Can you come over for dinner?"

It was a good thing she was sitting down so that she didn't fall down.

"Uh, who's asking?"

"Jasp's idea. Something about maybe we just needed to try each other on for size. I make a pretty good lasagna."

"I'll bring a salad," some autonomic part of her responded.

"Cool, we'll be home by six. 'By—"

"Tamara?"

"What?"

"Does your dad know?"

"Nope. Don't tell." And the connection went dead.

Perrin had found a new level of "completely nervous" that she'd never known existed. If she could have called back to beg off, she would have. But if she called on Bill's phone, she'd get Bill. And she didn't have the numbers for the kids' emergency-only cell phones. Her level of nerves definitely ranked as emergency, the national-level kind, call out the Red Cross and the National Guard.

She couldn't even think of what to wear. She almost called Maria before deciding that she just needed to breathe deeply. She wasn't going to dinner with the King and Queen, no matter how it felt. A dress was too far over the top. A skirt probably too much as well.

What would she wear for a casual evening at home? Tattered and faded Vassar College sweatpants and a fleece hoodie sweatshirt were her usual first choices. Too far the other way. She really needed to get a grip.

Perrin finally settled on jeans and sandals with some crazy-colored socks that Patsy had made for her from something she called magic yarn, the opera t-shirt, and the fleece hoodie just because she needed the extra level of security.

She was fifteen minutes early and drove past the house to park on a back street to just sit and wait. As the minutes stretched, her nerves became so bad, she knew she wouldn't make it the whole time without deciding to go home. With five minutes to go, she drove up to the house.

Perrin had sat in the kitchen once before, after dropping off Tammy, but she'd been too wired to notice much. Now she was so hyped up that she noticed everything.

Their house was in the Greenwood neighborhood, just a few miles north of downtown; a remodel of a remodel of a remodel Bill had informed her. The street was steep and narrow, enough room for two cars to pass, if they were careful and everyone parked close to the one curb that had parking.

The blue-gray two-story house with forest-green shutters and trim had a surprising amount of privacy in the crowded neighborhood. It stood on a rise a dozen steps above street level behind a massive old hawthorn tree. The porch light was on and she could see the living room light through the original diamond-cut window.

When she klonked the big brass door knocker, it felt as if it echoed throughout the quiet neighborhood. "Here be an interloper!" it announced. The desire to turn and run surged through her again, defeated by being too nervous to do any running. She thought she heard someone call out, "Dad, can you get the door?"

Oh crap!

Then the door was open. Bill stood there, backlit by the bright living room and looking really, really good in bare feet, jeans, and an open flannel shirt over a blue t-shirt.

"Perrin?" he barely managed a whisper.

She might have to kill Tamara and the conspiring Jaspar later, but for the kids' sake, she took the bit. Clearly it was up to her to make it work.

"I was invited to dinner by your children. That is, if you're willing to invite me into your house."

"The kids?" His eyes widened and his jaw dropped like in an old, silent movie.

She tried to fight down the smile, but knew she wasn't succeeding. "I brought a salad." Perrin held out the covered bowl as if that would make everything make sense.

Bill closed his mouth, then both his eyes. He opened one as if checking that she was still standing there. Then he looked up toward the ceiling, "Thank you, God." He almost launched himself at her, but stopped when she warned him off with a slight shake of her head.

His careful nod acknowledged both the wisdom and the regret of that choice. Then he held open the door and she walked in.

"Well at least that explains the lasagna mystery."

She looked over at his whisper.

"It's Tammy's signature ultra-special-occasion dish. She cooks a couple nights a week to help me out, but we don't get her lasagna very often. It's good. That little sneak."

The front door opened right into the living room. It was comfortable rather than being austere. More bookcases than art. A couple of well-used couches and chairs sat on a rug that had definitely seen years of children. A big, octagonal coffee table that appeared to have sixteen different projects on it, as well as three relatively clear spaces where they probably set their dinners on most nights. A big television hung to one side, though not one of the monsters—available, but not the center of attention. She could easily see them all hanging out here together.

Bill took the salad bowl, brushing her hand as he did so. The electric shock shook her. Distance and time had increased her reaction to him rather than decreased it. Standing here, barefoot in the center of his domain, he was so incredibly, perfectly male. His eyes darkened just looking at her. Well, at least that hadn't changed between them.

Perrin turned away to continue the tour.

A wide, carpeted stairway led up to what must be the bedrooms. Off the other side of the living room, was a pair of rooms connected with an open arch.

"Our offices, though they spread bigger projects out over the dining room table for weeks at a time. We actually don't get to eat at it much." Perrin peeked in. Two smaller desks were in the front part of the room. They were mostly neat, though it was easy to see which was which. The wall around Tamara's had numerous fashion magazine photo spreads torn out and taped up. The growth looked fairly recent. Jaspar's was actually neater, mostly dinosaurs and a half-dozen well-done model airplanes dangling overhead from bits of thread. A book open on the desk had a diagram just like the one Richard had been using to map out his stage lighting design.

Beyond the arch, was Bill's larger desk, that looked as if it had been hit by a hurricane. A new facet to the man, so terribly organized in his public life. She liked that he had a messy side.

"It's all so...normal, Bill. You've made a magnificent home for them."

He stood beside her looking about the room as if he'd never seen it before. His glance at her registered that he was aware in this moment of just how different it was from her own childhood, and that maybe she could judge better than he did.

"Think about it. How many kids share an office with their dad?"

"I, uh... It just seemed the right way to use the space when I did it."

Then he finally nodded, acknowledging that maybe he hadn't done so badly after all, as if there was any doubt.

On the far side of the living room from the front door, they stepped into the connected dining room and kitchen, separated only by a long counter with a gap in the middle. It was the only part of the house she really remembered from her prior visit. Last time Jaspar had been asleep, or had been pretending to be, Tamara headed that way, and the front room was dark. Now there were lights on everywhere and an oldies station playing.

Bill rolled his eyes when he saw her noticing it. It was as if the kids thought she and Bill had been adults in the 1960s rather than the twenty-first century.

Jaspar greeted her with a quick wave from where he was busy half-tossing a fourth setting at the table one-handed. Apparently that was all he was willing to offer, but she was glad to wave back.

"Scamp," Bill accused him and received back a glowing smile for his insult.

Tamara ran out of the kitchen area and, after only the briefest hesitation, threw herself into Perrin's arms. They held each other hard, like sisters too long apart. She kissed Tamara on top of her head. Then, continuing to forget all of her hard-won thirteen-year-old decorum, Tamara rushed back into the kitchen to make sure everything was all right.

The last room was a big space beyond the dining room. It had tools, toys, some miscellaneous furniture, and a forlorn-looking vacuum cleaner. A room they didn't use much.

"The house was really too big for us, but the kids fell in love with it, and it's right near a very good school."

Perrin smiled slightly as she moved to help Jaspar light candles and Bill headed into the kitchen to assist his daughter. Perrin only now noticed that once through the door, she'd relaxed. Somehow, all of her nerves had remained out on the porch.

BILL CONSIDERED SIMPLY SLIPPING under the table in a small puddle of contentment. In some ways this meal had been less casual than the dressed up dinner. It felt a little foreign to be eating at the dining table. Also, he'd been far more aware of the dynamics as the conversation had ranged over school projects, books, and the upcoming opening at the Opera.

Tammy was so glad to have Perrin sitting at the table that she was even more incoherent than Bill was. Jaspar was now the one he was being forced to see differently. How was it that his children kept growing up around Perrin? One moment he'd be wondering what it must be like to ride an elephant as Kim did in Kipling's tale. The next, he'd be watching Perrin and his interactions as if they were lab animals to be observed.

Tammy had told Bill more than once that Jaspar was really smart about people. Now he could see it. But he could also see that his son would make a fearsome poker player some day—he was far too good at keeping his thoughts to himself. He felt sad, the boy's spontaneity was another thing Adira had taken with her to the grave.

"Okay, Tamara," Perrin sighed happily. "You have to feed that lasagna to Angelo some night, it will make him crazy it's so good."

Perrin's compliment had Tammy positively beaming. She was first to stand from the table and started to gather plates.

"Cut that out," Bill told her. "You cooked. Cook doesn't clean."

"But Jasp can't—"

"Grownups will clean up. We still know how. C'mere."

She came straight into his arms.

He held her tightly and whispered in her ear. "You did it perfect, honey. I'm so proud of you." Then he raised his voice, "Now scoot, I'm sure your homework is waiting for you somewhere."

She scooted, with a hop and a skip she hadn't had since Jaspar broke his arm last week. He was shocked at how much he missed it, how easily he took her naturally bright nature for granted. He had to cut that out and remember what a gift she was. That both of them were.

"And you," he aimed a finger at Jaspar who was just clambering out of his chair. He was already a little gawky, just as Bill had been at that age before he'd started to really hit the growth spurts. "I don't know what your part was in this, but whatever it was, you did it right."

"Thanks, Dad."

Oddly, rather than coming to his chair, he went to stand by Perrin. The two of them had some form of silent communication that he couldn't follow.

"You're okay," Jaspar finally informed her so quietly Bill could barely hear it.

"Thank you," Perrin mouthed just as softly.

Then Jaspar was gone.

"What was all that about?" Bill asked her.

Perrin went coy. Her black-and-blond hair swirling across to hide her features as she stood and looked down to begin gathering plates.

"Perrin?"

"Jaspar and I appear to have negotiated a truce, perhaps even a peaceable settlement."

"Really, how did you do it?" Bill looked out into the living room as if he'd be able to discern the change inside his son wrought by the amazing Perrin Williams, but Jaspar was long gone.

"I didn't," she headed to the kitchen with the first stack of plates. "He did. Jaspar's the one who invited me tonight, convinced Tamara to cook her best meal for me."

Bill tried to get out of his chair to help. Really he did. But he couldn't seem to manage it. His children were just as mysterious and astonishing as the woman making herself at home in his kitchen.

CHAPTER 20

errin arrived several hours early for the opening night of *Ascension*. She dropped off a clothes bag with Jerimy, though strictly forbade his opening it. Her opening night dress still hung at her shop, where she'd meet up with her friends for the "official" arrival at the Opera House, but she couldn't wait.

Though the theater was pretty quiet still, the air vibrated. It took a little time to track down Bill. Perrin had expected him to be at the center of some whirlwind, instead he was sitting quietly reading through his own notes in his office.

She leaned on the door for a while and simply enjoyed watching his neat movements. Studying a page of the score, adding a tiny note in the margin, then checking it again before moving on. She could watch his hands for hours and never know discontent.

"Anywhere we can go for a quiet picnic?"

When he turned to smile at her, she raised the wicker basket with the red-and-white cloth that she'd put together herself in some fit of excessive domesticity.

"I have the kids. They're next door doing their homework. I know it's Friday, but with performances tonight, tomorrow, and Sunday matinee, I figured sooner was better."

"Sounds perfect," Perrin readjusted her libido a bit, but not much. She'd expected the kids to be around and had filled the basket for four. "But somewhere quiet so that you get a break. All three of you probably need it."

The kids didn't complain for a second about escaping schoolwork. Bill took her hand, and Jaspar didn't appear to mind, though it was clear that he noticed.

"There's this one place..." Bill led them to an elevator that went up several stories.

Perrin could hear in his tone that it was a place that had other possibilities if they were ever alone here. The elevator opened to another linoleum corridor, but through a heavy door they entered another world. A narrow steel catwalk led off into the darkness. Tiny lights hung on the railing about every ten feet.

It was Jaspar who pulled her up to the edge and then pointed down. They were at the very top of the stage, way farther above the floor than the audience ever saw. Down below she could see the set like a doll's house.

What on stage was a thirty-foot high wall of impenetrable forest, looked like a child's play set from up here. It was actually a series of a dozen trees that would disappear upward into the "fly loft" where they stood right now, an area just as big and tall as the stage right above it. The space was also occupied with other pieces of sets, lights and cables, and a dozen things she couldn't even identify.

The rest of the forest, she knew from looking it over at stage level, was three stories tall and full of shape, texture and color, but it was barely five-feet thick. The back was made of thin tubes of square steel, knit together as intricately as her costumes. They were made of interlocking eight-foot sections that rolled around on wheels. From up here she could see the Prince's castle sat off to one side, the Princess' homeland off to another, so massive up close, they were play toys from here.

Bill led them up a narrow flight of stairs and through a small door.

She couldn't make any sense of the space.

This time it was Bill who led her across the plywood flooring toward a low wall.

"Careful," he took her arm. "It's a bit of a drop."

At the rear of the platform, she understood where they were. They were in the ceiling of the auditorium. The deep red seats ranged in neat rows far below. So close, you could almost jump to it, a steel gantry had a half-dozen big lights.

Jaspar came to stand beside her.

She clamped a hand on his shoulder to make sure he didn't go over this rail unexpectedly. He just grinned up at her.

"See," he pointed with this good hand. "Jim, Marissa, Camille, and Jess sit there and run followspots. That's those big lights that they can aim down at the stage and steer to follow people. They let me try it once, it's fun."

Beyond the gantry, the inner structure of the ceiling ranged off into the distance, a maze of steel supports, air conditioning pipes, and tiny walkways.

"This is your idea of romantic?" Perrin asked Bill as they turned back to spread out the picnic on the floor that was actually the auditorium's ceiling.

"No one will look for me here at least."

Jaspar helped Tamara spread out the lunch as much as he could one-handed and they all sat. Sandwiches, sodas, and laughter told her she'd done well.

She hadn't worried about that though. Old Perrin would have, making sure each thing was thought out, planned, replanned. New Perrin had simply made lunch and was enjoying herself. Her usual mode was to sort of sit outside herself and observe how naturally, or unnaturally, she was interacting with those around her and make the necessary adjustments. Now she sat inside herself and simply observed that she wasn't busy second guessing herself.

When at length they returned to the main stage, Bill looked relaxed and the kids excited, exactly what she'd been hoping for. Though she'd never have pictured a picnic in the ceiling. Once on the stage, Bill pointed up to where they'd been sitting. That's when the nerves hit her, it was so far up in the air. She closed her eyes and looked away quickly.

Most of the crew leaders had shown up during their absence. It was only minutes before Bill was whisked away.

Jaspar and Tammy took her on a tour of the Opera House. Both tugging on her hands, often in different directions to show off favorite places.

From Bill's office, Tammy led them down the hall to visit Jerimy. She admired it as if new, though it was one of the only spaces she'd seen before. Smaller than her design studio, it had two sewing machines and a bin of fabrics, zippers, and the like for emergency repairs. A bank of washing machines was for removing stage blood before it set and made a stain. All of the clothes would be dry cleaned between every performance.

Next was the Green Room where Jaspar headed for the sugar until he noted Perrin watching closely and he turned for a fistful of trail mix instead.

Mika was already set up in the Makeup Room, six assistants hopping to his commands to make everything ready for the steady stream that would be coming through. With the chorus, they would be adorning well over a hundred people during the next two hours. Perrin retreated out of his way as quickly as Tamara would let her.

She liked the way that the technical crews made time for Jaspar. And not just because he was the Stage Manager's kid, they appeared to genuinely like him. He introduced Perrin to so many people that she never stood a chance to remember their names.

The bewildering lighting setup in the back corner of the stage was clearly Jaspar's favorite. The console reminded her of when the TV news showed the controls of the space shuttle. Screens everywhere, rows and rows of sliders, a bank of controls for the intelligent lights, which sounded creepy… Jaspar seemed to know what it all meant and how to use most of it, though he was careful not to actually touch anything as he explained it.

She didn't like to be reduced to saying "Uh-huh" at appropriate places, but maybe that was all he needed from her in this moment.

Perhaps that he wanted to share it with her was enough. She'd have to ask Bill later, maybe he'd know. But maybe not. He'd surprised her when he'd tried once to explain that he wasn't some amazing father acting from a secret fathering manual. He insisted that he was just making it up as he went along. Perrin decided that for the moment, "Uh-huh" was going to have to be sufficient.

Even more bewildering was the sound console. Not for the singers or the musicians, they didn't need any help he informed her, "not even Tam," he said with some pride. It was for sound effects, backstage monitors so that everyone could hear where they were in the opera, even the headphone system. It seemed that everyone had on a set of headphones all hooked into little battery packs clipped to their belts.

By now, people were scurrying around everywhere with intense purpose. Almost everyone. A whole group of men and women dressed in black right down to their sneakers and gloves, lounged backstage ready to move the set pieces that looked so real up close even if they had looked like toys from above.

When the kids headed to makeup, she retreated to the tall stool at Bill's station, just off stage right, not ten feet from where the actors would be onstage. "Stage right" was different from "house right" for the audience. Perrin heard people switching effortlessly between the two. It made a subtle invisible barrier between performer and observer, the switching of whose right and left was important.

Bill's station included a half-dozen little computer screens. One showed the overly early arrivals milling in the lobby. Another, a view from above the audience, showed the three-thousand vacant seats. A third offered a clear image of the still-empty conductor's stand in the orchestra pit, though Perrin could hear a piano tuner checking the concert grand down there.

One of the pair of larger screens showed the closed red curtain as seen from the audience, but it would show the full stage when it opened. The second one had an incomprehensible display that Bill told her he mostly ignored because it was the feed from Richard's lighting control console.

The biggest screen on Bill's console was the cue list. Every few minutes, Bill would breeze through, brush a hand down her arm that sent warm shivers up her spine, then start checking items off the list.

"Hour-thirty to show," he called over a PA that she could hear echoing about the backstage area. "House open in an hour. Chorus to makeup and costumes." Then he was gone again.

Four assistant stage managers swirled about. One was Bill's hands and feet on the stage left offstage area, another chased cast members, a third worked with crew chiefs from lighting and sound, to checking in with the prop masters who had set up long tables at strategic points in the off-stage darkness, every single piece sitting in its tape-outlined area. The fourth one appeared to be everywhere at once.

"Be dead without Jenny," Bill had remarked as the so-named assistant whisked him away to check on some last-minute detail.

"Pretty excellent, huh?" Jaspar appeared at Perrin's elbow, now dressed as the Young Prince, right down to his sling and sword.

"It makes my head hurt there's so much going on," Perrin confessed. "Is it always this crazy?"

Jaspar scanned the goings-on about him with a practiced eye. "No… " then he grinned at her,. "usually it's much worse!"

"Gee, thanks so much!"

He just smiled.

She'd learned during lunch when to recognize that Jaspar had something to say. She did her best to sit quietly and wait.

"Are you and Dad okay again?" His question sobered her.

Perrin had made a promise to herself to only speak truth with Bill's children, so she shrugged. "I think so. Remember, I've seen way less of him than you have."

Jaspar offered one of his sage, ten-year old nods. "Hadn't thought about that. He sure gets mushy when he talks about you."

"Seems fair. I get mushy when I talk about him."

He shook his head, "No, you don't. Not mushy. You get all quiet and happy at the same time."

Perrin desperately needed a subject change. "I made a surprise for you for the party after the show."

"More clothes I bet," he groaned but gave her a smile as he rested his good hand on his sword pommel to show his thanks.

"You'd win that bet."

He was right, she did feel all quiet and happy as he trotted away toward makeup and she left to get ready and meet her friends.

PERRIN CLIMBED out of the limo with Melanie, Jo, Cassidy, and Maria. She moved Melanie to the center, so that their dresses would work correctly together. The flashes were blinding. Russell brushed by close in front of them, kissed Cassidy quickly, and whispered, "Don't squint, and smile," before moving off to a new angle and raising his own camera.

Only Melanie appeared at perfect ease. The others looked a little wild, but then they shared smiles among themselves and it was somehow alright. Arm in arm, like they were following a red-brick road, her friends moved forward with her.

E! network stopped them along the way. Totally overwhelmed by the big glass eye of the television camera, Perrin kept her mouth shut. Melanie, barely missing a beat, stepped in and answered their questions emphasizing repeatedly that the woman beside her had indeed designed both these dresses and all of the costumes for *Ascension*. Her acknowledgement that she was indeed still seeing the Italian tenor star of the opera was brushed aside so quickly that Perrin barely saw it go by.

E! had apparently already done backstage interviews with several of the stars. When asked where the amazing ideas had come from Perrin couldn't answer, "While listening to Bill Cullen's lovely voice." Melanie cut her off gently when she tried to stumble out an answer and led them inside.

"Never answer such questions, Perrin," Melanie advised her quietly as Perrin slowly regained her equilibrium. "Designs always come from your heart, somewhere mysterious and unfathomable. It makes your line of designs more unique and enhances the perceived value of your work. Coco never explained her work, nor should you."

They drank overpriced champagne from tall, thin flutes and waited for the time to go in. Perrin began noticing that there were distinct categories of men and women approaching them.

Cassidy was soon at the center of a small circle of vintners and wine connoisseurs, apparently oblivious to her best friend's beauty. Jo had board members of both Pike Place Market and the Opera, as well as one of her former law partners, clustered close about her. Her quiet power so enhanced by her dress that each word she softly spoke stilled the group for them all to listen.

Perrin with Maria close by her side, was swamped by women wearing her designs. They were no competition for the power of the five new dresses, but still the gathering created a spectacle that kept many heads turned in their direction. Melanie continued to run interference for her, because it was all far too big for Perrin.

It was a huge relief when an usher rapped three notes on a small brass xylophone announcing it was time to take their seats. It was the same three notes as the little wooden door harp on her bedroom door. It provided memories that made it easier to smile and remain calm.

The opera itself was a bit of a blur. She knew the story and the music so well that she could simply enjoy the emotional journey without having to pay attention to all of the little details.

Carlo sang beautifully of hope and love; his first costume, for he alone had needed several, attempted to deny the foreshadowing of his pending failure that the music so broadly suggested.

The Magister's dark tones rose in threat until cut short with a magnificent low note produced by Geoffrey Palliser as the presence of the Overlord. He and the Empress were announced with overwhelming force and power. Perrin barely felt Melanie's squeeze on her arm at the magnificence of the costumes under Richard's lighting.

Carlo ceased being the singer and became the character. The Prince struggling against his fate despite its inevitably. Perrin could see the parallels of Bill as he struggled to hold his family together despite the tragic loss they had suffered.

When the Princess and the True Love both vied for the Prince's favor, Perrin felt as if she were being torn in two. She wanted both to win; both to triumph and achieve that which they sought.

The True Love's murder by the Magister's least servant came as such a shock that Perrin barely masked a sobbing breath, many in the audience did not. The Empress' intervention too late, the Overlord a moment behind. The Prince broken forever at her loss, crying out from his madness. The haunting tunes somehow captured Perrin's running rhythm as she'd run away from the hospital. How had she ever done such a thing to Bill?

Before she could truly hate herself, a light, sweet soprano offered the faintest glimmer of hope. The Empress and Overlord-to-be, Tamara and Jaspar, rekindled by the very darkness that surrounded them, glowed forth brighter than beacons in the night.

The opera, so dark, so rife with doom, was rescued from the very brink with a gentle duet of the elder Empress and her protégé. The Overlord's final benediction offering hope for all.

All but one. *Ascension* closed with a grim reminder of human fragility: the softly-weeping lullaby the Princess sang to lull the mad Prince who lay with his head upon her lap.

A shocked silence was all the stunned audience could offer. It stretched out long enough for her to glance at her friends. They all wept unaware, untended tears trickling down their faces. She checked her own cheeks with a hand, dry, though not through lack of—

Practically as one, the audience erupted to its feet.

ASCENSION HAD LIVED up to all of the hype created by the yarn-bombing and other advertising efforts. Bill told her that Seattle audiences were notorious for not giving standing ovations and had never demanded an encore in the four years he'd been at Emerald City Opera. *Ascension* would be headed straight into the majestic heights of major opera house repertoire, an unprecedented opening. No one was even worrying about the reviews. Well, not much.

She let the others go ahead to the restaurant while she rushed backstage. With Jerimy's assistance, she'd helped Tamara and Jaspar into their matching outfits from the bag she'd delivered earlier. These were the idea she'd had when she'd made the other dresses for her friends. The children were now attired to be the shining stars of the emotional progression she'd made with the five dresses and with the opera itself.

Tamara's dress was easily recognizable as the Empress-to-be, but shifted in two ways: into high fashion and unbridled joy. It wouldn't be appropriate for any lesser party, but it would be a smash hit tonight.

Jaspar's suit combined the fulfillment of the Young Prince's eternal promise with the Overlord's majestic power. She'd designed the sling right into it, in a way that turned the "accident" of both the sailboat and the supposed sword accident, into a representation of the small cost of his ultimate triumph.

Jaspar had declared it "Most excellent!"

Perrin had to agree.

By the time they were ready, Bill had arrived, changed into an elegant charcoal suit for the party. Hand in hand, the four of them walked through the warm May evening for the couple blocks to Angelo's new restaurant.

Perrin felt as if she was floating on air, Bill with Tamara on one arm and her on the other, and Jaspar holding her down to the earth with his good hand in hers.

Forewarned, Russell had been waiting at the entrance with his camera. No matter what else happened, Perrin knew that whatever her past might be, she would have photographic proof of just how much joy was possible.

*P*errin *followed Tamara and* Jaspar's instructions to the letter, and once again been unable to resist arriving at Bill's house early. She went with casual but pretty. The same outfit she'd worn the first time they met: the flirty fall skirt, clingy spring blouse, and the same filmy batik summer scarf. She'd substituted the leprechaun-green hat just as a fun tease. And not one single color of the opera, which was actually a relief.

When Bill answered the door, she handed him the large pizza she'd brought with her.

"What are you doi—" He smacked his forehead. "That's why the kids wanted to sleepover at Lucy's. Why those conniving, sneaky, pint-sized—"

"Would you rather I leave? If I do, I take the pizza with me." She offered him her most innocent smile as she reached out to take back the box.

He yanked it out of reach, wrapped his free arm around her waist and hauled her against him so fast she barely had time to laugh before his kiss crushed down on her smile.

"The pizza's still hot," she teased him.

He dropped it to the floor, landing it flat she was glad to see, and dragged her to the sofa, the bedroom being much too far away.

The pizza was long gone cold by the time she let him leave her long enough to reheat it, so that finally they could have some dinner in bed.

IT WAS in the shower the next morning that Bill learned something new about Perrin.

"You're shy." It was so unexpected that he actually said it aloud.

She didn't turn to meet his eyes as she rubbed a soapy washcloth over one of those impossibly long legs of hers, foot propped on the edge of the tub.

"How many women are you, Perrin Williams?"

"What?" that made her look up at him over her shoulder. "I'm not schizoid."

"No, you're impossibly healthy. Both of body, which we've gone to some trouble to prove once again, and of mind, because you are the most magnificent woman I've ever met. Not schizoid. But definitely multi-faceted, like a jewel."

"How Irish are you, Bill Cullen? Because that sounded like total blarney." She switched legs, offering him something else to admire.

"The name is, but I don't really know. We're pure American melting pot mutts. So fess up, how many Perrin Williamses are there?"

"You tell me." She pushed him out of the flow of water to rinse herself off, with her back still mostly toward him. Okay, there were scenes like this in movies. It was just odd that he was in the middle of one. He leaned back against the end of the shower stall to enjoy the view of the water sluicing through her hair and down her back and hips while he thought about it.

"Okay, there's the Perrin Williams born the day she met Jo and Cassidy. Still wild and crazy, but finding ways to control herself, to break from her past. Then there's the amazing designer who had to find a creative channel for all of the incredible energy and joy that had been buried for eighteen years too long and was desperate to find expression."

She turned beneath the water to face him, the shower still cascading over her, blurring and softening lines, only her face clear of the water. She looked amused, but not very.

"I think I count two more, three if you count the sexual goddess whose body I can never tire of."

That earned him a brief smile.

"There is the quiet genius who really doesn't want to be noticed. The scary smart one. The one who, whenever anyone even glimpses her existence, ducks behind the old familiar cloak of craziness as a distraction."

That widened her eyes and wiped away any remaining hint of amusement. He reached out and brushed his hand over her cheek, she leaned briefly into the caress, then returned to watching him quietly.

"I'm not sure that anyone other than Maria has ever seen her clearly."

Perrin slowly shook her head, then added softly, "And you."

"And me. Cassidy knows she's there," he continued. "That's why you're so close. But she can't quite hold focus on that Perrin."

"What's the last one?" Her voice barely sounded over the falling water. She hooked one hand over her opposite shoulder, masking her breasts. Bill was aware of the protectiveness of the gesture, even if she probably wasn't. One last shield?

"It's the Perrin Williams that I always see. Though, now that I think of it, maybe I'm the only one. No, my kids do, too. But I'm guessing that even you don't. She has a quiet center and a heart that is so open that it's always right there. It's the heart that let Jaspar and Tammy come straight in with no games, no defenses. They've learned to love you, but you loved them from the moment they roared into the Costume Shop before the first piece of paper was torn. She's the Perrin who shines before me every time I look at her."

"I don't know her."

"Oh, but you do, my love." He moved forward and kissed her ever so lightly, though her crossed arm still separated them. "Every time you are with me, those other Perrins aren't the ones that leap to the fore. Except at that first meeting with Wilson in your shop when I was being such a jerk, you've always showed me the true you. Every time you turn shy, it's because you think you don't know her, but you do. She is the Empress, powerful *and* vulnerable. She is the Princess, gorgeous *and* unaware at the same time. And she is most definitely the True Love, brilliant *and* caring *and* sharing. She is so loving that she can't help but pour her heart out into the world. And Perrin? All those many facets of you… "

"Yes?" her voice was slow and careful. Immensely cautious.

"That's who I always want beside me when I wake. I want her to be the mother of Jaspar and Tammy. And I want to have a child with you, Perrin Williams. That child would be a true miracle with you for a mother."

She narrowed her eyes, having to blink them a few times to clear them of the water trickling out of her hair.

"Did you just propose to me?"

"Yes, I did." Bill hadn't really planned on it, at least not yet, but he'd meant it with every cell of his being.

"In the shower?"

He looked up at the spray still cascading over them and slid his hands onto her hips, pulling her partway out of the water.

"Well, at the time I thought it was a waterfall in a tropical paradise, but this would appear to be a shower that we're standing in. So yes, I seem to have proposed to you in the shower."

"Oh."

"Oh? That's all you have to say, is 'Oh'?"

"Would you prefer if I said, 'Oh yes'?"

"That was sort of the point of asking."

Without breaking eye contact, she slid her arm out from between them, and wrapped both of her arms about his neck. Pulling him beneath the water with her, she kissed him hard.

Then she eased back just a bit, the water streaming over them. Her impossibly brilliant smile lit her blue eyes and stunned him speechless as she so often did.

"We have to ask the kids, but otherwise that's a really big, yarn-bomb sized, 'Oh Yes!'" Her kiss was wet, but there was no question about it being totally heartfelt. Perrin had always kissed him with her heart wide open.

But she had never before kissed him with the taste of tears running down her cheeks.

CHAPTER 22

*P*errin *had insisted that* she had one last load to fetch at the apartment before the move was complete. Bill thought they'd left it clean, but he must have missed something.

The family had all sat together and decided that she should move in and unpack in the days before the wedding, so that after the ceremony she would simply be home when she arrived. She and Tammy were even staying in Cassidy's spare bedroom tonight, so as not to spoil tomorrow, neither the wedding nor the first homecoming.

Perrin's home studio was mostly put together in the spare room off the dining room. A small cutting table, an eight-foot set of shelves full of fabrics on one side, an open-style closet down the other. At one end, beneath the row of north-facing windows, stood the Feather-weight sewing machine. And by the door, a pair of small desks.

She'd insisted that the kids would always be welcome there to do their homework or anything else, even if she was working. When he'd asked where his spot was, she'd pulled out one of the tall stools from beneath the cutting table. His name had been knit into a soft seat covering.

Over Tammy's desk, Perrin had mounted a massive crochet hook on which had been carved with burned-in letters, "Chief Assistant

Empress Tamara Cullen." Over Jaspar's hung a wooden sword, exactly like the one he'd worn on stage, with the same-style letters saying, "The True Prince Jaspar Cullen."

The kids had almost died when they saw them. If either of them could have loved Perrin more after she did that, they would have.

Bill had offered to go with her for the last load, but she'd insisted it was a one-woman job. Then she'd turned right around and asked the kids if they wanted to go with her. He'd watched them drive off in her van, as perplexed as ever about what she was up to. He knew that she would keep him on his toes for years, no, for decades to come. He also knew that it would always be a joy. Even the hard times. She would stand beside him and he beside her.

Tomorrow, they would all stand together as a family for the first time. They had made it a combined wedding, adoption, and name change ceremony. She'd tried to hold onto her own fabricated last name out of respect for their mother, but the kids had overruled her.

At the wedding, Tammy would stand as maid of honor, with Jaspar making sure his dad didn't screw up or collapse from sheer nerves. Despite his probing, Tammy had only said that her and Perrin's dresses were, "Totally Killer!" It was the same judgment Jaspar had declared when he and Bill had tried on their tuxes together. Bill had checked, but the girls had been smart and kept Jaspar in the dark about the dresses. Bill was trying to be patient, but it was really hard.

He finished breaking down the last of the moving boxes and stored them in the garage. They were gone long enough that he'd just finished installing the last shelf she'd asked for when they pulled into the driveway.

Bill could hear the excited laughter of the three of them as they came into the house, the best sound he'd ever heard. He went to meet them in the living room.

The kids were grinning like lunatics, of course they'd been doing that all week as the wedding came closer and closer, but then so had he.

Perrin looked tall and beautiful and majestic. He noticed two things.

"Your hair!"

"See, I told you he'd notice," Jaspar informed Tammy. "Our dad's not a total dork."

Bill chose the safe course and ignored the aside.

Perrin had dyed her hair gold-blond and cut it short fully revealing her astonishing neck and delicate face. For the first time since college, Perrin Williams had returned to her natural hair color and perhaps the first time ever, ceased hiding behind her hair.

As if she'd finally become herself.

"You've bypassed the Empress, my love," he moved down the hall toward them. "You've tipped right over into goddess."

Her smile was radiant. This was the Perrin he'd always seen.

It was as he leaned in to kiss her over the kids' heads, that his mind fully registered the second thing.

Tucked in the crook of Perrin's arm lay the tiny brindle-colored Cairn terrier they'd seen at the dog show. It had grown from one handful to two.

"I kept the breeder's card," she scratched the dog behind the ear. "She was just finally weaned last week. We figured if three-to-one couldn't win the vote to adopt her, maybe we just needed a fourth vote. All in favor, raise your paw."

The kids each shot up a hand. Perrin lifted the paw on the tiny ball of fluff—who perked up both of her ears at the attention—as his fiancée grinned up at him.

"Oh man." Well, it took a wise man to know when he was beat. Just as it had taken a wise man to see the real Perrin, then be smart enough to fall in love with her, and tenacious enough to win her heart.

As their children danced around them, he raised his own hand to make it unanimous.

WHERE DREAMS ARE WRITTEN

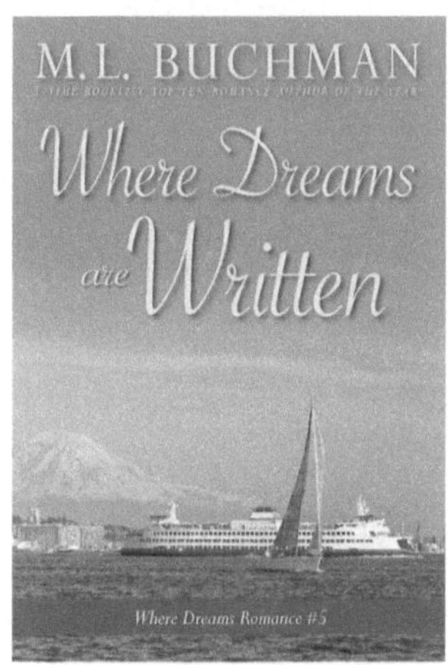

CHAPTER 1

Melanie stood, poised, at the edge of the "wedoption" of her friend Perrin. The ceremony had tradition, spontaneity, and so much heart. A wild mix, just as Perrin was. She had taken vows with her husband as his two children stood by them in Angelo's Tuscan Hearth Ristorante in the heart of Seattle's Pike Place Market.

It was Perrin's new ten-year old son who had named the ceremony. The wedding of Perrin and his dad, and her adoption of Bill's children—the "wedoption." The kids were adopting Perrin as much as she was doing so for them.

It was all so sweet that Melanie felt mushy and sniffly inside, not that she'd ever let it show. She pulled out no handkerchief, had no pockets in her sleek dress to carry one. She only showed emotions carefully, and never mushy and sniffly ones. Being one of the fashion industry's leading models, she'd learned long ago that showing her own emotions was almost never appropriate. Everything she presented, both on the runway and off, was very carefully considered. She occasionally wished she could simply react, but that never seemed to work out.

She let her present boyfriend, Carlo, swirl her into a dance across the space cleared at the middle of the restaurant.

"That was *magnifico,* Carlo. Your *Ave Maria.*" The operatic tenor, just finished with a highly successful production at Emerald City Opera, had indeed filled the restaurant with liquid soaring tones that evoked the sanctity of a small church set in the Italian countryside rather than Angelo's fine dining restaurant in the Market.

"This place and Angelo's food made it simple. It looks and smells so Italian, I sing from heart. The couple..." he slipped his hand from her waist for a moment to toss a kiss to the sky.

"Yes, *molto bello.*" Melanie had dressed carefully, to not outshine the bride, but she needn't have worried. One of the most innovative designers working today, Perrin had judged herself and her maid-of-honor daughter perfectly despite their sharply contrasting coloring. Perrin's golden hair and fair skin and Tamara's darkly flowing curls and her birth-mother's dusky complexion had both radiated in Perrin's designs.

"I could marriage her myself. So pretty." Carlo swirled her among the other dancers with effortless control. Carlo's French was as poor as her Italian and his English was non-existent. So, she always spoke in her school-girl Italian and he spoke to her in a child's rudimentary French. That way they always understood one another and the inability to discuss more complex topics had not been a major issue. Carlo was not a deep man.

But he was a kind and considerate lover. Also, his Mediterranean-dark skin, classic Italian good looks, and international fame had made them a stunning couple, frequently gracing the tabloid covers. But his limitations had soon become apparent and were now wearying. Soon they would be finished.

"I have received call on phone," he whispered as they pulled together for a slow passage of the song. "Marko Lerano has taken ill and they need an Alfredo for *Traviata* at La Scala."

"That's such wonderful news for you. La Scala," at least she thought it might be, so she offered her support. "When do they need you?"

"I have already called the taxi. They say the tickets at the airport will be. You keep hotel room as long as like."

Well, that was abrupt, but she knew such contracts were rare, vital to a career, and lucrative. Still…

"There is more, isn't there, Carlo?"

He nodded sadly.

She needed no other cue, she was about to be dumped. People didn't dump Melanie, she dumped them. She considered getting angry, but she wasn't, and hated people who put on a show for others. This was the perfect opportunity for a drama queen: a large audience, grinding someone else's celebration to a total, upstaged halt. Why did some women do that? She'd never understood.

What she did know was that, being Italian and male, it would be hard for Carlo to say the next sentence. They had done well together but she too had known it was over, for her at least. She wouldn't have minded if he had been left to pine away for her *un petite moment,* but if such was not to be, *c'est la vie.* She could at least be kind.

"It was a good run, Carlo, *oui?*"

"*Si.*" His appreciation shone on his face and the sagging relief in his shoulders. He kissed her on each cheek. "You are wonderful woman, Melanie. Never let persons tell you not."

"You're wonderful as well," she patted his cheek.

He leaned in for a final kiss, but if they were done, they were done. He was wise enough to hesitate then pull back and nod. And just that easily, their six months was over. Moments later he had led her gracefully to the edge of the dance floor, offered a final bow, and, after offering congratulations to the groom once more, slipped quietly out of the restaurant.

She stood pillar-still at the edge of the room as dancers swirled about the dining room floor. Those still at the tables shared stories and smiles among candlelight and buffet dishes.

Melanie sought inside herself for pain, or relief. And found neither. Merely irritation that she had been dumped. The Ice Queen they often called her, due to that perfect mix of self-composure and immense sexuality she could project. It had earned her so many accolades: four swimsuit covers, Victoria's Secret signature model, ever increasing offers of obscene amounts of money from *Playboy* that she kept refusing.

Melanie didn't need the money and would never pose nude. She had caused two major photographers to be fired for taking candid shots while she was changing clothes during a shoot; her contract was very strict on that point. She wore sheer and skimpy, posed naturally with a well-placed arm and little else, or wore only a Godiva of her trademark waist-length blond hair. But that's where she drew the line. The stories of those high profile firings had ensured that all her photographers were very careful around her. Neither of those images had made it out of the studio; the second one she'd had to shatter a five thousand dollar camera in order to make her point. But it had been made and no one in the industry was likely to forget it.

It was *Playboy's* first offer years before that had led to the final fight, of so many, with her mother. She had taught her daughter many lessons. Melanie had discarded most of them, but two lessons she took to heart: care with her money, and only the work mattered. The professional standards and practices Melanie had worked out on her own.

Carlo had left her by two towering vases filled with lilac and rhododendron, not far from the front door; the flowers nicely accented her maroon dress. She could easily slip away, but found herself unusually reluctant to do so. Melanie never stayed until the end of a party—it might look too desperate—but she remained despite that.

People came and greeted her and were greeted in return, having no idea that for only the second time in her life she had been dropped by a lover. She could forgive Russell because he hadn't known that's what he was doing at the time. Carlo however, was a sign. Of what? That things were changing?

Jo, one of Perrin's best friends, and her husband Angelo dropped by.

"So glad you could attend," Jo's touch was friendly as they traded cheek-to-cheek kisses. It really touched her and she let her façade melt enough to let them know it. Angelo was Russell's best friend and knew of their failed relationship all too well. And Jo, the calm, cool clear-thinking powerhouse lawyer who now managed the Pike Place Market. Of all the people she knew perhaps Jo was the only one who didn't judge her as anything more than who she was—inside.

"The food. Angelo. Holy *Merde!*" Melanie flapped her hands as if she couldn't think of enough to say. And she couldn't; his cooking really was that good. Yet another reason she was still standing on the far side of the room from the banquet table. He was one of the best Italian chefs in the country and she'd already had too much to eat, but would eat more if she happened to pass too near the sumptuous table.

He positively beamed.

How odd that she and Jo knew each other so little, but knew each other so well. They had cemented their relationship in an airport bar over two photographs, both by the same photographer. One photo, the moment she had fallen in love with Russell as he captured an image he didn't understand; the other of the same moment for Jo and Angelo, though they hadn't yet known.

She and Jo didn't need to speak to recall the moment where they had set the photographs side by side and Jo's life had changed as she saw the images of herself with her future husband. Jo simply held her hands a moment longer and pressed their cheeks together, no air kisses, no need for whispered words, just understanding and acceptance—both rare items in Melanie's world.

The couple moved on but Melanie felt a better than before they'd arrived.

She took a glass of champagne from a passing waiter so that her hands would have something to do. She didn't really want any. The merriment that resounded around the crowded dining room brushed by her as lightly as the smell of Angelo's amazing marinated lamb— that must be wafting out the windows to tease the tourists walking the cobblestones of Pike Place Market this cool May evening.

Perrin, Jo, and Cassidy—friends since college. And Angelo's mother Maria. They were all so close. You could see it in every gesture. What would it be like to have such friends? She watched them, all happily married. Perrin and Bill dancing to a Fleetwood Mac tune that for some reason was causing their children no end of amusement. Jo and Angelo now with Maria, all tasting the latest dish to come from the kitchen. More food. *Impossible.* Cassidy and Russell also moving across the dance floor.

Melanie took a sip of champagne to hide the pang of envy. Russell was so handsome, having just the right kind of roughness to him, and disgustingly wealthy. Though she had been very careful and was quite well off herself, so that had been less of a factor. Still, they would have been a perfect couple...for about a year. Whereas he and Cassidy looked quite content enough to be together the rest of their lives. Again, she resisted the sigh of longing.

Marriage and lifetime were not for her. Still, she could envy the group of friends their stable husbands and their close friendship.

While the other three women were starting college together, Melanie had dropped out of high school to pursue her modeling career. By the time they'd graduated, Melanie had nailed her first swimsuit cover and had put out a restraining order against her ex-manager mother ever contacting her again.

That had been the day she'd legally dropped her last name forever —she wanted no ties to her past. She'd earned her GED through a correspondence course and her business skills through the college of hard knocks and intense study.

Melanie now hid her desperate, New Jersey past behind careful emotional control and a soft French accent acquired from a learn-at-home computer program and perfected on international photo shoots.

Yet Perrin had made her feel included and welcome rather than the supermodel outsider unexpectedly in their midst. And those who Perrin accepted, her friends accepted without question. It was so unlike Melanie's own world where everything was move and counter-move; where the only things that mattered were image and your latest contract. The one escape she allowed herself was into novels, every-thing else she kept focused on her career.

She allowed herself to simply observe the wedding reception

crowd packing the restaurant, taking microscopic sips of champagne to portray herself as content with standing alone.

Angelo's Tuscan Hearth was warm with mahogany tables, blues and yellows on the walls and the midnight dark tablecloths. The wall art was all photographs of the old country by Russell. She had never looked as good as when he was the one photographing her—his retirement from fashion photography had been a blow to the industry.

The dance floor had become more crowded in the few minutes since Carlo's departure. The women wore DKNY, Lauren, Armani, and a fair number of innovative Perrin's Glorious Garb designs. Perrin's work stood out, by not suffering from the classic couture problems. Wearing her designs, a woman could walk out the door and not be out of place strolling through Pike Place Market. They would stand out for their beauty or eye-appeal, but these were not runway-only showpieces.

Perrin's fashion design friends, her new husband Bill's Emerald City Opera companions, and both of their personal friends all jostled happily together, mingling one table to the next. It was a joyous event, laughter an ingredient more common than the regional wines or the amazing food. If she knew how, she would swirl down into the crowd and appear to be enjoying herself. But the artifice usually so readily at hand eluded her and she remained, standing among the flowers.

Perrin swirled by in Bill's arms, laughing and shining with joy—a joy she had created in herself, despite her past.

Melanie found that the most surprising thing of all. She had always seen herself as too damaged to find a true relationship, yet Perrin's past had been far worse than hers. Here she was, Perrin outshining them all so effortlessly.

The bride's dress was a conceptual and technical masterpiece. The dress, and the complementary one that Tamara wore, empha-sized a fairy lightness, a magic that made them both appear to float about the room; both too joyous to touch anything as mundane as the real world. The diaphanous gold over a form-fitting sapphire sheath—like sunset glistening on the ocean. On Tamara's emerging curves and mahogany red hair it modestly promised the woman yet to come.

"Truly, Perrin," Melanie had told her over appetizers, "even in Milan, such work would be valued." It was no less than the truth.

Russell came by, nudged her slightly closer to one of the flower vases and snapped a couple of quick photos. He may have retired from fashion photography, but his skills had grown rather than diminished. Without doing it consciously, she had watched him move through the room, arranging groups but making them look candid.

Jaspar, Perrin's new son, had taken to following Russell around and the two were now consulting on which shots to take and how to set them up. The boy drank it up like a sponge. Russell with children. Melanie put a hand over her heart to stop the pain at the image. He would be such an amazing father even if they were not to be hers.

The shutter clicked again. She stuck her tongue out at Russell, but pulled it back in before he could raise his camera once more. He laughed, then he and his protégé moved on to other subjects.

She felt her phone buzz. Business. She always let the business line through no matter where she was, except during the wedding ceremony itself. Early in her career, jobs were offered, negotiated, and scheduled in the time span of a week. Now, if they didn't reach you immediately, the job could be gone before you called back. This was a text.

There was only one line: *Sorry. Swimsuit cast now set. Maybe next year. Sue.*

This should have been a contract, not a brush off. This should have been a shot at the cover; her chance to tie Elle for the record of five covers. Instead, she wouldn't be in the issue—for the first time in eight years. There had to be a mistake, but no matter how many times she reread the message, it didn't change. She never begged. She was Melanie. The demand for her modeling time was constant and costly. But this one time she texted back to make sure.

Sue answered immediately, *So sorry. If in my hands, you'd be in. S.*

White lie there, Sue was the editor-in-chief and could easily override any underling's decisions, but you never burned bridges in this industry. So, she wrote back a quick *Thanks and looking forward to next year. M.* White lie back.

It happened.

To others.

Not to Melanie. She'd never lost a contract before. Ever. Not since that photographer's cat had scratched her moments before her first big hand-modeling contract when she'd been eleven. The scar had healed long before the memory of her mother's head-wrenching slap for the lack of caution.

Melanie stood on the periphery of the wedding crowd and used all of her control to remain calm. Passive. *Immobile.* She had known it was time to start planning for her next step. She'd seen too many girls fall by the wayside with no backup plan and many, unlike Melanie, had not been careful with their earnings. There was always some seventeen-year old with perfect skin waiting to be discovered.

But she hadn't been ready for it yet. Tyra had her talk show and acting. Iman had her cosmetics and had married David Bowie. Naomi was still working, though not as often as she'd like, for a variety of reasons. There were whole chains of supermodel restaurants, as if the skill in the studio and on the runway somehow translated across industries, which it almost never did. And there was only one Kate in the world, only one Claudia, only one Heidi.

It wasn't the death knell of her career, but people would hear that she'd lost the swimsuit issue. Soon, not this year but probably next, her contracts would start to go down instead of up in both money and frequency. She hadn't worked this hard to become second-rate. Even if Victoria's Secret renewed her as their signature model, the writing was on the wall.

She moved along the edge of the room to find a chair in which to sit, her *équilibre* was not being reliable at the moment.

Russell, of course, chose that moment to emerge from around the gently flickering fireplace and step in front of her.

She sighed and strengthened her shields.

"Wow! You look like you've just been gut-punched, Melanie. What's up?"

Russell. Of course. The one person who could see when she was upset. Kind, frequently oblivious, and married to Cassidy Knowles instead of to herself. Russell didn't know everything about her but he knew more than anyone else ever had. Ever. Including how to read the Ice Queen's true emotions if her guard had slipped in the slightest.

There was a time that hadn't been true, but her single failure at making their relationship a lasting one had changed everything, and now he could read her when no others understood. She had been the one to make the mistake of falling in love with him; he had been the one to not notice and leave her behind.

"I appear to have just lost my boyfriend and the next swimsuit issue in the same ten minutes." The shock of saying it aloud cut her inside, despite wearing her cloak of calm for the rest of the world.

"Carlo dumped you? Where is that shit? I'll kick his damned ass for being so stupid." Russell was tall, taller than she was if she hadn't been wearing heels, and began scanning the crowd looking for him.

"Already on his way to Italy, I fear."

"Does he have any idea what he just threw away? Asshole." He sounded truly pissed on her behalf.

Melanie smiled to herself. Although Russell had done the same to her, worse because she'd been in love with him as she'd never been with Carlo di Stefano, he was ready to leap to her defense. She pulled Russell close for just a moment, to share an instant of his strength, then kiss him on the cheek.

"Hey, no falling for my husband." Cassidy came over to join them, she said it with a smile.

"*Excusez-moi*. Too late." Melanie could have bitten off her own tongue. Not that it was a secret, for Melanie had told Jo and whatever one of the three friends knew, they all knew. But the truth behind her words shifted her light joke over closer to envy.

Cassidy's gentle hand of sympathy on Melanie's arm made it both better and worse. The understanding was kind though, and Cassidy was always kind to the very core.

"What's going on that's made Russell so angry?"

Melanie told her.

"You lost the swimsuit contract?" Cassidy sounded deeply shocked on Melanie's behalf. She at least understood which bit of news was actually important.

"Wait," Russell spun to face her from his continued search for the departed Carlo. "You what? Crap! Is Sue even dumber than Carlo?" Melanie had met Russell while working on a swimsuit issue, had become a key model for Russell Morgan Inc., and shared his bed for almost a year. "I'll give her a call and—"

"And," Cassidy interrupted his growing tirade, "ruin any chance of her ever working with Sue again. No, Russell." Though she was half a head shorter than Russell and looked even more slender than she was when compared with his broad-shouldered frame, it was clear that Cassidy was indeed the right wife for him. She smoothed out Russell's hair-trigger emotions so effortlessly that neither of them probably noticed. They were that much in sync. Like Perrin and Bill, they were each so much better together than apart. Melanie would have gotten right up in his face and they'd have gone at it.

Once again, Melanie felt the stab of envy. Would she ever find a man to love her that much?

<hr>

"Now what the hell am I supposed to do?"

Silence. No one answered. Because no one was there.

Josh Harper stood at the doorway and listened to the odd quality of his voice echoing about his empty Chelsea condo on New York's Lower West Side. No wife, not anymore according to last week's small sheaf of papers and a court ruling. No lawyer, done and paid off the following day. Not even a realtor, "Just leave the key on the counter. The new owners will be changing the locks tomorrow anyway."

He didn't know anything anymore. The underpinnings of his life had been abruptly pulled when the woman he'd adored had decided she was no longer interested in men, or being married to one. No acrimony. No alimony, their incomes were near enough identical. No hurt, at least on her side, just sadness and apologies and a chaste kiss to end the five happiest years of his life.

With the wondrous and painful insight of perspective, he could now see what she meant, who she really was that neither of them had noticed. But that did nothing to ease the pain. Rather it only added to his sense of feeling foolish. He'd been naïve...or dense...or stupid enough to marry and love a woman who...wanted another woman.

He ran a hand over the Gaggenau cook top where they'd made a thousand meals together, the big double oven that had delivered turkeys and pies to large gatherings of friends. Mostly her friends, he could now see. Mostly women, though she swore that hadn't been conscious.

Josh still couldn't understand the echoing emptiness that had so recently been his cozy home. That had included his wife. Worse, she'd known for over half a year but had delayed telling him because she couldn't figure out how to approach the subject without hurting him.

At least she didn't have a girlfriend yet, she'd always been true to him just as he had to her.

One thing was clear, he needed a fresh start.

A completely fresh start.

And he could afford one. With his half of the money from the sale of the condo and furnishings, added to his half of their savings, he was set for a while. For several years if he was careful.

Josh pulled out his phone as he stood there at the door with his computer bag over his shoulder, his only constant companion. He'd left a dozen or so boxes, mostly cookbooks, with a storage company that would ship them if he ever figured out where they should go. His other belongings hadn't even filled the trunk of his BMW waiting for him downstairs. Perhaps he'd been too severe in shedding his past, but that was done now too.

He hit speed dial on his phone. When Shirene answered, he kept it simple.

"I quit."

"Don't be an idiot, Joshua. You can't. You're my senior editor. Your prose is part of what makes *Gourmet Week* hum."

"You have my four emergency articles already on file in case I was sick or something went wrong. Well, it's gone wrong. Consider them and my unused vacation as my thirty days' notice."

"No, Joshua, my friend. For ten years you've dedicated your life—"

"To reporting about food. And it was fun. But it's not what I set out to do in the beginning. It's not what I want to be doing ten years from now. Call Elric, he'll come aboard happily and do a great job for you. Give you a fresh viewpoint."

"But Joshua—"

"I'm so done, Shirene."

There was a long silence before she finally responded, "If you ever need a job in the industry, I get your first call?"

"You do."

"Promise?"

"Promise."

"And if you need a friend to talk to, you call me anytime, day or night?"

"You're the best, Shirene." A friend to talk to. That finally gave him an idea of where he was going. "If you're ever in Seattle, give a shout."

"Seattle? What the hell's in Seattle?" Spoken like a true New York publisher.

"Me. Bye." Josh hung up, tossed the keys on the counter, and closed the door behind him without looking back.

***

"Josh, buddy! What the hell are you doing here?"

Josh had chosen a quiet corner in his favorite restaurant, Angelo's Tuscan Hearth Ristorante in Seattle.

"Eating lunch? How about you?"

"Cooking it. Rush is over now, so I'm taking a break before we switch over to dinner prep." Angelo scanned the last few occupied tables and dropped dramatically into the opposite chair as if totally wrecked with exhaustion, which he belied a moment later by sitting up quickly and asking, "Why didn't you come in the back?"

Graziella, the pretty woman who ran front of house, had suggested the same.

Josh shrugged. He'd wanted to just sit. For two years he'd been coming here each time he was in the city. He'd seen it when it was a typical upscale restaurant, and again after Angelo and Russell had transformed it into a Tuscan hearthside with gas fireplaces, understated décor, and Russell's photography of cliff-side vineyards and quiet donkey-wide Italian streets. Angelo's cooking had been the only other element needed to rocket the place into the restaurant firmament. His own reviews had been a part of that process.

"Just wanted to sit and enjoy this wonderful place you've built." Tomorrow he'd start his novel. He was gambling his life savings on his ability to pull it off. But he'd give himself one day to just sit in a corner and pretend that he belonged somewhere. Maybe he could pretend, at least to himself, that he was here to review the restaurant like old times.

Old times.

One of the last four articles he'd kept on file with Shirene was a fresh take on this one chef's influence on the entire country's standard for Italian-American cuisine and the impossibly high bar Angelo had raised. He'd titled it "The Gauntlet" for the challenge of excellence and creativity that Angelo had thrown down before all other chefs. It was probably coming out this week.

"So, how long you in town?" Angelo signaled Graziella as she swept by and asked her for a bowl of pasta. "Long enough for me to roust the others for a meal? Might take a bit, you missed a hell of a wedding party I threw night before last for Perrin and Bill."

Josh actually felt the world spin. It was a little disorienting. In the past he would be in Seattle for just twenty-four to forty-eight hours with *Gourmet Week's* corporate travel department making the travel and hotel arrangements. He never stayed longer because he always wanted to get back to his wife. His ex-wife. Now *his* car, not some rental, was parked three blocks away with all of his life stuffed into it.

"Uh, sure, long enough to arrange a meal. Anytime. This week. Next. Whatever." He knew he wasn't making a lot of sense, but ten days ago he'd still been in a Chelsea condo on Manhattan's Lower West Side. Now, he didn't even know where he'd be sleeping tonight.

Angelo looked at him a bit strangely.

"Hey Angelo," Russell barged in through the kitchen door carrying a bowl of pasta. The last patrons startled under the abrupt assault of his big, deep voice. "Josh! When did you get in? Missed a hell of a wedding."

"I already told him."

Russell dragged over a chair from another table and sat on it backwards. He took a big forkful of the pasta that had probably been for Angelo. Angelo didn't look the least surprised, he just waved a hand at Graziella as she came out of the kitchen and then indicated Russell eating his pasta. She rolled her eyes and doubled back into the kitchen.

Josh realized that he hadn't done much damage to his own serving though he'd been sitting here for some time. He took a forkful, but didn't really taste it.

"I took photos of the wedding buffet for you," Russell spoke around his food with the skill of much practice. "You know, in case you wanted to do a write-up but were too late to see it all pretty. But you never showed. You did RSVP, didn't you?" He turned to Angelo, "He did, didn't he?"

"He did." They both turned accusing gazes upon him, as if he hadn't been busy losing his mind all month.

"I'm not with *Gourmet Week* anymore." Okay, there was something he certainly hadn't intended to say out loud anytime soon. It still surprised him.

"Crap, Angelo. There goes one of your biggest fans. Now we're going to have to break in someone new."

Angelo just shrugged. "So, who are you writing for now?"

"No one." He couldn't breathe; it felt like he'd just jumped off a cliff into nothingness. It was supposed to get easier to say these kind of things.

"God damn it!" Russell almost choked on his spaghetti and booming exclamation combined.

Angelo and Josh both glanced around the dining room, but the last of the midday patrons were gone.

"Did they fire you? Jerks. There's way too much of that going around."

Angelo shrugged when Josh glanced at him for clarification.

"No," Josh paused as Graziella came up.

She set another bowl of pasta in front of Angelo and smacked Russell on the back of the head which only made him smile.

"I quit."

Graziella had been headed away, but stopped and turned back to look at him.

"Fed up with it?" Russell grinned at his own pun. "Food reviewing gone sour?" He clearly thought he was on a roll.

"Something like that." The bitterness on his tongue only supported Russell's teasing.

Angelo and Russell nodded as if that explained everything, which was fine with him. There was plenty of explaining he'd rather not do.

Graziella on the other hand, looked immensely sad. She held up her ring-clad left hand for a moment out of sight of the two guys. It took him a moment to realize that she'd noted the white tan line on his ring finger.

He jerked his own left hand under the table, he still felt naked without the simple circle of gold.

She rested her hand over her heart for a moment and looked incredibly sympathetic. He had told her on his last visit about his wife and how much he loved Constance. He and Graziella had been seated side-by-side the last time he'd been out for a meal and he'd stayed to close the place.

Then she walked up behind Angelo and Russell, smacked them both on the back of their heads at the same time, before returning to other tasks.

While the two guys rubbed their heads and looked after her curiously, Josh did feel rather better.

CHAPTER 2

Melanie sat in Perrin's design studio because, sadly, she had nowhere better to be early on a Wednesday afternoon.

It was soothing to at least be surrounded by the process of fashion design: her high stool at the green rubber cutting mat-topped table, the sewing machines lined up along the wall, the wall of cubby holes filled with hundreds of fabrics all neatly folded and organized by the rainbow, the bright steel rolling rack of designs in progress, and the small changing area behind a gaudy Victorian screen. Even the designer sitting across from her doodling away at her sketchpad made it feel so normal when her world was so impossibly not.

Perrin looked elegant, she always did. No matter how crazy her designs, the tall slender blond made her clothes look exquisite and sexy. And Melanie had not missed that the two of them looked enough alike that what looked enticing on Perrin looked good on her as well. Melanie had a bit more chest and a couple of inches in height, but they were much the same. She'd worn a number of Perrin's pieces that had garnered attention, including the fabulous gown for the opening night of Carlo's opera just four weeks before.

Perrin looked far better than Melanie felt: dressed in a French peasant blouse, a modern-sleek skirt, and mid-heel sandals, she looked so alive and youthful. In that outfit she shouldn't, but she did. Was it the simple headband the same color as the skirt? Or the contrast of the styles? Melanie wasn't sure. But this look that no designer in their right mind would put together was light and fresh.

"You would have made a good model, Perrin."

Perrin vibrated with a vivacity that would play well on the runway.

"No. As much as I enjoy being a spectacle sometimes, I actually don't enjoy being in front of crowds like that. I like to grab their attention at a restaurant or on the street, but what you do…" she made a mock-shiver with her shoulders, "I'll leave that to someone else."

Melanie had always liked the runway. Enjoyed knowing that she could absolutely command the space so that viewers were dazzled and unable to look elsewhere. Some walkers felt they should be merely perfect "hangers" for the clothes they were paid to display. Melanie didn't agree. It was her job to make a designer look so exceptional that the show ended with people lined up to place orders.

"I like that *énergie* of throwing myself into the walk. It is the magic of a twenty-second declaration of power and control. There, I can unleash that which I must hold under such careful control in the rest of my life." Though she was grateful that she had no show at the moment. Or a shoot. One of the reasons she was so marketable was that she could take that twenty-second runway energy and provide it on demand throughout an eight-hour session in front of the camera. Right now, she didn't know if she could even bring that energy up for a candid.

She felt as if she never would again. As if… The next images were so morose that Melanie really needed a subject change. The last thing she wanted was to impose on her friend.

"You know to throw me out if I'm in your way?"

"Why would I ever do that? You're always welcome here. Actually, I'd love to work on some designs with you again. That dress we made for you for the opera opening, that was so much fun."

"It was," Melanie agreed. Perrin had made her the smash of the opening. And, in turn, Russell made sure that the dress received national attention as part of his marketing support for the opera and for Perrin.

"Besides, you aren't bothering me at all." Perrin began drawing a sketch of something that might have been a large hamster. "I just can't focus to save my life. I never thought I'd be married at all; not really. Always figured I'd find a way to screw up any relationship before it really stood a chance. Now, suddenly I have a husband, two kids, and a dog. I now can't imagine how I lived without them all these years."

Dog. That's what the sketch was. "*Un peu* alarming, *n'est-ce pas?*"

"More than a little bit. We're having such a fun time settling in that the kids are almost melting down. And me too. We all just have to keep our head in the game. Bill has one more opera before the summer break. Once it's over and the kids are out of school, then we'll get our honeymoon."

"South of France? A Caribbean island?" Melanie had done many shoots in both and wasn't sure which she'd prefer.

"We were thinking of Disneyland. The kids haven't been in years, not since their mom died, and I've never been. It sounds like fun."

Melanie laughed. She couldn't help herself. Perrin made it sound fun, and, of course, it would be with her involved. She pictured Tamara charging around Disneyland with her brother. And her parents. Melanie had only been a few years older when she landed her first magazine cover. *Teen Vogue* had offered her one great prize in addition to the exposure; it had shifted her thoughts into plotting her escape from her mother. Disneyland. How different their worlds were. How glad she was for Tamara.

"Perhaps I shall stow away in one of your valises."

"Nah, all dark and cramped in there. You wouldn't like it." Perrin's smile made Melanie feel welcome and as if she belonged here. Which she did as much as anywhere. She should be getting out of Carlo's hotel room—she really didn't want to spend another night there—but she had nowhere else to go except back to her apartment in New York. There was nothing to do there either. She'd blocked out a long window of time for the swimsuit issue and now had nothing to take its place. But that didn't mean she should impose.

"I should leave so you can work on something other than a dog coat." Melanie began to rise but Perrin waved her back down.

"I'm interviewing a seamstress in a few minutes anyway, several of them I think. I just can't keep up. Before the success of the opera we were already selling stock far faster than I could sew. And with a family now, it's completely overwhelming. I won't miss sewing the same thing over and over anyway; I'd rather design. But the business side and marketing and everything else is so overwhelming I can't think. I'm afraid I'm going to have to give up some control, but I hate doing that."

So did Melanie, yet another thing they had in common.

Melanie enjoyed watching the interview. She started as an observer. But she could see Perrin hit a wall far too soon. So, Melanie asked a question, eliciting Perrin's near-panicked relief. After that, they both ran the interview.

Karissa was smart, quiet, and loved to sew. She knew her own limitations, had tried designing and simply not taken to it, but she loved the feel of a well-crafted garment and appeared to know what that meant. Her interview dress was a piece of immaculate construction of her own doing, but not much imagination.

Melanie too knew her own limitations. She'd only ever loved one thing, the business and process of modeling. Some models enjoyed nothing more than the clothes. Others wanted the fame, going for the bad press with wild flings and parties when they couldn't generate the good press.

She'd tried, in the safe seclusion of her Upper East Side apartment, to both design and sew. The Sudanese supermodel Alek Wek had done just that and created her fabulous line of Wek handbags, one of which sat at Melanie's feet. While Melanie had managed some bit of skill, neither had held her interest nor sparked her imagination.

Perrin was all set to hire Karissa on the spot, but Melanie suggested one last step. Karissa was sent to the fabric racks and then the other end of the big cutting table to reproduce one of Perrin's designs, but in a size four instead of a size two—using no pattern but the dress hanging before her.

Raquel, Perrin's store manager, had lined up four candidates who arrived at half hour intervals. The next two seamstresses didn't make it as far as the sewing test: one due to poor skills, and the other one had irritated them both so much that they'd simply shown him the door. Even Karissa had sighed quietly with relief from her assigned sewing machine when the bombastic East European was gone.

The last one, a young gay man named Clem, arrived in a flamboyant suit that bordered on the ridiculous, jacket lapel points almost up to his ears and Capri-length suit pants in dark pinstripe with white socks and cordovan shoes, but the construction was amazing even if the taste level was a bit bizarre. He landed at the machine beside Karissa to create a size six. In moments they were chatting and teasing each other, despite the competition of the interview.

"Do you need two?" Melanie had taken Perrin aside after she watched Clem ask for guidance from Karissa and how easily they each gave and took direction.

"I don't know, really. Let's go out front and ask Raquel."

The front of Perrin's shop was such a treat; a 1950s diner of chrome and red leatherette, populated by amazingly well-attired mannequins. Melanie always made a point of spending time here each trip to tour the display booths. Everything had changed once again. Prohibition was back, and she'd added Cotton Club and speakeasy posters to the décor. Glam flapper dresses, updated with modern colors sat next to Zoot suits rethought for women.

The best of it were the two booths at the end where she always did her wedding displays. There, snuggled together, looking as if they were waiting for their ice cream, were the sleek wedding dresses. They had the lace shoulders, sleek profiles, and tea-length hemline of the 1930s, and the elegance of Perrin's Glorious Garb. A mannequin poised as a waitress was shockingly attractive in the demure pink satin that didn't feel the least bit demure.

Melanie forced her attention back to Raquel—a striking and buxom redhead, an exemplar of the tradition of that name. With an admirable efficiency, she laid out the orders. Already there was a two-week wait for dresses and business suits that weren't in stock in a particular size. Wedding dresses were booked for two months out.

Melanie glanced at the store's racks, they'd been sufficiently ravaged that Perrin's Glorious Garb was in danger of becoming a custom-to-order shop with nothing to satisfy the impulse or tourist buyer. When a customer strolled in, they needed to be greeted with an abundance of options. A glory of them. Not the almost painfully thin displays she now had.

"*Deux*," Melanie informed Perrin.

"But that's two salaries."

"You need two."

Raquel nodded agreement then set out a sales chart representing the last four quarters.

Melanie inspected it for several long moments. She'd rarely seen such a growth curve. She shared a look with Raquel and they both laughed.

"I know! I've been telling her."

Melanie turned to Perrin, "You had need of two seamstresses two months ago. How have you been doing this by yourself? You'll need another in a month. They'll pay for themselves twice over based on these orders. Restocking the racks and working on the new designs... *Assurément! Deux*. Let us go and see how it is they do."

Neither was done, Perrin's designs weren't simple. But based on the work so far, and with Melanie's confirming nod, Perrin hired them both on the spot with instructions to return tomorrow and finish the dresses.

When the buoyantly giddy pair had been turned over to Raquel for paperwork and the studio was once again quiet, they dropped onto stools to catch their breath.

Melanie was thrilled. The depression that had skirted close beside her for the last two days, as it always did whenever she contemplated her past, had been driven back down into the depths where it belonged.

As they chatted back and forth, oddly about the coat design for Figaro, Perrin's opera-named Cairn terrier presently asleep in a small doggie bed under the table, Melanie had mentioned her need to get out of the hotel room she'd shared with Carlo.

"Oh, you must stay in town until your next contract. Please Melanie? We'll have so much fun." Perrin had grabbed her phone without awaiting a reply and called Mama Maria.

In an eyeblink, Melanie was a bit befuddled to find herself heading off to check out of the hotel. Maria would meet her in half an hour in Pioneer Square. Angelo had a condo there, at the south end of downtown, that he had lived in before marrying Jo. Maria had, in turn, lived there before marrying and moving in with Hogan.

"See," Perrin had insisted, "maybe it will bring you good luck as well."

Why it was that married people always thought their unmarried friends couldn't help but want what they had? Melanie would like to be married someday. But though her career had stumbled, it was far from over and she had no intention of slowing down anytime soon.

That wasn't the issue. She liked the idea enough to let Perrin sweep her along. Besides, the woman was an unstoppable force anyway so resistance really was pointless. The problem was that she didn't know what was now expected in return. Help with a few interviews didn't balance a pleasant and free accommodation in the heart of Seattle's old town district.

Despite her misgivings, between Perrin, a very helpful concierge, and Maria, Melanie soon found herself ensconced in a charming condominium just off Seattle's Pioneer Square. On the seventh floor, it peeked over the present Alaskan Way Viaduct elevated roadway, offering a stunning view of Elliott Bay and the Olympics.

"Imagine the view when they finish the tunnel," Maria had said, "and they take down the Viaduct."

It would be stunning. It would offer a premier view in a premier location. Pioneer Square was the founding site of Seattle. And while it was small and quaint, it felt more like New York than much of the city. The area burst forth with more tiny shops and galleries than Soho. Restaurants and bars were tucked in out-of-the-way corners.

Maria told her the best bookstore in the city was just two blocks away and had a coffee shop; Melanie would have to be very careful there—bookstores were a major hazard to her careful budget. The International District offered a small Chinatown that guaranteed good eating. If she had to be somewhere in Seattle, this would do nicely.

That the condo sat empty most of the time was apparent by the emptiness of the refrigerator, but Melanie preferred to eat out anyway. She only cooked on rare occasion and then very simply. Fruit and yogurt would cover most of her at-home needs; she could practically live on fresh-made smoothies.

It had rich, oak-wood flooring, a heavy-beamed ceiling—high enough to feel open rather than oppressive, and sunny yellow walls sporting pretty framed pictures of Italy: Tuscany, Liguria, and the Piedmont. The living room furnishing could have been her own, an IKEA selection. She'd never felt the need for more in her own personal space.

The masterpiece of the décor was the kitchen. Everything else was comfortable yet little more. But the corridor kitchen clearly belonged to a chef with its generous space, built-in cutting boards, and fierce-looking stove. It had a large walk-in pantry with northern light that stood mostly empty. The two bedrooms were done prettily. She found them to be cozy and took the one that had clearly been Maria's based on the feminine touches in bedspread and art.

Maria fussed and pampered her, which was very kind and did indeed make Melanie feel welcome. If only she didn't have the constant kneejerk reaction against every possible form of mothering. But she did, and she had to suppress it hard and often. *Maria is not your mother, don't react. Don't react. Don't react.* And she didn't; at least not on the outside.

Permission to stay at the condo also added another checkmark on the ledger sheet of life; she now clearly owed Maria as surely as she owed Perrin. She had no concept of how she'd ever repay either of them.

"As long as you like, Melanie. We have no plan to sell it. It is so convenient, we just haven't found a use for it at the moment. It's free-

and-clear and costs us almost nothing, so it is yours to use. No guilt," she'd waggled a finger before Melanie could protest, forcing her to keep her guilt to herself. "It's obvious, young girl, that you need somewhere to stop and breathe for a moment. This is where."

She did turn down an invitation to dinner with Maria and her husband, but carefully accepted the hug Maria offered. Such kindness was so rare and precious. And she simply couldn't bring herself to trust it.

Melanie unpacked into one corner of the generous master closet and the built-in dresser designed properly to accommodate a woman. Men always thought four drawers covered all needs—which was all she needed for her current suitcase-sized wardrobe—but she appreciated the design. She liked this room very much and settled in for a quiet evening. She actually didn't need much dinner, and for some reason she was so exhausted that an energy bar with a cup of tea was all she could really stomach. A luxurious rose-scented bath and she was in bed with a book by eight and asleep by nine.

JOSH PARKED his Beemer in the garage. He grabbed his computer and a pack with some clothes, figured everything else could just wait for tomorrow. At this point he simply needed somewhere to collapse.

This morning he'd woken up six hours and a speeding ticket away in Spokane, after crossing the country in five remarkably long days behind the wheel—the Great Plains went on for bloody ever—without any tickets. *Welcome to Washington.* Some greeting.

He hadn't driven across the whole country since a college road trip when he and two buddies had punched straight through from New York to San Francisco in just fourteen minutes under two days. It was Spring Break so they'd spent five days freezing their asses off on the fog-bound coast and then turned around and hammered back. Clancy had gotten the speeding ticket on that trip.

Angelo had dragged Josh into the restaurant kitchen for dinner. He'd served a venison and baby squash skewer drowned in a morel mushroom sauce with a slow, spicy heat that built and warmed without burning. It almost made Josh wish he was still working as a food writer so that he could dedicate a whole article to this one dish. Russell had called his wife Cassidy to join them. The three of them had spent a merry evening harassing Angelo and his crew from a side prep table while they made dinner service look like an art form rather than a duty.

Angelo's kitchen was a magazine photo-worthy creation; Josh knew because he'd done a feature article on just that kitchen. At the far end was the patissier station that Angelo's mother Maria ruled over. It was now occupied by the night service chef, but all the prep had been done hours before by Maria.

The friturier hovered over his fryers and the grill master and soup potager hovered to Angelo's other side. He anchored the center of the line passing prepared plates to the aboyeur Louisa, who cajoled, pleaded, demanded, and absolutely controlled the final dressing of each plate. She also made sure the timing would have the product hit the tables at its very peak moment of perfection.

Josh had avoided most of the unwanted questions by sticking close to Russell so that Graziella couldn't get him aside. And he kept his left hand out of Cassidy's sight as much as possible. When she finally rolled her eyes at him, he caught on that she'd noticed right away: both the missing ring, and his lack of interest in discussing it. After that he relaxed a little.

He'd stayed through closing and cleanup because of the company, but now he just needed to sleep. Angelo had insisted that he could stay in the condo for as long as he wanted. It was just sitting empty. Angelo said he'd sell it once the old Alaskan Viaduct roadway had finished coming down which would shoot up the property value.

So tired he could barely stay upright, he let himself in, dumped his computer on the first chair he spotted, and headed for the bedroom, not bothering with a light—there was enough light coming in through the uncovered living room window to steer around large objects. He opened the door to pitch darkness. As he reached for a light switch, a small suitcase slammed him square in the chest.

More due to surprise than the force of impact, he crashed backward to the hardwood floor, good thing he'd already dumped his computer on the chair, and had a brief impression of long legs sprinting by as he struggled to catch his breath.

"Who the hell are you?" A woman. Pissed woman. From New Jersey by the accent. Wasn't he in Seattle?

Josh rolled up on one elbow as the light flicked on, temporarily blinding his weary, night-adapted eyes. In between cautious eye blinks and narrow squints, he was offered a sideways view of the legs that had flashed by a moment before. They were even longer than his first impression. Atop them was a faded t-shirt with "Versace" across it in large, scripted letters. He was on the verge of admiring the great stream of tousled blond hair that covered the woman's face when he focused on her hands.

They were clasped directly in front of her and were aiming a…Taser.

"Whoa!" Josh held his hands palm out.

"Answer the question, you bastard!"

He sat up very slowly, keeping his hands in view. A shake of her head flipped most of the bounty of hair back over her shoulder. He recognized her immediately. You couldn't be anywhere near the print magazine industry and not know Melanie, perhaps not anywhere on the planet. He'd only met her the once, while having lunch with Perrin on his last trip to Seattle a couple months before. He'd been unable to speak a word to the breathtaking beauty.

Normally it was the truly amazing chefs he had trouble speaking with even though interviewing chefs had been part of his job. His first meeting with Eric Ripert had nearly killed him and he was sure that it was only because the man was so old-world civilized that he hadn't declared Josh a complete idiot. It had been a total "fan moment."

But Melanie had been worse than that, so stunning and so impossibly real that he'd become totally awkward despite being happily married, or so he'd thought at the time. He could still remember the way she'd smelled from the moment when she had kissed him gently on the cheek in greeting. He'd planned to laugh with his wife over it, except she'd dropped the divorce bomb on him as soon as he walked back into their condo from that trip. Now he'd better get past being tongue-tied if he didn't want to get zapped.

"Hi, Melanie."

She didn't blink or lower her weapon. Well trained by whoever had been her self-defense instructor.

"We met once. Josh Harper. A friend of Perrin and Cassidy's. Actually Cassidy and Perrin's; I've known Cass years longer. Ever since we both did a review of a gourmet burger place that opened on East Fourteenth." And he was babbling.

The weapon lowered partway. Now rather than being aimed at his face, it was more in line with… He casually brought his knees together though he didn't try getting to his feet.

He had to admire the effects of her rapid breathing on the thin t-shirt that ended teasingly high—high enough to indicate if she wore anything underneath, it didn't include shorts.

"Josh Harper?" It started as a question but ended more as a statement. He also noticed her voice shifting out of New Jersey and into New York. "What are you doing here?"

"Angelo gave me a key. And you?"

"His mother was kind enough to do the same."

Josh did his best to offer a laugh, but she hadn't finished lowering the Taser all the way. "I do wish family members would communicate more, don't you?" After a heartbeat or five had passed and she still hadn't lowered her weapon, he nodded toward her hands.

She finally lowered her aim, sliding the Taser back into a large designer handbag resting on the dining table. "It would certainly have made my heart happier if they had done so. That was not an *agréable* way for waking up."

By the end of the sentence her voice had shifted again, this time to the one he remembered from interviews and their one meeting. A soft, gentle French accent offered not as a coo, but rather as a gentle mask. And now he knew just what it masked. The New York fit her well, the New Jersey made no sense with who she appeared to be, *the elite member of the New York social and fashion scene.*

He risked climbing to his feet. Damn she was tall. With her bare-foot, they were the same height. If he shed his sneakers, she'd be... Josh thought about something else as rapidly as his tired brain would allow.

"Sorry for scaring you. I'll just, uh, go find a hotel. Do you know any around here?" He picked up his pack and did his best not to stare. He'd only ever seen Melanie presented to perfection, both as a model and at that afternoon lunch a few months before. Here, she stood in a t-shirt with no makeup and her hair mussed, and she was even more astonishing, as if by dropping the French accent she was truly revealed. Breathtaking. It was just as difficult to not stare at her deli-cate, patrician features as it was to not stare at her legs. The power of those intense blue eyes that so defined her public image were no less powerful in private.

She shook her head, "I arrived here just a few hours ago. I only know the hotels uptown."

They shared a smile. Uptown in Seattle was all of a dozen blocks away, not halfway up Manhattan with clear lines of demarcation for the diverse neighborhoods in between.

"It is late," she glanced around until she found a clock. Past midnight. "You should stay here. There are two bedrooms."

"But—" His throat went dry picturing being in the same apartment with Melanie. This wasn't right. He was...no longer married. *Separate bedrooms, separate doors. Get a grip, Josh.*

"You sure you don't mind? It's been a hell of a long day."

With an elegant wave of her hand she indicated another door. She didn't have that painful thinness that so many models cultivated, she looked incredibly fit, just lean and perfect.

Melanie returned to her own room, wishing him a neutrally pleasant goodnight. She passed close enough that he could just catch the slight rose-scent that must be her soap, warm on the gentle breeze of her passage. Not quite close enough to get past that to the woman who had brushed her cheek against his in a French-style greeting back when he'd been a different man, but still it suited her very well.

He couldn't help but admire her careful knee bend, revealing nothing, to pick up her suitcase from where it had landed after knocking him back. Also the view of her departure. Damn but the woman could walk. And this was flat footed, without really trying. In heels and couture, she was generally acknowledged as the best walker presently working the runways.

Josh stood in the middle of the living room after her door closed, wavering as he did so. Whether that was from the exhaustion, the fall, or seeing her so close, he didn't know.

He headed to the other bedroom, didn't bother with the light, and simply collapsed onto the bed. Too exhausted to move, kick off his shoes, or reach for the covers; he lay there. He thought about how Constance would laugh when he told her that he was sleeping one thin wall away from one of his short-list women.

They'd had a merry date once as they'd each discussed the five people in the world that they would want a free pass on if they ever had a chance at an affair. Melanie had always topped his personal list ever since he'd seen the model's first-ever cover on his high school girlfriend's *Teen Vogue*. He'd looked into buying the back issue years later, but it was one of the very first issues and quite the collector's item, especially when paired with Melanie's subsequent success; far too expensive for a whim.

Constance had bought it for him for his birthday one year. They'd had a laugh over it, then he'd slipped it back into its archival plastic bag, tossed it in his desk, and forgotten about it. It was now in a box down in his BMW, one of the few gifts he'd kept from her.

Constance had joked that she couldn't argue; should the opportunity ever arise Melanie could easily top her own list. He fell asleep before the irony of that long-ago joke could make him break down completely.

CHAPTER 3

$\mathcal{J}$*osh woke up to* an internal alarm clock, one still located on another coast, and couldn't get back to sleep. He took a quick shower and donned fresh clothes before he slipped into the still-dark living room.

No light under Melanie's door. Of course it was barely five in the morning, no sane person would be awake yet.

By the streetlight's glow still coming through the large west-facing living room windows, he surveyed the space. It was mostly a great room made up of entryway, living, and dining all in one space with a generous kitchen in the corner. For that he had to turn on a light.

The space was practically orgasmic. Angelo's hand was clear here, a kitchen designed from scratch by a chef for a chef. All of the equipment top grade, cutting boards, and a second prep sink all perfectly placed. The solid cabinets of natural oak, the counter space broad, even a marble section for pastries.

Then he discovered the massive pantry. Barren except for one rack which sported an awesome collection of kitchen machines, you could easily move a desk and chair into the space. If he could squeeze in a cot, he could happily live right here next to that kitchen. He already had a couple of ideas of what to cook; there was no way he could live here another day with this kitchen and not play in it. Except this was Melanie's place first. Maybe she'd let him come by and cook.

First thing it needed was coffee. An impressive home espresso machine sat in the corner of the main counter with a grinder standing right beside it, but he had no beans. He checked the freezer. Nope. Besides, the grinding would wake Melanie. And there was no way he could start his First Day, *drum roll please,* of his writing career without his morning boost.

He shut off the light, took his computer in a sling-pack over his shoulder, and tip-toed out the door.

Seattle wasn't quiet at this hour, it was silent. Pioneer Square's bars and restaurants had been vibrating with energy when he'd arrived last night. The warm May weather drawing crowds out onto the streets and the small tables set up outside hip bistros. Couples had wandered the art galleries arm-in-arm and small mobs of overdressed and overly-effervescent teens flashed fake IDs at anyone who even pretended any interest.

Now the streets belonged to him and some tall guy going into the back entrance of a homeless shelter's kitchen, based on the brief flash of bright lights and shining stainless steel. He wandered up First Avenue toward Pike Place Market looking for a place to go, not even the coffee places were open. He checked his watch, still too early for the first chefs to hit the Market's stalls. The air was saltwater fresh, but after the traveling he'd done and the sleep he'd missed, he'd need the air to be highly caffeinated as well if it was going to make any difference.

For ten years he'd been reviewing restaurants and food festivals all around the country. From the Bite of Seattle to the Food & Wine Classic in Aspen to the New Orleans Wine & Food Experience, he'd been to them all and written about them all. He had a press pass for the Experience next week, but he wouldn't be headed to New Orleans to attend. He could hear people congratulating him on "getting out of the rat race" then shaking their heads sadly as soon as his back was turned. He knew it, for he'd done the same thing himself often enough.

No. A fresh start was better. If he could just find some coffee.

Pioneer Square gave way to a few unrestored blocks that had seen better days sixty or seventy years before, as he walked up First Ave. But then he hit the theaters and condo towers that had sprung up in the last decade. Still not a one of their ground-floor coffee shops was open yet.

As he crossed Marion Street, he looked downhill. The day's first ferries for Bainbridge Island and Bremerton on the far side of Puget Sound were pulling out of the docks, the deck lights blazing as they headed to fetch the first big loads of morning commuters. He'd bet they had coffee on board. The sky was brightening, the stars that had reached through the streetlights were slowly fading away.

Even Pike Place Market at the top of the long First Avenue grade was still silent and unlit. The only vendor up and about was the fishmonger. He and his assistants were already pitching ice into the big display cases preparing for the arrival of the day's catch. Their fish were always the freshest. Angelo or Manuel, the executive chef at his second restaurant, would be here right after the fish arrived to make sure they had the very best of the selection.

They traded friendly waves, but Josh felt a little disconnected from the world around him and simply continued along the old brick street lit by the bright "Public Market" sign glowing bright red above the market. The hundreds of other shops were still shuttered.

Then, up Post Alley, he spotted a single light. The back door leading into Angelo's kitchen stood open to the morning air. As he approached, he smelled coffee. Rich coffee. Then he spotted Maria working over her baked goods, the patissier always had early hours to get the ovens up to temp and the breads just right.

Coffee, he could just go begging; he'd need at least a lame excuse. It seemed only right that he should go in and apologize for missing her son's wedding party for Bill and Perrin. Yeah, really lame, but he was desperate.

He barely had time to blink before he was seated across the baking prep station from her with a cup of rich Italian roast and a *cornetto* filled with dark Venchi chocolate still so warm from the oven that the chocolate ran down his chin when he bit into it.

"I ran into Melanie last night."

"Oh, where?" Mama Maria Amelia Avico Parrano Stanford was the short version of Sophia Loren: beautiful, very-nicely figured, and aging splendidly. Josh knew that her son Angelo was at least thirty, but it was difficult to equate that as being possible when observing the flour-spattered beauty working across from him.

"Around midnight. At the apartment," he kept his tone dry.

Maria put her fingertips to her lips but they did nothing to hide her smile.

"It's not funny. The woman nearly Tasered me."

"As she should have, intruding on her in the middle of the night."

Well, clearly he was going to get no sympathy here. He'd have to try the guys later. But he'd bet it wouldn't work there either. They'd have absolutely no pity for him once they heard just how scantily clad his assailant had been.

Maybe he'd just keep his mouth shut; he had to protect her reputation after all. He sipped the coffee again and felt himself waken a little. By tonight his body would be shifting over to West Coast time.

Maria slid another tray of *cornetti* into the oven before sitting on a stool across from him. He liked the restaurant's kitchen at this time of day. It was dark outside. The only light came from the single overhead that cast its light on the stainless steel table, but not beyond. Maria was a shadowy figure except for her hands brightly lit as she tore off a corner of her own *cornetto*.

"You must have loved her very much."

Joshua's coffee cup slipped from his nerveless fingers, the black liquid cutting a dark river across the floured work surface. His attempts to apologize were waved off as Maria wiped the surface and poured him a fresh cup.

At a loss for what else to do, he nodded. He still couldn't see the chink in their marriage. Couldn't find the place where they had gone their separate ways and their love had become a façade. Because it hadn't. Their last night together hadn't been filled with anger and biting words, they had simply sat all night on the couch and held each other and cried. Well, she had cried, he'd still been too numb.

"Well," Mama Maria re-dusted her table and began rolling out the next batch of dough, "it is good that you feel so much."

"So that it hurts this badly?" He sounded angry even to himself.

"So that you could have loved so deeply. Your heart is shattered, but it is not broken. It will heal as long as it continues to feel." She brushed a long curl of dark brown hair, with just the slightest hint of gray, back into the kerchief she wore and began rolling out the next batch of dough with the confidence of decades of practice.

He thought about what she was saying. His heart certainly hurt enough to believe it would never heal. Though it did hurt less than it had a month ago, even a week ago when he'd walked out of the New York condo and pointed his car west. As unimaginable as it seemed, maybe someday the pain would ease enough for him to take a breath without whimpering.

Josh didn't see it happening anytime soon, but just maybe it was possible.

"You are either scary smart or just plain scary, Maria. I'm not sure which."

Her smile was radiant, "When you figure it out, could you let Hogan know? My husband often claims that he would very much like the answer to that question."

"Will do." But he wasn't ready for whatever other insight might be coming his way. "Would it be okay if I went out and worked on my computer in the dining area for a while?"

"Of course, Joshua. If you take the small table to the left of the server's station, that is always the last one we seat. You can sit there right through meals if you want to. Now go, do something to fix your heart; I suggest you spend the day pretending it is fine and work on a task that will distract you. I have breakfast to make and then desserts for today's service. When I have the Pandolce Genovese ready, I will bring you a piece."

He gathered up his computer pack, coffee, and *cornetto* before turning for the swinging doors. Just before he crossed the threshold Maria called out after him.

"And don't give Melanie a thought. These things have a way of taking care of themselves." She'd timed her comment perfectly so that he'd actually have to step out of the dark restaurant and back into the dimly lit kitchen if he wanted to ask what in creation she meant by that.

And of course, the woman—who he'd barely given any thought to at all this morning—once again stood in the forefront of his thoughts. Stood there in a worn, too short t-shirt, watching him with the most amazing eyes in the world.

***

"He was very cute," Melanie admitted. Still at something of a loss as to what to do with herself, she'd returned to Perrin's store. She felt some responsibility for helping Perrin choose the two seamstresses and she wanted to follow up on how that was working out. It was too little to repay the kindness of the lead on the condominium, but it was a deposit on account.

Karissa was faster and Clem was more accurate, they complemented each other well.

"I always liked Josh," Perrin admitted as she sorted through a shipment of fabric. Colorful bolts of mid- to lightweight summer fabrics covered most of the cutting table.

Melanie had ended up at a small desk in the corner that was buried in a storm of untended paperwork. For something to do with her hands, she began sorting and stacking it as they talked.

"I never jumped him though. Happily married and all that." Perrin clearly enjoyed her ability to shock, but such things didn't faze Melanie. Instead she agreed, that was a line that she too would never cross.

"No ring," Melanie had noted that as he'd lain on the floor at her feet. "Just the tan line for one."

Perrin disappeared behind a stack of greens: Lime, Hemlock,

Apple, and Loden. "Well, if that's true, something major happened. He was one of those guys who never stopped going on once you got him on the subject of his wife."

"Well, he certainly didn't mention her while I had my Taser aimed at him."

"You aimed a Taser at him?" Perrin popped back up to look at her. She looked like a mischievous modern-day angel wrapped in a tight, over-scale herringbone-print hoodie. "Did you shoot him?"

"*Non!*" She'd never shot anyone except a training mannequin. "Though I came close, he did very much scare me." And then this morning he'd been gone before she'd woken up. No note or anything, not that there was any reason he would leave one. She was nosy enough to peek in the other bedroom and see that his pack was still on the floor and the covers looked as if he'd slept on top of them and then not bothered to straighten it all up afterwards.

Did she like or dislike the implication that he would be returning? She wasn't sure. They would have to talk it over, she wasn't exactly in the mood to cohabit with anyone. Especially not mere days after breaking it off with Carlo. She sighed to herself. After Carlo breaking it off with her. It might be nice to have a man-free zone while she re-gathered her self-esteem.

Perrin turned back to her fabrics, testing the drape and lie of a couple of them.

Melanie focused on the papers before her. There were bills to pay with completed but unsigned checks, probably prepared by Raquel. Good, that meant Perrin wasn't letting others make her payments. Sign your own checks for your own business. None were over seven days old. Also good.

There was a fair wad of fan letters. Melanie was used to these, but was surprised to see that a designer also received them. Most were harmless, only a few creepy ones, and no gross ones; her own mail had the reverse ratios.

There was also a thin stack of general correspondence. She started reading without really thinking about it. Then she read another and a third.

"Perrin?"

"What do you think of this one?" she held up a swatch of Malachite Green.

"Not with your skin, *non. En réalité,* I'm not sure any woman could get away with that unless they were going to a costume ball as a harlequin."

"That's what I thought," Perrin tossed it aside and continued her sorting. "Don't know why I ordered it in the first place.+"

Karissa and Clem were conferring over whether they needed to hand roll the hem. When they decided that was what the fabric called for, Melanie relaxed. They did have a proper sense of what was required to execute Perrin's effortless styles. She was also pleased to note that neither had to ask the other how to execute it.

"Perrin," then Melanie realized that she already had Perrin's attention, the woman was just multi-tasking. "I hope you do not mind that I—"

"If I did, I would have stopped you before you got to the fan mail."

Melanie had only seen a few times how sharp a person Perrin was, in addition to her design work. She wore a cloak of wild craziness that distracted like…ah. It distracted like Melanie's accent. A revelation she'd regretted making to Joshua last night, but he'd scared her all the way down to her core.

Whenever her childhood New Jersey accent slipped back to the fore it made her feel unclean. She'd had to take a shower to scrub it off before she'd been able to go back to bed. Still, she'd lain awake far into the night. She couldn't write it off as adrenaline let-down, her heart rate was unexceptional. It was… She pictured the moment again. How Josh Harper had looked after getting over his surprise. No, not how he'd looked, how he'd looked at her.

She knew that her legs were one of her best features. And while he had obviously noted them, he had spoken neither to her legs nor her breasts. Disconcertingly, he had looked right at her. As if having heard her original, hated voice, he somehow saw the real her. No one did that, not Russell or Perrin. Maybe not even herself, but somehow Joshua did.

"Some of that fan mail stuff is pretty weird," Perrin shrugged uncomfortably. "I don't know what to do with it."

Melanie waved at the thick stack of letters, "I send them a signed photo." Except for the creepy and the scary ones. "You should use this pile to create a mailing list. Just give them to Raquel and she can use them to send out your season-line brochures."

Perrin suddenly became very interested in sorting a stack of reds. She set aside a Persimmon and a Cayenne, not a color combination Melanie would have expected, but she did like the way it felt to her eyes.

She nodded when Perrin sent her a questioning glance.

Taking up the two fabrics side by side, she walked over to the wall of fabrics stacked on shelves down one of the studio's long walls and began holding them up to different fabrics, both complementary and contrasting.

Melanie read between the lines, "You have no season-line brochure."

"I barely have a season-line," was Perrin's whispered response.

Melanie moved up beside her and rested a calming hand on Perrin's arm. She was practically vibrating with nerves.

"Perrin."

This time Perrin looked up at her and Melanie could see the incipient panic so close below the surface. That's when she realized that Perrin's success had already overwhelmed her and now she was losing control.

That also would explain the letters that Melanie had sorted aside from all of the other untended business. Those were requests for major blocks of work. An Off-Broadway show, five society weddings —three of them complete ensembles from mother-of-the-bride on up, even a request from Shelley at *Fashion Alive* magazine. She was just a junior editor at the magazine, but she had a discerning eye and was looking to make her mark. She wanted to come for a visit and see a show.

Perrin took one look at the letters in Melanie's other hand and shied away toward a horrid Cyber Yellow that had nothing to do with two reds she was still holding.

Melanie took the letters back to the desk, found a folder and tucked them inside. No wonder they'd been at the bottom of the pile of unfinished business, they were scaring the woman to death.

"Come here," Melanie called her over.

Perrin came, still clutching her two pieces of red fabric and a swatch of the Cyber Yellow.

Melanie knew when a little harsh therapy was needed and pushed her into the chair. She relieved Perrin of the reds with a bit of a tug, secured the yellow with an extra sharp tug, and then put a pen in her hand.

"First, you sign these checks and pay all of your bills. Then we give the bills and the fan mail to Raquel to deal with."

Perrin nodded mechanically and began signing.

"What about the other—" the poor woman couldn't finish the sentence.

"We forget about those and I take you out to lunch."

Perrin didn't protest about the unsorted mounds of fabric awaiting her. She nodded again and worked her way through the bills.

Aubrey James paced the tables as if he were inspecting a firing squad rather than judging a cook-off at the county fair. He was a tall, spare man who walked with a pronounced stoop and clenched his hands firmly behind his back. A frock coat and a beaver top hat would have placed him comfortably in the eighteenth century where...

JOSH GLARED at his laptop's screen, "Where mystery novels go to die." It was his tenth opening just this morning and not a single one had led anywhere. At least this one had the decency to die quickly unlike the three full pages of crap he'd given to Felicity James, clearly Aubrey's evil twin sister.

He reached for his coffee, but it was long gone cold. He took a sip anyway.

Then he looked up in some shock. The restaurant which had been comfortably dark, only the soft worklight over the server's station lighting the entire space, was now vibrant with light, patrons, noise, and food. His stomach rumbled. Angelo's had filled with a lunch crowd without his consciously noticing. There were chattering tourists, small family groups for whom lunch at Angelo's was obviously a splurge—dinner being out of their reach, and many wearing Seattle-casual who were so underdressed that they were clearly labeled as being very well off.

Thinking back, he could remember hearing things. But he'd been lost in trying to grind out an opening scene to the novel. He'd been meaning to write a foodie mystery since, well, forever. So, despite the miserable openings he'd created, he'd take it as encouraging that he'd become too absorbed to be distracted by what was going on around him.

His was one of the few tables not filled with patrons. Paying patrons.

Graziella swung into the server's station to collect some menus to take back to the greeter's station.

"Ah. The writer emerges," her smile lit her beautiful Italian face. Her English had only the slightest trace of an Italian accent. She ruled the front of house with an iron hand, but she added an Italian greeting and the Mediterranean flair for warmth and an ease to her seamless service. That the girl was also drop dead gorgeous and glowed with joy anytime you mentioned her chef-husband Manuel, only added to the charming atmosphere she created.

"I guess. Is it okay that I'm—"

"Angelo has declared this table as yours. Most *patroni* paying our prices and eating our food don't want to sit so closely beside the wait staff. We usually only seat our personal guests here. You look hungry, I'll bring you a bowl of chicken skewers marinated overnight in white wine and baked with an Umbrian spice rub served over fresh-made pepper linguine."

He was too busy salivating to protest about not wanting to mooch before she whisked off to greet some new arrivals.

He was again scowling at Aubrey James to see if he was salvageable, when someone joyfully called his name and practically launched herself into his arms.

"Perrin!" he gave her a tight hug. "I'm so sorry I missed your wedding, but—"

She kissed him on the tip of his nose then snagged his left hand.

"But," she said with a sudden, soft sympathy. She rubbed her thumb over the spot where his wedding ring had been and it all slammed back in. Then, with her flawless timing, before he could once again feel all of the gloom of the world crashing down on him, she turned on one of her radiant smiles.

"If only you'd told me sooner, Josh, I wouldn't have fallen in love with Bill and his children. Our children," she corrected herself and her smile bloomed even brighter. "Then I could have been all yours as I always promised. Alas, now we're not meant to be."

Perrin had made any number of flirty passes at him over the couple of years since they'd met. Always harmless fun. She was a truly enjoyable woman, who'd have driven him nuts trying to live with that wild energy of hers.

She dropped into a chair and turned to address her companion, "But he'd be perfect for you."

That's when Josh focused beyond Perrin.

Melanie stood there: quiet, self-contained, and breathtaking. In sharp contrast to the last time he'd seen her, she was impeccably dressed. Her long hair pulled back in a tight ponytail, a designer cashmere sweater that draped down to mid-thigh captured at the waist with a wide belt of hand-tooled leather that slid down over one hip like a caress, tight slacks that had clearly been made with her legs in mind. Actually, seeing as this was Melanie—they probably had been designed specifically to be modeled by her. Leather sandals and unpainted nails finished off the delightful picture. He could feel his brain knotting up again and nothing he did seemed to fight it off.

Perrin waved Melanie to join them.

"We do no want to disturb..." Melanie's soft French was firmly in place.

"Oh, yes we do." Perrin pushed the lid of his laptop closed with a sharp snap.

"It was just as well. Aubrey James had been no more interesting than Sheldon Taylor or Percival Cummings or..." he shrugged his apathy, even if his shoulder cramped a little on the way up.

Melanie settled with a grace and poise that Perrin thoroughly lacked. But to see them sitting side by side was actually pretty surprising. Perrin's personality was always so big that it overshadowed her beauty. But side by side with Melanie, the two women could almost be sisters.

Yet there was more to Melanie than looks. She might think she was hiding behind a tall protective wall of French elegance and reserve. But Josh had heard her true accent and seen her street-fighter's stance. There was a strong and tenacious woman in there as well; such a sharp contrast to her outer mien that he had trouble crediting it. But he could see it in her eyes.

He shoved his laptop into his bag and smiled at the two of them. "I'd be thrilled if you two would join me for lunch." He'd also be the envy of every man in the room. He nearly said it aloud, would have if it had been only Perrin, for she'd have been tickled by the idea. But for Melanie, it was probably something she heard far too often, being credited only for her beauty. Well, if that was how she was perceived and treated, he would be the exception to the rule. He'd start with being real.

"I'm so sorry that I scared you last night. 'Course you scared the crap out of *me;* turnabout is fair play, I guess. So, we're kind of even on that. But are you comfortable with me there in the condo? I can find somewhere else to go if you aren't. Though I'd hate to leave that kitchen before I had a chance to try it out."

Melanie studied him and he learned something else about her in that moment. In addition to being beautiful, Melanie was smart. He could see her weighing factors, assessing him, a quick glance to Perrin as if factoring in Perrin's greeting of him.

He now knew that the model's stellar career had been no lucky coincidence of fate and fortunate genes, but rather a success engineered by a highly intelligent woman. Then she offered a smile that knocked him back in his chair, not with its force, but rather its genuine unaffected nature. In a funny way, it made the gorgeous supermodel into a beautiful woman.

"I think it will be *agréable* if you were to remain," Melanie offered and sipped at the water and ice tea that Graziella had somehow spirited to their table with none of them noticing.

He would like very much to know what factors had just been included in her decision.

HAD JOSHUA HARPER done more than a cursory appreciative look at her outfit, or had made some stupid guy comment about "having two tall blondes for lunch," Melanie would have asked him to leave the condo before nightfall.

But he hadn't.

Instead, he'd cut straight to the first thing between them. No comment about last night, no leer because he'd seen her in a state of *déshabillé* that few men ever had. And he'd offered to move out rather than asking if he could stay. Obviously a friend of both Angelo and Perrin, the latter opinion carrying a surprising amount of weight…

Melanie looked again at Perrin in surprise to see if she'd reacted, but she was still doing that cheerful, exuding-joy-at-the-whole-world thing she did so well. She was still the same woman; so whatever had shifted had been inside Melanie. Some part of her had decided to trust Perrin's instincts, beyond the world of fashion and now extending out to people.

She'd decided it would indeed be very agreeable to have Joshua Harper staying there and had told him so. And again surprised herself. It was one thing to think it, but why had she added "nice" to her statement? Perhaps he wouldn't know that *agréable* implied more than the English "agreeable."

This time it was Joshua she turned to assess. She sometimes wished that she could turn it off, step back and simply accept people, but she'd learned to choose even casual acquaintances very carefully as a survival trait. She'd done it for so long now that she could only be amazed that others didn't do the same.

Joshua leaned in to laugh at some tease by Perrin. He was handsome, with softly curling dark hair and a well-defined chin. He had an easy smile. However, just as she'd noted the first time they'd met months before, it was mostly for Perrin.

He began telling her of last night's events and Perrin was listening as if she hadn't already heard it from Melanie. Joshua did leave off the part of how scantily clad Melanie had been, but was entertaining Perrin with a description of his being sprawled at a beautiful woman's feet and facing a fearsome weapon of death as if she'd wielded a machine gun, or perhaps an entire Schwarzenegger-esque arsenal based on his embellishments.

Melanie felt a pinch as she watched him regaling Perrin. Of course Perrin was smiling at him and what was she doing? Remembering from last night that he was as tall as she was, and liking that. Assessing, calculating—gods, she'd shut it off if she could.

His story over, Perrin had asked him what he was working on.

"A novel," then Joshua had blushed.

"How's it going?" Perrin ordered a shrimp *panino* and salad. Melanie selected the same, slightly envying the lush bowl of pasta that Joshua was served. This was her carbs-allowed meal, but pasta was for splurge, not for everyday.

"It sucks!"

Melanie laughed. She didn't know why. It just came out. His clearly conflicted emotions about his book didn't stop his wry humor. She hadn't expected him to be so...unforced.

He looked at her in wonder as if she'd just sung an aria.

She was tempted to snap out "What?" but his smile had answered her laugh. So, she changed her path.

"And why, Mr. Harper, does it suck?"

"Nah," he shook his head. "Been working on it all morning and I'm sick of it. Tell me something from another world. What is amazing and new in the fashion world?"

That easily, he turned the topic away from himself. She began to feel suspicious now. Nobody was that thoughtful, were they? Or had she truly become so calloused and suspicious of everyone's ulterior motives?

Maybe—just while she was in Seattle, which wouldn't be for long anyway—she would try being a different person.

Perrin had begun discussing her new fabrics and some of the textural ideas that were sparking already for her next creations.

Melanie waited. She'd suggested lunch to get Perrin out of her workspace and ready to talk about her business. She'd dismissed the idea when Perrin had chosen to sit with Joshua. But now... He had opened a door out of kind consideration rather than talking about himself as any normal man would. She waited her moment and joined the conversation just as the salad was served with a balsamic vinaigrette on the side.

"The amazing thing, Joshua—"

"Josh."

"*Non.* I will call you Joshua."

The polite bow of his head tickled her. She always called people by their full name to keep them at a distance. With a simple gesture and smile, he had shifted it from a formality to an endearment. So simply that she couldn't help but feel charmed by him.

"The amazing thing, *Joshua,*" she smiled back despite her normal practice of reserve, "is the other requests that Perrin's Glorious Garb is receiving."

"It's just letters—" Perrin tried to cut her off.

"Society weddings, an Off-Broadway show. Next, Hollywood will come calling."

"Well, actually..." Perrin was studying her salad. "I got a couple of e-mails, but they scared me." Then she looked up. "Melanie! I can't do what I need for the shop. How can I do the rest of that?"

Before Melanie could begin to explain, Joshua rested a hand on

Perrin's arm and drew aside her attention. Melanie wanted to snap at him for interfering.

"The first question, Perrin," he withdrew his hand as the sandwiches arrived. "Is do you want to do those things? I heard you absolutely killed at the opera, but did you enjoy it?"

"Are you kidding?" Perrin waved her *panino* in the air in her sudden excitement. "The chance to build a three-hundred piece collection was fabulous. Defining the anchoring three styles and fifteen main costumes. And big weddings are just another grand story. If I could only…"

Joshua cut her off with one of his marvelous laughs; Melanie could really get to like that laugh. It made her feel cheerful, though she was irritated with his interruption.

"So, do it!" Joshua told her.

He was right. He had cut directly to the core. Did Perrin even want this? That was the key success factor and she hadn't even thought to bring it up.

Perrin stopped chewing and stared at him. Her body, normally vibrating with energy had suddenly gone still.

"How?" It was barely a whisper.

"Not a clue."

Perrin gasped, swore in a quite unladylike way, then stuck her tongue out at him.

"But," then Joshua turned those warm, dark eyes on Melanie. "I'll bet she knows."

Now it was her turn to be stunned to silence. People only ever learned the hard way that Melanie was a businesswoman first and a model second. She had studied, even paid for two night courses and private tutoring from an attorney to make sure she understood contract law well enough to negotiate her own. Her contracts were the best in the business. She'd seen the crap offered to most other models and, after soliciting Melanie's advice, they took them; which was often head-shakingly stupid, but not unusual.

But no one had ever seen that about her until they were on the wrong side of the negotiating table. With Joshua she'd shared two meals and a mutual scare and somehow he saw—

"Do you?" Perrin was asking her. That wide-eyed innocent girl shining through despite her dark past.

Melanie took a bite of her own *panino* to buy herself a moment. Oh, Angelo was so good. The taste of the simple toasted sandwich unfolded in layers. She shook off the invitation to a playful journey that the food attempted to lead her along, and shifted her attention back to the discussion of Perrin's business.

Her friend's talent, work ethic, and dedication to the craft weren't a question. She was one of the most innovative yet effective designers working today. She understood how to elevate both everyday wear and wedding wear without forcing them onto the runway. Melanie herself had worn some of Perrin's styles out on the streets of New York and simply felt fabulous, not out of place.

And she knew how to make a woman look incredible; she really understood the female form. And not just the model thin; she'd seen Rubenesque women shining in Perrin's dresses.

The demand was there as evidenced by Raquel's numbers and the folder of requests resting in Melanie's handbag. And if there were e-mails in addition to those… She began calculating assets. Russell had already done some ads for Perrin—his fashion-photography name still had immense clout in the industry. She'd need—

Melanie pulled back, would have sat back except for the years she'd spent training herself into a perfect posture. It was a fascinating puzzle, but not one she was a part of.

"Do you?" Perrin asked again in the voice of hers that none could deny.

"It's not a small project."

"I get that," suddenly the business side of Perrin was at the table as well. This was a woman Melanie had only glimpsed the once before. "Do you, Melanie, know how to do this?" This was no longer a vague question by a hopeful excited beginner. This was a fellow professional.

"No, I don't," Melanie had to be honest. She'd never taken a design house to market before.

Perrin looked deflated.

Joshua looked at her as if he didn't believe her. He even had a bit of a smile. Then he said, "But…" and left it hanging.

"But," Melanie conceded, "I do know what it would take to figure out."

CHAPTER 4

ours later, Melanie still didn't know why she'd said that. It had unnerved her enough that she hadn't rejoined Perrin at the shop. Instead she'd gone down to Elliot Bay Books at the south end of Pioneer Square, a few blocks past the condo.

As promised, it was a magnificent store; a labyrinthine collection set in interconnected lofty, bright spaces. A little wooden ramp led up to Pacific Northwest history and women's fiction. At the far end of the ramp, bookcases of age-worn wood were crammed to bursting with an excellent humor collection.

In the room beyond ranged a vast collection of science fiction, romances, mystery, and more, simply poised and awaiting their moment to leap from the shelf into a patron's hands. She found new books by two of her favorite mystery authors, and a military romantic suspense that she didn't know but promised a strong heroine. She did enjoy reading about strong women.

She and her stack of books had ended up downstairs in the coffee shop with a pot of peppermint tea and a Bing cherry biscotti—another carb, but at the moment, she needed it. It looked as if Seattle might have been founded in this very room. Age-darkened wood tables, stout but comfortable chairs, and soft lighting perfect for reading and relaxing. Just beyond lay a line of heavy wood pillars supporting the floor above, a large array of chairs and a podium for author readings; she'd need to get a schedule to see if there was anyone interesting in the next few days. And everywhere there were colorfully filled bookcases wrapping the walls and defining spaces.

This was as close to heaven as Melanie had been in a long time. She poured her tea and settled in to choose which book she would read first, and thought of Joshua.

What had the man been writing? A novel, but he'd never said more. She'd never dated a writer; truth be told, she found them a little daunting. Her five new books—she'd managed to cut herself off at five—showed the diversity that could imply. The walls around her only reinforced that there was no way to guess.

Nor could she guess how he had seen through *her* careful walls. No one saw past the supermodel. Jo had only seen the model who had loved Russell. Russell could see something of her emotions, but no matter how protective of her he was—which was quite charming as she really didn't need it, but it was so kind that she let him think so— he saw her only as a celebrity and former lover.

She and Perrin had designed a few dresses together, which had been an exciting and fascinating experience. Perrin's creativity and her own knowledge of the industry had combined to make a truly special gown for the opera's opening. Perrin had also shared Melanie's own need to leave her past behind and start clean, something they'd easily recognized in each other. It made them compatible, but even Perrin didn't see who she really was.

Only Joshua walked right past the supermodel and addressed Melanie directly. It didn't make sense, but it was the only way she could describe the feeling.

She'd created a career based upon a chance crossing of genetics and an attitude she'd always known how to control and deliver. Those were the tools of the persona that she presented the world, and the world had paid her very handsomely for that. But the money had been paid to the exterior mask, not the woman within.

Her business-side skills, those she had created from scratch through intensely hard work and painful experience. It was the business person who felt most like her because she'd earned every single bit of that knowledge on her own.

Joshua had not only seen, but complimented the second woman. No man had ever seen past her beauty, not even Russell.

Instead of settling in with her books, she slipped out the folder of Perrin's letters and read through them more carefully. It was an interesting problem. Design houses were often based upon a single person's genius. It was a matter of developing a support system that both leveraged their skills and isolated them so that they could do whatever it was they did best. The finest designers possessed some kind of synaptic connections that were as unique as her own genes.

Designers could be wildcards like Karan, eccentrics like the reclusive Zoran, or born marketers like Hilfiger. They could lead their own companies, for better or worse, or turn it over to a CEO who understood and worked with them.

It was the shoestring years that were the problem. Perrin was trying to add the occasional seamstress, but she'd need to have a great deal of preparation in place to handle the requests now spread across the bookstore table. She'd been right to be afraid of these, but the opportunity nearly sizzled in Melanie's fingers it was so hot. She could feel the potential radiating off them.

Melanie left her tea for a moment to return upstairs and purchase an attractive, leather-bound journal she'd spotted earlier by the cash register. Back to her book-lined corner downstairs, she began sketching out just what it might take for Perrin's Glorious Garb to climb the next level. Her tea was long gone cold by the time she remembered it.

JOSH HAD SPENT the afternoon doing a market run to stock the kitchen. There was nothing like it in New York City. The produce here should be on cooking shows, not sitting out for purchase. The freshness and unblemished quality was astonishing and he ended up buying far more than he needed.

What did supermodels eat anyway? Thinking of Melanie's healthy look, he'd guess that she ate less, but very high quality. She had none of the gauntness so common in her profession, so he worried less about calories and more about being nutrient dense and flavorful.

He'd begin with a minestrone soup. He wandered Pike Place Market, selecting the root vegetables he'd need, spring spinach for iron, and fresh herbs. It was crowded with jostling shoppers browsing the stalls. He bought a fresh-orange gelato that tasted of California sunshine.

And the flowers were everywhere in the Market. Spring in Seattle meant buckets of flowers. The strange weather this year had crossed late tulips and irises with early dahlias. He'd gone certifiably nuts, buying more flowers than food and then had to cart them all down the ten blocks to the condo.

He didn't know if Melanie was planning to be back for dinner or not, but he'd felt like cooking anyway. And he wanted to bring the Seattle spring indoors.

If he stuck around Seattle at all, he'd see if he could find some herb plants so that he could have them right in the kitchen. The mid-afternoon light shining in the condo's south and west windows would make a windowsill garden easy to cultivate.

He built the soup and started it simmering as quickly as he could. Then he unloaded his car, stacking his meager collection of boxes along the wall. The new finish on the old wood floor shone in the spattered sunlight just begging for a few nice accent rugs and new furniture, especially a decent writing chair. He resisted the urge to unpack his boxes into the large bookcases Angelo had placed near the kitchen, obviously for a cookbook collection now probably in his high-rise home with Jo.

For the moment, he pulled the laptop out on the dining room table, but made no new progress on the novel. His attempts to distract himself with his e-mail totally failed after deleting the few messages "congratulating" him on making the leap into the unknown. An inbox he'd never caught up with in the last decade was empty in minutes. Not a single message from Constance. He slapped the cover closed before he could ask why he was expecting one. Five years of marriage and all he'd proven was that he was even stupider about women than writing novels.

He went to check on the soup, but it didn't need anything other than more time.

He'd noticed the way Melanie had left much of the bread from her *panino* behind at lunch. She hadn't made a show of it, but it was there. So carbs were an issue, but you couldn't have minestrone without good bread. Rather than a big loaf, he'd purchased small ciabatta rolls. Also, he left out the handful of pasta that he'd normally have tossed in for Constance. Constance's mom had always done it for her little girl and it was the key ingredient of minestrone, according to his wife.

No, his ex-wife.

He had to brace himself against the counter and let his head hang while trying to remember how to breathe past the pain. It was no longer a constant companion, but it did slap him when he least expected it.

"It smells wonderful in here."

Josh almost strangled himself as a gasp for breath—far too close to a sob for his taste—jerked him upright to see Melanie relocking the door behind her. He couldn't speak as the vision floated toward him. Again, that soft, unconscious sway of hip and the natural smile.

"I…" *Get your shit together Josh!* "…didn't know if you'd be around for dinner, but I made plenty. I do have to warn you, it's disgustingly healthy."

"As long as it smells the way it tastes, I'm all in." She dropped her large, wood-handled, leather designer bag on a chair and came over to stare down into the pot and breathe in deeply, releasing it with a soft sigh.

This close, he could smell her despite the aromatic minestrone. She smelled of…*if you're going to be a writer, you can find the right word*…hope. Of glorious possibility. Simply being in her presence made him feel as if the world was a better place. Standing so close that he could easily have run his hand over her long, lovely hair, the world was filled with promise.

He stepped back, "I'm such a mess."

"You are, how?"

"I didn't mean to say that aloud."

"Too late!" She leaned back against the counter, crossed her arms comfortably and looked at him with the bluest eyes on the planet. "Give."

Evade! "First let me say: this accentless New Yorker fits you better than the French."

He shouldn't have said that. She tensed up as if he was the one now wielding the Taser.

"The slightly French supermodel is strong, foreboding, unapproachable. I can see why you chose her; she is an exceptionally formidable woman positively radiating mystique. And I can see why you left behind the…other." At least he had enough sense to not throw Paramus, New Jersey in her face.

She tensed more anyway; her arms clenched so tightly he wondered if she'd hurt herself.

"But this version of you, with the trace of Manhattan in your voice and leaning back comfortably—until I was dumb enough to start on your accent to avoid answering your question—is an equally wondrous and alarmingly attractive woman."

"Alarmingly?" She didn't sound pissed. Okay, not only pissed. Melanie also sounded intrigued, though she was keeping it off her face with that perfect control of hers suddenly clamped into place.

"Way!" was the only answer he felt safe giving before returning his attention to nursing along his soup. The silence stretched but he didn't dare look up. He took a small taste of the rich broth and decided that a little salt…no, anchovy paste would bring it to life nicely.

Speaking truth to power was said to be a very dangerous action undertaken only by the brave or the foolhardy. Well, he'd just made a total fool of himself, for what greater power was there over man than beauty? Maybe he could work that into his book somehow. Who was he kidding? If he ever managed to write one.

"Alarmingly."

He nodded at her choosing to make it a statement, but didn't look up.

"And you think that by turning my own judgment of myself on its head is going to get you out of answering my question of how are you a mess?"

This time when he glanced up, he could see the humor showing on her face.

"I had kind of hoped."

She flashed that killer smile that was never seen in any of her ads or photo spreads or runway shows, then told him he was a, "Sucker! Now give."

He laughed. He couldn't help himself. Something about her filled the world with a joy he'd forgotten existed.

"How am I such a mess?" he reframed the question.

"Yes."

"Because three months ago, on the day I first met you as a matter of fact, I had a wife who loved me, living together in a condo that we'd decorated just right for us, and a great career as a food writer. Within twenty-four hours I was well on my way to losing all three."

"I know the food reviewing part. I always read your articles and reviews first, just in case I didn't have time to read the rest of the magazine. You write beautifully."

"Okay, I'll try not to grow wings and float about the room on a sheer burst of ego."

She glanced at the heavy-beamed ceiling, then back down at him, her tone dead-flat serious. "Watch your head if you do."

MELANIE COULDN'T THINK of the last time she'd had a conversation like this with a man, or a woman. It was easy, fun. Even if Joshua had just torn off her mask by… How had he done it? By being nicely normal and making her soup.

Men bought her sumptuous meals she didn't want, hoping it would work in their favor—it never did. Men didn't cook one of her favorite comfort soups from scratch or make a show of ducking their heads just in case they did sprout wings. No one understood her humor. But someone just had. How curious.

So, he'd had a wife and a condo.

"What happened?"

"After five years together, Constance," the poor man winced at merely saying her name aloud, "discovered she was more interested in members of her own sex. It was amicable, and yet I still—" He turned away, not even pretending to fuss at the stove. He braced both hands on the sink and bowed his head, much as he'd been standing when she entered.

Melanie was unsure what to do, but she knew she couldn't stand to witness such pain and do nothing. She moved up beside him and began rubbing her palm up and down his back. There was no fat on his frame. He wasn't "built" like Russell or muscular from weight-lifting like Angelo. He was long, lean, handsome, and hurting.

"I'm okay. Sorry," he forced himself upright. "I'm fine."

"*Oui,*" she went back to her French accent hoping to elicit a small smile, but it didn't work. "You look as fine as Caesar the day his best friend stabbed him."

"No!" he faced her. "It's not like that! She—"

"Shhh…" she brushed a hand down his smooth cheek. He was trying so hard to be fair and brave no matter how it tore him up inside.

"Shhh," she stopped his next protest with her fingertips on his lips.

Quite how she came to be kissing him she would never be sure, no matter how often she thought about it. It was definitely her action to replace her fingertips with her lips, not his. And it hadn't really lasted all that long. Not really. Just long enough for Joshua to return the kiss. Just long enough for her to moan briefly as their bodies slid together like a custom fit.

She took a half step back.

Joshua didn't move to follow.

But when she went to step back farther, he reached out to stop her; just resting his fingertips on her arm, but it was enough.

"Just give me a moment."

She nodded, unable to speak.

Joshua swallowed hard, then blinked. "First, let me say thank you."

"And second?" There was a softness there she didn't often allow into her own voice, but she really wanted to know what was second.

"Well, we can never do that again."

"What?" That was about the last reaction she'd expected. What was it with the world that everyone was suddenly rejecting her? Why were—

"Wait! Stop!"

"Stop what?" She looked down at herself. She hadn't moved an inch. They still stood close enough for her to feel the heat from his body, his fingers resting so lightly on her forearm still kept her in place as if glued. Close enough to see the obvious reaction his body was having to hers. "I haven't moved."

"No, but your brain just went somewhere nasty. Here," Joshua turned down the burner under the soup and tossed a cover on the pot with an overloud clatter that made them both wince. Then he took her hand and, leading her over to the dining table, guided her into one of the chairs. Not releasing her hand, he sat in the next one after turning it to face hers.

She liked the way his hands felt. Clean, muscular. Not callused, but someone used to using his hands. He didn't crush his grip down on hers. It was the lightness of his touch that held her in place far more surely than his grasp.

"Okay," his voice was deep, husky, one she could easily melt into under different circumstances. "First—"

"You do like your lists, don't you?"

"I do. First, a kiss like that could kill a man. Way more dangerous than a Taser. You know that, right?"

She could only shake her head. He wasn't what she expected from even one sentence to the next.

"Well, it can. Damn, Melanie, that was amazing. But second, there is no way you want to waste that kind of amazing on me no matter how much I enjoyed it."

"Why not?" The man wove words around her in circles more neatly than Donatella wrapped the latest Versace fashion.

"Remember the part where I'm a mess?"

"And I'm not?"

That rocked him back in his chair. He let go of her hand, more let it slip from his grasp than actually let go. She missed the contact.

He rubbed at his eyes for a moment. "Sorry. Wow. Told you I was a mess. You hit me with a kiss like that and you expect me to remember that you aren't some fashion goddess for whom everything is perfect."

Perfect. She was so many kinds of not perfect. She was sick of men thinking that because she was "oh so stunning" and had a successful career, that somehow made everything automatically okay.

Then he slid down a little in his chair, crossing his feet under the table—rather than outside her chair as if to cage her in—and catching his thumbs in his jeans pockets with just that exact amount of casual that men made look so easy and natural. He might be a mess, but he was a damned handsome one. He assessed her with those dark eyes. She'd worked with too many intense designers and photographers to fidget, but it was the first time in a long time she'd wanted to.

"You're in Seattle. In a borrowed condo. What is the world's best model doing hiding out in Seattle?"

"I'm not hiding. And I'm not the best."

"Don't be ridiculous," he dismissed her second statement so lightly. "Yet still, you're here."

"Okay," she had to admit, "maybe it looks like I'm hiding, but I'm not." Then why was she sounding so defensive? "I'm helping Perrin."

She could see that he wasn't buying it. She could prove it, even if it wasn't technically true. Reaching into her handbag, Melanie pulled out her newly-purchased journal and dropped it into his lap, forcing him to stop looking so damn comfortable with himself in order to keep it from falling to the floor.

She went to the bath off her bedroom to let him look through her ideas. The first step away, she regretted exposing herself to him that way, but couldn't very well take it back. She had to get some space, and rinse the city off her skin with cool water. Instead, she stood staring at herself in the mirror and tried to see how he saw what he did. Melanie looked at her reflection, and only saw herself.

That was the problem.

Joshua saw the same woman she did.

JOSH FLIPPED through the two dozen pages covered in Melanie's sloppy cursive and some sketched charts that he'd have to ask her about, though two of them might have been a workload analysis. Then he went back to the first page and began reading.

Analysis of Perrin's Glorious Garb business structure and present standing in cash and orders. It was bigger than he thought, though some of the numbers were really wonky. He noticed that Melanie had returned from her bedroom and stood in her doorway looking at him still seated at the dining table studying her work.

"Did she really only have a manager and a shop clerk and herself until yesterday?"

"Day before, I helped her interview and hire two seamstresses."

"I don't know fashion, but she looks really understaffed."

"She was. Still is," Melanie admitted.

He continued reading. Growth curves, analyses... "What's a mob show? Is that like a runway event for the mafia or something?"

"A runway show can cost hundreds of thousands of dollars to stage. She doesn't have the cash for that and won't anytime soon. A mob show is hiring and dressing the models, but turning it into an informal show at the entrance of a major runway show. It gets attention, perhaps decent press if it's good—and it goes without saying that hers would be good—it can be almost as effective at a tenth the cost."

He looked at the timeline sketched out, "but not for six months?"

"You have to build a capacity so that you can address success when it occurs. To have a hit show and then not be able to deliver subsequent orders to customers…"

She trailed off at his nod.

"What?" She looked surprised that he understood.

"I was just thinking of some restaurants I reviewed. The chefs were masterful. And in the early days, I'd review them. Then they collapsed beneath their own inability to perform and maintain standards after the notoriety packed their establishment. It was pretty sad actually." He tried shifting in his seat, but couldn't find a comfortable position. Those first failures had been so horrid.

"I took more care later in my career, starting reading their financials and inspecting their kitchens before I'd write them up. I used to hurt for some of these poor guys, they finally land a visit by the Senior Editor of *Gourmet Week,* me, and cook their hearts out. What does he do? He sits them down and tries to explain why he won't write a review until they get their shit together. Not a pretty sight. I may have made Angelo cry back in the beginning."

Melanie moved into the room, slowly coming from the doorway back to the table. The sway of her hips, the smooth slide of long hair onto her shoulder, the way she looked at him…

And then all she did was sit back in the chair she'd occupied only minutes before. Something had changed, but he'd be damned if he knew what. He dug around in his head for what he'd just been talking about.

Soup?

No. He needed to check on it, but that wasn't it.

How they were both a mess?

She hadn't answered that; which was a lady's prerogative.

Perrin's Glorious Garb. Right. He tapped the pages filled with Melanie's writing.

"I can see this working, but do you think she can pull it off?"

Melanie didn't play coy or pretend; she simply shook her head.

He liked that clarity and honesty. He flipped through the pages once more, "There's got to be a way. This is solid. You did a really great job here."

He failed to notice the casual brush of fingertips that Melanie used to wipe away the tear sliding along her cheek.

"SO, WHAT ARE YOU WRITING?" Melanie had to talk about something to stop herself from getting a second bowl of the minestrone. It was beyond delicious.

"Crap. That's what I'm writing, drivel and crap. I didn't really expect anything else at the outset, so I'm not really upset." Joshua mopped up the remains of his second bowl with his roll. "I wish it wasn't quite such forced, amateurship, totally lame crap though."

"Tell me about it." Somewhere along the way the Ice Queen hadn't quite shattered, but she'd certainly been star-cracked. Actually, she knew the exact moment. It was when Joshua had read her notes and said they were "solid." She knew he was one of the most respected writers and business analysts in his field. She'd learned a lot about how to manage her own career from reading the business column he put in each issue of *Gourmet Week*: "Basting the Business."

Why did one outside validation from such a near total stranger mean so much more than the evidence of her banking and investment accounts? She didn't know why, but it did.

"I always thought a foodie mystery would be fun. Murder and food. There are so many great weapons: knives, poisons, gases, walk-in freezers... It just seemed like a fun idea. I've been thinking about it for years." He took up his third ciabatta roll and, finding nothing more to mop up, simply began eating it.

"But..." Breaking down, she took the last piece of her first roll to wipe her own bowl.

"But," Joshua shrugged. "I never thought about what plot I would write, who I would kill and who might be the murderer. So, I'm starting out pretty cold. An article I can fake.

"Because you've written four or five columns a week for the last decade," she cut him off.

"Okay, granted. I've had some practice so I know how to do that. Can't fake a novel. That's real writing."

"What if it wasn't?"

"Huh?"

She rested her chin on her fist, elbow on the table. It placed her a bit closer to him than she'd anticipated, but neither did she want to draw away.

"Well," she began, "I've watched designers become completely snarled when trying to create a 'showstopper'—a truly breakthrough dress. Perrin does it right. She surrounds herself with dozens of sketches and specific fabrics. I think that's part of the reason she has so much success. She keeps the results unimportant until it's done. She just plays."

"Unimportant?"

Melanie so enjoyed watching him thinking. Every expression was right on the surface.

"You mean just start writing and let it go where it goes?"

"*Absolument!* If the words aren't so precious, if the stakes were lower, wouldn't it be easier to write?"

He narrowed his eyes at her, "How are you so smart?"

She could only sit back and blink at him.

"No, don't stop now. You're on a roll."

Melanie went and dished up one more ladle of the soup, more to buy herself a little space for the new emotions running through her. He had cooked her dinner, but there was no *quid pro quo* that she could sense, he'd been generous and she'd accepted. She checked her internal tally sheet and still found no entry on it except gratitude. Joshua was gaining a presence in her thoughts in just an evening's time. That was disconcerting.

Returning to the table, she casually nudged her chair a few inches farther away. She needed the extra distance from this man if she had any hope of keeping her shields intact.

The extra few inches didn't feel nearly far enough.

"No! No! No!" Melanie waved her licked-clean soup spoon at him.

Josh fooled around in the kitchen cutting up a pear and some cheese for dessert.

"You start with a bang. Here, I will show you." She dug into her big purse and unearthed five novels.

"What else is in there?"

"Shut up and listen." And she began reading. It wasn't some sotto voice recitation. She read the first half dozen paragraphs of each book, giving a voice and drama to the writing. By the second one she was on her feet, by the third, she began acting out the speeches. By the fourth he'd forgotten about dessert and at the last one he was mesmerized.

Each book opened with a punch. Some character in trouble. The trouble varied. The military romantic suspense had conflict with a new commander, the mysteries with a dead body, the thriller with a car chase, and the humor book with a hilarious situation that Melanie refused to read past the first few lines.

"*Non!* What is *de la plus grande importance* isn't what they are saying. It is the punch with which they open. The first scene, the first dress in the runway show—POW!" She actually came up to him and slapped her palm against his forehead. "That is what makes the audience excited about the show, that first kick says 'just you wait.' The one at the end of the show is the showstopper, but the beginning, that is the powerful one."

Josh still didn't have the least inkling of where to start his book. But watching Melanie stride back and forth in her excitement, he definitely understood that a powerful woman had to be at the heart of the story. Because, *Damn!,* he had the perfect model for that character right in front of him.

CHAPTER 5

osh woke at his usual five a.m. Apparently being on the West Coast simply wasn't working its way into his biorhythms. He showered, and slipped out of the condo. He exchanged a wave with the now-familiar shelter cook going in the back door just as Josh passed. The bit of routine helped ground him in the quiet city, it made him feel a little more as if he belonged.

Which was a welcome change, because nothing about last night fit into any sort of a coherent reality. Normal guys didn't spend a long quiet evening chatting with a supermodel. For the life of him, he couldn't recall what they'd talked about.

Maybe his nervous system was still in overwhelm.

He'd headed up the ten blocks of the First Avenue grade and tried to get his brain working again. Every time he did, he simply thought of Melanie.

That was it. Just Melanie.

The words had been fun. She was intelligent, well-read, and had a dry sense of humor that he tripped over every time.

Her laugh. He loved her laugh.

It had lit the condo, made it warm, filled it with life.

They'd—he could do this if he focused—talked about favorite

305

books through a dessert of tea and crisp slices of New Zealand pears. Okay, he'd recovered that much. Oh, and powerful characters. Didn't the woman use a mirror and see herself clearly? She held herself under such tight and careful control with apparently no idea of how truly formidable she was.

He watched the ferry once again leaving the Seattle waterfront under the brightening sky. Right! Travel. They'd gone on to talk favorite destinations: he and Constance had vacationed in several spots that had been promoted in the backgrounds of Melanie's photo shoots. Melanie had eaten in any number of the restaurants that he'd reviewed. They were forming a nice little mutual admiration society. J&M Mutual Admiration Society. She'd suggested they needed a logo and t-shirts.

Melanie had tried to insist on cleaning the dishes, but he hadn't thought to buy rubber gloves and he wasn't letting her risk her hands.

"I'm not frail," she'd protested.

"But I know that my fingers are not worth a gazillion dollars an hour. Go on, tell me what your hands are insured for by Lloyd's of London."

He'd meant it as a joke, but when she quoted a number in the mid-seven figures he'd responded, "I am so throwing you off the clean-up detail."

And her bright laugh had wrapped around him in thanks.

Like Odysseus, he followed the siren call of coffee through the warm spring darkness still hovering over the silence about Pike Place Market. Mama Maria would assuredly have coffee and a *cornetto* ready and waiting.

Melanie had reacted strangely to him, which shouldn't surprise him, as she was running his own emotions through the blender—on the Utterly Destroy setting. She'd smile at him and his pulse would rocket upward. She'd look grateful for being let off the hook of washing dishes barehanded and he'd felt...strong? Chivalrous? Something.

Once he'd thought about it, it made perfect sense how smart she was. Even if it was unexpected at first. Careers like hers didn't happen by accident. No matter how delectable the food was, the restaurant failed if not properly run. When he learned that she was her own manager and agent and negotiated her own contracts, he knew he was in the presence of greatness.

He arrived at the back door of Angelo's faster than expected. Again it was open to the soft morning. Maria, in a pale blue dress and floral apron worked once again beneath the lone light in the darkness.

"What are you making today, Maria? It smells heavenly." He reached for a *cornetto* but she slapped his knuckles with a long wooden spoon so fast that he never saw it coming. He sucked on his knuckles; they really stung.

"What?" she turned to face him. "Is that the proper way to greet a woman? I expect at least a hug and a kiss upon the cheek before you steal any of my breakfast."

"Right. Sorry." He came around the counter and bent down to give her a hug and a European-style peck upon each cheek. He kissed her on the forehead for good measure. It was only after he did so that he felt the heat rising to his cheeks. He'd never hugged Maria before, felt he barely knew her.

"Good, boy." Maria waved him toward the coffee pot. "You're family now, you can get your own coffee." She returned to rolling out the dough, then looked up at him as he stood rooted to the ground. Maria smiled and patted his cheek with a floured hand.

He shuffled off to get his coffee. By the time he returned to the stool he'd occupied yesterday, a pair of *cornetti* were waiting on a plate. Even the walk and the strong coffee weren't enough to clear his head.

"What are you doing to me, Maria?" She'd cast some sort of strange spell over him and he couldn't shake it off.

"Me. I do nothing. You do it to yourself."

"If that's true, then I'm in real trouble."

Her laughter was bright and musical.

"I can't believe some cad married you before I came along."

"Ah," her smile turned radiant. "Hogan Stanford is the perfect man for me. Fear not, you will find the perfect woman for you."

"I did," his own bitterness mixed with the next sip of coffee and he set it down with an overloud clatter in the quiet kitchen, only barely managing to not spill it again.

"No. You may think you did, but she proved you wrong. It is clear just from looking at you that she is the one who left, more the foolish woman. The right woman does not do such a thing. Men are often foolish, but a smart woman would know what she had and keep it close."

He was tired of telling the story, of defending Constance. Even as he had the thought, he recalled Melanie's fingertips on his lips. And then her kiss. It was totally inappropriate. He didn't want a rebound relationship, especially not with Melanie because she deserved so much more than assuaging his need to be with someone again—no matter how briefly.

But—and he tried his best to ignore the feeling of disloyalty to Constance—Melanie's kiss was far more powerful than her beauty. One of them had moaned with how glorious it felt, and he still wasn't sure whether or not it was him. The sheer power of his desire to devour the woman on the spot had been so startling that it was enough to break the spell of that brief kiss, at least for that sufficient instant to allow him to step back.

"Well," Maria was staring at him with her hands resting on her hips, "that was clearly a very pleasant thought." Her smile said that she knew much more than she was saying. Well, he didn't want to hear it.

"Perhaps I should go write."

Maria returned to her preparations for the day, "If you can."

Unwilling to face that question either, he retreated to the darkened restaurant and the table that Angelo had said was his. He sat down and began setting up.

Maria followed moments later with the coffee and untouched *cornetti* that he'd forgotten to take with him. She gave him a hug from the side and kissed him on top of the head.

"Such a good boy."

He watched her walking back to the kitchen. What did she know that he didn't?

"Perrin, I need to see those e-mails," Melanie had done it. It had only taken ten minutes walking around the Belltown neighborhood before entering Perrin's Glorious Garb, but she'd found the nerve somewhere.

Perrin flapped a hand toward a stack of paper at the corner of the cutting table. "I printed them all." She had finished clearing the far end of the table and fluffed out a couple yards of royal blue. A tall pile of jewel tones stood as a protective barricade between them down the middle of the table.

Karissa and Clem glanced at her with interest, but then each noticed that the other had stopped working, so they both returned to the woman's business suit they were copying in two different sizes—a little competition was a useful thing. The suit hanging on the rack between them was a powder blue, with a thin black pinstripe that just reeked of femininity and power. The overall cut and lapels were so retro that they could well be the next "new."

Melanie turned from the enticement of closer inspection, or perhaps trying it on. She could see on the rack just how masterful she'd look in it. With a dark-charcoal blouse for daytime and the jacket open, without the blouse and the jacket buttoned in the evening —the closures high enough that even a strongly figured woman could wear it. Most clothes like this could only be worn by the most flat-chested. Perrin designed for women who had shape as well.

By the time Melanie had finished her inspection, Perrin was whacking at the royal blue with a rotary cutter. Smooth efficient slices with no pattern. Were the designs so clear in her head that she could cut them freehand, or was that only for mockup? Melanie was a little too daunted to ask, just in case Perrin really was that skilled.

Perrin was so studiously ignoring her, that Melanie knew every move she made was being closely observed.

Melanie turned to the stack of e-mails and began to read. There were many more e-mails than there had been letters, but the quality was mostly lower. She rapidly sorted aside the stupid "offers" from agents and managers who wanted to control Perrin for however much they could bleed out of her. Two she didn't simply set aside, she tore them to shreds and threw them in the garbage. She knew those scam artists and didn't want their name in Perrin's shop—what they'd done to some models they'd managed to latch onto had been horrible, career-ruining horrible.

"These two names, and I will give you a list of three more, you must delete their e-mail as soon as it arrives. They are pollutants, not people."

"What names?"

Melanie rattled them off, added another for good measure. "I will write them for you so that you do not forget."

"No need, I've got it. Thanks, I was worried about that kind of thing."

Melanie never needed to write down such things either. Her respect for Perrin's mind went up another small notch. How much had she made the same mistake about Perrin that others made about her? They saw the flighty artist and missed the sharp businesswoman so easily.

Well, she would take a lesson from Joshua and no longer underestimate Perrin. It would be difficult, Perrin's chosen self-protective persona was as polished as her own.

Back to the e-mails. The wanna-be designers were all so overeager. Some of the more professional ones had included images from their collections. On one set of images, which didn't have an attached e-mail, Perrin had made some notes down the side. The designs were interesting, but the eye was young. Perrin designed for women, but this designer sketched for teens. And did it well.

"Perrin, whose are these? If you ever want to do a youth line, you might consider hiring this designer. It would be a very fine place for beginning."

Until that moment, Perrin had been assiduously focused on cutting and pinning more of the royal blue. As soon as Melanie held up the sketches, Perrin stopped and her entire manner shifted. Her smile was huge, "Those are Tammy's."

Melanie looked at them again in awe, "I thought she was thirteen."

"Fourteen next month."

"*Merde!*"

"I stuck them in hoping you'd like them. I can't judge because I love her too much. I never imagined a step-daughter. Actually she's my daughter since I adopted her the same day Bill married me, but that freaks me out too much to really think about. She's young enough that I could have had her if I'd had her while still in high school. But a step-daughter, okay, daughter who is so skilled at design already just makes me all..." Perrin did a shimmy that might have been a lot like a firecracker about to explode.

"They are: well done, creative, age-appropriate," she ticked off on her fingers, trying not to feel as if she was channeling Joshua's passion for numbered lists. "You seriously need to consider these designs as the basis for a product line. A separate product line."

"Her own line?" Perrin tasted the idea and stared at the ceiling as she toyed with the idea.

Melanie realized just how little prepared Perrin was for what was about to happen to her; no matter how smart. That should have been an automatic next-step thought, instead it had to be given to her to think about.

Melanie went back to her sorting. Several of the e-mails were overlaps with the letters. She checked the dates; frustrated by no response to their electronic messages, they had gone to paper-based pleas. But for the most part, there were at least as many new opportunities here as in the folder. If only twenty percent of these came through, Perrin's business wasn't going to grow, it was going to skyrocket upward. Whereas her own was...

Melanie clambered off the stool and to her feet. She looked for somewhere else to sit, but realized she didn't want to sit. She didn't want to sew. She saw Perrin—still glowing from the compliment to her new daughter—leaning in to explain a particularly tricky pattern piece to Karissa and Clem.

The soft-rap tune on the radio was getting on her nerves; something about a geek in pink. Next one would be about models no one wanted to see any longer.

Out front would be no better. From here she could see customers in the front of the shop. There was so much purpose here, everyone had something to do and she...was useless.

Melanie had never been useless. More importantly, she would never again depend upon another person for her state of mind. She closed the folders, picked up her bag, and wished Perrin *À bientôt*. No one on the outside looking at her must ever know what was wrong.

Yet Perrin clearly sensed something by her surprised expression, but Melanie made it out the door before it registered fully enough for Perrin to do more than look at her oddly. A clean getaway.

That's what she had to do. She had to get away. She didn't belong here. She belonged in... She didn't even know where the swimsuit shoot was this year. That was insider-only knowledge, and for eight straight years she'd been in the know.

Well, the magazines weren't going to control her mind either. Her mother had done her best to twist and control Melanie's mind, as well as Melanie's body to her own ends. That too was done. So, perfectly in control—calm, collected, and throwing a walk that made men stop and stare—she strode past the shops of Belltown and then headed south.

It was late morning. Hole-in-the-wall restaurants were blocking as much of the sidewalk as they dared with small steel tables and artfully rusting chairs throwing off her purposeful stride. Little boutiques were displaying wares not half the quality of Perrin's. These were shops she might have normally browsed, but it would be a pointless waste.

When she reached Pike Place Market it meant she was a third of the way back to the condo. She would pack, find a flight, and go home. Hopefully she would get there before the wave of depression crushed down on her and left her unpresentable to friends and fodder for her worst enemies, the paparazzi. With a single unguarded moment, they could capture and damage a career, even one like hers.

And news of the swimsuit issue loss would be out by now. Add that into…

She stopped. She couldn't breathe. Bending over to rest her hands on her knees, her hair almost brushing the dirty cobbles, didn't help. All she could see was the cobblestones. No air. She leaned against a handy wall until her head stopped spinning enough for her to think. To recognize where she was so that she could continue on her way. She was in front of…

Angelo's?

She'd been headed to the condo; straight down First Avenue. How had she ended up in the heart of Pike Place Market? Granted it was only a block aside from her escape route… Oh. Some part of her that was still functioning knew she should say *merci* to Maria and *au revoir* to Joshua. He hadn't been at the condo when she woke, so maybe he was here writing.

JOSH LOOKED up from the pit of despair into the warm sunshine of hope. The transition was a shock to both his brain and his libido. If yesterday his writing had been crap, this morning he had crawled into the outhouse, then ducked down the hole for a long swim.

He took a moment to appreciate the wonder that was Melanie. Her casual wear could shame, well, any supermodel that wasn't her and all mere mortals. Rumpled leather cavalier boots to mid-calf, skinny jeans that showed the advantage of perfect legs even when hidden away, a sunshine yellow blouse whose loose form didn't reveal, but a sharp leather vest that suggested very strongly. And those eyes. Cornflower blue offset against her light golden hair.

"I'm leaving."

"Thank god."

She looked at him quizzically.

"I think Mama Maria put a special hex on me. If yesterday was crap, today is completely unmentionable in decent company." He slapped his laptop in his bag and rose to his feet.

It was only when he was standing eye to eye with her that he saw the stiffly square set of her shoulders, the grim determination in her look. He knew that look. Head down and striding straight into a headwind come hell or damnation. It was the only way he'd survived the last three months.

Her words finally registered. She was leaving? Like leaving Seattle? *Nope. Not no way. Not no how.* He didn't know why the voice in his head was so vehement on that point, but it was.

"Uh huh. Leaving? Good. Let's go." Purposely misunderstanding her. He offered his arm, and when she hesitated, he took her hand and tucked it into his elbow simply because he wanted to. She left it there as he guided her out of the restaurant. He liked the sense of connection.

She seemed almost nerveless, even ethereal as he led her down the rough brick of Post Alley. The late morning crowd of tourists swirled about them. The piano guy had his little roll-around upright piano on a street corner and was knocking out a very creditable version of Joplin's *The Entertainer.* Josh tossed his spare change in the busker's bucket; he didn't want to risk dislodging Melanie's hand to reach for his wallet.

In silence he led her deeper into the Market. He'd expected her to unravel at least a little bit as they moseyed past the overflowing flower stands, but their lush scents and brilliant sprays of color didn't touch her.

So, keeping them in pace with the slow-moving crowd—but not stopping to admire the sights—they were soon clear of the flower, produce, and artisanal sausage merchants. They bypassed the pasta stall with over thirty flavors of pasta from chocolate to strawberry to —he had to glance over his shoulder to be sure of the last—licorice. He made a note to try that someday, perhaps paired with honeyed peaches for a dessert—the black pasta and golden fruit making an interesting contrast. Down the stairs by the tea merchant, they passed the parrot store and a bagel shop.

It only took a few minutes before he had led her under the viaduct highway, across Alaskan Way, and out onto the vacant Pier 62. All of the other piers along Seattle's deep waterfront were filled with tourist or commerce activities: restaurants, giant Ferris wheel, ferry terminal, the Seattle Aquarium. For some reason this pier and the adjoining one created a couple of acres of unoccupied rough wood planking. A few people wandered the open expanse, but it was actually a very private place right at the heart of the Northwest's largest city.

He led her out to the far corner of the pier. Behind them the city soared and bustled. Ahead of them the dark blue waters of Elliot Bay were dotted with green-trimmed white ferries, container ships headed for the big orange port cranes to the left, a couple of sailboats skimming along under the light breeze. A massive cruise ship was just pulling away from the next pier to the north. The city proper was bordered to the south and north by house-dappled hills, straight ahead the snow-capped peaks of the Olympic Mountains were so bright in the sun that it was hard to look at them.

Melanie remained beside him, unmoving, unspeaking.

Josh bided his time, letting the soothing breeze—pleasantly cool off the water on a calm day—wash over them. When he turned at last to face her, because he couldn't stand not seeing her a moment longer, she looked a little calmer.

"Okay, Ms. Secretly-I'm-a-mess-no-matter-how-incredibly-I-present-myself-to-the-world. What happened?"

In answer, Melanie simply turned into his arms and lay her head on his shoulder. She clung to him as if he were the Rock of Gibraltar rather than a lost soul himself. Well, if she needed him to be strong, he would be.

His arms naturally slid around her and he came to appreciate so many things at once. Slender yet strong, hair even softer than it looked, just meant to be stroked gently, and he was right the first time —she absolutely smelled of hope, hope and summertime.

MELANIE COULD FEEL the day brightening, one tiny bit at a time. She knew she was being irrational, knew her past wasn't really a vicious bounty hunter seeking to repossess her soul; it only felt that way. Except it didn't feel that way with Joshua.

From the moment she'd taken his arm, it was as if all her willpower was gone. Her panic-level desperation to run, to get somewhere safe, had simply drained away. When she was losing control, he had simply taken it. Then he'd led her here where the people didn't press about her so.

She had meant to give him a brief hug of thanks, but her body had other ideas and she'd clung to him like a lover, never wanting to move again. His arms were strong, solid. His shoulder perfect to lean her cheek on. Right at the base of his neck was a place she could go to hide for a long, long time. Not even to hide. She could almost…what? Be content here?

His skin was warm against her nose and forehead. His soft dark hair, which needed a trim soon, tickled her temple. Her nose couldn't place him except to say, "male." Joshua exuded "strong male" as if it were a new designer fragrance. So, instead of a brief hug or a tentative embrace, she simply allowed herself to appreciate the soft stroke of his hands down her back. To enjoy the moment.

Before she was ready, his chest rumbled with the repeated voicing of his question. How was she supposed to know what happened? She'd simply needed get away before the world collapsed on her head.

Her desire to leave her momentary haven was non-existent, but Joshua kissed her atop her head and then pushed her back a half pace to study her, keeping his hands on her waist. She wanted to imagine that her shields were up, but knowing that he always saw straight through them, she stopped trying.

"Well, whatever it was…" he continued as he studied her.

She could still feel the deep rumble of his voice where she'd left a hand resting on his chest.

"I'm guessing that you've given yourself a pretty thorough scare. I find it hard to imagine you being scared of anything, but that's my guess."

"Will you cut that out!"

His grin told her that he knew exactly what she meant and the answer was: no, he wouldn't. "Bugs you, huh?"

"No one sees past my shields."

"Superman and me, we're tight. Drinking buddies, you know."

She didn't know whether to smile or poke him sharply in the solar plexus, so she did both eliciting a satisfying whoosh though she hadn't hit him hard enough to do more.

He took his hands from her waist to rub at his chest and looked at her in surprise.

"You better just keep your x-ray vision to yourself. You start looking through my vest and I really will Taser you but good."

"Yes, ma'am. I can't speak for my imagination, but I can promise on my x-ray vision. It's very limited in such cases."

"What is it with men and their imagination? Women spend very little time mentally undressing men."

"Damn and I had such hopes."

Melanie, having said that and having returned her hand to the center of his chest in apology for striking him, now found that she could imagine Joshua unclothed. As a matter of fact, it was disconcertingly easy to do so.

"Distract me," the request sort of blurted out of her.

Joshua looked her right in eyes for a long moment, appeared to be on verge of suggesting a sure-fire distraction that would earn him a truly sharp punch in the solar plexus; a Taser was not the only element of her self-defense training. But rather than speaking his thought, his eyes slid aside and studied the world around them. Something across the water had him narrowing his eyes for a moment.

"How's your blood sugar?"

Not, "are you hungry?" It was a more personal question of whether her current chaos of emotions was due to low blood sugar. In the body condition she maintained, blood sugar was at times a delicate balance. She tested her own feelings. Nope, that had been genuine panic.

"I'm fine for the moment," she told him.

"Excellent, c'mon," he brightened like a little boy. "Got a treat for you if you have the afternoon free and don't mind spending it with me." Once again Joshua offered his arm. This time she was glad to take it, enjoyed the connection through the light cloth of his button-down shirt, just open enough at the throat to hint at the strength she'd felt there.

He led her south along the waterfront until they reached the big ferry terminal. She was always amazed at how many of the big white and forest-green ferries there were, shuttling back and forth from the Seattle waterfront. Of course with the island-cluttered Puget Sound nearly chopping the state in half from north to south, it made sense.

"I reviewed this great little place over on Bainbridge Island a couple of years back. Perfect for lunch."

When the boat arrived, he guided her not to the bow of the boat pointing out to the Sound, but to the stern of the passenger deck several stories above where the cars loaded. Most people passed into the main cabin through the big doors heavy enough to keep even the nastiest storms at bay. She and Joshua stood in the late morning sunlight at the rearmost point and watched the loading process. A small fleet of bicycles and motorcycles zoomed aboard, then a long stream of cars, shuttled off to the correct spots for the crossing by orange-clad ferry workers.

A glance up revealed the city, close and looming above them. The massive double-tiered roadway of the Alaskan Way Viaduct, so crowded with cars and trucks, as if they were trying to use it as much as possible before it was replaced by the new tunnel being bored beneath the waterfront. Skyscrapers capped it off, made far taller than they actually were by the steep hill climbing up through the city.

"They all look so intent, don't they?" Joshua's words drew her attention back to the loading. "Even the ones too out of their element to follow the ferry loader's instructions; all in such a hurry to arrive."

Without Joshua's words, it would have been no more than a stream of cars, but it was more. She began to see and appreciate the scene, but her interest paled soon enough. There was a sameness to all of that focused intent and she found it exhausting to witness.

"Let's go explore." The ferry was huge, holding a couple hundred cars in the lower two decks and at least two thousand passengers in the two upper decks.

"They're almost done," he assured her. "There's something I want you to see."

So she waited, rubbing shoulders with Joshua and waiting for the world to finish and get on with it. After the last car, there was a lot of very coordinated activity: stringing up ropes and safety nets, hand signals with some shore-side worker, raising of ramps. A glance at Joshua, but no, that isn't what he was waiting for. He remained still, quiet, a calm center.

She did her best to emulate him.

The ferry engine's roared to life with a deep rumble that shook the steel decking.

"Here," Joshua was leaning on the fresh-painted dark-green railing staring intently down.

Melanie followed his gaze. The ferry slowly dragged itself from beneath the overhanging ramp, and then she spotted a narrow gap of water. With a bellowing blast of its horn, loud enough to hurt her ears and big enough to claim the ferry's right of passage out into the waters, the boat began gathering speed. The propellers kicked up a massive swirl of aerated water, temporarily disrupting the Sound's dark blue.

And then she felt it like a breath of fresh air. As hypnotized as the proverbial deer in the headlights, she was mesmerized by the spectacle of Seattle slipping away from them. It was a visceral rush that coursed through her body as if they were leaving the world behind. *Parfait!* Absolutely perfect!

"This must what it's like to go into space," Joshua's voice mixed with the engine's deep rumble.

It truly felt as if she was leaving the planet. There was a heady sense of liberation. Any worries or memories she'd been having were now back there on the land. And with each passing second, this great steel behemoth of a boat was taking them farther and farther away, out of trouble's easy clutches. She felt light, free.

Melanie took Joshua's face in her hands and kissed him, really kissed him. Not that intriguing brush of lips in the condo last night. This was a toe-curling kiss and his need was no less than hers. But what had started as a first burst of joy, grew deeper, gentler, but more intent. She was soon wondering just what the other men she'd kissed in her life had been up to, because this was like none of them.

Finally Joshua pulled her into a hug too close to kiss. They simply wrapped their arms around each other, leaned their cheeks together, and held on.

He whispered in her ear, "I was right. Your kiss. One hundred percent lethal."

"Guess we've died and gone to heaven."

"If it isn't, don't tell me, because I don't want to know." Then he took her hand in his before turning to look at the boat. "Now we should go explore."

CHAPTER 6

They wandered about the ferry from one end to the other. Josh led Melanie up into the wind of the mostly open upper deck where her hair streamed behind her like a great banner, dancing in the brisk wind. He pointed out the Alki lighthouse perched at Seattle's westernmost point with Mount Rainier soaring skyward as a glorious backdrop and joked that they were beyond anyone finding them now.

"Free at last. Free at last. Thank God almighty, we're free at last!" he shouted to the shining sky as Melanie sparkled the air with her laughter. She made him feel a dozen feet tall.

As if her kiss hadn't already done that.

For just this afternoon, for just this moment, he would allow himself to simply enjoy the company of a gorgeous and fascinating woman. He wouldn't be Mr. Food Writer. Nor would he permit Mr. Divorced Loser in either. Not even Mr. Wanna-be-novelist who kept writing drivel.

He'd be simply Josh, who had just received a life-changing kiss that simply couldn't be real. No one gave of themselves the way Melanie had just given to him. If he didn't know he was on the rebound, he could start thinking some pretty amazing thoughts about the woman who had yet to relinquish his hand.

For their arrival at Bainbridge Island, he led her to the very bow of the boat in time to be at the forefront of the crowd. That gave them prime viewing space along the front rail as the boat cruised into Eagle Harbor and snuggled up to the ferry dock.

"I only had an hour to explore this town when I was here. Bainbridge Island, both the town and the island are actually called B. I., has a lot of money. High-end rural but within commuting range to Seattle. So there's a lot of tasty eating and shopping here."

They wandered the streets, actually the street. Most of Bainbridge was on a single street a few blocks long. They stopped at a wine store, where Josh was talked into a local loganberry wine. Then the shop owner went on to sell him a local artisanal blue cheese to go with it for a dessert.

"Wine and food shops are as dangerous to me as hardware stores to most guys. Just," he made a point of opening the shopping bag once they were out of sight of the shop and looking down in overdramatic disbelief. "Just stop me if I ever do that again."

"Deal. If you'll…" Melanie came to a halt beside him and looked in a bookstore window. "You can't let me go in there."

Melanie didn't look the least bit like a bookworm, but her near lust for the bookshop was impossible to mistake. Then he recalled that she'd hauled five novels out of her handbag last night, one still sporting the charge slip. He held the door for her and shooed her inside.

"Hey!"

"I can't be the only weak-fish on this outing. Go find a book."

She did come away with a book on Northwest weavings. But he ended up being the big spender with two new thrillers, a mystery, and four books on the history of Seattle.

"Okay, we just have to get off this street," he complained when they were back in the sunlight. "How's the peckishness level?"

"Rising. I saw that cute diner by the ferry."

"The Streamliner. Yep, they're tasty. I have their cookbook too. I'm going to do you one better."

MELANIE STARED at the bright blue sign on a stainless steel diner two blocks off the main drag.

"The Madison Diner, founded in 1953? This looks like the sort of *dîneur* that hasn't changed the grease in its fryers *since* 1953," she teased him, though it did smell splendid; comfort-food smells wafted through the doors so thickly she could taste them on the air.

She wore her French accent in public like a second skin. It kept people at a distance, though Joshua simply ignored such barriers and continued to treat her the same. She was having a terrible time this afternoon remaining focused on any one thing that wasn't Joshua. She turned firmly away to inspect their diner.

It did look as if it had been teleported right out of the fifties. Stainless steel as far as the eye could see with metallic blue panels. The roof and building corners were all rounded. Once inside, she wasn't the least surprised to find round steel stools along the counter with red leatherette padding. Small booths that really were perfect for shooting greaser movies.

It all looked...cozy.

For an instant, the outside world was juxtaposed. Perrin's beautiful and quirky store was also a 1950s diner motif. Take away the tables and the cook line, replace the chattering tourists with fashion-forward mannequins... She shoved the image aside hard. She didn't want to think about the real world. She wanted to remain here, in the present, with Joshua.

Melanie closed her eyes for a moment and breathed in deeply. It smelled heavenly. Not as heavenly as Josh, but enough to make her stomach rumble a little. The waitress, a pretty brunette, obviously recognized Melanie but made no big deal of it which was a surprising change from the standard.

Soon they were tucked in their own booth, he with a fresh-squeezed lemonade and her with ice tea.

"Let me guess," Joshua was using the little-bit-too-full-of-himself teasing tone of his, "a bowl of soup or a salad."

"*Non.* With such a menu, there are too many choices. But I see one something, so there is only one choice for me." He made many guesses, but none were even close. "You however, would appear to be a mushroom Swiss cheese burger guy. Extra fries."

"Nailed."

He snorted with laughter when she ordered the Blazing Buffalo Chicken Burger marinated in Buffalo chicken-wing hot sauce, with no bun but an extra side of hot sauce.

"I may have to eat French and *une très petite portion* when the reporters find me, but I think we are sufficiently far from any reporters here."

"Don't know. The *Bainbridge Island Review* could be desperate for a front page story. They're sending some poor stringer this very moment to interview the most beautiful woman to ever mosey through their shops."

She ignored him. Well, not entirely. The booths weren't designed with two people six-feet tall in mind. Their knees kept bumping as Joshua decently tried to move his aside. She finally leaned her knee against his and left it there. Not as connected as holding hands, but far more welcome than unwelcome.

She'd never been one to hold hands. Melanie had deigned to parade on many a man's arm, though rarely with any of the benefits that the paparazzi always assumed. This was the first moment all day that she'd thought about her hands. They were one of her highest paid features and she protected them assiduously. Her first million had been made on her hands alone.

Even as she surreptitiously inspected them, she knew that she would hold hands with Joshua again if he offered the opportunity, despite the risk of an unsightly stretch or crease.

"So, are you ready yet to talk about what freaked you out this morning?"

"*Non!*" But he'd surprised her. She gently tested her emotional state. No sign of the looming depression that had her scurrying back to New York. Instead, she had been quite enjoying herself. Was still enjoying herself.

"If you don't, it's just going to lie in there and fester."

"That does not sound so enjoyable, does it?"

"*Non!*" he replied clearly to tease her again about her chosen accent.

"Crap!" She gave it full Jersey-twang which earned her the laugh she'd been hoping for. It also made her feel just kindly enough toward him to begin the story of the last week.

"THEY DROPPED you from the swimsuit issue? Damn it! I always looked forward to—" Josh tried to stop his mouth, but it was a moment too late.

Melanie lowered her fork slowly back to her plate of half-finished chicken burger. If he didn't stop the ice shield descending like a cloak from above before it covered her, Melanie would be as surely gone as if she'd run straight to the airport.

"Wow! Did that ever come out wrong or what?"

"*Oui!*" Her accent was back in full force.

"Don't I get one screw-up? You admitted to ogling my restaurant reviews."

"*Mon dieu!* 'Ogling' is not the operative word and you know it." She was carefully dabbing her mouth with her napkin; her eyes no longer focused on him, instead inspecting the cook line as if the fry cook who clearly sampled too much of his own wares was suddenly of greatest interest. Soon her knee would no longer be against his and he'd be a goner.

"Hey, if I can't admire your art, why is it okay for you to admire mine?"

"Because, it was not my art you were admiring."

Josh saw his one thin chance of recovery and leapt for it like a man drowning.

"But it is."

The cloak's descent paused, but it had already covered her perfectly still hands.

He took a bite of his burger to appear casual, but didn't taste it. With a single phrase, he'd become just like every rutting goat out there. Which he really wasn't. The chance to see that much beauty in one place had always stunned him. There was something else…but he couldn't quite put his finger on it.

"How is it my art?"

"You have studied how to place yourself, how to present yourself in such a way that you create an emotion. Lust in some. In others, and I like to think I'm one, it creates a deep appreciation for the beautiful, the powerful, and—" The thought that had skittered aside moments before crashed back in on him and he stopped, unable to continue, unable to think. If he didn't swallow soon, he'd choke and he couldn't manage even that except by great conscious effort.

"It creates what?"

He looked up at Melanie and tried to make sense of her question, but he couldn't.

"It creates—" she must have finally noticed his shock.

Josh knew the shock was there. He could feel it. A wall that momentarily locked him safely away from the worst of his own emotional storm.

"Joshua?" Melanie had dropped her accent and reached her hand tentatively toward his arm.

He shook his head. "I never bought a single swimsuit issue. I saw them. Enjoyed them. Enjoyed you in them. But I didn't buy them." His voice sounded so neutral, so perfectly normal.

"I don't understand."

"Neither did I." His ex-wife was the one who'd always bought them, year after year.

"So," Josh leaned back on the bow railing of the ferry. They had their own little section of the foredeck to themselves. Slouching back, facing away from the view, provided him the perfect position to watch Melanie as she watched the approaching city.

She'd caught her hair back in some intricate French braid that appeared effortless to create and was exotically beautiful to look at. But from his vantage, what it did was keep her hair—as much as he liked it down—clear of her face. Her emotions were so visible against those fine features, it was incredibly intimate.

Especially after talking through his marriage and divorce in such excruciating detail. That she still looked on him at all was a wonder.

And he liked that intimacy, ignoring that it couldn't last once they were ashore. For once they landed, she would again be the world's most sought after supermodel—one blip did not destroy a career like hers no matter what she thought—and he would continue to be an unholy mess who couldn't write.

"So," he started again, hoping he could recover his train of thought when faced with such breathtaking beauty. "You never did explain what upset you this morning."

"*Non,* I did not explain such a thing and now I shall not, not to such a cur."

"Why am I a cur now?"

"Because you did not buy your own issue of the magazine. If you had, instead of mooching your wife's copy, I might still have been in this year's issue. *Tant pis!*"

"Say what?"

" 'Too bad!' Loser."

"Can't win for losing."

"Precisely. And you, my tall and handsome *chien,* have lost this round."

"At least you didn't call me *chienne.*" Being called a bitch was never his first choice.

"You may be a dog, Joshua, but you are definitely a very male one."

He could spar words with her forever, she made it so much fun.

Though he'd definitely need to work on his high school French if they were going to spar in two languages.

A glance over his shoulder showed the half hour crossing was about fifteen minutes gone.

"Okay. From here to the shore is a quarter hour. If you answer the question, I promise I won't ask again."

"Ever?"

"At least not for tonight. Best offer I've got."

She grimaced and turned her back on him, leaving him to admire other features of her. With her hair back in its thick braid, the line of her neck was revealed. A trim waist his hands actually ached to touch again. And her curves continued not as emaciated waif, but rather as elegantly feminine.

He was about to do something to let her off the hook when she spoke, it was soft enough he had to start forward to hear it over the brisk wind and the rumble of the ferry's engines.

"I was sitting with Perrin. And I knew what to do. I knew what she would need to be a huge success rather than be closed within a year without knowing what hit her. There is no third path, no safe middle ground. Her talent will have too much impact."

"Wonderful. Take the high road," he spoke over her shoulder because she didn't turn and he didn't dare touch her.

"You don't understand, Joshua. I said that *I* knew what to do. She doesn't. She couldn't; not even if I were to explain it all. And she wouldn't want to. But I could."

Josh waited. They were so close. He knew the shore was sliding near, but he didn't look away; couldn't risk her changing the topic.

"But I don't know this woman, the one who thinks she knows what it would take to launch Perrin. I know the model. Her I invented. Her I know how to control. I don't know this other person. I don't know her any better than..."

She didn't need to finish the sentence.

He knew that the person she didn't know was the one that was sweeping him off his feet—the one that was Melanie and not the model and business superwoman. He took her gently by the shoulders and turned her to face him. There were tears starting from her eyes.

"Melanie."

She nodded uncertainly.

He kissed her.

She kissed him back, but there wasn't any heat behind it, nor did he expect any. "What was that for?"

"Because I wanted to."

She scowled at him through her silent tears. He brushed them aside with gentle strokes of his thumb.

"Melanie."

"Kiss me again and I just might get around to actually Tasering you."

"You are the most magnificent, powerful, exceptional woman I've ever met. The mere idea that you could lose yourself while you're doing something you love is laughable. It's so laughable and fallible that it takes you down from the ridiculously high pedestal you live on and makes you momentarily accessible to us mere mortals. When you're down here, I get to kiss you."

"So," Melanie blinked into the wind. "You're saying I have to keep screwing up to get a kiss."

"It's one way."

MELANIE COULD SEE the shore fast approaching, the Seattle skyline once again towering above them.

Melanie was no closer to making a decision about how to help Perrin. Working for her temporarily wouldn't be enough. Stepping in and making sure Perrin was a success would be throwing away a career that Melanie had spent two decades building, and she wasn't about to do that.

She did know one thing though.

So she threw herself at Joshua and drove him back against the thankfully stout railing hard enough for him to grunt. And then she wrapped her arms around his neck and kissed him the best she knew how.

Kissed him until the madness in her head quieted enough for her to relish the heat and the power of this man in her arms.

Kissed him until she no longer feared she'd shatter and be dispersed to the four winds. Until she felt totally present and there was only the here and now and their shared need for each other.

It was heady, breathtaking, and it left her torn between singing and laughter, both of which she only rarely did, and then did it alone —until Joshua had pulled the laughter out of her and into the open.

Her singing? She'd keep that in the shower.

CHAPTER 7

s they were walking off the ferry, discussing dinner ideas, Melanie's phone buzzed with a message. It was the first call in days and she scrabbled for it. Perhaps one of the models on the swimsuit shoot had broken a nail—she'd seen beginners panic for less —or had been eaten by a shark—she could always hope.

But the text showed a local number.

Meet us at 5- the Fabulous Five

It was four thirty now. And she knew exactly who the four were and where they were meeting, the fifth puzzled her. She slowed to a halt at the top of the exit gangway where commuters were queuing up to board the ferry back to their island homes.

All of the surety she'd felt moments before evaporated. Joshua noticed, of course. They were so in tune that their bodies practically hummed in harmony. Maybe she'd let a little of her singing out of the shower. Was Josh down with Tunstall or B.o.B,? Maybe he was more of a Taylor Swift-Carrie Underwood cute blond country-singer sort.

Gods she was losing her mind.

"Kiss me."

331

He only hesitated a moment. She thought something dark wandered across his thoughts, but it was gone by the time their lips met. The kiss grounded her but did little for her suddenly jittery stomach.

"*Merci.* I think that you are on your own for dinner tonight, *mon ami* Joshua."

"Good news, my friend?" he nodded down to the phone she still clutched like a baseball ready to pitch across a mound or a plate or wherever they pitched such things.

"*Je ne sais pas.*"

"No idea? Do you want me to go with you?"

"*Non.* Go write, find Russell, something like that."

She turned to go but he stopped her with strong hands until she looked at him.

"Are you sure you will be okay?" The warmth and care... She wasn't used to it. It was always just a ploy... By anyone, except for Joshua. How many more things would she think, "except for Joshua?"

"No," might as well be honest. "I'm not at all sure. But you tell me that I am invincible, *oui?*"

"Damn straight!" he sounded far more assured than she felt.

"Then I shall simply go and be *incroyable!*"

"Of course you will. You already are incredible." Then he swept her into a kiss that had her winding her arms and a leg about him and holding on to her newly discovered personal anchor.

The round of applause they received from the outbound commuters did little to boost her certainty, other than knowing she too had to go.

<hr>

"Russell, dude. Rescue me." *From myself!* Josh thought loudly. *I'm head over heels with a woman totally out of my league.*

"Hey, that you, Josh?" Russell answered over the phone.

When Josh admitted that it was.

"I really need a high-octane distraction."

"How about a high proof one?" Russell gave him directions to his place. He'd never been to Russell and Cassidy's condo just a few blocks north of the Market in Belltown, but it was easy enough to find.

When he arrived, Russell let him in and pointed toward the kitchen. "Grab a beer or something. We're out on the deck."

Josh dropped his and Melanie's shopping bags by the door, one of hers was bright pink and clearly from a dress shop.

"Thinking of walking the other side?" Then Russell grimaced. "Sorry, forgot. Your ex. Not funny. Just come on through."

Josh found the fridge had two really smashing whites and he'd bet the cupboard had an exceptional red or twelve. Cassidy's reputation as a wine entrepreneur was starting to surpass her reputation as one of the nation's leading food-and-wine critics. Though they'd been friends for years, she still humbled the hell out of him. He took a Heineken.

The condo boasted such an amazing view out the window, over a dozen stories up right on top of the hill overlooking the waterfront, that he didn't notice the apartment at first.

There was their ferry, already headed back across the water.

"Did that really happen?" he asked the empty living room.

The condo didn't answer.

If he were in any condition to judge, he'd say that he'd just had the best date of his life, but he knew he was still awash in the aftereffects of Melanie's final embrace and did his best to push the thought aside. He could still feel her kiss burning on his lips.

He was in so much trouble here.

When he finally focused back on the condo, it was almost a comedy. Clearly, it had been purchased and decorated by Cassidy. Her taste was elegant and understated: pale greens and soft golds set on a base of white carpet. Except for a big, dark-blue recliner with a stack of books spilling off the table beside it. A very high-end camera dangled precariously from the edge of a low shelf.

Apparently the neck strap was too enticing for a small black cat with a ridiculous amount of hair for such a pristine apartment, who was deeply snarled in the strap in a fight to the death. Josh managed to nudge the camera back to safety without strangling the cat.

Art covered the walls. Most of it was clearly Russell's photography, except for a line of small photos over the couch. A dozen pictures of sailboats and lighthouses. The last picture was of the two of them getting married at the Mukilteo Light. Josh remembered that; it had been a hell of a party. He'd gone with Constance and… Crap!

He shoved the memory aside and moved quickly out onto the balcony. There was a set of iron chairs and small side tables. Enough room for four guys to sit comfortably and watch the busy waterfront like gods on high. It was bright, the sun was shifting west, though still a ways from setting. He kept his sunglasses on.

There were two other guys there. He didn't know them, though one looked vaguely familiar.

"Angelo's cooking tonight. This one's Bill Cullen, Perrin's other half," Russell waved a hand at a man to match Josh's six feet, but he was a big-boned guy without an ounce of fat. Josh wouldn't want to wrestle him. A tall, lean, older man—more patrician—was introduced as, "Hogan Stanford who is still trying to prove he's worthy of Mama Maria."

"Six months since we were married, Russell. You have to let a fellow sailor into safe harbor sometime."

"No, I don't." By Russell's smug and relaxed attitude it was clear that he long since had. "Marrying Mama Maria is not a get into jail free card."

"A cell I plan to stay in forever."

"Good thing," Russell drank his beer, "or Angelo and I will have to kill you."

"C'mon man." Bill tossed in his own two cents. "You think Maria would leave even a tiny piece of him for us to kill off? Wouldn't happen. That woman is scary. She threatened me about treating Perrin right the first time we met. Actually threatened me." He shivered as if a chill had just washed over his soul.

"She made me breakfast the first time we met," Hogan looked immensely pleased.

Russell covered his ears, "Na-na-na-na. Don't want to be hearing that shit, man. Can't believe that Mama Maria slept with you on your first date. Just not right. Na-na-na-na."

By Hogan's grin, Josh could see that there was a web of half-truths that the man had been feeding Russell for some time, and would probably get away with continuing for some time more. That's when he figured out why Hogan was familiar.

"You're the shelter cook. Down in Pioneer Square."

"I am. Volunteer there five days a week. Why—oh, you're the early riser in Maria's building." Then Josh saw Hogan aim a wicked smile at Russell while he was looking out at the water. "Yep! I know that building well. Maria and I—"

Russell again covered his ears, "Na-na-na-na. Shit, Josh, don't encourage the man. To hear him tell it, they probably had sex on the kitchen floor. He and Mama Maria. Just such a bad image."

Hogan's suddenly soft smile indicated that may have just been the first fact Russell had gotten right.

Josh could get to like this. He settled into a chair between Russell and Hogan. This was exactly what he needed. A night with the boys to get his libido back in check.

Then Bill leaned forward to look at him around Russell, "I'd be careful, Josh. I hear Russell is even more protective of Melanie than he was of Maria."

"Sure," Russell nodded. "Melanie needs more protecting than Maria. But what does she have to do with this?" He went to take a drag on his beer.

Bill's smile was wicked, "Perrin says that Melanie and Josh here are shacking up together in Angelo and Maria's condo."

What the hell? Josh had never met him before and he was getting thrown under the bus by the man?

Russell choked on his beer, hacking and sending spray everywhere —over his jeans, even dribbling down his chin. "You what?!" he thundered loud enough to be heard on the ferry now halfway across the Sound.

Josh wondered if he was about to die from a dozen-story fall.

Hogan tapped his beer bottle against the one Joshua had yet to raise to his lips, then leaned in and whispered as Russell continued to splutter, "Welcome to the club, my boy."

MELANIE ARRIVED at Cutters Crabhouse with her heart still skipping every third beat. She should have brought Joshua for support, but that wouldn't be appropriate. Besides, since when did Melanie need someone else's support? Still, a part of her admitted, his little pep talk about how she could do anything should give her heart. Did give her some. But would it be enough to face the *Fabulous Five?*

The bar was already hopping though it wasn't quite five o'clock yet. An upscale urban hangout with an amazing view of Pike Place Market and the southern Seattle waterfront, it would be packed and roaring with the after work crowd within the hour. Her history in Seattle had been cluttered with this place.

Her first trip here had included a dinner with Russell in the main restaurant beyond the bar, set against one of the best views in all Seattle. That was back when— She shuddered from the thought and lost some of her confidence. That was the weekend she had fallen in love with him and then broken up with him. Her heart had been an impregnable fortress ever since… Right up to Joshua. And she was too busy at the moment to decide whether or not he was somehow gaining entrance past that protection.

Her last visit had included lunch with Perrin, and it was where she'd first met Joshua. At that table, close by the window, now occupied by a pair of couples clearly enjoying themselves. She hadn't paid too much attention to him at that meal, but she would take strength from their having been here together, even in a group.

Though Melanie had arrived early, four of *The Fabulous Five* were already there. And waiting. She lurked a moment in the shadows, dropping her heart rate by sheer willpower as she assessed them. While she did so, she pulled out her French braid to let her hair flow free. She would find strength in arriving as Melanie the model. She finger-combed the worst of the twists free until it should billow properly. No time to retreat and brush it out.

The four women stood out in the chi-chi bar with its dark wood tables, tall chairs, and amazing view just beyond the glass. The afternoon sun streamed in through a softening screen and lit the four women so that they glowed like a runway show frozen in time.

Russell's wife Cassidy Knowles, the founder of the Washington Wine Cooperative, already a growing force in the national and international marketing of Puget Sound wines. She'd dressed in her classic black slacks and turtleneck, her brunette hair spilling to her shoulders. They really needed to do an intervention and get some color into her wardrobe; she definitely had the figure for it.

Jo Parrano, who had married Angelo last fall, should have been a model. Her native-Alaskan dark hair and skin, and her voluptuous curves accented by one of Perrin's custom powersuits clearly identified her as one of the most powerful women in Seattle.

Maria was dressed perfectly, as she always was. She understood color and flow. She was both beautiful and clearly the calm center, the true anchor of the group. If she could age the way Maria was, she'd be thrilled. It was patently ridiculous as Maria was almost a foot shorter than Melanie, but she was living proof that life began at fifty.

Perrin sat beside the still empty fifth chair and, as always, was a study in fashion. Her hair was golden rather than the dye jobs she used to sport. She wore a dress of jet black velvet. It had one sleeve that started as a fingerless glove. At her shoulder, it broke into two waves that draped and cascaded down her slender figure so dramatically it would have made her face hard to focus on—the eyes just wanted to travel right down to the short slit-reveal at her calves. Except, the other shoulder and arm were bare and relieved the eye of its downward journey. Rather than losing the pale-skinned woman in the dramatic dress, she shone.

Who belonged in that empty fifth chair still eluded her. And where would she sit when she crossed the room? There should be a sixth seat. Unless she were being called in and dismissed for some reason.

Cassidy, Jo, and Perrin were obviously the original core group.

Maria had joined in as much as a mother to the three grown women as a friend. And now all four were happily married to amazing men. Tamara, Perrin's new-adopted daughter, was too young to be the fifth. A great girl, but just a young teen. They were sitting in the bar at Cutters Crabhouse.

Well, she didn't need a mother. She was Melanie, she didn't need anyone. Joshua's face came to mind, but she ignored the thought.

Deep breath. Forge ahead.

She knew how to make an entrance. You executed the most powerful entrance by *not* making one. No grand gesture, no hard walk. Simply stroll naturally into the middle of the room, hesitate for just a second—not long enough to make you look uncertain, just enough to catch the eye of anyone even partially looking in the right direction—then you hit the walk hard.

Melanie did it this time not to make the statement of her arrival, and not to silence the crowded upscale bar perched over the waterfront. She did it because it was the woman she felt most secure being in public. Melanie the model always controlled any room she entered and she controlled it this time as well.

"Damn, girl, but you can really walk," Perrin beckoned her over for a hug. "I've tried to do that, just in my studio, but I always feel stupid."

"That probably means you're doing it *correctement*. It is a crafted walk designed to make other women sweat and men weep with desire. While it is not normal, at times I find it to be useful."

Maria glanced to either side of Melanie. She herself of course didn't turn to watch the effect she'd caused; though she could certainly hear just how slowly the conversations were returning.

"Well, you seem to have done your job this time. A wide collection of stunned puppy looks." Then she smiled up at Melanie. "You'll have to teach me how to do that someday, so that I can do it to Hogan."

Melanie liked Maria. And while she didn't need a mother, the woman was unfailingly thoughtful. Her kindness ran even deeper than Cassidy's.

"I could not do that," Melanie tried not to look uncertain as she remained standing by the fifth chair. Who was the other person?

"Trade secret, huh?" Perrin sipped at a Cosmopolitan.

"*Non!* I don't want to kill Hogan. Maria, you are already the perfect embodiment of a woman. If you do anything more, it is sure to slay the poor man."

That won her a round of laughter, a blush from Maria, and gleeful agreement from the three younger women who clearly loved the older woman deeply.

"Who else is coming?" The fifth chair was making her nervous. She felt exposed. Was she indeed supposed to just stand all evening?

"No one," Maria reached out to take Melanie's hand and gave her a slight tug to sit between her and Perrin. "We were *The Fearsome Four-some.* Not anymore. The chair is yours."

Melanie's knees went weak, so it was good that the seat was vacant to settle into before she collapsed. *The Fabulous Five.* This wasn't some test or a setup for a future favor. No entry on the tally sheet This was a welcome. She had thought her invitation to Perrin's wedding was merely thoughtful. But they were offering her so much more.

They were treating her as if she belonged among them.

Well, wasn't that just as surprising as all hell?

JOSH SURVIVED, but it was a close thing. He'd never quite understood the full significance of the phrase "steam coming out his ears" until Russell rounded on him.

Suddenly two hands as big as meat cleavers were inches from his throat. Hogan pulled Josh back toward him for protection—or so he first thought. Instead, Hogan wrapped an arm around Josh's throat, not quite choking him.

"I've got him for you Russell. Go for it."

Josh didn't know whether to feel betrayed or terrified. Then he realized that Hogan's move had neatly blocked Russell's first instinct to simply strangle Josh with his bare hands.

"What do you mean, 'shacking up with Melanie'?"

"I—"

"Hey," Hogan cut off Josh's attempts to explain. "If you had Melanie—The Melanie—practically living with you, would you throw her out of your bed?"

Russell flinched as if he was the one who'd been struck. "I already did that to her," his voice was barely a whisper, but Josh heard it.

"You did?" Bill and Hogan echoed Josh's thoughts.

Russell Morgan... And Melanie...?

"Is that why she's so damn gun shy?" Josh could feel his own heat rising. "You slept with her and then threw her out?" That last wasn't all that much softer from Russell's first shout.

Russell tried a wry smile, but it came out looking sickly. "I didn't know what I was doing at the time, but, yeah, that's pretty much right. Except it was worse. Damn woman fell in love with me...*then* I threw her out."

Josh didn't know what to say. Should Melanie have told him? They'd shared a few amazing kisses and a hug he would remember for the rest of his life, but it wasn't as if he expected her to be a virgin. It was just a shock that he knew one of her former—lovers was too uncomfortable a word—guys. The fact that Russell looked more upset than Josh felt actually made him feel a little better.

Hogan got up and went into the apartment. He came back with a tumbler with three fingers of scotch in it and handed it to Russell who knocked it straight back.

"Hey," Josh tried to make it light, "where's mine? I'm the one who almost got killed here."

"Yes," Hogan acknowledged as he settled back into his chair without fetching another glass. "But he needs it more."

Josh looked back at Russell.

He really did look like hell.

"Nachos? I haven't eaten nachos in years." Melanie looked at the spread of appetizers before them. The clams weren't fattening by themselves, but eating them without the focaccia bread, which was practically dripping with butter, would be a crime. The deep fried calamari was popular with the table, though she'd never been a big fan of it. But nachos. She had a totally ridiculous weak spot for nachos.

"It's okay," Perrin dipped a piece of the bread into the clam juices, bit off a chunk, and sighed happily as she bit in. "Nothing here has calories or fat. Not as long as we're all together. It's one of the rules."

Melanie could already feel that second glass of wine. She never drank two glasses. Hell, she never drank one. She tried closing one eye, then both. But the nachos were still there teasing her nose. She opened one eye, the others were watching her.

"You are all bad influences."

There was a small cheer and much pride displayed around the table. "Don't make us suffer alone!"

Melanie didn't. She dipped the crab nacho into the dish of fresh-made guacamole and decided she was going to have to marry the chef.

"So, how far along are you?"

"With what?" Melanie really hoped Perrin was asking about her business. Even if Melanie hadn't told Perrin she was working on it, she really hoped that's what it was.

Perrin's eye roll informed Melanie that her hopes were dashed.

Jo and Cassidy looked perplexed, so no one was talking behind her back at least. Though Maria's smile looked far too knowing for her comfort.

Melanie looked back at Perrin and assessed the situation. Nope, no way out of it. So, she'd give a little.

"We spent the day taking a ferry over to Bainbridge Island for lunch."

"So, that's why you left my shop so fast," Perrin nodded and Melanie would leave her with possession of that bit of misinformation. It had been embarrassing enough sharing a full panic attack with Joshua; she didn't intend to share it with the rest of the world.

"Wait!" Cassidy held up her hands. "Wait just a second." She leaned forward as far as she could without upsetting the table. "You and who?"

She opened her mouth but Perrin leapt in on her moment of hesitation.

"She's sleeping with Josh Harper."

"I am not!"

"You're both staying in Angelo's condo; so you're sleeping together. If you're doing that in separate beds, you need to have your head examined. He is majorly cute."

"He is not!"

All four women turned to her at her protest and she knew she was caught, because Joshua most definitely was cute on any woman's scale. Discretion apparently lay at the bottom of her now empty wine glass. Well, if she had put her foot in it, she might as well go all the way. With a shrug, she flicked her hair back over her shoulder.

"He's *not* cute." She pictured him standing by the ferry ramp, still watching her when she turned back to check. The afternoon sun had lit his dark hair like the finest walnut furniture. His face, the brightening of his smile as she'd turned to look back and found him still watching her. The way he made her feel.

"He's beautiful."

"ANSWER. THE. GOD. DAMNED. QUESTION." Russell's growl sounded positively feral. Great, Josh was caged on a high and narrow balcony with a guy Hulking-out to twice his already substantial size.

"Which god damned question?" No way he was going to make it easy for the man.

Russell's glare deepened, if that was possible. "Are you sleeping with her?"

"Not that it's any of your god damned business, but no."

Most of the anger-bloated Hulk went away, and the slightly sad man had returned. "Why not?"

"Why am I not sleeping with the woman you just threatened to kill me over? What kind of a stupid question is that, Russell?"

"My kind. Cassie's always telling me I'm an idiot, but Melanie's really special. I don't want anyone messing with her."

Joshua considered ramming Russell's words right back down his throat as he was obviously someone who'd obliterated his own rules.

Russell held up his hands in resignation.

"I know. Just don't go there. Let's just acknowledge that I was a goddamn idiot before I met Cassie and she straightened me out."

So, Josh didn't go there. That's what friends were for. Or at least what you did for someone who'd resisted killing you outright. He bought himself some time to think by going in to get a glass of scotch. After a moment's consideration, he grabbed three tumblers and brought back the bottle, refilling Russell's before he handed round the rest.

They all raised a toast to the setting sun and knocked it back, at least he and Russell did. Bill and Hogan showed a little more control and left some in their glasses.

"I'm not sleeping with her for a lot of reasons. One, I've only known her for about two days. Two, I don't want someone as amazing as her to be my 'rebound' girl from my divorce because she deserves better than that. Three, because she deserves better than me. And four, because she deserves someone who sees Melanie, not the supermodel, and I can't seem to get around that entirely because the woman is so bloody breathtaking. Happy now?"

Russell studied Josh long enough in silence for Josh to feel that his throat was dry, so he sipped his beer rather than risking a look for where the scotch bottle had gone.

Then Russell turned to consult Bill and Hogan who nodded in response.

"Shit!" Russell cursed softly. "I always thought you were a decent enough guy, Josh. Did you have to go and prove it so that I look like more of an idiot than I am?"

"Sure," Josh tapped his beer against Russell's empty scotch glass, then sat back to enjoy the view and the company. "What are friends for?"

"Oh," Perrin placed a hand over her heart. "Dreamy kiss on a ferry boat. I hadn't thought of that. I need to take Bill out on a ferry crossing and get a kiss that sounds that dreamy."

"I've always liked Josh," Cassidy started with a nod that probably continued far longer than she intended. She was looking distinctly blurred and Melanie was pretty sure it wasn't only her own perception through several glasses of wine that was causing it. "He's a wonderful guy. Not as amazing as my Russell, but a good guy. Known him since forever and I always liked Josh. He's a good gu— Hey, Melanie?"

"What?"

Cassidy had stopped nodding and come slightly back into focus. "You and Josh would make an amazing couple."

Perrin jabbed Cassidy in the arm, "Hello. Welcome to the conversation. Can you picture the dress I could make them?"

Jo shook her head, "No." She shook back her long mane of dark hair, even drunk her posture was upright and elegant.

Melanie suspected that nothing disturbed the woman's lawyerly manner.

"You can't get Josh to wear a dress. You have to make the dress for Melanie. Suit for Mr. Har-penter," she interrupted herself with a lady-like hiccup. She found her water glass on her third attempt.

"I don't know," Perrin's smile said that she was clearly still the most coherent of the three, though maybe not by much. "Josh is so pretty. We could put him in the dress and Melanie in a suit."

"I," Melanie drew herself upright to protest the conversation going on without her. "I am not marrying anyone."

Cassidy, Jo, and Perrin ignored her.

Maria Parrano took her hand, drawing Melanie's attention. With a gentle pressure, she pulled Melanie close enough for her to speak softly despite the noise of the bar and the ongoing debate over Melanie's wedding day.

"You will, you know."

"Will what?" Melanie wondered if it was her or if Maria's words made no particular sense. Melanie had switched over to water some time ago and was pretty sure she was only a little tipsy.

Maria's eyes were perfectly clear. "Oh dear girl," Maria kissed her on each cheek. "You will make a beautiful couple."

MELANIE WASN'T sure who was leading who home. Cassidy lived only a few blocks up the hill and had offered her a spare bedroom. At some point after Maria's comment, Melanie had switched back to wine without quite noticing how.

She suspected that Cassidy had been more coherent than she appeared and filled Melanie's water glass with a refreshing white wine when she wasn't paying enough attention.

No matter, she had neither the energy nor the inclination to return to the Pioneer Square condo. Joshua would probably be there and she wanted a little distance from him, at least enough to stop herself from jumping him. Because after the four women... No. After her four friends poking and prodding her and talking about their own husbands, both the appreciated quirks and the not so appreciated, she was certainly feeling ready to jump one Mr. Joshua Har-penter.

Somehow between them, she and Cassidy climbed the nighttime Seattle streets; the night still alive with music from bars, their doors open and people enjoying late night treats around little tables at side-walk cafes. They made it into Cassidy's condo. She aimed Cassidy into the master bedroom, where Russell's soft snores indicated that he hadn't waited up.

Cassidy reappeared a moment later and handed her a big shirt to wear as a nightgown. Then she was gone and Melanie stood in the hall lit only by the few streetlights that could reach this high.

She washed her face and changed in the guest bath. She was glad to see that Cassidy had given her an oversized woman's t-shirt rather than one of Russell's. As they'd once been lovers, that would have been too strange.

Russell's fluffy black cat was waiting outside the bathroom door to inspect her when she emerged. Without really thinking, she reached down and scratched it between the ears eliciting a happy buzz. She snatched her hand back and the animal eyed her strangely.

"I'm not explaining to you why cats freak me out. Go away." Her hand itched where that photo shoot cat of her childhood had slashed at her. Melanie slipped into the guest room, making sure that the cat, however disappointed, ended up on the other side of the door when she closed it.

In the vague light, she spotted a chair and dropped her belongings onto it. She turned for the bed, a vague outline of white that was her sole concern. After tonight's excesses, and this afternoon's emotional upheaval courtesy of Mr. Joshua Har-penter, she could sleep for a week.

That's what they'd called him for the entire rest of the evening, the memory made her giggle a bit.

A voice sounded out of the dark, "Please don't throw a suitcase at me."

"Joshua," Melanie's voice was a breathy whisper.

Josh reached to turn on the bedside light, but thought better of it. He'd woken in time to see Melanie's unmistakable silhouette slipping in the door, but not soon enough to be sure she was clothed. He was instantly sober. Or at least sober enough to not assume he was hallucinating.

"I shall go somewhere else. Back to the condo." He could hear her gathering her things.

He could also hear her exhaustion. "No. I'll go. I can sleep on the couch or something." He remembered in time that he wasn't wearing anything under the covers, so he stayed in place.

"Cassidy—" she said at the same moment he said, "Russell—"

They both hesitated.

"You don't think it was some master plan?" she really did sound wiped out.

Joshua reached around on the floor and found his underwear. He slipped them on under the covers as surreptitiously as he could while he responded.

"I like Russell and Cassidy, but neither one is sufficiently sneaky. Perrin, maybe, except she'd have first made you a nightgown out of taffeta or something. Maria is definitely sneaky enough, but not Russell or Cassidy. So, I'll just count myself impossibly fortunate and burn some candles of thanks to our Lady of Chance." He started to get out of bed. "I'll go."

"No. I—" she stopped, but it didn't sound as if she was gathering her things either. They were both exhausted and both too considerate. Well, she was. His body's reaction would prove him to be a complete and total cad if she turned on a light before he could find his jeans.

At an impasse—he knew that she'd leave if he insisted on going and neither of them would sleep soon.

"Melanie, how about this? You climb in here and I'll behave. I will promise that you will remain completely safe. We'll just sleep."

"You're being ridiculous."

"No. Completely and unbelievably stupid considering how much you've been occupying my thoughts today, but a promise has been made and a promise will be kept. C'mon."

She hesitated for several long moments, then he saw the faint outline moving toward him, followed by a soft *Merde!* as she stumbled on the clothes he'd dumped on the floor before crawling into bed.

"Get in this side; it's already warm." He held up the covers and slid over to the far side as she took the covers.

He lay there having no idea what he'd been thinking. The woman of his fantasies now lay possibly naked a mere foot away. Everything he'd promised himself to not think about—insane pedestal and all. Each motion of the mattress and the sheets as she settled sent bolts of electricity rocketing through him.

And his fantasies were becoming an issue. The pin-up fantasy of the most beautiful woman he'd ever seen was fast being replaced by the flesh-and-blood one who had kissed him with such abandon on the ferry; the one who had kept him chastely entertained and intrigued through a long date to Bainbridge and back; the one he really wanted to get his hands on.

He had to get up.

Go to the couch.

Sleep on the floor.

Something.

Before he could force himself to go, she rolled toward him. In moments her head rested on his shoulder. Her body, thankfully clothed, lay along his or he would have lost all control—promise or not. One of her legs, not the least little bit clothed, draped over one of his.

"You're a good man, Josshhua." Now he heard the slur in her voice, not the least trace of French in her speech. Maybe not drunk, but he'd guess pretty damn loose or she wouldn't have crawled in. That made her completely and totally out of bounds, whether or not she offered. No way was he taking advantage of her.

She settled in, draped an arm across him, and fell asleep with a soft sigh.

Now what in hell was he supposed to do?

CHAPTER 8

elanie woke the way she normally did; one moment asleep, the next wide awake.

Wide awake and nestled in a man's arms.

Joshua. She didn't need the soft morning's light edging in around the closed curtains to know instantly it was him. If felt as if they'd always slept together.

By the rise and fall of his chest, she knew he was asleep. One hand wrapped around her back, the other one resting on her hand which in turn rested on his chest. She had crawled in and curled up against him —what a total Jersey Shore hussy.

Except she didn't feel like one. Instead she felt like a woman who had her best night's sleep in recent memory while nestled safely in her lover's arms. Though he wasn't her lover.

She'd certainly never slept with a man without having sex before. Was something wrong with him? With her?

His chest slowly rose and fell several times before she remembered what he'd said. She'd been drunk and half-passed out on her feet, and Joshua had promised she'd be safe. Those were not words that any man had ever offered to her. Especially not offered and meant. Actually, no one had *ever* offered her safety, including her own mother.

349

And then he'd given her the warm side of the bed when she'd been chilled from the cool wind off the Sound and utterly exhausted.

She'd not only been safe, but felt safe. Exactly as he'd promised.

She considered making him break that promise right now. But they were guests in someone else's apartment. In Russell's! If someone had told her before last night that she'd ever sleep in Russell's home again, she'd have laughed in their face. She absolutely wasn't going to have sex here, no matter how incredible Joshua felt.

She managed to slip from his arms, gather her things, and make it to the guest bathroom with no one the wiser. Dressed, hair brushed, and face fresh scrubbed—she never wore makeup except on a shoot— ten minutes later she entered the kitchen.

Cassidy was sitting at the kitchen counter with a big mug of coffee and her computer tablet, though she didn't appear to be focusing well.

"Hi."

"Uh, hi," Cassidy looked up at her. "How in the hell can you look so together when my head feels like mush?"

"No hangover. Whatever wine you slipped me, it must have been the best quality."

"Actually," Cassidy wrapped her hands around her coffee mug like gripping a lifeline. "I think that was Jo. She appears all demure, but in truth she's very sneaky. You've got to watch that woman like a hawk. My mistake was letting Perrin switch me over to Cosmos. Help yourself to coffee."

"You really don't look like you slept much." Melanie took her time about making a cup of tea instead, moving softly in sympathy for Cassidy's condition. Espresso from French roast was among the French habits she'd never learned to enjoy.

"Russell greeted me very nicely—" Then Cassidy blushed hard and looked aside. "Sorry. Too much information. I know. I just—"

Melanie rested a hand on Cassidy's arm to stop her. "Russell and I were lovers. It didn't take, for many and valid reasons. He married you and loves you. Let us simply leave it at that. *N'est-ce pas?*"

Cassidy did her head nod thing again, nodding a couple too many times.

"You know. I think that's the first French you've spoken since last night," she squinted her eyes as if concentrating. "Maybe not even then. It fits you. You sound uptown New York."

Melanie blinked in surprise. How had she been so relaxed to let down her shields? Last night, too? She thought back, but couldn't be sure. What she did remember was immensely enjoying her inclusion in *The Fabulous Five*. And she couldn't feel the slightest sense of an entry on her internal tally sheet. She'd simply been welcome, just for herself. That too was a new experience.

"Joshua said the same thing, but he is a man, I'm not about to trust a man on such things."

"Like I think I said last night, Josh is a good guy. I've known him forever, since before he met his wife back when we were both upstart restaurant reviewers. Just friends, no spark there, then he met Constance. Who wasn't so constant. God I'm rambling. If this coffee cup were bigger, I'd just put my face in it."

"Maybe I should start trusting Joshua," Melanie topped up Cassidy's coffee. Then she decided that if her instincts were relaxed enough to drop her accent around Cassidy that just maybe she should trust that feeling all the more. "Besides, he also greeted me very nicely last night, if a little bit differently."

"Joshua?"

"He's asleep in your guest bedroom."

"Joshua?" Cassidy was blinking hard trying to get her brain going. "Josh!? I sent you to bed with Josh? Oh my god! I'm so sorry! It wasn't planned. I swear it wasn't. I—"

Melanie had to laugh. It really was too funny. Joshua had been absolutely right. Russell and Cassidy were sincere friends, but not conniving ones.

Melanie sat down across the counter and told her new friend about how her evening had ended.

JOSHUA SLEPT LATE into the morning and woke to the smell of frying bacon and coffee. He dragged on jeans and a t-shirt before padding out into the kitchen to find Russell battling the stove like a ship's cook on a stormy sea.

"Shit, Russell. You look worse than I feel."

"Yeah. You sleep okay?" Russell tossed in some more bacon and nodded toward the coffeemaker.

That's when Josh remembered.

He spun to look around but there were only the two of them. None of Melanie's things had been in the bedroom. He doubled back to check. Nothing. Gone as if it had never happened.

But it had. The other pillow was dented, the covers were mussed on both sides of the bed. Her pink bag from the dress shop was gone.

The memories were slowly returning through his foggy brain. He'd held her for hours, imagining what it might be like to do so every night. He'd buried his nose in her hair for a long time—long enough to actually sober up—just in case he never had a chance like that again. His idea of heaven had been wholly redefined by simply holding a sleeping woman.

"Huh," he looked around the condo again as he returned to join Russell in the kitchen. She was definitely gone. Without waking him. Now what did that mean? "I slept great."

Josh made eggs and toast while Russell brought the bacon in for a landing. They took their plates to the balcony high above the bustle of a Pike Place Market morning.

CHAPTER 9

elanie was determined. For the first time in days, maybe weeks, she felt as if she had Things to Do. Much more her natural state; she first went back to the Pioneer Square condo to change into her exercise clothes and do a virtuous workout.

Melanie padded into the great room, cool and dim with the indirect morning light through the western windows. She liked that Maria and Angelo had left much of the main space open. Clearly, they'd only really cared about the kitchen. Even the dining table wasn't much. They probably planned to only test recipes here; any entertaining would be at the restaurant. A couch and a couple of big chairs were all that defined the living room. A television sat off to the side, not at a comfortable angle to any of the furniture, so that too was unused.

It left her a large open area of gleaming bare wood. From her point of view it was perfect. It gave a six-foot tall woman room to do her yoga stretches without fear of running into furniture or inopportune sections of wall. She'd become lax since the loss of the swimsuit photo shoot. In just one week she could feel the loss of flexibility and tone.

That would never do. She did a double session until a sheen of sweat made it hazardous to continue until she had the chance to purchase a mat. Carlo's hotel room had a large oriental carpet that worked well, but this expanse of shining oak was a slipping risk.

She almost didn't want to shower. When she did, she'd lose that scent of Joshua that…wasn't clinging to her so much as following her around. A pleasant companion.

But she had things to do, so into the shower she went. She grabbed the last bowl of Joshua's minestrone soup for lunch, thanking him with each luscious spoonful. She considered feeling guilty about eating it without asking first. But if she wasn't going to feel guilty for sleeping with the man, she wasn't going to feel guilty for finishing his soup.

And she certainly didn't. Cassidy had sighed romantically when Melanie recounted how Josh had declared she'd be safe, then delivered on that promise.

"I wouldn't tempt him again though. You'd risk ruining a perfect story." Cassidy had looked serious, as if the story was the most important part. Well, maybe it was. Josh was a writer, he would understand the importance of careful beginnings.

Melanie had walked halfway up the First Avenue hill, opening an effortless path through the Seattle crowd with just a small dose of New York attitude, when she stumbled to a halt. If she'd stopped on a sidewalk in New York she'd have been trampled—you broke the Big Apple's pedestrian flow at your own risk. In Seattle, one person bumped her lightly and immediately apologized.

What had ground her to a halt was that word "beginnings." She'd selected lovers, knowing that's all they were. She'd fallen in love with only one of them. Dear Russell had also thought they were simply two people who enjoyed each other and the sensation they created on the New York scene. She was the one who'd broken that bargain and fallen for him. But their "beginning" had been like any other.

A party. Did she remember whose?

A passing brush on her shoulder got her moving again, though more slowly than before.

It was the meet-and-greet party for her second season on the swimsuit photo shoot. He'd been handsome, charming, and acting very single. Melanie had googled him to make sure, leaving the other girls to fawn on one of the handsomest men she'd ever seen. He was indeed single. It was buried fairly deep, but she also found that he was a billionaire's son as well as owning his own photo studio.

That had caught her attention, but with a second shoot under her belt—and she hadn't known it yet, but her first cover as well—she wasn't doing badly herself. He'd hooked up with another of the models who knew nothing about him, and that had been fine.

Whatever else Russell did or however he acted at parties, behind the camera he was both professional and masterful. He drew the very best out of his models. He had done the simplest things, which evoked emotions inside her that she didn't know were there—buried or otherwise. After a session with Russell Morgan, a girl needed a cold shower simply to think clearly. He made it easy to lose herself in the role of sexual goddess; he made her believe it of herself.

But their eventual "beginning" had been like any other of her affairs. More intriguing, more artfully played, more fun, but not so very different. He'd dragged it out over a year: a chance meeting here, hiring her for a small ad shoot there, finding out that he'd referred her to a shoot with an up-and-coming designer that no one had heard of but had then burst on the scene.

Then he'd taken her to lunch, and to bed. Or perhaps she'd done the taking. It had been as mutual as it had been expected.

But with Joshua she already had stories and promises and steamy kisses. *Merde!* They'd slept together and held each other through the night, not like *lovers,* but like she imagined people *in love* did.

She'd never had a real beginning even as a teen. At the time she'd discovered boys, or rather boys had discovered her, she'd been foolish and naïve, giving up her first kiss before her first handholding, her virginity for empty words. She'd wised up fast and remained that way ever since.

Melanie didn't feel wise around Joshua; she felt...

Again she stopped in the middle of the sidewalk, blinking in surprise to find herself outside of Perrin's Glorious Garb with no memory of the last half dozen blocks. It was a wonder she hadn't been killed in traffic crossing the street.

Around Joshua she felt… Still the word eluded her.

Melanie smiled to herself as she entered the shop, the doorbell jingling brightly.

Maybe tonight she'd find out just how Joshua made her feel. She'd wager it would be *incroyable* and was a little surprised at how eager she was to win that bet.

"YOU WANT ME TO WHAT?" Joshua shook his head. "No way."

"C'mon man," Angelo leaned forward over the plate of Baci—hazelnut and chocolate "kisses" Maria had made this morning—that they'd been pillaging since lunch. "I'll even… I'll even—"

"He'll even pay you," Russell nursed an ice tea, looking a little less gray and bleary-eyed than he had this morning.

Now it was Angelo's turn to turn a bit gray, but he nodded.

"No," Joshua shook his head. "First, you can't go on feeding me gratis no matter how damn much I'm enjoying it. Second, I don't want to write any more food articles."

Russell slapped the table, and then winced showing his hangover was not wholly cleared.

"That's it," he continued in a softer voice. "You don't do this and Angelo cuts you off. You write for him, he goes on feeding you guilt free."

"But I don't want to write any more of that—"

"Don't say it," Russell stopped him suddenly clear-eyed.

Joshua glared at him.

"I did that for a while, called my photography crap because it wasn't what I thought it should be. I'd look at a Bourke-White print, and then my latest spread for Prada and feel like a total sell-out. But I've learned that I'm damn good at what I do. Don't call your art crap. You really don't want to do it? Fine. You're an idiot, but fine. But just from one artist to another, don't put it down."

"Why the hell am I an idiot?"

"You're staying in the same condo as Melanie. Have you at least kissed her yet?"

"I have." But no way was he going to tell Russell that there'd been more than that. Especially not that they'd slept together in his own condo.

"Okay," Russell sighed a bit sadly. "At least you're not a complete idiot."

Joshua would keep his thoughts on that point to himself.

"Write Angelo's press release," Russell made it a suggestion. "Give it the pizzazz that I can't seem to find on this one. You get to keep eating Angelo's fucking awesome food."

"Damn straight you call it that," Angelo pitched in.

"And the words might prime the pump a bit. Maybe it gets your novel moving because it sure isn't doing squat now, is it?"

"How did you know?" It wasn't—not even a little—but he hadn't been advertising that.

Russell simply looked at him steadily.

"Crap! I didn't think it showed that badly."

"It shows, buddy. So say you'll write the damn thing. Then you can tell us about when you kissed Melanie and why you didn't mention a breath of it last night."

"Perrin," Melanie traded a surprisingly warm hug with Perrin back in the workroom of her shop. "I actually wanted to talk to you about something different last night, but never got around to it."

"About you making it with Josh?"

"No," Melanie sighed. She doubted that Cassidy would have called Perrin to spread the news of last night's adventure, but somehow the story of last night had traveled. Perhaps these three women were telepathic with each other.

"Can't blame a girl for trying?"

That's when Melanie noticed the fabrics Perrin was working with today. A pure silk Duchesse satin that breathed with the faintest pearlescent sheen and a medium-weight silk crepe back satin in the palest, most perfect sky blue. She couldn't stop herself from reaching out to stroke the materials.

"Soft, huh?"

"Oh my god, Perrin. Aren't these like forty dollars a yard?"

"Fifty and fifty-five, wholesale. Sometimes a dress calls for the very best."

"Well, it is a lucky woman who will be wearing this dress."

"She won't let me help her even measure it," Tamara came in and dropped her school bag under the counter. She was a sharp contrast to her new mother, dark curly hair flowing to her shoulders versus Perrin's short golden blond. Their skin was a sharp contrast as well, Tamara a permanent sun-kissed gold and Perrin almost as pale as the silk spread across the table.

Perrin hugged Tamara hard in greeting and Melanie was glad to see it was fully returned. She felt a dozen different pulls inside. The pull of a mother and daughter who clearly loved one another and were happier together than apart, the exact opposite of her own maternal relationship. And the pull of mother with child. Melanie had never pictured herself with a child, but watching the two of them together, she could almost see it.

"You," Perrin leaned down to kiss Tamara on top of the head before letting her go, "can spend the afternoon on a project here if you promise to do your homework tonight."

Tamara offered an indifferent shrug, exactly as you'd expect from a teen.

Perrin winked at Melanie before continuing. "First you have a clothing line to start designing."

"I do?" Any affectation of disinterest evaporated in that instant.

Melanie did her best to hide her smile, but sliding on her model shield couldn't suppress it. Tamara's eyes had gone wide.

"Yes. I showed your sketches to one of the best professionals in the business," Perrin smiled at Melanie.

Tamara's jaw dropped as she turned to face Melanie for a moment then turned back to look up at her mom.

"And she said that they were a great start, really pretty, and you needed your own youth line. You get to name it, brand it, and design it. I'll help you with all of that and the business."

"TJPW!" she blurted out. "That's what it's called. Tam, Jasp—my little brother is named Jaspar," Tammy told Melanie as if they didn't already know each other. "P is for Perrin, and W for dad. I know. I know. Everyone calls him Bill. I thought about TJBP and got an oil company, the other way around I got Peanut Butter, so he gets W for William. The weird acronym will be cool. I've got a design for the logo at home. I really get my own line?" At the last she went from an effervescent rush back to breathy disbelief.

At Perrin's nod, the girl leapt into Perrin's arms.

Melanie had to look away from the sheer power of such joy. What might she have become with even that little bit of encouragement?

A gentle touch on her arm drew her attention back. Tamara stood close beside her. She mouthed a silent thank you and hugged Melanie gently. Melanie returned it the best she knew how.

Then, with a cry, "There's so much to do!" Tamara turned back into a thirteen-year-old whirlwind, digging a sketchbook out of her pack and flipping to pages filled with more sketches. Without hesitation, she moved to the fabric wall, grabbed a pair of scissors and began trimming samples off the corners of different colors and materials to tape down beside her designs.

Perrin leaned in close to Melanie and added a kiss on each cheek to add to Tamara's thanks. "So much to do, she isn't kidding."

"That's what I wanted to talk to you about," Melanie had thought the moment had eluded her again, but instead it had returned reinforced. The time was now.

When Melanie pulled out the file folder of letters and e-mails, Perrin grimaced. Then, she sat on the stool beside Melanie, close enough that their knees were brushing. Melanie was reminded of her lunch with Joshua and let that help her confidence.

"Okay," Perrin took a deep breath and tried to offer her a smile. "Okay. How do I survive what's happening to me?"

"*Bon.* At least you see the problem." Melanie pulled out her notebook that she'd worked on at Elliot Bay Bookstore and Joshua's notes of a few strategic enhancements.

"What are you working on? And what is that divine smell?"

Joshua jerked back up from typing, inhaling like a diver emerging from the depths after his air tank had run out. Once again he'd missed Melanie's entry into the condo.

He could only watch in stunned amazement as she crossed from the front door over to where he was set up on the dining table. She always walked like magic, every motion was a joy. But there was something more today. A lightness in her step, the damn woman shone like the springtime outside.

That she came directly to him and hit him with a kiss as powerful as any Taser, left him stunned speechless.

"Joshua? Melanie to Joshua? Hello. Anyone there?"

"Uh-uh." Definitely not. He didn't trust himself to try words yet, even mustering up a grunt was a hard-won victory.

She moved over to inspect the oven. His eyes continued to track her even if his brain couldn't. He knew he was reacting badly, like some gobsmacked schoolboy, but he couldn't stop.

One of the most beautiful women on the planet had just greeted him as if they hadn't spent last night curled up together. Or rather she greeted him as if that's exactly what they'd done. He still couldn't believe it.

She squatted down and eased open the oven to peek. It was a fluid motion that sent heat rippling along his body. His mouth had gone dry and neither swallowing hard nor taking a slug from the long since gone warm lemonade sitting beside his computer helped in the slightest.

"It's," he managed in a lame croak. "It's lasagna."

She turned to grimace at him, then tried to cover it for his sake.

"No. No carb-laden pasta. Instead I used thin slices of roasted eggplant, low fat cheeses, and homemade red sauce. There's a tossed salad in the fridge, just needs some avocado sliced over it right before I serve it."

"Oh my god that sounds amazing." Melanie flowed back to the table.

"I…" his pulse jumped significantly as she settled in the closest chair. "I cheated. I used Angelo's red sauce, mine takes a couple days to meld flavors properly. So does his, but he always has a large batch of it going. I actually stole his recipe." Babbling again. Since last night, her smell was such a part of his memory that he could pick it out despite the aromatic kitchen.

"What are you working on?"

"An article for Angelo. Did you have a good day?" *Do you have any idea how constantly I was thinking about you?*

"I did. I sat with Perrin and showed her the business plan we wrote up. It took away some of her fear, but she hasn't bought in the whole way yet. Which is not a bad thing. The plan is still very rough and she has more than enough common sense to see that. I'm not sure what is missing, but we made progress."

Joshua nodded and tried some more lemonade.

Melanie smiled at him coyly.

Joshua tried to remember how to breathe, because his autonomic systems had just shut down.

"It would be a shame to waste such a meal."

"Waste? Why would it be wasted?"

Melanie took his hand and pulled him easily to his feet.

He stumbled after her as she returned to the kitchen, leading him like a puppy on a leash.

She turned off the oven and the timer. Then she led him toward the bedroom. Her bedroom.

"No. Wait. No!" His brain finally cut back in and he dug in his heels, her fingers almost slipping from his.

She looked at him in surprise, "Don't you want this?"

"Like I want a glass of Côtes de Rhône after eating Robuchon's Steak au Poivre," Josh swallowed again. "That means yes, desperately. But you don't want me."

"How do you know what I'm thinking?"

"Oh. Okay, I don't. I'll admit that."

"Excellent," she tugged on his hand, but he resisted.

"You don't want me. No, scratch that. Speaking for you again. I. Me. I don't want to do this."

"And yet you said, *Oui, désespérément.*"

"And I meant it." He pulled his fingers from her grasp so that he stood some chance of thinking coherently. "But I'm a mess."

"So you keep assuring me. And I'm not any better. I simply know that I want you in my bed and you are now the first man to ever tell me no."

She reached for him, but he backed off. Dragging his hands through his hair did nothing to help.

"Melanie," he tried to sound calm and rational. "I don't want you as my rebound lover. I don't want to bring my feelings of hurt and betrayal from my ex-wife into your bed. You deserve so much more than that. So much more than…me."

Melanie laughed at him. She actually laughed at him. "Cassidy was so right about you."

"Cassidy? What does she have to do with this?"

"She said," Melanie took his hand again and once more led him, "that you were one of the most decent and *charmant* men she'd ever met. She was right." She stopped just inside the bedroom and closed the door behind them.

He felt as if he was now on the wrong side of the bars around a lion's cage. Lioness' cage.

"Joshua, just answer me one question. Honestly."

He looked into that perfect blue of her eyes and nodded, "Always. That's what I'm trying to do is be hone—"

"Shh," she rested a finger across his lips. "One word answer: yes or no. Okay?"

He nodded, not wanting her to remove her finger.

"Do you want to be with me?"

"Gods yes. So much—"

"One word, Joshua." Her laugh sparked his own smile to life. "Just one, Mr. Writer."

There was only one answer to the question. He pulled her into his arms, buried his face in her hair and held her tightly against him. So tightly that he never wanted to escape.

MELANIE HAD NEVER MET such a man. He didn't grab, grope, pinch, didn't even kiss her. For a moment she half feared it might be a hug and then a "no." But it wasn't. It was a man holding her so close simply because he wanted to. As if the holding was more important than the lovemaking. It was, but no man ever understood that.

In turn, she simply wrapped her arms around his neck, rested her head on his shoulder and hung on. A gentle swaying motion came over them, building to a slow dance in which their bodies rubbed, nestled, warmed, heated, and finally burned.

When at last he kissed her, any sign of the gentle lover had vanished. Joshua was replaced by a man with need. *Désespérément* indeed. His hands roved over her, not grabbing, but rather studying, learning, memorizing. Such strong hands, as if custom-made to appreciate a woman's shape. Her shape.

Though the bed was a bare two steps away, that was too far. He pushed her against the door as she wrapped herself about him. Most men were too rough, and she had to warn them to take care as she bruised easily. Not Joshua. Without holding back, he perfectly judged where pleasure soared without harm.

Except that his kiss was overwhelmingly powerful. For all he was doing to her body, their kiss had yet to end. He swallowed her purr of raw pleasure and his deep-throated moan in response vibrated right down her body.

She had unleashed the wild beast inside the gentle man.

Melanie gave herself to him to be consumed.

JOSH FELT the moment of change. He wasn't sure from which of them it had come, but it was change. One moment he'd been holding Melanie the gorgeous supermodel. The next he'd been holding a woman with no name; not that she was nameless or faceless, but rather that no single name could describe her or contain such a person. A woman who offered her very being for him to hold, to discover, to revel in. A woman who embodied desire and passion and joy.

He lost himself as well. There was no Josh. There was only a man who wanted to bring this woman pleasure like none she'd ever imagined. There would be no tender moment. Not this time. The need was too great, as if they were male and female genders personified and all passion, heat, and fire of the species must be expressed only through them.

At times she whimpered, at times he did. Clothing was shed or torn aside. There would be time to marvel at such skin, such curves later. Now there was only hunger. Beyond sex, beyond need, beyond desperation. Their bodies knew what they themselves couldn't possibly. They simply belonged together in a state like none he'd ever tread before.

Somehow, somewhere, they stumbled to the bed and found protection. And when she took him from above, when she arched her head back and her hair had showered over her like sunlight, he wanted to unleash a cry of triumph that would rattle off the very heavens.

MELANIE HAD DIED. She knew it for a fact. And she had slaughtered the best lover she'd ever had. She lay upon the chest of the dead man and listened to his heart continue to hammer just as hers did. She'd never felt such a release, had never so lost herself to the act of sex.

She almost blushed at the thought. Calling what they had just done "sex" was like calling Josh's gourmet eggplant lasagna a Stouffers frozen dinner.

When making love, Melanie always had retained control, maintained command. Even when appearing submissive, she still stood a half-step aside to monitor, shift, or shape the moment. Not this time. *Dieu!* Not anywhere close to control. She'd thrashed like a wild woman, taking everything he could give and begging for more.

And now they were both dead. Had to be after that.

Impossibly, showing a muscle control she knew she lacked, Joshua placed a hand on her back and began slowly stroking up and down her spine. As he went, she could feel him slowly sorting her hair from the tangle it must be, finger-combing it back to some sense of order. They must still be alive. Heaven, even if it felt this *incroyable,* would never include Melanie having tangled hair.

"There's no way we can ever repeat that." She tried not to feel sad at the thought. She was glad to have been there even once.

He kissed the top of her head. "Maybe not, but we can sure try."

She nodded. That was encouraging.

THEY ATE A SILENT, candlelit dinner. Words would be too much, too big. Joshua had pulled on jeans without underwear, and Melanie had slid on one of her overlarge t-shirts that kept sliding off one of her shoulders. She kept pulling it back into place so that she could watch Joshua's eyes go dark with heat each time it slid off again.

The only thing that kept her from completely fawning over the food was that if she started to talk about the amazing food, then she'd give voice to the incredible sex. And she liked that a man so full of words wasn't able to speak in her presence.

But the pressure of the silence built. Finally it grew until it wrapped so thick and warm between them that it filled the condo wall-to-wall, floor-to-ceiling.

She set down her plate, removed his from his nerveless hands and set it on the table.

He didn't move. He simply looked up at her with those wide dark eyes.

She straddled him in the chair and held on as he took her once again. This time with all the care and tenderness that had been lacking before. Their need had gone quiet and careful. The candlelight caught highlights in his hair, glimmered in his eyes, and made her feel understood and welcome.

He leaned her back to gain access to her chest. She rested her back on the rounded table's edge, dug her fingers into his soft hair and hung on. He murmured his appreciation as he sucked the warmth, heating her womb, heating her chest, until it flooded over her and all she could do was hold him tight to her as her world shifted.

Joshua was not some casual lover. This was not a night of shared sex and a few weeks or months later, *c'est la vie.* She'd always thought the phrase "life-changing sex" to be a naïve and unlikely phrase. Even if this sex didn't change her life, it had certainly tossed out any previous standard she'd ever had.

When they'd both gone over the top as quietly this time as they'd roared over it before, they didn't move. Joshua held her in his lap, resting his head on her shoulder, her own cheek on the top of his impossibly soft hair.

"So," she whispered, just loud enough to be heard over the distant jazz music coming in through the open kitchen window. "Are you going to resist me in the future?"

"I don't know why I was dumb enough to try the first time. Your slightest whim is my command."

"Well, there is this flower that only grows in ancient Tibet—"

Joshua groaned, "I'll wager that going there will not turn me into Batman, which is a pity. I've always lusted after his car."

Melanie rewarded him with a kiss atop his head for understanding her joke. She'd gone to the movie to see Christian Bale, he was ever so enjoyable to look at. She used to do that, make obscure comments, but no one ever understood. It made people uncomfortable, including her. But Joshua kept getting her obscure jokes. One more piece of herself that she could be around him.

"Okay. Here I have for you *une question* that you have carefully avoided every single time I've asked. This time, you have to answer it." It was fun to tease him with the French model, especially because he saw the real Melanie so clearly.

She could feel his nod against her chest. The motion almost made her drag him back to bed. It was so close and personal.

"What are you writing, and why is it making you so *très misérable?*"

"What makes you think—" Josh didn't bother finishing the question. Even Russell had caught on that he was unhappy with his writing, which meant he was being pretty damned obvious about it.

He shifted so that his face was turned directly into Melanie's shoulder. It felt as if he could hide there. Her well-defined collarbone lined up with the bridge of his nose. His nose snuggled into the softness of the muscle just below, his lips on the first suggestion of the rise of her breast. She still rested her cheek atop his head and he could feel her hair sliding over his arms and bare back like a cloak of safety.

"I've had this idea since forever. A foodie mystery. Hercule Poirot meets, I don't know, Julia Child. But every time I try writing, it just sounds contrived or pompous. I write, wrote for a living. And now I'm wondering if I should get my old job back." Had Shirene already contacted Elric? Yes, he'd left New York and quit the magazine almost two weeks ago and she had a magazine to run. She'd probably hung up the phone with him and speed dialed Elric. No call back for other suggestions probably meant he'd leapt at the opportunity as predicted.

Melanie didn't say anything. He'd seen her in the bookstore at Bainbridge. He knew she was an avid reader. Maybe she was thinking what an idiot he was to imagine he could jump from journalism to novel-length fiction.

"I tried opening with a punch like you suggested, but since I don't know what I'm punching, it just comes out lame. Angelo and Russell cooked up this deal where I'm writing him a set of marketing press releases and website copy for the restaurant. A phased campaign. He's thinking about a third restaurant but wants to build up some attention beforehand."

"It is sidetracking you from your novel?"

Melanie smelled so spectacular. He ran one hand up her back beneath the t-shirt, again appreciating her deceptive strength. His other arm remained cinched about her waist to anchor her securely in his lap.

"I see. I am the one sidetracking your attention."

"Perhaps tonight a little more than usual," he admitted. His hands, his senses, his brain was reeling from the floodgates this woman had opened inside him. "Not that I'm complaining."

"Nor I," and she made a motion with her hips that took his breath away. Then she shifted out of his arms until she was once again sitting across from him. She stretched out her forever-long legs, the tail of her t-shirt hiding almost none of their glorious length—or much of anything else—and rested them on his knee.

He began massaging her feet.

"But that is not answering my question again, *monsieur*. And that will never do. Tell me of your story."

Again the image of the lioness struck him. The deadly, powerful, beautiful queen of the savannah, with the power to transform herself into passionate lover, or abandon herself to the moment.

"That's the problem. I don't have one."

"Okay, tell me of your characters."

"They're all bland, or flat, or… Hell, I don't know!"

Melanie closed her eyes as he found a knot down in the arch of her foot. Her breathing picked up pace a bit, her breasts lifting enticingly against the loose, worn-thin Michael Kors t-shirt.

"Oh," she breathed when the muscle had loosened up and he'd eased off. "If you ever want anything from me. Sex, personal shopping, someone to order takeout, just do that again."

He'd have to remember that. He didn't think it would be hard to recall. He was well into the other foot by the time she spoke again.

"Maybe your problem is like a runway show."

He couldn't imagine how, but was glad to listen. She could read the *Wall Street Journal*, all of it, and he'd be glad to listen to her voice. Especially if she was wearing nothing but that thin t-shirt.

"You are starting with the finished show."

"Huh? What? No I'm not. I've got nothing finished. I haven't written a single paragraph worth saving." He forced his gaze up from her amazing breasts to her amused eyes.

"You are starting with the show. A designer never begins with a show. They start with a piece: a jacket, a dress, or..." she wiggled a toe against his ribs which tickled, "...or an emotion. Then another. It is only then that they can build an entire outfit, when they have found the unique qualities of all of those pieces."

"Then you have a show."

"Silly man," she rubbed a foot along his leg, impossibly eliciting a response from his body that he'd have bet was long past recovery. "Then you have one outfit. A twelve-outfit show can easily take twenty or thirty outfits to discover, for some designers it can take hundreds to put together a twenty-piece fall line. Then, it must all be in the right order. Do you write reviews?"

"Sure."

"*Non!* You write about a restaurant, you set it in a city, perhaps a neighborhood. Then you tell the story of its ambience. You might give a hint of a dish as a tease, but you do not describe the whole dish at once. That is for later, to be discovered by the reader as they wind through your review. That is why I like your reviews so much."

Josh had to fight down the distinct urge to preen a bit at the compliment. However he could see what she was after and it made sense. He went to speak, but Melanie was on a roll, sitting up, leaning forward, her feet now on the floor.

"You think I just walk. Any girl can just walk. It is all most girls do is walk. Look, I show you."

Oddly, with this different kind of impatience she didn't slip back into New Jersey, but actually back into her model-world French. No, it wasn't impatience or anger. That's why. It was excitement.

She jumped to her feet. "This walk. The *Grand Pas*, 'Big Stride.' This one. Watch the walk, not me." She set off across the living room with a hard punch that made the t-shirt flounce and bounce in an interesting way, but did look a bit ridiculous.

"Or this one!" Her abrupt tone forced his attention wholly onto the walk. A purposeful stride, more appropriate to a power suit at a Fortune 100 meeting than a t-shirt in a condo.

She continued back and forth, showing him a dozen walks or more, each so unique he could still identify them, even if he didn't know how she did it. Each as unique as a character. She started giving them names. Veronica was practically a streetwalker. Jessie clearly wore a tennis skirt. Razz would be in leather and chains and was so smokin' hot that he wouldn't mind running into her a time or two.

"This one. Her name is Shelley. A new fashion editor I have only met a few times. She is a powerful woman, if a little unsure of herself. She shows that to no one. But there is a tiny slice of it that only the right man can see, that least bit of vulnerability." And she walked away from him with a near perfect, almost military confidence. Three steps from the front door, she half turned to look back over her shoulder, but didn't quite finish the turn. Just that flash of uncertainty totally changing the character. An eyeblink and he would have missed it. If she hadn't told him, he'd certainly have caught the feeling though not why he felt it.

Melanie stood at the far side of the room, her fists on her hips. "*Oui?*"

"*Oui,*" she was absolutely right. He was trying to write a novel. He needed to write a character first, after that maybe a scene.

Then Melanie came walking straight toward him rather than up and down the length of the room. She walked with a perfect awareness of how the t-shirt skimmed the top of her thighs, shrugged the t-shirt off one shoulder at just the right moment to jack his libido through the roof. Head down. Just enough tilt for her face and chest to be wholly hidden by her swinging hair, forcing all attention to her legs and hips. She let each leg carry her weight in turn and her hips completely relax. It caused them to sway in a way that was making him sweat.

She strode up then halted abruptly, her knees a breath away from his. Her feet spread to either side of his own, fists once again on hips, hair swung aside with a sharp toss of her head, revealing bare shoulder, neck, face, and intense blue eyes. This wasn't the lioness, female or not, this was the lion—the greatest hunter of them all. The grandest alpha of the whole pack, no matter her gender.

"Holy crap, Melanie! Who the hell was that?"

"This," she brushed a hand down her length from neck to groin, "is the woman about to drag you back to her bed."

Josh staggered willingly to his feet to be led to his doom.

MELANIE WOKE ABRUPTLY in the dark. Alone. She knew it without having to roll over and look. An empty bed felt different. A shiver rolled up her spine; some dream, barely forgotten, but one that had racked up her heart rate and breathing.

An odd noise came from the living room. A soft sound she couldn't identify.

She donned a t-shirt and sweatpants and crept to the door. A single light lit the kitchen table.

Joshua. The dream retreated a little further.

He sat with an untouched glass of milk rested beside the small laptop. His bare back so beautiful in the softness of the indirect light. Once again he wore jeans that rode low enough to show he wore nothing else. His focus was absolute.

Melanie watched him type for a long time. He'd pause, stare off into the darkness, seeing something, searching in the shadows. Then he'd put his head back down, his fingers flashing across the keys once more before he even had time to look down at the screen.

She was in such trouble with this man. They had been here together days, merely days, yet it felt as normal as if it had been forever. At some point, she'd get a call and she'd be gone. New York, Paris, Milan, Tokyo. The only reason she wasn't gone already, other than the stupid swimsuit issue, was that she hadn't updated her website to show herself as available for bookings.

It wasn't rebound. Yes, Carlo had left her, but over the years she'd been single as much as she'd been with anyone, more. That wasn't the problem. The problem was Joshua Harper.

It was his doing that pieces of her shield lay unrecoverably shattered on the condo's floor. The protection she'd always kept so close about her heart didn't keep out Joshua. And the rest of *The Fabulous Five*. What did they now see and know that she'd never shown to anyone in her life?

Her anchors were gone.

Perhaps he was right. He wasn't good for her. Not safe. She shouldn't have pushed. After five years of marriage it was too soon for him. He'd latched onto her like a breath of fresh air, but that was all. And she'd latched onto him as a fantasy of… She couldn't quite make up an excuse for herself, but it was there. Wasn't it? Domesticity? Of belonging, if only for a moment of time?

Joshua would get lost in some novel, or settle somewhere, put down roots, and never want to leave. He struck her as a complete homebody.

Then she'd be totally screwed.

What if she could adapt? Settle in…Seattle? The runways were New York, Milan, Paris. The photo shoots were mostly New York. Seattle connected to nothing in her life.

Better to just end it, be done with it, and get the hell back to New York where no one knew her. Declare it as one night of marvelous sex and cash it in while she was still ahead before—

"Hey, you. Didn't see you there. I tried not to wake you."

Joshua stood a single step in front of her. His chest all shadows; safe to hide in. But Melanie had never liked hiding from her problems. She'd done it—when the dark clouds of pending depression had threatened to stomp her ass—she'd done it. But she didn't want to hide from this problem.

"Melanie?"

Or did she? "Sorry to interrupt your writing. I'll just go back to bed."

"No, wait. I'm done anyway. I just had to get something down. You inspire me, pretty one."

"Pretty one? *Pretty one!* Is that what I am?" Fuck! That's what her mother always called her right before she struck. When Melanie was a powerless little girl. Well she wasn't powerless any—

"Whoa! Whoa! Whoa!" Josh held up both hands.

If he'd stepped forward, she might have struck out at him. Pay back all that pain, all that fear that—

"Melanie."

"What!"

"Take a breath."

"What?"

"Take a deep breath."

"Look, I'm breathing just fine." She waved to her chest. That's all men saw of her anyway.

"You're on the verge of hyperventilating."

"If I do, it's my own damn problem!" Then she heard her own voice; heard the shrillness that sounded so like her mother's. How had it spun in on her? And tonight of all nights? She and Joshua made such love and here she was... She could feel her cheeks flash hot as she bolted for the bedroom.

She didn't make it. Josh stopped her easily; his casual, unthinking strength a comfort rather than a cause of fear. He led her away from the safety of the bedroom, from the safety of the bathroom where she could lock the door, the shower where she could weep and no one would hear. He guided her to the couch. Sat her down. Wrapped a throw around her shoulders. Then he fetched his untouched milk.

"Sip this. Slowly."

When she didn't unclench her fists from inside the blanket where they were bunched close below her neck, he held the glass to her lips. She was forced to take a swallow or have it dribbling down her chin.

It was warm, soothing.

She could feel it moving down, into her belly. Her breathing slowed, damn him. And her heart rate along with it.

Finally, she simply leaned her head into the middle of his chest. He set down the glass of milk and wrapped his arms around her blanketed shoulders. She was unable to speak past her own embarrassment. Now was when he left her. Now was when he decided she wasn't worth the trouble. In the past... Actually, no one had been allowed to see this in the past. No one had ever seen The Melanie at her most fallible.

"Well..."

Here it came.

"You did mention being less than perfect, didn't you?" His voice was light, amused.

She had.

"I'm still not seeing it."

Melanie jerked upright to protest. But in the motion, she clipped his chin with the back of her head.

Hard!

His curses and intermittent, "Ow! Ow! Ow! My tong-ga!" would have been funny. Was funny. God she was such a mess that she started to laugh. Beyond funny, it was ridiculous.

The laugh swept her. They were two such ludicrous people.

She wiped at her eyes to see Joshua's expression shift slowly from pain to amusement to laughing himself.

"Ow! Ow! Don' make me laugh! Hurth!"

That tipped her right off the deep end. She collapsed into his lap, right onto... Well, wasn't that interesting. No questioning her effect on Joshua's body, not even when he was in pain.

His bare belly was right there. She put her lips against it and blew a loud raspberry.

His laugh turned into a high and silly giggle, intermixed with "Ow! Ow! Ow!" Gods he was so cute.

She blew another raspberry against his ticklish spot.

He twitched. Pushed at her.

She managed one more before he leveraged her away.

The next moment his mouth was on hers and if his tongue was still hurting, he showed no signs of it.

He swept her up in his arms, blanket and all, and carried her back to bed without once breaking the kiss.

CHAPTER 11

"*here does it come* from, Melanie?"

They'd woken together, sometime well into the morning. Rather than simply expecting sex first thing, Joshua merely held her. Again, they had slept wrapped around each other.

She discovered that she was past keeping secrets from Joshua. Past being coy, or pretending to be. When had that happened?

"What are your parents like?" she had to know his frame of reference.

"They're all right. Retired a couple years ago to Florida. How stereotypical New York can you get? I try to see them a few times a year, whenever I'm, I was, in the area to review a restaurant. We're good. Not close, but good. Why?"

She held onto him hard, hoping against hope that he'd still be there when she was done telling him about hers. No one on the planet other than Perrin knew anything at all about her parents, and even she didn't know the details. Melanie would bet that was one story that hadn't traveled to Jo and Cassidy. There were some things they wouldn't understand. Of the three of them, only Perrin had also known fear.

"I don't know how to tell this," she rolled her face into his chest looking for strength and, oddly, found it.

"Just say it. I'll still be here when you're done."

Some little girl part of her wanted him to promise. Maybe he already had. In Joshua's arms was the safest place she'd ever been. *Just do it, Melanie.* She took a deep breath and began.

"When I was eleven, I woke up to hear a terrible fight going on outside my bedroom. Apparently my father had decided I was pretty enough for him to spend some time with."

Joshua's body went rigid. His voice, at least an octave lower, ground out, "Did he touch you?" It was the first time she'd ever heard anger in his voice and it would have been terrifying if it was aimed at her. He'd shifted in a heartbeat from thoughtful lover to powerful bull-male. The kind you didn't want to upset.

"He never had the chance. Mom caught him halfway through my bedroom door on his first foray. In minutes, we were in the car and gone. I had clothes and school books, not much else. We never went back."

"Three cheers for her."

"No," she tried to sit up to judge his face, but he was holding her so tightly she couldn't move even that much. "You don't understand. She was yelling at him about the risk of damaging me. My first big photo shoot was scheduled for the next morning."

"At eleven?"

"I started out as a hand model," she held up one before her eyes as if she could see what was so special about them, but had never spotted it. "In the first years I made over thirty percent of my income from my hands. I still accept a dozen or so hand shoots a year. Sometimes for the oddest thing. Jewelry sure, but also holding a Coke can, a fine ink pen... No soap commercials. Risk of rash."

"How did the shoot go?"

"The photographer's cat scratched me and they had to get another model. My mother slapped me so hard we had to cancel two face shoots as well because my face was swollen. I missed a week of school because you could still see the palm print on my cheek. Those first months living in the car together were hard."

"You—" His voice choked off. His anger beyond speech.

"Mom ran my career with an iron fist for seven years, though she never struck me again anywhere that would show. By the time I was eighteen, I was a lot smarter. She'd been waiting for that moment, had been focusing all her efforts toward the big payouts. She had *Playboy*, *Hustler*, and a couple of porn movie companies all lined up for the day I became legal."

Joshua merely ground his teeth.

Usually when she'd thought of those years she felt ill, misused, and so very alone. But now she simply felt disconnected. She could have been reading a school report aloud for all she felt. Again, the safety of Joshua's arms.

"Did you—" There was no doubt as to his feeling on this. He wasn't some man asking if there were salacious photos he had missed somewhere. This was a man angry almost past tolerance.

"No. Never. If you see a naked photo of me, it's a fake. Not even a peep shot from the changing areas backstage at a runway. I gained a rather fierce reputation by smashing high-end camera equipment pretty early on."

"Well done!"

"I did a family divorce, got custody of myself, so to speak. Put out a restraining order against my mother. Shed myself of her name, that is why I use no last name. I let her keep the money she'd embezzled as my manager."

"You let her keep—"

"I didn't want it. Not after her slimy hands had been all over it. Actually, every account I was a signatory on, I signed over to charity. I'm sure she had accounts I didn't know about, but I bet I got most of it. The day I turned eighteen I was broke, but I was my own woman. And I was in demand. I'd studied business like hell and have been my own manager since that day. I own a small studio apartment free and clear in a secure building in Manhattan. Everything else—everything, went into savings." She smiled and kissed Joshua's chest. He still hadn't let her up and it felt wonderful. "I'm very well off."

"Shit!"

"What?"

"I was wrong before." She tried to read his voice, but she couldn't. The anger was gone but she couldn't tell what had replaced it.

"Wrong about what?"

"About the whole perfect thing."

"Blew my cover, did I?" She tried to smile as she said it. She really hoped this wasn't where he pushed her away. And she should never have mentioned all the money. Bad slip.

He finally released her. Rolled slightly until they lay face to face, just inches apart. His dark eyes were intent, warm, welcoming. No signs of disgust or avarice. Every time she second-guessed his motivations, she'd been wrong.

"Totally blew your cover," Joshua acknowledged with a brush of knuckles along her cheek. "What's the word for someone who's better than perfect?"

She shoved against his shoulder which barely moved him. He was far stronger than he looked.

He leaned in and kissed her.

She let herself melt into the kiss.

"Wait," he murmured against her lips. "What's better than that?"

Then he showed her just what he really thought of her.

For a whole week Melanie let herself play house. During the days she worked with Perrin on her business plan and consulted with Tamara after school on her new line.

In the evenings she and Joshua began exploring the local restaurants from the old tradition of The Merchant Café to the little Pho noodle shop on the corner. At night she had the best lover imaginable.

And they never shut up around each other. Joshua's characters were starting to take shape. He was cast-building and between them they worked out how his characters walked and talked, their backgrounds and how they reacted to different stresses. Teaching Joshua how to do the walks enough to feel them with his body had left them both in tears with laughter.

Joshua held Melanie's hand when they took long strolls along the Seattle waterfront. They would walk an hour or more because they were so enjoying the discussions.

Shelley was now one of his main characters.

"She walks just like you did that night," Joshua's eyes went dreamy at the memory.

She had more where that came from.

"Though I gave her thick dark hair. She's a military trainer."

"Who lives where?"

"How should I know? In a renovated missile silo?" he'd tossed it out flippantly.

Melanie's spontaneous laugh had apparently settled that idea for Joshua. So, they'd gone about the task of designing the levels of her missile silos. Two silos: one to live in, one to run training sessions in. It was all a great game.

During the day while she was at Perrin's, he'd be at Angelo's or the Pioneer Square condo pounding out words. In the evening she'd read through them, marking the bits she liked and the bits she didn't. He had a turn of phrase that made her smile when she least expected it.

One afternoon she'd received a text to meet him at the urban park on the high side of Second and Madison. She found him sitting on a bench in the bricked yard, shaded by leafed-out maple trees. Melanie could easily spend the day just watching him work.

But the sixth sense Joshua had developed about her presence had him turning within moments though she'd come up behind him. The afternoon traffic was loud, the metro buses shuffling and roaring.

"How?"

"Me and Superman."

A quick scan and she spotted the tall coffee shop window in which they were both clearly reflected. "No, Joshua. Just you. Superman didn't have eyes in the back of his head."

JOSH LOVED that Melanie had both spotted his cheat and let him have the win anyway. He kept his kiss brief because they were in a public place and he didn't want some random scandal photographer to get a photo and make her life miserable.

"C'mon. I just discovered this place that I've got to show you." He offered his arm.

She slipped in her hand and he led her two blocks up the hill and toward a building that filled an entire city block, six or seven stories of diamond-shaped glass. He waited until she spotted the sign.

"The Public Library." He could hear the blasé tone. Nothing was as good as NYPL; the New York Public Library was one of the best libraries on the planet after all.

"Trust me," Joshua was grinning as he led her inside.

"Stacks. So what's the big deal?" The place was bustling, but it was just stacks on the first floor.

Without a word, he led her up the escalator. And the world opened above them. Computers and comfortable meeting rooms ranged far and wide across the floor. Light poured in from above. The modern version of the NYPL's Rose Main Reading Room, with lines of reading desks and fifty-foot ceiling muraled like the sky.

"It's pretty."

Rather than speaking, he led her to an elevator and took them to the top floor. The view from the top was nice, but nothing spectacular. Without comment he led her down the ramp that circled downward. Level bookshelves ranged off to either side, but the aisle descended in a spiral row by row.

They were in the 100s before she noticed the numbers painted on the floors, the walls, the bookcases. By the 200s she was looking a little dazzled as they completed the first lap of their descent.

"How many stories?" she barely whispered.

"Four full laps to go from 000s to 900s. This isn't New York. You can just walk into the stacks without a catalog query and a request to a librarian. Any subject. Look!"

He led her into 391 and there was costume and history. Just as he'd hoped she got all gooey-eyed. She reached out to touch some of them like old friends.

"I'd show you 746, but I'll never see you again if I do."

She leaned and began whispering in French close by his ear. It took him time to translate, especially as he didn't know some of the words and he had to kind of cobble together the sense of them. Then he caught on.

The gorgeous lover of his was describing things that maybe even the *Kama Sutra* didn't know about. Things she'd do tonight if he led her to that section directly.

He considered blushing, considered it seriously as they were standing in the middle of the library stacks. Instead he took a deep breath.

"You are not motivating me to do anything but drag you back to the condo right away."

"Then you get *zéro. Rien. Nada. Zilch. Nichts. Ny—*"

"I get the idea. I get the idea. Why do you know how to say 'no' in so many languages."

"It is, how you say, useful around men."

"You're killing me with the accent." One of the things she'd started doing was that all of their sex was done in French. It was definitely improving his language skills, but it also made him horny as hell every time she said even a word or two in the language.

And she bloody well knew it. *Merde!* But the woman was going to kill him yet.

He zigzagged her through staircases that cut across the middle of the loops instead of walking the descending spiral of the full catalog.

Joshua let her walk into 746 on her own. Textile Arts and near the very end of the category, one of the most impressive fashion collections he'd ever seen.

MELANIE RANGED ALONG THE BOOKCASES. There were references here she hadn't known existed. Other volumes she'd only seen in Óscar de la Renta's personal collection.

But the greatest surprise was that Joshua had found this for her. He'd had clearly scouted out the two non-fiction sections she'd most care about and given them to her as a treat.

He stood in the "bead embroidery" section pretending interest so that she wouldn't feel rushed. What was he doing to her? How had she come to care so much about the man?

Melanie didn't "fall" for men; she chose lovers. Carefully, with forethought and discernment. Joshua simply swept her feet from beneath her.

This week held other surprises. Apparently, having been beaten back twice in the same week by Joshua, her depression had given up its attacks and fled. At least for now. Melanie didn't even feel it lurking, though it couldn't be completely gone. That was too much to ask.

It was often six months or once whole a year between attacks that drove her to go to ground for a week. She'd always managed to hold it off when there was work scheduled, but this time it had been driven away by the man now browsing through the fabric dyeing section. Future retribution worried her somewhat, but she did her best not to contemplate the problem.

She and this man had bared their hearts to one another. They'd spoken of their pasts, the cracks in his marriage—only visible in hindsight. Her failure with Russell. It was as if the revelation of her childhood had taken down the last of the walls between them.

The one thing they carefully didn't discuss was the future. They curled up each night as if it might be their last together, and woke with a shared look of surprise and wonder.

This was as close as they'd come, his showing her something he knew she would love, this beautiful fashion collection just begging to be studied and enjoyed over time. She wondered if he was conscious of it, that he was trying to find reasons for her to stay in Seattle even if there was no possible way for it to work without destroying her career.

It was an eloquent statement and she would gladly repay him for the effort by delivering every single thing she had whispered into his ear.

But they both knew it was impossible.

About that there could never be any words.

CHAPTER 13

ngelo's two restaurants were open over the weekend and closed Mondays and Tuesdays, so everyone had shifted their schedules to match. Jo managed the Pike Place Market on that schedule. Russell and Cassidy were freelancers so they were always busy, but were more likely to take time off on Monday and Tuesday.

Perrin was caught in between, with the kids in school and her husband as the stage manager for Emerald City Opera. So, she worked Monday through Friday, but the shop ran Wednesday through Sunday.

When Melanie arrived on Monday morning, the front door on Second Avenue was locked. But she spotted the light in the back of the darkened shop. She went around to the alley door, picking her way around a couple of city-ugly dumpsters to tap on the back door, though the alley itself was open and totally harmless.

Perrin let her in. No seamstresses today, so apparently they too were working the Wednesday through Sunday schedule. The shop was quiet and peaceful, but Perrin was still a whorl of activity with a half dozen projects spread about.

"Tomorrow is Tuesday, you know," Perrin stated as if that explained something.

"Which means what?"

"It means that you and Josh are coming to dinner. We all go to Maria and Hogan's every Tuesday."

Melanie blinked. It was no longer a shock that she was included, but still a pleasant surprise. "What do we bring?"

"Oh, first timers just show up."

She reminded herself to talk to Joshua. Melanie didn't like the idea of being a "first timer," of being somehow different from the others. They'd think up something appropriate.

"They're also probably going sailing tomorrow."

"That's so not going to happen," sailing was not a Melanie sport. Not even a little. She recalled touring Russell's boat on that wonderful-horrible Valentine's Day that had been the end of their relationship as lovers. She felt slightly nauseous just remembering the oil swirl of water across the bilge exposed through the missing floorboard.

Perrin laughed, "Yeah, our first trip didn't work out so well either." By Perrin's grimace it must have been something spectacular. "I almost lost Bill and we both almost lost Jaspar. The boys still go out with Russell, but Tamara and I almost never go with."

They chatted a while, talked business for a bit. But something was bothering Perrin. She was holding back, which wasn't like her. Neither was she working on a design or a construction while she talked.

Melanie tried prying it out of her without success, so finally she just asked.

"Well, you've been so kind to me, I hate to ask. But Russell said I should."

"Perrin, spill it or I'll force you to make me a dress out of that very expensive fabric you had the other day."

Perrin's eyes slid aside for a moment, but her smile increased rather than diminishing. "Not yet," but declined to explain that comment when Melanie pushed.

"The thing is," Perrin went to a clothing rack in the corner and fussed with a line of garment bags. "I answered the phone yesterday. I really shouldn't do that, but Raquel was busy with a customer and I happened to be in the shop with Tammy and… Well, I…"

Melanie waited her out until Perrin spilled it all forth in a single breath. "It was *Fashion Alive* magazine. Not that editor; the ad department. They had a last minute cancellation—after they were already in layout—so they have to fill the ad space. The editor told them, I have no idea why, that I could fill it on short notice. They're giving it to me gratis if I can send the images by tomorrow."

"Are you kidding, Perrin? That's great! They're on the verge of challenging *Marie Claire*. A third-page ad is almost ten thousand dollars. Gratis is enormous."

Perrin's nerves were wilder than usual. She began folding and refolding a piece of blue corduroy that must be for one of Tamara's projects; the blue had pop, it was a thoughtful selection. Melanie grabbed Perrin's hands to still them and sat down on a stool. That forced Perrin to come to rest opposite her.

"It's a game changer, isn't it, Melanie? You told me one was coming, but it's too soon. I'm not ready."

"Yes," Melanie had to acknowledge, "stepping into *Fashion Alive* is a game changer. Even a small ad will have a real impact on your business. But this is really too important an opportunity to miss. You're far more ready than I thought you were at the beginning of the week. I'll commit to staying at least another week so that I can show you how to tweak the plan to make it work. You'll have to bring on more people. I already talked to the owner of the shop next door. He said he'd love to rent the back room, it's empty right now. So you could just punch a door right there," Melanie pointed at the wall, "and create a sewing room pretty easily."

"Okay, I kinda hoped you'd say that it made sense, but that isn't the favor I wanted to ask."

Melanie kept a tight hold on both of Perrin's hands as she could still feel Perrin's nerves humming.

"Russell is willing to take the pictures for me, but would you be my model? I can't pay very much, but you'd be so perfect for these designs and it really freaks Cassidy and Jo when I make them pose and—"

Melanie cut her off. "Yes."

"Really?"

"No, I said that just to get you to calm down," Melanie laughed at the abrupt disappointment that flashed onto her friend's features. "Of course I will, Perrin. I love your designs. They always make me look so at the edge of new ideas. I'd be thrilled to pose for you."

"Wow! Uh, how much do you—"

"How about that dress I mentioned?"

Perrin's smile was electric. "Well, that might be cheating, but it's a deal." She didn't explain her enigmatic comment.

"It's a deal!" Melanie and Perrin spoke in unison and together shook their still-clasped hands up and down.

"Two other things I should probably mention."

"What are they?" Melanie was pleased. It would be fun to do a shoot, even a little one.

"First, Russell rented my old apartment upstairs as a studio and he said to call him as soon as I found you. I should have called you earlier. I was trying to get up the nerve when you came by. He wants to do it right away."

Melanie took a deep breath and checked in with herself about modeling for Russell. She was feeling wonderful, much of which was Joshua's doing. And it *would* be great to work with Russell again. He always found a way to make her look so alluring. Even if it was just a third-page ad, the discards would create some fresh material for her website.

"Call him now."

Perrin squeezed her hands hard.

"What's the other thing?"

Perrin reached for the phone and began dialing. She kept her head down as she spoke.

Melanie could barely hear her mumble.

"The cancellation was a four-page spread in the first twenty pages."

MELANIE WAS STILL TRYING to digest that bit of news as she worked her way into the first dress and did her own makeup.

When Tamara arrived from school, she was instantly tasked with brushing out Melanie's hair. Not a single snarl or twist allowed. Her hair was always either a straight fall or in a ponytail. Her trademark hair was never up, never teased, and god forbid never colored. That was part of her contracts; it also vastly simplified styling choices for the designer. Which many complained about, but ultimately seemed to appreciate.

A four-page spread in the front twenty. The only thing that caused a cancellation like that was a revelation of illegal activity, like design theft. Even the buyout of a fashion house wouldn't cause that late a change. All of the space was prepaid and they were way past the late-cancellation deadline, so the magazine would have no financial loss and could afford to give away, she did the math, almost eighty thousand dollars of space.

Melanie considered kicking out a text to some industry friends to find out who had choked and how. There were only a dozen or so advertisers who could afford that major a spread to begin with. The front twenty was the stomping grounds of only the very best and the very well-funded who typically reserved that space over a year ahead. She'd text later.

"The editor was one of your customers," Melanie knew it was right the instant she said it.

Perrin shrugged in the mirror. "I don't work front of shop much anymore, so she mostly dealt with Raquel. But after she'd bought three pieces in a single fling, she insisted on meeting me. I only had a few minutes before Bill picked me up, but she was very excited. She looked great in one of my day dresses, very chic and flirty."

"That's a true fan, Perrin. They are rare and precious people who can make all of the difference." Thinking of fans, maybe she should call Joshua. She'd come to accept that he was a fan of her public image, even forcing him to unearth the *Teen Vogue* when he'd confessed to owning a copy. She'd looked good. Young, but good. She couldn't be angry because Joshua had also proved time and again how clearly he also saw the real Melanie.

"Look who I found just hanging around to carry my gear for me," Russell announced as he burst in the back door.

Joshua peeked at her over Russell's broad shoulders.

Russell winked at her from where he'd stopped, completely filling the back doorway with his broad-shouldered frame and two camera cases.

Joshua had to shove past the grinning man. He crossed the studio and reached for her.

"Don't touch the hair. Tamara's been working too hard for you to muss it up."

She could see the temptation cross his features.

"Don't even think it, Harper. Just don't."

Instead, he held her hand and kissed her on the lips very sweetly. She gave him a careful hug, then turned back to the mirror to check the damage. Well worth it.

THE SHOOT ITSELF WAS A BLUR, they always were. Melanie let herself become a vehicle for the photographer's instructions. She'd done photo shoots with Russell: before, during, and after they'd been lovers. It had made little difference; they were professionals doing the jobs they both did best.

But Joshua affected her, she could feel it. She'd walk toward the camera and recall the heat she'd seen fire up in Joshua's eyes when she'd worn only a t-shirt instead of one of the sexiest pant suits she'd ever seen.

She would turn to look over her shoulder at the camera and see Joshua standing behind Russell with a smile so wide she wanted to go and kiss it off his face.

They went through a dozen pieces, Perrin and Tamara scrambling back and forth between the downstairs design studio and the upstairs apartment-turned-photo studio. Russell had Joshua stand in to give her positioning for a pose—something about them being the same height was desirable, but Russell didn't stop to explain—and then move him carefully aside without jostling her. Even after he was gone, she could feel herself leaning on his shoulder and smiling from somewhere down inside.

For some reason that he never explained and she'd never asked, Russell never used to use her face in his ads. He always hid it with hair, hat, shadow, or other composition. Not this shoot.

The time flew. At some point, they fed her. Later, Bill and Jaspar came to pick up Tamara and instead ended up being recruited by Russell to the dozens of odd jobs involved in a shoot: angling reflectors, holding meter cards, shifting umbrella lights, moving props without disturbing the model's position, flapping boards in front of a large fan to create little gusts, and a myriad of others.

Melanie and Joshua were actually reentering the condo by the time she came back to herself, just like a couple returning from a good day's work. Both chattering away about how fun it had been as he unlocked and held doors for her to pass through first.

The afternoon had been an extravagant whirlwind of innovative clothes and immense fun. Joshua had taken to making the occasional funny face over Russell's shoulder, several causing Melanie to crack up and lose a pose.

"I *love* photo shoot modeling!"

Joshua laughed at her passion as she set her purse in its usual spot then did a twirl in the middle of the living room.

"It's the single thing I loved the most. More than the runway. It's that back and forth with a truly skilled photographer."

"Uh-huh."

The man was slouched against the wall with his arms folded across his chest. That sparkle in his eyes and grin on his face whenever he was just watching her. He never tired of it and she never felt self-conscious in front of him. She just felt...appreciated.

"It's like you were saying when you got that first scene written." She spun over and pinned him to the wall for a moment with her lips and body. Even when she pulled back enough to continue, she used her body to keep him there. "That energy the character gave you and you gave her. It just hums inside you."

And it had been such a joy. None of them were being paid and none of them cared. They were all there to help a friend. Well, she'd get a killer dress out of it, because that was the only kind of dress Perrin made. She'd felt a little guilty about requesting such luxurious fabrics, but a free four-page spread would pay it back in the first day's orders.

"Joshua, we have to totally re-do Perrin's plan. A big spread wasn't supposed to happen until next year."

"You also didn't factor in having the most beautiful woman on the planet being the signature model."

She giggled at the compliment. Melanie never giggled, but she couldn't help herself. Joshua simply made her feel that special.

"Let's go dancing!"

And that's exactly what they did. They hit Pioneer Square.

"Hey look!" Joshua pointed at the sign above a bar right in the heart of the Square.

"The J&M Café. Oldest bar in Seattle." Melanie read in wonder. "The J&M Mutual Admiration Society now has a base of operations."

They drank one beer each, laughed like they'd had a dozen, and rocked out to the live band right up to the two a.m. closing time.

Russell had called them to come early to Maria's Tuesday night dinner. Cassidy and Russell lived a few blocks north of the Market in Belltown. Maria and Hogan lived in a building that looked directly down on the cobbled streets, booths and the water-front. The apartment was cozy for a couple rather than spacious and begging for expansion like the Pioneer Square condo.

They'd decorated it with a tasteful eye and an old-world elegance that fit them. Kitchen, bedroom, and office all opened off one wall. The living room boasted a large brown leather sofa facing the view and several comfortable-looking armchairs to either side. Bookcases down the left wall. The back of the living room was the domain of a massive oak table that could easily seat a dozen.

Josh hadn't been sure what to bring. Just a bottle of wine seemed lame. And going up against a patissier of Maria's skill also kept desserts off the list of possible things to bring. He'd settled on a platter of build-it-yourself bruschetta. He premade and toasted the thin rounds of French baguette and rubbed them all lightly with garlic. Then he'd made a large plate with a pile of fresh-made mozzarella cheese at the center and surrounded it with mounds of slivered olives, chiffonaded basil, diced sun-dried tomatoes, and a half-dozen other toppings.

It had earned him a hug from Maria and had earned Russell a swat from her when he'd tried to grab a fistful of the toasts to munch on. So, Joshua would count that as a two-fold success.

"You know," Russell absently flexed his sore knuckles as he turned to Melanie. "I won't use any image without your approval. But I think you'll like these. I really hope so, because I didn't have time to make any other variations. I already ran them by Perrin and she's over the moon." He rubbed his mouth where Josh would bet she'd planted a smacking kiss of thanks.

"But no pressure to like them," Melanie had laughed that beautiful laugh of hers then tugged Josh along to go look at them. The four prints were laid down on the bright oak of the big dining room table.

Josh had never really looked at Russell's work, except the landscapes on the walls of Angelo's restaurants. Those evoked a specific, soothing emotion making it a comfortable place to dine rather than merely eat. But these fashion photographs were something else again. Even to his untrained eye each was a straight-shot punch to the gut.

Melanie was posing—with herself! That's why he'd had to stand in to help her find the right poses. Rather than four images of her, there were a total of nine on the four pages. In the first, the pantsuit clad Melanie was resting a casual hand on a friend's shoulder, except the friend was also Melanie, dressed for a night on the town and laughing at a joke just told.

In the next, she leaned against her own back, clad once in a dynamo black powersuit of jacket and skinny spring-green dress, the other in the slacks, blouse, and loosened tie of waterfall silk of a woman supremely competent and confident—enough so to not need the powersuit. Each appeared to be scoffing at the other's presumption.

Sportswear was clearly the subject of a grudge match between two ponytailed Melanies somehow glaring at each other but also, just as clearly, giving the camera a nudge-and-a-wink look that made him want to laugh.

The last page. He wanted a life-size poster of that last image. Melanie three ways. Three brilliant evening gowns the color of new leaves—each radiating sex in its own way. But it wasn't just sex, it was the raw power of the incredibly feminine form within. One with deep cleavage and soft flowing folds, the second with a form-hugging sleekness, and the last dress so thoroughly covering her body that it was impossible to avoid imagining the woman beneath.

Separately they were beautiful, together they were astonishing.

Josh could pick out each woman. Could see the powerful, the shy, the playful, and all of the others she'd told him about and walked for him. But there was something more, if he could only identify it.

Melanie gave Russell hands-down approval. They went to the computer in Hogan's small home office to sign the model releases and send them off to the magazine.

Josh stayed to study the pictures and see if he could figure out what he wasn't seeing.

"She loves you so very much."

He startled to see that Maria had come up beside him to look down at the images of Melanie. Then Maria's words registered. "She what?"

"Look," she nodded down to the nine figures looking back at him. "If you can't see it in how she looks at you, it is right there in all of the pictures. Russell is very skilled, but even he couldn't have done that if it weren't in her to give."

And now Josh could see it. He could see that all nine of the women before him were also the final woman. It was a woman Melanie hadn't shown him before. It wasn't the lioness who had devoured his heart. It was the beautiful woman who had offered hers to him.

She reentered the room from the office door not ten feet away, laughing about something with Russell. Then she turned to him and her face shifted. It was subtle. If he hadn't been studying the images before him, if Maria hadn't pointed out the common thread, he wouldn't have understood the change.

There was no question, Maria was right.

Melanie loved him.

Just maybe she loved him as much as he abruptly realized he loved her.

"WHAT IS IT?" Melanie had asked Joshua three times during dinner, but he had only shaken his head and looked away. Something had shifted after he'd seen those wonderful ads Russell had made.

He took another bite of his Italian cheesecake, clearly to avoid answering her question.

"You begin to scare me, Joshua." She kept her voice low. She really hoped he wasn't somehow seeing her again as the supermodel. He was the only one who saw past the external beauty; past the make-believe she presented to the world. At first it had scared her, but she had come to cherish that about him.

Russell had indeed made her look fabulous. These ads were going to, as Perrin would say, kick ass. But if they'd made Joshua lose that unique perspective he had of her, it wouldn't have been worth it.

Maria and Hogan had propped up the first three images for display along one of the bookcases and tacked the fourth on the wall which was covered with candid shots, mostly of the people in this room. The photo shoot was definitely the news of the evening and the images were a near constant topic. Only now did it strike her that Maria might intend to add that image permanently to the family collection.

To keep Russell's ego in check, Perrin and Tammy had started a campaign of teasing him horribly about anything they could come up with. Cassidy had joined in on the side of her husband and Jo was refereeing in such a way as to make it more lively. Cassidy had been right; Jo was sneaky.

As the sun had set beyond the Olympics, candlelight had replaced the sunlight. The room was crowded and loud, filled with the sounds of friends simply glad to be together.

And no one was treating her strangely at all. Not because of the photos, not because she was a supermodel. No one, except Joshua.

Maria and Hogan sat at either end of the main table, but with the restaurant staff and other friends, there were sufficient numbers that they spilled over into the living area, returning to the table only to restock plates from the vast trays of food that had been prepared and to add a tease to the merry battle surrounding Russell. It was cheerful mayhem.

She became aware that Joshua was studying her closely. The noise around the table was sufficient to create something of a bubble around them.

"You," Joshua whispered softly enough that only she would hear it, "are the one who is scaring me."

He must have seen her confusion.

His answer was to lean in and give her a kiss that reassured her more than any words could have done. It was a kiss flavored of ricotta, chocolate, and strawberries—Maria's Italian cheesecake. It lingered, tested, and asked. She didn't know the question, but she answered and felt the shift inside her as she did so. Her heart didn't pound, instead it beat as smooth and silky as the texture of the dessert. Joshua's kiss was a place she could go to be lost forever. Time, sound, the external world stopped. Nothing existed but them, their connection, their being together in this lingering moment.

When the kiss ended, her ears were buzzing. And that was the only sound in the room. From one end of the table to the other, everyone was looking at them. Even those sitting in the living room chairs and sofa were silent. Cassidy and Perrin actually had tears in their eyes. Jo had rested her head on Angelo's broad shoulder.

Tammy broke the silence with a thirteen-year old's sigh that sent a ripple of laughter around the room. Then Jaspar offered a ten-year-old boy's view with a loud, "Eww!" which shifted the sound of the laughter yet again and slowly rekindled conversations.

Melanie didn't blush when she was kissed. More than one of her clinches had ended up on the cover of *People* and a fair number had graced the cover of the *National Enquirer.* But now the heat roared to her face.

She considered facing the laughter in defiance. But it was a friendly sound that made her feel both welcome and fortunate. So, rather than pulling on her imperious cloak, she did as Joshua did and turned her full attention to her dessert—only too aware of how closely their legs pressed together beneath the table.

osh had wanted to help, but Melanie only let him do so when she was stuck on some particular aspect of Perrin's business strategy.

"Your job, Joshua, is to write. You wrote those two press releases for her, which were wonderful, thank you. But that is not your passion. You have quit your job to write a novel. Go, write your novel."

As if he could just wave a wand and the typed pages would appear. So, he'd gone alone to his usual table at Angelo's and sat down to write.

He tried waving a fork of the boar-sausage pasta that Graziella had served him for lunch, but all it did was waft the delicious smell of garlic, sausages, and fresh basil; no novel magically appeared on the table or under it. He checked.

So he ate the pasta, ignored the gentle conversations of the late lunch crowd, and, as he'd done all week, turned back to his computer. He had his fictional world built. It was a crazy one that was nothing like he'd imagined.

He'd thought it might be a cozy murder mystery, a poisoning, half the people in the house guilty, the other half wishing they'd thought to kill the victim themselves, no one knowing who to trust. Not just cliché; way overdone cliché.

Melanie had pointed that out and he'd thrown away almost five thousand words.

Hard-boiled had been another dead lead. The Sam Spade of the culinary world, still referring to women as "dames" and guns as "heaters" though he lived in the modern world. It simply hadn't come together. That had only cost him a thousand words or so.

He'd tried to force it to be a police procedural: *CSI* does Pike Place Market. So not. Another thousand.

But this? He didn't know where it had come from. It was as much political thriller as anything else.

It had Shelley his female soldier, a television celebrity chef with Hubert Keller's graying ponytail, and the first female President. The cast reminded him of last night's second dinner at Maria's, just as diverse and off-the-wall fun as the first. Melanie's triptych, now framed, had still hypnotized him and he still hadn't found a way to talk about his revelation. In love, both of them, and neither daring to say it aloud.

That's all his novel's plot needed to make it a complete train wreck —a love story.

Josh stopped with another forkful of pasta halfway to his mouth and stared at his screen.

He'd built his world: a tableau of people rife with quirks and short-comings. He had a cool opening murder, there were so many inter-esting ways to kill off a chef.

But what if it wasn't a mystery? That's how these people fit together! It wasn't a foodie mystery, it was a foodie thriller.

And a love story.

He couldn't think the words without thinking of Melanie. All week, they still hadn't spoken a single word of the future. Telling her that he loved her could ruin that. With love went commitment. Not just committing to relationship, but the mere act of loving meant connection.

And that had worked out so spectacularly badly for each of them.

With their track record they shouldn't even start. There was a thought that hurt like hell.

Rather than speaking—rather than forcing a conversation neither of them had wanted to have—they lived the future one day at a time. They went for walks, made dinner plans, lunched with friends, and worked hard. Perrin's business was consuming Melanie's days and the novel his, but the nights were their own.

They bought little things for the Pioneer Square condo. Not for themselves but for the condo, because anything more might imply some form of permanence. A poster that would look good there. Bright pillows that cheered up the sofa. A couple of yoga exercise mats that Melanie was using to prove to Joshua just how inflexible he was. "I should teach a class called, 'Yoga for men who don't bend'!" She should, he for one would gladly pay to watch how she could move.

They were living a love story, one day at a time by continuing to pretend that tomorrow didn't exist.

His novel needed a love story. Not only wasn't his book a murder mystery, it wasn't a foodie thriller either. No. It was a foodie romantic suspense. It was crazy; that same kind of craziness that somehow made sense. Like him being in love with a supermodel who loved him back—ridiculous from the outside, wonderful from the inside.

The woman would be the chef...no, too stereotypical. She'd be Shelley's protégé. A shapely, ambitious senior airman with a cheery blond bob. Penny Baker, bright and shiny like the copper coin, with a cooking last name to intrigue the chef hero.

The man, the older chef's protégé... No, too much the same as Penny. He needed another story...

Josh startled to realize that Melanie was sitting quietly on the other side of the table. They had brainstormed so much, that he didn't think about it, he just leapt in.

"I need another character. Interesting guy. Cooks a lot. Professional chef or the potential to be one. Not sure yet. He needs to be someone for my heroine to fall in love with."

"You."

He opened his mouth, then closed it.

Melanie took a deep breath and let it out slowly. Then her smile shone to life. "Wow! That was a surprise."

"I'm noticing that."

"Well," Melanie reached over to take a forkful of his pasta. "Oh that's so *délectable*. Angelo is definitely a food criminal, because this is sinfully wonderful."

Then she looked at him more seriously.

"Any woman with the least common sense would fall in love with you, Joshua Harper."

He tried to catch his breath, but it was sticking somewhere in his chest. "You always struck me as a woman with immense common sense." How lame was that? He was begging.

"Thank you," she reached over to take another forkful. She made him wait while she ate another bite, her eyes remaining locked on his.

She took her time chewing, swallowing, reaching to take a sip of his ice tea.

He remained mute.

"Yes, I'm not sure that it is sensible, but I have fallen quite in love with you, Joshua. I find that it complicates things quite badly."

"I've *been* noticing that myself for over a week." There. He'd as good as said it. But it wasn't enough and he knew it. "I don't know if it was at our first meeting a couple months ago or the moment you threatened to Taser my ass, but I have discovered I am so very much in love with you. I'm sure this isn't just rebound. It's too big and too wonderful to… What?"

Melanie's smile had grown huge.

"What?"

"You are a man of many words."

He looked down at his computer screen, and then back up at her to make his point. He was.

"So, my man of words, what are you thinking?"

"I'm thinking I can write anywhere I have a laptop." He said the next part because it was true. "And you. I need you like I need to breathe. You inspire me. You make me want to be better—" He clamped his jaw shut. He was doing it again. Too many words.

Melanie tipped her head, her long hair making a blond waterfall over her shoulder. "You are more romantic than I am, Joshua. But you are right. I have never looked as I did in those photos. I have spent the week since puzzling over that difference. I finally found it. During that entire photo shoot, I was thinking of you. I was thinking of the joy you bring me."

"So, what do we do?" Josh was sorry the second he asked, for the smile slid off Melanie's face. She bowed her head and her hair shuttered part of her face from him.

"This I don't know."

So, it was up to him. "Okay. Here's what we're going to do." His voice seemed confident, declaring that he had the answers, even if he didn't. Yet.

She looked up at him in uncertain hope.

"First, we will continue as we have been."

"Playing house as if we are a couple?" there was an edge to her voice.

"Making the most of each day because we choose to be together."

She brightened at that interpretation and nodded.

"Second, we start talking about what tomorrow may be. Not what are we committing to. Let's make it...ah!" There was the metaphor he wanted.

He hit Save, then closed his laptop, shoving it and the now empty pasta bowl aside.

He nudged his ice tea closer to the middle of the table in case she wanted some more. "So, what are we really good at together?"

"Making love." She said it matter-of-factly but it sent the air whooshing out of his lungs. He continued when he got his breath back.

"Okay. I'd say better than 'really good' but I'll accept that. No, I was thinking that we're really exceptional at ideas. At coming up with ideas *and* making them happen. Do you know how rare that is? People have a thousand ideas, but never seem to get around to them. Those people make me crazy."

"Me too. Okay, so we make up ideas and do them. I still do not understand where you are going, Joshua." She ran a manicured finger down the side of the sweating tea glass as she tried to see the path he was following. That would be a good trick, as he only saw only a little of it himself.

He tapped his laptop. "We need to make up our own story, our own novel. We've already got the first meeting."

"Me trying to Taser you."

"Right. Thanks again for not pulling the trigger."

"It's a button."

"Whatever, thanks."

"*De rein.*"

"And we've both just admitted that we're quite completely gone on each other."

"You can say 'in love,' Joshua," her smile mocked him.

"I can. But I don't want to scare you."

"I'm already scared enough for it not to make much difference."

"Okay. I don't want to scare *me,* because being in love with a woman who is beyond perfect is definitely an unnerving experience. I keep waiting for you to snap out of it and look at me with utter disdain."

She reached out to brush the moisture-cool finger along his cheek. He took the opportunity to capture her hand and leave a kiss in the center of her palm. He loved watching her response to him as her lids half lowered and a sigh rippled through her.

Graziella passed by their table, "Get a room, you two." She dropped off a second ice tea and a spare napkin, leaving a smile in her wake. Gone too fast for Josh to even say thank you.

He turned back to Melanie, "My idea is, before you distract me any further. Let's brainstorm it out. We can't build a relationship any more easily than a runway show or a novel. We've got a great basis: we love each other, and we both want to find a way to make this work."

"We're supposed to write our own romance?"

"Yes. With its own happy ever after." He shrugged, "You have any better ideas, I'm open to them."

She studied him for a long moment in silence. He could see the brilliance that she hid so carefully from most others. It clicked away behind her eyes like a finely-tuned mechanism. The business woman analyzing the idea slowly gave way to the sensual lover who made his head spin.

"I think you are right."

"I am?" Could have shocked him—about a Taser's worth.

"Yes, we are both too smart to not find a way to make this work. But there is one thing that you must first do, Joshua."

"Name it."

"You must, without any extra words, tell me that you love me."

He almost started with "You make such difficult requests," but caught himself in time.

He still held her held her hand, so he rubbed a thumb over the kiss on her palm as if making sure it stuck there. He looked into the most amazing blue eyes he'd ever seen. He let the brightness—that shone on him from the most unlikely of women—wash over him.

"I love you."

Her own response was equally simple and he knew his life had just been changed forever.

Graziella's quiet "Hallelujah" in the background he simply ignored.

Fashion Alive *landed on* the racks eight days later and the response was instantaneous and overwhelming.

At Melanie's advice, that evening they all retreated to Bill and Perrin's house in North Seattle, made a huge pot of decaf, and crowded around the dining table to confer.

"You'd think that my first ad spread in three years wouldn't create so damn much noise," Russell complained and Cassidy patted his shoulder in sympathy. "I should never have put my logo in the corner. I didn't put my name, just the damned logo. Designers are coming out of the woodwork looking for me. I got so effing tired of repeating that I'm retired and only do the work I initiate. So, I shut off my blasted phone and put a 'go away' auto-reply on my e-mail."

"My personal advice, Perrin," Jo's voice was definitely in her serious legal advice mode and they all stopped to listen. "Is duck and run. Don't stop until you and your family hit Tahiti at the very least." That got the laugh she was clearly aiming for. "How many hits did your website get again?"

"I stopped looking after the first five thousand," Perrin shuddered. "That was in the six hours after it hit the first newsstand. Over a thousand of those were on the catalog request list. Russell, if I don't move to

Tahiti, I'll need you to build me a catalog so that I can send it to them. Wait, Melanie, can I afford to print and mail that many catalogs?" She didn't pause for an answer. "Two hundred on the quote request list. I'm so glad I never got an online store set up or I'd be so screwed."

Bill sat close with his arm wrapped loosely around his wife's narrow shoulders. Good man.

Melanie glanced at Joshua and knew he would react the same way if the crisis was landing on her shoulders.

"First," Melanie decided it was time to take some control. "First we have to stop and say congratulations to Perrin. Yes, you've just traded up for the next set of problems, but they are great problems to have."

"Why am I not feeling so lucky?"

"Because you're a very smart woman," Jo chimed in.

"You will," Melanie corrected Jo who actually winked at her. "Wait until the shock is over."

"Does that happen any time soon?" Perrin sounded very doubtful.

"No," Melanie reassured her and got the laugh. "Second, if we ignore everything for a week or a month, it won't matter. All it will do is make you more mysterious. Zoran has turned mysterious into an art form. One of America's top fashion designers for the last three decades and he doesn't show up in Wikipedia except on the French site. He doesn't do runway shows or give interviews."

"But she has to fix it sometime, right?" Jaspar spoke up from where he sat close beside his sister. "Tam still gets to make her new clothes? I don't care about that girly stuff, but she does. Can she get a fashion spread like you, Mom?"

Calling her Mom clearly struck Perrin like a slap; a really good one that snapped her out of panic and back into thinking. She leaned over to hug both her kids. "Tamara still gets her new line whenever she's ready. Even if we run away to Tahiti. I promise."

Melanie kept an eye on Jaspar. Perrin had totally melted at being called "Mom." Almost as if it was the first time. Just how smart was the boy, maybe sensing how much she needed encouragement at the moment? Or more likely, just feeling some connection and responding to it? His frank look back when he noticed Melanie's attention told her that it was the former and he just might be that insightful about people.

Had she been that smart at ten? No. She'd still been a naïve little girl. She'd certainly been that smart by the time she was eleven though, living in a car with her dangerously unpredictable mother.

"We need to come up with a plan for you to expand sooner than expected, but still not outstrip your income or your sanity."

"I'm glad to give you a loan, Perrin," Russell offered. "You know that. Whatever you need." The advantages of having a multi-million-aire in the room. Actually two of them. Melanie might not have Russell's immense family wealth, but she too could lay down some serious money if necessary.

"No," Perrin held up both hands. "No loans. I don't want to be beholden to anyone. This is my business. If I fail, fine. But I don't want something I might not be able to repay."

"Shit, Perrin, you know I wouldn't miss—"

"No," Melanie cut him off. "She's right. Different people make different decisions. Perrin needs to trust herself on this."

Bill and Perrin both reacted to that one by holding each other tighter. Melanie didn't know why what she'd said was important, but she could see the two of them becoming more solid, more supportive of each other in that moment.

What was it that Joshua had said? She inspired him. Well, he grounded her. Just as she could see what Bill and Perrin did for each other, Joshua grounded her more deeply in who she really was.

They all jumped when the doorbell rang and Perrin cried out in surprise.

Jo's dry voice was barely louder than Bill's crossing to the door with Joshua close behind in support. "Told you to run while you still had the chance."

AT THE FRONT DOOR, Angelo was waiting with a large thermal bag and several cloth carrysacks.

"Candygram!" he called out as soon as he spotted Bill and Josh.

Josh snorted out a laugh. Bill looked at them like they were both nuts.

Josh exchanged a look with Angelo. Next time they had a boys' night, it was definitely going to include a screening of *Blazing Saddles.*

They helped Angelo lug his care packages to the kitchen. As they passed through the dining room, Angelo repeated his call. Russell barked out a laugh; most of the women just rolled their eyes.

"What have you got here, Angelo?" Josh lifted the heavy carriers onto the kitchen counter.

"I figured you needed some sustenance. As soon as the dinner crowd was fed, I dropped the rest of the night on my new sous chef. Graziella is going to tell me how he does. Manuel has the other restaurant under control."

While Angelo and Bill distributed plates and uncovered platters of food, Josh uncorked a red and a white and circled the table pouring glasses. He dropped a bottle of sparkling cider between the kids. Perrin opened that and served them.

Angelo and Bill delivered a lasagna and a pan of Chicken Marsala to the table.

When Josh asked Perrin which she wanted she said quietly, "No wine. I'm fine with cider."

Something happened around the table. The guys didn't react, but the women sure did. An itchy feeling between Josh's shoulders had him grabbing Bill's shoulder before he could return to the kitchen.

"What?" Bill asked him.

"Not sure. Give it a moment," then he turned back to watch what was going on.

Jo and Cassidy had turned to Perrin, then Jo's eyes had shot wide. Angelo continued around the table to Melanie. She was about to help him set down a plate in the center of the table, but it was as if she was moving in slow motion.

"I've got it," she told Angelo. But Josh could see that was the outer poise of the supermodel speaking. Inside, he saw the woman was also looking at Perrin with intense interest.

"Bill," Josh said softly. "I think you need to talk to your wife. Maybe out on the deck."

Perrin's fair skin, even lighter than Melanie's, blushed bright red at his words. "No. No, I think it should be here. In front of the children, in front of our friends."

"You okay, honey?" Bill moved up close suddenly solicitous and filled with worry.

Josh was going to retreat to give them space, but figured maybe he'd better stay close in case someone had to catch the man as he fell.

Perrin's laugh was bright and sharp. She was crying, but her smile was huge. "Am I okay? No, in so many ways." Again the over-bright laugh. "But in one way, really, really good. You know how we decided to try for one more kid right away?" Perrin shrugged. "It worked. The test this morning was positive."

"But we only just started last..." Bill trailed off.

Josh counted three seconds of dead silence before the man swept his wife off her chair and into his arms.

The room exploded with applause. Apparently the kids were fully on board with the plan of getting a younger brother or sister; they leapt into their parents' arms. Somewhere around their feet, a small dog who had been sleeping quietly in her dog bed began to yap until it too was scooped up to where it could lick someone's face.

Josh looked at Melanie. She was in profile to him. Somehow he and Constance had never reproduced. "Someday soon, first our careers." But someday had always been soon, never now. Looking at Melanie, Josh could easily imagine her with children. The lords above and below help him, but he could picture her with their children.

But there was no magic moment. No turn and locking of eyes. No instant silent awareness, as he would have written this scene. Instead Melanie was looking intently across the table.

Josh followed her gaze to Cassidy, who had gone sheet white. He couldn't make sense of why she was upset by what was clearly a very happy and welcome event.

Melanie was up and moving and Josh circled the other way to back her up for whatever explosion was coming.

It wasn't an explosion. He arrived just in time to hear a desperate whisper.

"The date? What's the damned date?"

Melanie placed a hand on her shoulder and told her.

Cassidy began swearing softly, at least at first. It built rapidly into, "Goddamn you, Russell. I'm not ready for this. I'm so not ready."

Melanie tapped Russell on the shoulder to get his attention.

"What? Hey, you okay, babe? You need some wine?"

"No." Cassidy's voice was suddenly very clear and silenced the room. "No. I don't want any god damn wine."

"What, honey?" Russell brushed Melanie aside as he gathered his wife to her feet and tried to hug her. She shoved him back until they stood a half foot apart, she glaring up at her much taller husband. Now everyone was on their feet around the table watching.

Josh still didn't have any idea what was going on.

"That night," she snarled up at Russell.

"Could you be more specific?"

"Just how much did we have to drink that night?"

"What night? Oh. I had a fair bit and I think you had… Wait… Just hold on." Now it was Russell's turn to go sheet white.

Josh didn't have it yet, but he was close. Melanie rolled her eyes at him, then momentarily rested her head on her own shoulder as if sleeping. As if sleeping on her own…no, on *his* shoulder.

He and Melanie had too much to drink and slept together without sex. Russell and Cassidy had the sex that night, but hadn't used any— Oh.

Cassidy gave a long-suffering sigh and leaned her forehead against her husband's chest. Russell automatically wrapped his arms around her. A moment later he stepped her back and looked down into her face.

"Really?"

"I'm late. You know I'm never late."

"Really?"

"Russell!" she ground out his name between clenched teeth. "Could you say something more useful than: really?"

"Holy shit! Really?"

She laughed and leaned back in against his chest. He scooped her up and sank back into his chair with her now cradled in his lap.

Josh pulled Melanie close so that he could slip a hand around her waist.

"Anyone else?" Cassidy's comment had just a touch of snide irritation, but Josh wasn't buying it as she delivered it from where she sat in Russell's lap.

Melanie held up her hands palm out.

Jo shook her head, but the look she sent Angelo told Josh that they might start trying very soon.

He and Melanie returned to the kitchen to take over the last of the unloading.

"Is that one of your future scenes in our story, Joshua?"

He took the time to kiss her slowly and thoroughly, the food could wait a minute. "Yes. A child with you? Very much yes. Not a deal breaker, but—"

Her smile answered him, "Too many words, Joshua. But I agree. If we can figure this out, that is definitely part of our story."

There simply had to be a way to make this work.

"Maria should be here, and Hogan."

She was right. At his nod of agreement, Melanie pulled out her phone and called them. Asked if they could come right away, they needed more advice about how to handle the business success.

"You are so cruel," he teased her. "You didn't tell them."

"And have them race needlessly? And ruin the surprise? *Non!* That is not for me to do."

Josh knew only one way to answer that, "You better-than-perfect woman you." He kissed her quickly and carried the last of the food to the table.

Dinner was about half eaten when Maria and Hogan arrived. Once again, the mayhem was complete.

MELANIE KNEW they had to return to the problem of Perrin's looming success or Perrin would be awake half the night and be overwhelmed by what was sure to begin happening tomorrow, no matter how they tried to ignore it.

When the dinner was done, she got the kids organized to clear everything off the table and into the kitchen. The table was far smaller than the monster in Maria's condo, but they all managed to crowd together as they once again faced the problem that had brought them there in the first place.

"There are things we can accelerate. The expansion of your sewing space and staff is the most critical. I can help you do that this week. And Russell knows contractors better than most. You may not want his money, but you should accept his advice and help."

Perrin nodded stiffly. It was passive, the shock of the news and the child enough to overload anyone's brain. At least tonight she'd understand that there were possible solutions, even if she couldn't remember them in the morning.

"The biggest problem is how to protect you. You are a business owner and a designer. Never, ever make the mistake Donna did. You are not to be the CEO. You need someone to run the business for you."

"Raquel?" So, Perrin was still listening and thinking.

"No. She runs your storefront. She'd be overwhelmed. You need a high-level manager as soon as you can afford one. Before then. Maybe you could get someone by offering them a share of the business instead of a salary at first."

Russell tossed out a couple names from the New York fashion industry.

"Georg retired since you came west," Melanie began ticking them off on her fingers. "He owns a fishing boat down in Florida. Kenalla and Perrin would kill each other in a week. It turns out that the reason Perrin got the ad placement she did was because your third suggestion is now in jail for embezzlement. He was caught trying to board a plane for Argentina. The company isn't even bankrupt, it was a shell that he gutted and now it is simply gone."

"And why do I want one of these people?" Perrin was back. Leaning forward, thinking. It was right. This was her business after all.

"You don't," Joshua cut off Melanie's reply.

Melanie turned to him. "Yes she does, Joshua. She can't do this herself."

"No. She doesn't want one of *those* people."

"I do know more about this than—"

He held up a hand to silence her. It was a commanding, peremptory gesture she'd never expect from him.

"Can we talk in private for a moment?"

Talk? He wanted to talk when he was obviously so wrong. When… No. Maybe he was trying to take their first fight out of the room.

She almost told him to go to hell.

"Please?" His whisper was a soft caress. She didn't like that he had that much power over her, to change her mood with so simple an action. But she couldn't deny the sincerity of his request.

"No!" Perrin called out as Melanie started to rise. "Look. This is family. Cassidy and I, we did our thing in front of everybody. So just do it here. We're all family."

Melanie would have flinched, but it used to give her mother too much satisfaction; Melanie had trained herself out of it. Family? Apparently not. She'd begun to think there was a way for her and Joshua to be family, but maybe she needed to step back and make sure she really understood his story first.

"Give us a break, Perrin. It's personal," Joshua kept his tone light, cajoling. Is that what he'd been doing to her? Manipulating her with kindness?

"Oh? And finding out you're pregnant isn't personal?" Cassidy shot out a second salvo. "Just try it, Josh. My whole world just changed." Then her look went impossibly soft and she turned to plant a kiss on Russell's cheek. "Oh man did it ever change."

"She's right, Josh. Melanie." Russell pointed a finger at their chairs.

"Sit your asses down and lay it out on the table. This is family. All of this." He looked directly at Melanie on that last statement.

It was a look she recognized, one he'd been unable to give her years ago. Whatever else Russell might feel for his wife, he had enough love in his heart that he also loved Melanie. She couldn't walk away from that.

She settled into her chair.

"Do it up, Josh," Russell shifted his gaze. "Whatever it is, spit it out."

Joshua looked at her uncertainly. Then turned to look around the table.

Melanie followed his gaze.

Bill with Perrin pulled so close they were practically in the same chair, their children leaning on their dad's shoulders. Maria and Hogan holding hands as were Jo and Angelo. Cassidy still sitting in Russell's lap with his big arms keeping her safe.

And Joshua.

Melanie folded her hands in her lap and stilled them. She was ready now. Her shields were back in place, at least mostly. No one here would see her reactions. No one except Joshua from whom she'd never been able to hide the slightest emotion.

He clearly read her irritation and her tightly held composure, offering a short apologetic nod that he'd made her feel that way.

Well, she wasn't going to start. No way was she making it any easier for him. Again he acknowledged her choice and began speaking.

"The reason I wanted to talk in private," he offered a scowl to the others around the table.

Out of the corner of her eye she could see Perrin stick her tongue out at him. Melanie wanted to cheer.

"The reason was, I need to preface my question with the fact that I love you—"

"Duh!" "We knew that." "That's all?"

They both ignored the others' comments. Joshua waited for them to die down. Melanie wondered if hope or horror was going to follow that statement. This was Joshua, she really, really wanted it to be hope.

She nodded for him to continue, offering him a slight smile of encouragement, as much as she dared.

His shoulders eased a tiny bit, but not much before he continued.

"And I wanted you to know that my idea, my question, if you are willing, is motivated only in thinking about what might be best for you and Perrin. It also could work in our, uh, novel project, but—"

"No codes!" "Cheater! Cheater! Pumpkin eater!"

"Okay!" Joshua turned on the table with a snarl that caused her to lean back as well.

She'd never seen or heard Joshua be openly angry. He'd clearly been furious when she'd revealed the story of her past, but this was completely different. She hadn't known he was capable of showing fury. It was a dark, fierce sound.

"No codes? Fine. I'll give you no codes. I'm trying to figure out how to spend the rest of my life with this woman without doing to her what her bitch mother did. I don't want to force her to be even the least bit different than she truly is because she is so perfectly herself. I love her so much that I'll just die if she walks away. I wouldn't change her for all the world. Is that clear enough for you all?"

Melanie's gasp was the only sound around the perfectly silent table. Thank god! She had misread Joshua. But she was getting better at trust, and he'd know that about her. How perfectly he understood her. Angry *for* her, not at her.

Apparently satisfied with the results of his tirade, he turned back to her. It was so quiet that her ears actually rang.

"I have an idea," his voice was impossibly back to a caress that she could now appreciate. "It's about your career. It would also be good for us, I really think it would. But I don't want that to influence your decision at all. I'll follow you, or be at home waiting for you when you get back. I don't care, I just want to be with you."

She nodded carefully for him to continue.

Then he began to lay out his plan.

The **Smashing Six** *had* gathered at Perrin's store to get dressed up before going out to dinner. Tamara was almost a-dither as much as Perrin over her inclusion in a girls' night out.

They'd coaxed Cassidy into a flowing dress of tropical fabrics which clung and revealed with every move she made. Jo had struggled against her fashion fate, but a cocktail dress of sky-blue jersey had revealed quite how impressive her voluptuous figure really was. Tamara wore the first of her own designs which was both edgy and inventive.

"Your turn," Perrin announced merrily.

Melanie had turned for the racks. There was a suit of dark blue she'd been itching to try, but Perrin simply shook her head and led her into the back, commanding the others to find something out front for Maria. Only Perrin and Tamara went into the back design studio with her.

The renovation had been completed in just two weeks. A door had been punched through into the larger space beyond. The area now smelled of fresh paint and new equipment. The first five stations were set up in the efficient sewing room that could hold at least five more.

Karissa, Clem, and the newly hired Celine would be starting in there tomorrow.

Melanie could only marvel at the changes that had been wrought, both in Perrin's shop and in herself. She remembered those first days, sitting here, knowing she didn't belong but having nowhere else to go.

Just a month-and-a-half later and she felt completely at home amid the whirl of conversations. Now it was familiar and welcoming. She loved being here.

At Perrin's command, Melanie's closed her eyes.

"But Perrin—"

"But Melanie!" she responded. "No peeking!"

She huffed out her exasperation, but closed her eyes.

She could tell the instant the cloth touched her skin. This was her dress. Nothing felt like fifty-dollar a yard satin. It wrapped, caressed. Perrin had built in support, so only the scantiest of panties separated her from pure unadulterated heaven.

Even if she'd have less reason to wear such things in public now, maybe she would model it for Joshua. If he were a good boy. And he was; a very good boy.

His grand plan was so simple, she still marveled that she hadn't seen it herself. She could still take the occasional modeling job, if she was in the mood. But she had something far more interesting to do now.

Perrin and Tamara fussed around her, reminding her every thirty seconds to keep her eyes closed until she'd almost wanted to snap at them. When Tamara tied a swatch of heavy corduroy over her eyes, it was a relief. Few designers minded her seeing the dress before the tweaks of a final fitting, but Perrin had been so insistent.

Her cell phone rang somewhere. The ring said it was her business line. A groping hand, someone placed it into her palm. She answered it blind.

"This is Melanie."

"Oh, I'm so glad I caught you."

"Hi, Sue. How is the shoot going?" It was easier to be civil now about missing the swimsuit issue. The passing month had helped as well.

"That's why I called. I don't know how to do this properly, so I'll just blurt it out. I need you."

Melanie remained stone silent. She didn't know how to react, she honestly didn't. Sue took that as an opening.

"That new girl we brought on, I can't even say her name I'm so upset. She's currently the cover shot—"

"Congratulate her for me." It took everything in her power to not end the call, to not say something snide and burn the bridge once and for all. Sue continued as if Melanie hadn't spoken.

"—in the London papers: *News of the World* and *The Sun*. It will be hitting the U.S. tabloids by the weekend. The little bitch was selling lap dances in one of those Russian discos. There were paparazzi shots; she was wearing nothing but one of *our* bathing suits that she kept when she stayed behind after the shoot. She wasn't drunk or stoned— not a single decent excuse I could use in the press—just a wild little bitch. Took money, let them… Let's just say I've seen streetwalkers with more class. I need you. I need the Melanie magic to offset this news. We go to press incredibly soon. We're in final photo selection right now and just had to throw away half of our 'Moscow in the Spring' collection, damn that place is so cold. Please, please, please. I saw that hot-hot spread you had in *Fashion Alive* and was just kicking myself. And now this. You have to save me. I'll grovel. Anything you want."

Actually, she thought that Sue was doing a pretty impressive grovel already. Melanie's brain kicked into high gear. She wanted this. Not like she had before, but she wanted this to prove that she still had it. Was still in the game.

Shove that aside. Think like a businesswoman. No. More than that.

"Hang on, Sue." She muted the phone.

"Perrin," Melanie called out into the darkness of her blindfolded eyes.

"Yes?" she was so close they were almost touching.

"Do you do any swimwear? Really sexy, short-out-a-man's-brain kind of swimwear?"

"Some. Oh yeah, on you, it would be screamingly hot. I did fluorescents this year, amazing with your hair and skin tone. And I can make more. I have the materials right here and some more ideas already sketched that I just haven't had time to build."

Melanie considered the factors. "Do you want to skip three or four levels at once and trade up for a whole different set of problems?"

"You're the CEO. You tell me." Melanie could hear Perrin's smile.

That had been Joshua's elegant solution. Melanie would step in as CEO. She'd also save the startup corporation, Perrin's Glorious Garb, a bundle of money while guaranteeing international quality marketing by being its signature model as well. She'd get to take Perrin global, and still do the modeling she so loved.

Melanie clicked the phone back off mute, "You still there, Sue?"

"Right here."

"Okay. Here are my conditions. If you say yes, we can deliver the images within seventy-two hours. Condition one: I will be using Pike Place Market and a fine Italian restaurant as my locations. Maybe throw in a Seattle ferry for a northwesty bonus."

That should boost Jo and Angelo's national profile significantly. And she'd bet she could talk Joshua into another ferry ride, especially if she was clad only in Perrin's swimwear.

"We can fly you there," Sue sounded eager.

"I am in Seattle right now, along with my second condition: I will have Russell Morgan do the shoot."

"Oh yes. He's amazing. I can't believe you found him. Seattle? Really? That's where he went? Whatever for? Never mind. Don't care. Yes and yes so far."

"I knew you'd like that. Third and final: I will be exclusively providing all of the swimwear, each piece of which will have the standard designer credit. Trust me, it will be innovative." Because Perring didn't know how to design anything that wasn't.

"Done. Contract within the hour."

"Standard rates plus my and Russell's rush fees."

"Okay," she gave a very insincere sigh about the rush fee, but she had to know that was coming. "You're the best, Melanie. By the way…"

"Yes?"

"We haven't selected the cover yet."

Melanie did the best to keep the smile out of her voice, "Always a pleasure doing business, Sue."

She hung up and held the phone out into the darkness. It was taken from her fingers.

"Holy shit!" Perrin breathed out slowly from where she'd apparently been frozen at Melanie's side. "Did you just get into the swimsuit issue?"

Tamara's squeal of excitement was loud enough that Melanie could hear all the others rushing into the back studio.

As Tamara cried out the news, there were numerous gasps and comments, some of which made sense and some of which didn't. The latter included a fair amount of shushing noises.

Melanie was still blindfolded and couldn't see their expressions to figure out what was going on.

"Can we lose the blindfold, Perrin? Please? Anyway, Lesson One in business: never burn a bridge." Joshua and his counting lists were rubbing off on her. "Lesson Two in business: there's no longer a me, there's only an us."

"Well, you may think that, Melanie, but you're wrong."

"Oh?" she tried to sound arch and haughty, but there was a merriness to Perrin's tone that made her attempt a total failure. The others were laughing as well.

Fingers worked at the loose knot of her blindfold.

"Sometimes," Perrin whispered in her ear over the noise in the room, "it *is* all about you."

And she slid the blindfold aside.

Melanie stood in front of a three-fold modeling mirror.

But it was a Melanie she barely recognized.

The bright sheen of the pearly Duchesse satin shimmered down her length like water. The strapless bodice was an elegant finger weave of the Duchesse and the palest sky blue of the crepe back satin. The slightest breath caused the satins to shift and shimmer, all the more so because of the contrast of the shiny and the crepe textures. The blue brought her eyes to light like sapphires without the hardness that some blues caused. Bright and soft.

The sheen of the dress had been complemented by a lacy, pearl-studded, flowing back veil that left her face exposed and, while covering her hair, still allowed it to spread and billow. It positively shone.

"*Mariée!*" Even to herself her voice sounded drifty with wonder. "A bride! You made me a wedding dress, Perrin. All this time, you were making me a wedding dress."

Perrin moved up beside her in the mirror and reached out to tweak a seam.

Melanie brushed her hand aside and then grabbed it and held on. "You don't mess with something this perfect. I can't wait to wear this for Joshua."

"Not before the wedding!" they all chimed in, and gathered close around to look at her in the mirror.

"Of course not. He hasn't even proposed yet. I won't let him. We both agree it is too soon." She turned in profile, unable to believe what she was seeing. In an entire career built on looking beautiful, she had never looked this *magnifique* before. Not even close. "But I can't wait."

"Oh, I got you an early wedding present. Maria and Angelo are giving you the condo—"

"Perrin!" Maria and Jo cut her off.

"Crap! I wasn't supposed to say that. You didn't hear that. But they are. This isn't nearly that impressive."

Perrin handed her a small card.

Melanie first gave Maria and Jo a hug.

The condo. It was so perfect for them. A gift she couldn't accept. She'd buy it. Though she'd insist on that later. That wasn't a problem.

It was a home.

A real home, with Joshua. They'd make the second bedroom into an office for him. Or perhaps convert the overlarge pantry just off the kitchen he so enjoyed cooking in. Then the bedroom could be for a child.

She had to blink aside the tears that threatened to overwhelm her. The circle of friends, *The Smashing Six*. These were the women she would have as lifelong friends. Have children with. Grow old with. Belonging with them was a gift beyond price.

She had to wipe away more tears before she could read the card.

Perrin's Glorious Garb. Her name and title: CEO.

CEO. The card made it real. She'd found her back door. Except it wasn't some safety net to the end of her real career. Instead it said that her entire career to date had only been building toward this new beginning.

She hugged Perrin, carefully so as not to muss the dress.

Perrin was looking at her strangely, "Read it again. Out loud."

"Perrin's Glorious Garb. Melanie *Harper*." She didn't manage to get the title out past the sudden tightness in her throat.

It took her a moment, and then it wrapped around her like lover's embrace.

Years ago she'd thrown away a last name that meant nothing.

And now she'd have the name that meant everything.

And always would.

WHERE DREAMS TASTE LIKE
CHOCOLATE

"*Madonna Mother of God!*" Tony Bosco would have had the crown of his head smacked with a wooden spoon by Grandma for saying it, but he couldn't help himself.

His cousin Vic looked up from where he'd been sliding the latest tray of dark chocolate orange truffles into the display case. Together they stared out the large plate-glass window that faced onto the Madison Street sidewalk, at the east edge of Seattle.

"Oh, yes. She is something, isn't she?"

Something? Tony couldn't even speak. He hadn't prayed in years but he wanted to drop to his knees on the linoleum and beg God himself to make her turn in at their chocolate shop's door. He'd been back in Seattle for only three hours and he had just seen a goddess—unlike any woman he'd found in his entire five years in Europe.

When she did indeed turn toward him, he considered maybe Grandma was right and he should start going back to church.

With a bright tinkle of the bells on the back of the door, she breezed in. Five-ten of statuesque redhead in a flirty dress—the shade of beaten copper that clung to her like a dusting of sugar—strolled into the shop. The calf-high boots and accompanying short hem on the dress didn't *imply* a thing; the combo shouted, "Amazing legs!"

"I need two of your finest, Vic. It's a beautiful Friday."

Tony couldn't have said it better himself.

Vic already had a pair of his ginger caramel dark chocolates in a tiny sack. He exchanged them for the six dollars she already had out in her hand, her long graceful hand.

With a cheery, "*Ciao!*" she was gone out the door and Tony was left listening to the ringing bell rather than that silky voice, American English, but seasoned with Italian. Gone so fast he didn't even have an eye color for her, though an impression of bright blue existed somewhere in his head.

"What the hell was that?" He still didn't have his breath back.

Vic laughed, "Don't worry. You'll never get used to her. But every Friday, if she's had a good week, she comes and buys two dark chocolate ginger caramels. Won't buy anything else, so I make sure to never run out on a Friday."

"And if she's had a bad week?"

"Don't see her, but thankfully that doesn't happen so much. I do so look forward to these days."

"Couldn't you have, like, slowed her down for a moment?" Tony knew he hadn't blinked, and still there hadn't been a chance to look at her clearly. Too many first impressions and too little time to sort through them. He sniffed the air, but could find not one hint of her. Only the rich smell of fine chocolate remained in the shop.

"Can't be done."

"Because you haven't tried."

"Tried plenty, Cuz. Not happening."

Tony rolled his eyes at his cousin. Vic had always been a lame-ass when it came to meeting girls. Actually, he'd been stellar at it, as long as Tony wasn't around. Tony always managed first choice, which he never complained about and only lorded over his cousin at every *other* opportunity, not wanting to be too obnoxious.

His cousin laughed at him, "Okay, Mr. Hotshot European Chocolatier. Next week, I'll keep my big mouth shut, you go ahead and try. Not a thing on this planet is gonna slow that woman down."

He didn't want her to slow down, he certainly never did that himself. He just wanted to move down the same path for a length or two, long enough for a wild affair. Tony turned back to the chocolate-making work counter and looked down at what Vic had given him on his return to the States just hours before.

His cousin had taken over the shop and the family recipes when their shared grandparents had retired and gone RVing. He'd never thought they were the sort, impossible to imagine them *not* in this shop. But they were off to tour every scenic byway in the country.

He'd never really thought he'd be back here. He'd worked in some of Europe's premier chocolateries, been trained by master chefs, but the old shop felt comfortable. It was the right size. A cozy front area for customers to stare into the large glass display cases, small enough for a friendly jostling of elbows as they picked and chose, but not cramped or crowded. The kitchen was behind, with no door to hide it away from the curious who wanted to peek over the cabinets. Light streamed in, bright through the front glass, dappled by trees through the high, kitchen windows in back.

This shop is where the two boys had spent every summer as kids. Once Vic had taken over, he'd increased business to the point where he could either manage the shop or make the chocolates, but not both. Seattle loved chocolate treats, and had plenty of companies catering to that craving. But even with competition, Granddad's recipes were making a name for The Chocolaterie Bosco.

Tony had been at his usual loose ends when Vic called. He'd been hanging in Milan where his latest girlfriend had dumped him. Normally it worked the other way, but when the captain of the winning Italian team of the Tour de France swept her up, he knew he'd been totally outclassed. They'd been close to done anyway.

Il Cioccolato Bello only needed him for pick up work. He'd learned all he was going to at Oui Chocolat in Chartres outside of Paris. He'd plumbed the depths of Die Schokolade Maestro in Hamburg. And even thinking of the head chocolatiers at Kāko in New Zealand or Callebaut in Belgium made him exhausted, he was so not excited about "going back to school."

So, Vic had given him an excuse to move once more half around the world and come make chocolate for a small but enthusiastic clientele. Just the two of them and a part-time clerk on the weekend, closed Mondays and Tuesdays.

He leaned on the work counter and stared down at the dozens of hand-scribed index cards laid out across the cool marble slab. Vic had set them out for him. Granddad's sloppy handwriting was faded on some to near illegibility, partially lost behind chocolate smears on others, but there was a voice here. A voice Tony had seen and loved, but perhaps never really heard.

He picked up one that he thought might entice *la belle signora.*

"I'll start here," he held up the card.

"Courvoisier-brandied cherry," Vic nodded his approval. They shared a smile. They both remembered the trouble they'd earned for dropping a pair of them down the back of Vic's older sister's dress one summer then smacking them so that they burst, just moments before her date arrived. The long red stains had never come out and they'd both learned an appreciation—over many, many tedious unpaid hours of manual labor at the shop—just how much fine girl clothes cost.

CHAPTER 2

*R*aquel *Wells sat in* Madison Park, counting an extra blessing that her favorite bench was open. It sat at the edge of the park, under the shade of a tall maple tree and faced Lake Washington. As she opened the paper bag she looked out at the lake: twenty miles long and three wide, it had halted the eastward expansion of Seattle a century before. Most of the park was fronted by a sandy beach and a very popular swimming area. Her favorite stretch was perched above a rocky rip-rap and nestled under friendly maple trees close by the shore.

From here, downtown Seattle was a comforting four miles behind her and the broad lake masked any thoughts of Bellevue on the far shore. Here is where she did her best thinking. Here is where she ate the best chocolate she'd ever found.

Vic Bosco's Ginger Caramel, the dark chocolate sheen ever so lightly dusted with sea salt, slayed her every time. This is what heaven was like: a sunny day, a beautiful view, and a multi-layered treat for her palate.

As an extra treat today, her outfit had totally gobsmacked Vic's new assistant. The guy looked as if he'd been paralyzed. Having an outfit that actually made a man's jaw drop, well, that was a definite bonus. He was six foot of terribly handsome and appeared to be one of those guys completely willing to wield it as a woman-slayer. Absolutely not her type.

Her dress was just one of the many benefits of working at Perrin's Glorious Garb. Four years ago she'd taken over as store manager on a wing, a prayer, and at the sharp prodding of two of Perrin's best friends. Perrin had been barely scraping by and Raquel had been doing no better as an underling in the corporate mayhem of Seattle. Perrin had offered her straight commission and a ten percent share in the company if it survived.

Many times it had been close, but Perrin's talent couldn't be stopped. Now, with Perrin's recent successes and Melanie Harper signing aboard as CEO, the company had gained global attention.

Raquel had kept the operation going, taken night classes for an MBA (Stage One of her Personal Life Plan), and scrabbled like a madwoman for four years. And at a very fine luncheon this afternoon, Perrin and Melanie had presented her with a brand new business card; it read "CFO." There had been champagne, there had been tears, and there had been many smiles of well-deserved satisfaction. Soon, if the five-year business plan that she herself had written came even close to being accurate, they were all going to be very wealthy women.

That was completely worthy of two of Vic Bosco's ginger caramels.

She'd promoted her clerk to store manager and was now free to focus on the on-line retail side of the business. Part of it was straightforward; Perrin's unusual designs built to stock. But Perrin's trademark was custom clothing matched to the individual. Turning that into an electronic platform was proving to be a fun challenge and a potentially lucrative one.

It was all running smoothly, or as smoothly as such things did. A lot of hard work lay ahead for all of them. But thankfully it was no longer about survival, rather it was about creating a stable success. That was Stage Two.

So, now it was time to focus on the next Stage Three of her

Personal Life Plan: find a suitable partner. That too promised to be a great deal of fun and, if all went well, that too would have life-changing results.

She bit into sweet, salt, and ginger and let her eyes drift shut to fully appreciate the chocolate flavors.

CHAPTER 3

The very first thing that Tony changed was how Vic was making the chocolate itself.

"Only the Criollo beans, buddy. Forastero is for wimps and Trinitario is only for wannabes and second raters."

"But—"

"Deal with it. Sell your stock off to some other shop. I won't be using it."

They had always mixed and ground their own nibs. The process of separating the cocoa solids and the cocoa butter was slow but worth the quality control it provided. Then they remixed them in precise portions with sugar, milk for the milk chocolate, and sometimes other flavorings. Granddad had always taught them to conch the chocolate for a full twenty-four hours. Chocolate was tenaciously gritty until it was ground with metal beads to break it down. Tony jumped the twenty-four hours to three full days—for mouthfeel, a trade secret he'd learned while sleeping with a pretty little Swedish chocolatier named Rosalie.

He forced Vic to buy a second conching machine so that they could run dark and milk chocolate batches at the same time. Vic went totally lame and bought a small machine without consulting him.

Tony dug into his savings and bought a large capacity machine for the dark chocolate. He'd never been a fan of white chocolate, so the small machine that Vic had bought got demoted to that role. Granddad's old homebuilt could run the milk chocolate.

"It's Friday, buddy. You ready, *mi cugino?*" Vic elbowed him sharply enough in the ribs to knock the air out of him.

"Not an idiot, my cousin," Tony waited until Vic's guard was down and slipped an ice cube down the back of his shirt. He'd been thinking about the Madonna Lady all week. How was it that his idiot cousin hadn't even learned her name.

It was a beautiful June day. What would she be wearing on this bright, breezy day by the lake?

The answer once again took his breath away. Parisians so proud of their fashion sense didn't have an inch of advantage on this woman. She breezed into the shop. A matching diaphanous lavender skirt that swirled about her knees and a matching leather vest, one of the sleeveless ones never intended to close, simply to enhance—a duty it performed admirably well because after all, it had a lot to work with. The luminous blue of her blouse matched her sapphire eyes.

She was looking at him with a single arched eyebrow, six dollars already in her fine-fingered hands.

Speak! Tony shouted at himself. "Greetings, Madonna Lady. How may I help you?"

"She—"

Tony cut Vic off with a scathing look. He knew what she wanted, that wasn't the point. The point was to get her talking.

Vic winced. His cousin knew he'd botched the play.

Raquel was smiling at him. Okay, he'd have to kill Vic later for making him look a fool, even if it had been his own fault.

"Two of your dark chocolate ginger caramels."

He offered her a small sample plate of chocolates, "Would you like to try my granddad's brandied cherries?"

"No thank you. Just my two dark caramels."

In moments the door was closing with its cheery bell and six dollars rested beside the register.

"Gone..." he couldn't believe that she'd slipped away so easily. Not correcting his "Madonna Lady." Not offering her name in its stead. And turning down the chocolate he'd made especially for her, as good a treat as Granddad had ever concocted.

"Told ya. No slowing her down." Vic slapped him on the back hard enough to really sting and turned to greet a mother-daughter pair who entered the shop.

Her departing wave had been offhand, too perfectly casual. Tony knew when the gauntlet had been thrown down and he wasn't a man to leave that challenge unanswered.

CHAPTER 4

aquel sat on her park bench and bit into the caramel. The chocolate slid over her tongue. It didn't simply melt in her mouth, it hesitated to play there a while, thick with teasing flavors she'd never noticed before. She tilted her head to one side, watching a sailboat skim along the lake while appreciating. The cocoa taste built and lasted, like a sweet, pure chord from a harp.

Perhaps she was extra sensitive today because she was launching Stage Three of her Personal Life Plan tonight. In two hours she'd be having dinner with Steven Tu. He was one of the partners of the law firm that Perrin used when her friend Jo was too busy. He was hugely successful and quite handsome. They'd met at business functions a few times. His sense of humor was a little weak, but his intelligence and taste more than compensated.

Raquel had always worked hard, unlike either of her parents. They came from money and were well on their way to losing it all through benign neglect. She was going the opposite direction and had been since she was seven. Her net worth had always been known to the penny and ruthlessly budgeted. She had started with hand sewing doll dresses for sale at Saturday markets; even working by flashlight under the covers until her fingers were poked to bleeding. Making clothes for junior high and high school friends, at least the ones who cared more about looks than designer labels, had given her a good training. She'd also learned that while she'd never be a designer, she could copy a name brand and knew how to reshape it to a body. She'd put herself through college working three jobs and still had been doing that when she'd joined Perrin.

Now after two decades, she was twenty-seven and all of that work was paying off. Raquel Wells was about to collect her rewards. Not that achieving her goals had ever slowed her down; she'd just set new ones and continue charging upward. Financially stable at twenty-seven. Next on the list was happily married by thirty. She'd allotted three years to make sure it was the right man for her, though she only expected to use six months of that time. True financial success and solid personal stability by thirty-two, plenty of time for a child at thirty-five.

When Raquel began considering which man she might choose to build that future with, Steven Tu's gentle manners and impeccable taste came easily to mind.

She had come up with a list of three initial candidates and hoped that one of them would be the answer she was looking for.

Another rustle of the bag, and the second caramel was gone before she managed to slow herself down enough to assess what was actually occurring.

The chocolate was different.

She didn't like that. Vic Bosco's chocolate was comfortable, familiar, it fit into her life. For the last year, since she first felt she could afford the splurge, it had been both exceptional and completely consistent. You could plan on exactly what you were going to get there.

This must be the doing of the one playing games at the counter, the one fishing for her name with "Madonna Lady."

She should go back and tell Vic to change it back, or get rid of the new man. But then Raquel realized that she was still tasting other aspects of the chocolate, though the treat was long gone. The flavors were different, but they were also lusher and richer. They continued to open and unfold despite how greedily she'd eaten both candies.

Maybe she wouldn't be complaining to Vic. Somehow it felt disloyal to Vic to even think that. But it was…better.

Rising from her bench, she smoothed the chocolatier's bag, folded it in half, and slipped it into her skirt pocket. Time to go change for Steven.

CHAPTER 5

*T*ony *was losing his* mind.

Three weeks. No joy.

She'd refused a Habañero Mango Crème. She'd scoffed at his Pear Brandy Truffle. And now she'd even turned down his taste of Christmas in Summertime Strawberry Eggnog with just a hint of nutmeg.

He'd tried slipping the treat into the bag with her invariant ginger caramels, but she'd caught him the first time.

The second time, he had placed it into the bag *before* she came in. She had actually brought that bag back after she was done eating her two caramels.

Placing the bag on the top of the glass display case, she'd simply said, "I didn't pay for this." And then shot him a wicked smile. With a swirl of red hair and a jingle of the door's bell, she was back out of the store. The shop was far too busy with a Seattle Chocolate Tour for him to respond. Vic had one thing right, the woman apparently never slowed down.

After that last failure to entice her, he didn't even try to put a third candy in the bag.

The Madonna Lady didn't even open it to check. Instead she raised it a few times as if weighing the bag, smiled at him, then paid and departed. He'd been left to watch the effect of designer slacks on mile-long legs and a well-toned behind. A fine view, but not what he was really hankering for.

Clearly she had a plan: to make him totally insane.

Just as clearly, he needed a plan. The problem with a plan was that it required thinking ahead. Even without his cousin's constant ribbing, he knew that wasn't his strongest suit. Vic had always been the thinker and Tony had always gone with the flow. He was only ever serious about one thing: chocolate.

Like it was yesterday, he still remembered the first time that he'd watched, really watched, his grandfather forming a chilled ganache into a perfect ball, swirling it in melted chocolate to coat it, then giving it a quick roll in cocoa powder and coconut. Granddad had popped it into Tony's mouth, still cold in the center, the chocolate coating still warm beneath the cocoa and coconut. In that moment he knew what he wanted to do. He wanted to awe someone the way Granddad had just awed him.

And there was the problem.

The beautiful redhead wasn't even giving him a chance to impress her. So why was this one woman so important that she was making him doubt his skills as a chocolatier?

Answer that one, boy, and you could conquer the world. Granddad's standard reply to so many of Tony's questions wasn't comforting, but at least it was familiar.

"Vic, I gotta go for a swim."

"Yeah, you look like you need to soak your head."

Tony punched Vic's upper arm hard, with a knuckle extended to ping the nerve cluster, and then headed to the apartment they shared above the shop to change.

CHAPTER 6

"Oh my god!"

Raquel looked up from her second caramel to see the assistant halted in mid-stride mere steps from her bench. She had to blink. Not wearing a chef's coat and slacks, he was almost unrecognizable. He wore an old pair of cut-off shorts that revealed powerful legs, a t-shirt that clung to his frame, and a towel around his neck. He was a very handsome man in his chef's suit. But out of it? Wow!

She primarily sold women's clothes, but Perrin occasionally did menswear and Raquel knew enough about the male physique to see that he had a swimmer's build. Not as a mere occasional workout; he obviously swam a lot to earn such conditioning.

"Madonna Lady," he breathed it out on a gasp of disbelief.

"That's not my name."

"So, what *is* your name?" he growled in frustration.

"Raquel Wells. And if you make one single joke about Raquel Welch and fur bikinis, you're a dead man." She'd heard that way too many times. That was one of the reasons she liked Steven Tu, he hadn't gone there once in their month of dating, without prompting. The man presently standing by "her" bench she knew she had to warn off, a fact confirmed by his smile though he asked a different question.

"Why didn't you tell my your name before?"

"You didn't ask."

He stared down at his flip-flops and then up at the leaves of the overhanging maple tree before shaking his head sadly and laughing.

"You're right, I didn't."

And as simple as that Steven Tu was crossed off her list. This hadn't been much of a joke, but the man had laughed at it nonetheless. Steven had not even a shadow of a sense of humor. She'd thought they'd been compatible enough on other fronts—both business people, both very forthright—for it to be a possibility. But the chocolatier's simple laugh had disproven that.

"May I join you?" he waved to the empty end of the bench.

Manners were appreciated, even from a man she could never be interested in, so she nodded her assent. "And what is your name?"

"Oh, I'm not nearly so easy."

"I could ask Vic." She wasn't easy either, but she wasn't above being sneaky.

"You could. My cousin is a complete and total pushover around beautiful women."

"Whereas you are…"

"…much further into the complete idiot category. You can call me Tony."

"But that's not your name?"

His shrug was eloquent.

Now it was her turn to laugh. There was a scream of five-year old giggles that rippled over from the nearby beach. She took the last bite of the caramel that had been melting in her fingers. "That's so good. How do you do that?" She licked her fingers clean.

"Family secret. I could tell you, but then…" he shrugged negligently.

"You'd have to kill me."

He nodded, "Sadly true. That or marry you. Then you'd be family. What do you say, is that secret worth being married to me forever and ever?"

Not a chance. "Maybe I'll marry Victor instead. That way I'd be family and you'd have to tell me." Tony didn't look even a little like a forever and ever sort of guy.

"It's Vicenzo. And if you marry Vic, then I'd definitely have to kill him," again the deep snarl sounded though it was belied by an easy smile. "I know fratricide is frowned upon, but you can't really get in trouble for killing a first cousin, can you? I mean if he goes off and marries the most beautiful woman I've ever seen, he deserves what he gets."

"He does." She felt another laugh bubbling up inside her. He was quick, this chocolatier perhaps named Tony. And charming. Raquel generally enjoyed her power over men. But she was looking for someone who: 1) saw past her beauty and, 2) had more to offer than charm. She'd estimate a poor rate of return on a bet that Tony could manage either one.

She rose lightly to her feet, "I really must go. I have a date."

"A date?" Tony slapped a hand to his chest, slouched in the bench and groaned. "Is it serious? Can you be cured?"

"Yes. No. And yes." She was actually going to go and break her date with Steven, no point in wasting more time there when she knew it wasn't going to work out in the long term.

Tony started to look hopeful, but kept his hand on his heart as if in precaution.

"But not for you, my bucko."

He collapsed onto the bench as if dead and she laughed.

Then she turned for home. With Steven crossed off her list, it was time to call Gary Thomas. Perrin's husband worked at Emerald City Opera and had introduced her to the new head of accounting there. A single father with a cute five-year-old girl. She'd met them both at Opera events and they were so charming together. In addition to their shared business backgrounds, Gary was clearly a sweet man with a big heart. Instant family could be both efficient and lovingly secure.

CHAPTER 7

It was while he was getting in an hour's swim on Lake Washington, the bracing water knocking some sense into him, that Tony figured out that he'd literally stumbled onto his plan. The next Friday he was ready.

Raquel breezed into the shop with her six dollars and ever-present smile. He took her money, handed over her pre-filled bag, then lifted one of his own and sent her a questioning glance.

Her smile quirked up on one side and lit her eyes. Damn! And he'd thought she was a knock-out before. That's when he understood that a regular smile was her default state. But it was only when it went sideways that he'd really tickled her funny bone.

She tipped her head to the side, causing her hair to cascade down over one shoulder in thick waves that just begged to be gently brushed back from her face. Then with a nod, she turned for the door.

Tony held up a hand palm out toward his cousin.

Vic automatically raised his hand, not really sure why. Tony slapped it with a hard high-five. This time it was Vic's jaw that was down.

Tony shed his jacket, grabbed his bag of chocolates, and bolted for

453

the door so as not to lose Raquel. She didn't slow down a moment and he had to jog to catch up with those long legs.

Her bench was taken so they strolled along the pathways of Madison Park, past playgrounds loud with pre-dinnertime mobs of kids, along the winding walkway above the equally popular beach, and under the small section of quieter trees. It wasn't a big park, so the view was constantly changing: the cluster of shops at the end of Madison Street, a beach full of kids, a pretty little garden of rose bushes, shade trees, and from everywhere the sun sparkling off the surface of the lake.

As they walked, they talked of what she did for a living. At first he thought she just sold clothes, but as CFO of a rising clothier she was way more. A bit daunting, in fact, because even he'd heard of Perrin's Glorious Garb. The only thing about clothes that he usually paid attention to was how to take them off a willing woman. But Raquel was part of a powerhouse company that had commanded the cover and a major spread in the latest *SI* swimsuit issue. The fabulous Melanie claiming her fifth cover.

One the other hand, he was an assistant in his cousin's chocolate shop. His only stake in the business was a shared heritage and a conching machine. It rapidly became clear that she was a very focused gal. She clearly ate, slept, and breathed the fashion business. He just didn't rate.

But as they strolled by the water and talked, he began to feel less overwhelmed. She wasn't some accounting nerd; she was as passionate for the business of clothing as he was for chocolate. It appeared to rise from that same deep core, reaching back into childhood and superseding all else.

That was a passion he could appreciate.

As summer drifted toward fall, they continued to walk or sit together on the bench each Friday. He'd never spent so much time with a woman he wasn't sleeping with, but it was hard to complain as he was so enjoying their weekly afternoons together.

She still refused to taste his chocolates, though he brought a different one each week. It had become a thing between them: he would plumb the depths of another of Granddad's recipes, and she would politely insist that she was happy with ones she knew.

CHAPTER 8

*R*aquel *finally gave in* and tasted the chocolate from Tony's bag after an entire summer of Fridays. Their maple tree was starting to change colors, and maybe that too was part of the reason she gave in. She hadn't refused because she was stuck in her ways, as he'd jokingly accused her. Nor that she was a one-track gal, which she was, but not about chocolate. It was that she'd found what she wanted and that's what she ordered each week.

But mostly, he'd finally looked so pitiful that she'd broken down. How was she supposed to deny those sad, puppy dog eyes on six-one of pouting chocolatier male.

But this she hadn't expected. Liquid coconut trapped in a dark, dark chocolate.

"Oh my god!"

"Madonna Lady likes?" he'd insisted on continuing to call her that.

She could only close her eyes and nod. It didn't have the comfort of her ginger caramel, but it was so very good. It revealed exactly how skilled he was.

This chocolate didn't indicate a level of mere competence, it revealed mastery. The coconut didn't overwhelm, it whorled with and enhanced the perfectly smooth chocolate coating. All of his years studying in Europe had definitely not been as idle as he'd made them sound; this small confection could only be the result of years of remarkably focused training.

She sighed again as she finished the treat. This time it was a sad sigh, so she kept it to herself. She was jolted out of her small ennui by Tony.

"So, how's this next guy on your list working out?"

Gary Thomas was sweet, thoughtful, and a good businessman. After three months together, they'd even begun talking about when it might be time for her to meet his daughter as girlfriend rather than friend. They both agreed that it was too soon, but they were talking about it.

The problem with Gary was that he was merely a good business-man, not a great one, and definitely not a driven one. There was competence, but no passion. No mastery like Tony's chocolate nor the desire to achieve it.

Raquel had worked her fair share of nights and weekends, both while attending night school for her MBA and since for the growth of Perrin's Glorious Garb.

Gary had taken the job at Emerald City Opera as a downshift from a Microsoft job. His wife, a software engineer, hadn't wanted the downshift which had ultimately caused the breakdown of the marriage. The only time she took off work was to spend time with her daughter; something Raquel easily understood, but Gary didn't.

Raquel was a long way from ready to slow down. She was just picking up speed.

So. That left only one more man on her first-tier list. Marco Mancini was a division manager at Ferragamo Milan and he was all about speed.

"Milan?" Tony looked at her cross-eyed. "Why would you go to Milan for a date?"

She hadn't really meant to talk about her love life with the likes of Tony Bosco, but somehow it had become a natural part of their conversation.

For three months he'd listened and offered no comment, other than the one time clutching his heart. After she'd walked away from that first meeting at the bench, a final glance back had revealed him lying on the bench, hands crossed on his chest holding up his swimming towel as if it was a lily. She'd left him with her laughter.

Sometimes their Friday walks had become Friday meals; the edges of Madison Park boasted several nice restaurants. He never pushed any intimacy, said he never poached on another man's ground, he never even asked to come in when he walked her the few blocks to home on the warm evenings.

He kept it light. Sometimes he made her wonder if she was losing her powers, then she'd catch him watching her at unexpected moments. No, the interest continued, but the decency stopped him, as she was seeing another man. But now Marco Mancini was next on her Stage Three list.

She and Marco had met at New York Fashion Week last February. The heat between them had been instantaneous. Their affair had been wild, crammed in between runway shows and designer meetings. Their postcoital conversations had been purely business and marketing—which had been fun; sometimes even during sex—which had been perhaps a bit much. His focus was incredible and his skill as a lover was amazing. He had made it very clear in several very suggestive e-mails quite how happy he would be to see her again. She would suggest a week's visit to start, and see where that led them.

CHAPTER 9

"*Milan?*" *Tony asked the* darkness above his bed.

"Milan?" he asked the bathroom mirror a couple of hours later, still unable to sleep.

He went back to bed...for seventeen minutes. It was the middle of the goddamn night, but his brain didn't seem to care.

"Milan?" he muttered to the chocolate conching machine grinding its way to a finish of the latest batch of dark chocolate.

He flipped through the battered wooden box of Granddad's recipes. He stopped at the one with a small heart drawn in the upper-right corner. It was the chocolate he'd made sixty years ago for the woman he'd been courting. So simple it was laughable, so pure that the least mistake would ruin it. Chocolate-covered blueberries. This one card was covered with a dozen tiny corrections. He'd clearly worked and reworked this recipe until he had it perfect.

But that was his grandfather and grandmother's story. He didn't want to give Raquel anything more of Granddad's, he wanted...

He didn't know what. He wasn't used to wanting more. Not when it came to women.

But he'd start by closing the old box.

The kitchen had filled with the fall morning's light by the time Vic

461

wandered into the kitchen, "It's time to open up. What are you working on?"

Tony ignored him and threw his latest attempt into the trash.

At some point Vic set a sandwich and a soda beside his marble work table. Tony could hear the noise of customers out front, of the Saturday crowd as it swelled, then later faded away. The windows were dark by the time he finished his creation.

Vic sat quietly in a dark corner of the kitchen with a glass of red wine, waiting.

Tony set the finished chocolate on a cut-glass plate and delivered it to his cousin.

In silence, Vic took it, bit off a small corner and closed his eyes the way Granddad used to when analyzing a taste.

Vic took his time, finishing the piece in three small bites, taking a long time after each.

When he finished and reopened his eyes, Tony could feel the nerves coursing under his skin. He was never twitchy about making chocolate, but this one was different. This one was…

Vic rose to his feet without a word. He crossed to the office nook and returned. He set a blank index card and a pen on the table in front of Tony before returning to his seat.

"You have to write that one down. And, as Granddad always said, 'Don't give me any crap about it being in your head, boy.' It's better than anything Granddad ever did. He's going to freak out the next time he and Grandma come through town. Christ, Antonio, it's amazing."

Tony wrote it down, his hand shaking with lack of sleep.

CHAPTER 10

"**G**one? **What do you** mean gone?" Tony wanted to reach through the phone and strangle the pleasant woman on the far end of the line. He didn't have Raquel's number, so he'd called Perrin's Glorious Garb as soon as he'd woken up. The front desk clerk hadn't been at all helpful about her boss' private schedule, so he'd bucked his way up the food chain, never expecting to be handed right to the owner herself.

"She's on vacation," Perrin's voice was polite and distant. "How may I help you?"

"Between Friday night and Sunday morning? She can't be in Milan already." Tony closed his eyes, struggling not to imagine Raquel in the arms of some hot Italian designer. His stomach twisted.

"No, she's staying overnight with some friends in New York." The voice shifted as if he suddenly had the woman's full attention. "Is this the One?"

"The one what?"

The woman on the phone sounded even merrier at his confusion. "Well, you better do something quick, Mister One. Raquel doesn't slow down for any man."

Where had he heard that before.

"When are you expecting her back?"

"Wrong question. Lose one turn. Ehhh!" She made a harsh penalty-buzzer noise.

He pulled the phone away from his ear and stared at it for a moment. "Then what's the right question?"

"Ehhhhhhhh!" Perrin made a longer buzzer sound.

"Oh." His only excuse was that he'd slept under six of the last forty-eight hours. He knew the right question now.

"She's only staying in New York one night?"

"Give the man a kewpie doll!" It sounded oddly as if the woman on the other end of the phone was now dancing.

CHAPTER 11

*I*t was *Monday afternoon* by the time Raquel came off the New York-Milan flight. She felt ragged. All of the expectation she'd thought to be feeling hadn't made the flight with her. Not even in her checked luggage. She'd slept poorly in New York and not at all on either flight. It wasn't supposed to be like this.

She must look awful. Marco was going to take one look at her after she came through customs and tell her to turn back around. Even her lack of enthusiasm had a lack of enthusiasm.

When Marco had said how excited he would be to see her any time, and Perrin had teased her about backlogged vacation time, she booked a flight and took a chance. She could keep up with the business on her tablet computer and enjoy Italy and Marco in between. Multi-tasking was her lifestyle.

Except it didn't feel that way.

At the head of the jetway she stumbled to a halt. A beautiful man in a white dress shirt, dark slacks, and mirrored sunglasses stood just inside the terminal. The sign said, "Wells."

Marco had said he'd meet her at the hotel. But he'd sent someone? No one should be waiting for her on this side of customs and security anyway.

Then she focused her tired eyes on the rest of the card, "Fur bikinis for sale—cheap."

She laughed. Someone had—

Finally she looked up at his face.

"Tony?"

"Antonio Alberico Bosco at your service. That's my full name, which oddly means 'invaluable elf ruler of the woods' if you can believe that."

He had her laughing despite her confusion and exhaustion. She couldn't make sense of it; of any of it.

"My flight made it in fourteen hours ahead of yours. I slept over there," he pointed at a row of seats close to the gate. With an easy confidence, he took her arm and led her to a quiet corner of the terminal's seating. The vast windows revealed the paved expanse of the airport and the city skyscrapers rising beyond.

"I'm..." she took a deep breath to steady her whirling mind, "...meeting someone."

"Yes, me."

"But—"

"Open wide."

"What?"

"Open wide or you won't get your treat."

She looked down. He held a small box marked with The Chocolaterie Bosco logo, gold on black. It had always looked abstract...but she now saw that it was an elf playing a trumpet beneath a tree.

"You flew all this way to feed me a piece of chocolate?"

His engaging smile had her opening her mouth against her better judgment. How ludicrous was it? She was here for a tryst with a highly successful Italian designer and now she was sitting and tasting—

Her brain switched off as she bit down on the chocolate that Tony had slipped into her mouth. The chocolate was, oh, magnificent. Impossibly smooth and luscious. There was a hint of...it took her a moment to pin it down, fresh apricot.

Then her teeth broke into the center releasing a flood of apricot liqueur, thickened into a syrup that lit up her sense of taste and smell too, and then she finally sunk her teeth into perfect texture of the candied apricot core. Triple apricot!

Somehow, impossibly, Tony had captured their summer's worth of Fridays in a single bite: from the first change of the chocolate, to the lush mastery of the liquid coconut but transformed from tropical to summer, and the candied core texture that she so loved in the ginger caramel.

"It's like a perfect kiss," she barely managed to breath it out. She opened her eyes. Tony's handsome face so close that she'd barely have to move to touch noses.

Then Tony's lips brushed hers. It was a question, no more.

When she answered, he opened to her and slid his hand to cradle her cheek.

The kiss coursed through her. Men mostly just wanted to sleep with her, but against all odds, Tony had first become her friend. She knew how impressed he was by what she'd done, how deeply he understood the drive that had pushed them both every day, even if it had been down different paths.

And his kiss, oh gods she was lost. His power overwhelmed her senses until she had to push him away so that she could breathe and think and hear something other than the pounding of her heart.

"How?" How had he known to be here? The passing crowd from her flight had thinned.

"Up 'til now I have always made Granddad's chocolates. Enhanced them. Built on them."

He disoriented her; he was answering a different question. He did that to her a lot. Tony Bosco the European playboy had also been the chocolate maestro. She'd watched through the summer as Chocola-terie Bosco had bloomed with him as the new chocolatier.

"I never understood how Granddad made such chocolate until I really looked at the recipe he'd used to court Grandma. He put his heart on the plate. You've done something to me, Raquel, and this is the best way I know how to show it."

She made herself focus on his words and resist her desire to kiss him again. His kiss was even better than his chocolate which should be impossible, but it was true.

"Since the first moment you swooped into the shop, there has only been one woman in my thought—" Then he burst out laughing. Not at something amusing, but at something impossibly funny.

For once she couldn't follow the joke, "What?" By the time he recovered enough to speak, she was ready to offer him a sharp jab.

"Your boss is a very smart woman."

Perrin was, but what did she have to do with apricot chocolate and the best kiss of her life?

"She said I was 'The One.' I had no idea what she was talking about, but I get it now."

Rachel tried to come up with an answer, but couldn't find it anywhere. "Okay, I give. You need to let me in on the joke."

His face sobered, then he brushed his fingers along her cheek. "I'm, uh, glad you liked the chocolate."

"It was magnificent, but that was also a subject change."

"It was," he nodded. "For perhaps the first time, I wasn't copying Granddad."

"You put your heart on the plate."

He managed a nod, but his lips were clamped tight as if he was unwilling to speak the next words.

He really had put his heart into it. No one else could have made that, could have captured their story in a confection. What had it cost him to do it? And he'd done it for her. He'd—

"You just told me how you made that incredible bite."

"I did," his voice was rough.

"So, having revealed your secret, now you have to kill me?"

He shook his head.

"Well, I'm certainly not going to marry your cousin in exchange for that secret."

All of his suppressed tension exploded outward in a laugh that had heads turning in their direction.

"Thank god for that." Then he slipped out of the chair beside her and knelt on the floor of the airport terminal without releasing her hands. "Will you marry me for it, Raquel? For I can't imagine ever designing a chocolate for anyone else but you."

In Raquel's neatly ordered life, it made absolutely no sense. Yet it made perfect sense. They shared passion and determination and he had a heart that she knew would never stop giving. He'd opened up a place in her that she didn't even know existed and filled it with light and smiles and flavors. It was so easy to picture a life with him, children with him, growing old with him.

"I guess that depends."

He blinked at her in surprise.

"It depends on whether you were smart enough to bring more of that apricot chocolate."

"I did. And I'll make you as much as you ever want once we're home."

She leaned down to seal the deal with a kiss.

"Then let's go home."

WHERE DREAMS ARE SEWN

CHAPTER 1

"*You've got to be* kidding me."

"The woman is a demon," Clem agreed with her. Anna, Kristin, and Mitchell leaned in to look over their shoulders.

Kari Jones flipped up the hem of the dress to inspect the lie of the fabric. "Look at this seam work."

"Beyond demon," Anna agreed over Mitchell's low groan.

"Am not a demon!" Perrin stood at the entry to the sewing room. Her designs were always immaculate and technically a challenge, but this one took it to a whole new level.

"Then what are you?" Kari wanted to grow up to be like Perrin. Too bad it was never going to happen. That Kari was three days older than her boss was the least of the problems. She had learned the skills and could pattern and sew as well as her boss, perhaps even better, but the talent and vision that had struck down like a lightning bolt and launched Perrin into the fashion design firmament had somehow bypassed Kari.

Her own designs looked...serviceable.

Perrin's designs had walked runways and were splashed across major magazines.

When she took the job almost a year ago, Kari had hoped that some "designer magic" might rub off Perrin and onto her, but it hadn't happened so far. However, the amount she'd learned about construction was huge.

"How did you even do this?" Clem was still inspecting the dress. Kari could see the secrets and looked to be the only one of the four sewers who had.

"I'm a *demoness!*" Perrin did a football end-zone style dance around the dress form.

Kari snorted, "That's for damn sure. A very pregnant one."

Perrin rubbed her belly and smiled. She wasn't due for another couple months, but the blond was already spectacularly round-bellied rather than her normal waif-slender self. Another reason Kari would never grow up to be Perrin; Kari was already six inches taller and far more curved—well, than Perrin's normal shape. Her non-descript dark hair curled to her shoulders instead of being a golden bob.

Still, she wished she could grow up to be Perrin someday.

Perrin continued a cha-cha toward the doorway of the room where the five sewers worked to reproduce Perrin's designs in necessary sizes for the shop and custom orders. The others continued deconstructing the new dress, learning from Perrin's prototype. Anna was a wizard with pattern-making and Clem was almost as good a seamstress as Kari was. They'd figure it out. Kristin and Mitchell were so fast that, once a design was understood, they could reproduce it as many times as necessary.

Perrin tipped her head for Kari to join her in the main design studio.

Kari loved this space. Folded fabrics shimmered along three walls, peeking out of floor-to-ceiling cubby holes abundant with color and texture. To the right a doorway into the storefront cut through the shelving and to the left a bank of high windows let in the Seattle sunshine, which today was of the typically autumn gray-and-wet variety. Down the center was a sprawling cutting table and another pair of sewing machines below the windows. Design heaven.

Tamara, Perrin's step-daughter, sat at the cutting table amidst a sea of fabrics. Even though they weren't related by blood, it was easy to see that the bolt of brilliance had landed on the fifteen-year-old's head as well. Tammy was piecing together a teen clothing line and it was some of the coolest work Kari had ever seen. With Tammy's work, she didn't feel envy; she felt awe.

Perrin perched carefully on a stool and Kari sat down facing her. Tammy looked up at her for a moment from across the table, but then returned her attention to the fabrics as if embarrassed; not even looking up long enough to offer a hello. Tammy Cullen was usually as effusive as her adoptive mother. And Kari had thought she was really close with the girl...but not at the moment.

Kari's nerves suddenly roared awake.

She turned her attention to Perrin and saw the worry there.

Kari couldn't imagine that she was about to be fired. Perrin's Glorious Garb needed to be adding more people, not cutting them. And she'd finally come to terms with not being Perrin...mostly.

But Perrin's worried look didn't go away. Not a good thing; she and Perrin tended to buoy each other up. The CEO could always calm them down, but Melanie was in Paris on her honeymoon.

"I—" they both started on the same breath.

Kari nodded for Perrin to speak first, and then had to wait her out.

"I," Perrin finally began again, "need you to do me a favor."

"Sure," Kari said in her most even voice. It didn't sound like she was being fired.

"Tammy's getting overwhelmed. Would you be willing to take over as the head fabricator for her line?" Perrin spoke in a mad rush. "I know she's just fifteen and you'd rather be a designer but I want her to have the best and she's good on a machine but you're way better and you can do fitting even better than I can and I can't think of anyone that would be more fantastic or that we'd both trust more and—"

"Oh god, yes!" Kari managed to cut in on the runaway freight train of Perrin's words. Fifty percent relief and a hundred percent excitement.

"—because it's my daughter's line and I want it to be perfect and you could do that and…really?"

Kari nodded. Head seamstress on a new line? Oh yeah. And if it came out of Perrin's Glorious Garb, there was no question any line would be major; especially when it was as good as Tammy's. She'd been dying to get her hands on those designs.

"I was afraid you were about to fire me."

Perrin's shock shifted quickly to mock anger, "You try to leave here and you and I are going to have some harsh words. You belong here."

Kari could only smile back at her. She did. It was hard to believe, but Kari knew that she'd found exactly where she was supposed to be. It gave her a bit of a thrill that a woman of Perrin's amazing skills agreed.

"Really?" Tamara whispered from across the table, looking up shyly beneath the dark brows and hair she'd inherited from her mother who had passed on several years ago.

Kari rose and circled the table to sit beside Tamara. They were the ones who looked like mother and daughter. Everyone remarked on it who saw them together. It had become a running joke between them by the second time they'd met. They'd rapidly settled on Auntie and Little Girl.

"Are you kidding me? Your clothes rock. I'd love to help with them." Instead of offering the hug they normally shared, she held out a hand. "Thanks for asking for me."

They shook on it like two serious adults.

Then Tammy gave out a very fifteen-year-old squeal and threw herself into Kari's arms. "Love you, Auntie Kari."

Kari hugged her tight. This is what she wanted. Not just the challenge of helping shape a whole line. She buried her face in Tamara's hair for just a moment and wished she had a girl of her own.

"Love you…Big Girl."

Tammy squeezed her even tighter and squealed again.

CHAPTER 2

he moment he walked in the shop, Richard Nyberg knew he'd made a mistake. *Always have an emergency book with you.* His wife had told him that any number of times before she'd left him—left them—two years ago. It was the one piece of her unending streams of advice he should have listened to, but he was always forgetting.

In seconds, his Lana and Tammy Cullen had hugged and were giggling together like he supposed a pair of fifteen-year-old girls were supposed to. Tammy dragged his daughter off for a whirlwind tour of the shop.

He slowed down a minute to check out the place. The dress shop felt welcoming and successful. Part of it was the thoughtful designer who had staged the store as carefully as the colorful designs. The other part was the surprising number of customers in a relatively small shop. Women swirled in and out of changing rooms, sipped tea while inspecting skirts and blouses. There was a happy buzz of voices from people glad to be there.

The stage manager at Emerald City Opera, Bill Cullen, had married the owner of the shop a year ago. Lana had hung out with their kids a lot during long rehearsals and shows, but he'd never thought to bring his daughter here. He could see that he should have. He supposed that a high-end women's clothing store was one of those "girly rights" that no one told single dads about.

Tammy was towing Lana from one display to the next. It was set up like a 1950s diner. Chrome and red leather booths were populated by mannequins in clothes hot enough to remind his libido that it had been a damned long dry spell. Single dads with young kids didn't date. There was never enough time and it got way too complicated the few times he'd tried it.

The girls slowed down at the wedding dresses and he heard their oohs and aahs despite the general noise level of customers chatting around the busy shop. Girls who were fifteen should not be admiring wedding dresses. Daughters who were twenty-five shouldn't be doing that. Maybe at thirty-five he'd let Lana out on her first date...like he'd have any say in the matter.

The shop manager, an elegant redhead, whisked past him in a dress that said, "I'm hot, powerful, and you couldn't handle me." She had a smile of welcome that invited and a ring that attested to the fact that some man thought he could, indeed, handle her.

"You're looking lost," she eased to a stop close beside him on a return loop.

"I'm with the blond one," he hooked a thumb toward Lana sighing over evening gowns with low cuts that his daughter would never, ever, under any circumstances be allowed to even dream about wearing.

"It was so nice of your daughter to agree to be Tammy's model," the redhead sounded delighted. "We truly do appreciate you helping her out. However, it looks like they're going to be a while. If you want to wait, they'll end up in the back room eventually. There are places to sit there out of the fray."

He took one last glance around the room. He was the only male present and was receiving the eye from several of the very well-tended women in the shop. That had been Lana's mother's trademark —he still did his best not to think her name—she was always well tended. And had finally found herself a sugar daddy who had offered to make sure she stayed that way—far beyond the capacity of the opera's chief lighting designer who had merely loved her.

"Yeah, that would be good."

The redhead guided him through the swinging doors to a diner's cook line that was filled with women's accessories. It was such a creative space that he had to slow down to admire it. Someone here knew what they were doing. Handbags dangled from pot hooks, pantries were filled with fine boots, and a walk-in freezer was lined in lush winter coats. The ceiling was hidden by dozens of inverted open umbrellas, splashes of color to delight the eye. It would be even better if they were backlit and the light shone through them—not his place to point that out. Still a very cheerful effort.

Another set of swinging doors and he was in a space that would almost put the opera's costume shop to shame. It was far smaller in scale, but there wasn't a wasted inch; it was a dressmaker's dream.

The redhead pointed him to a chair at a sewing machine, then whisked back to the shop while he admired the departing view. She might be too high-end and too married for his taste, but that didn't mean he was dead.

At the same instant a tall woman swooped in from the next room with her arms full of a gaudy mish-mash of fabric. Some of it looked like it had been graffitied all over, like girls used to do to their notebooks when he'd gone to high school. Now Lana stored all her school stuff in her tablet computer and he couldn't even check the outsides of her notebooks for doodles of boys' names.

She'd gone on dates; group dates, but even she called them dates. It had taken him a lot of careful prodding to discover that "hanging out" was a bunch of people and that a "date" meant little more than that the bunch of people had an even number of boys and girls, not necessarily paired off thank god. If there was a boy in the next-level "going out" category, she hadn't let him know about it yet.

The woman dropped into the chair in front of the machine beside him.

"You applying for a job?" she nodded toward the machine he was seated at. Like the ones at the opera, it looked oversized and immensely complex.

"Not likely."

Then he looked at the woman. She was a knock-out in a different way than the store's manager. Long dark hair curled past golden skin. She was as shapely as the redhead, but because she was so tall it looked right on her. The redhead was more in a powerfully voluptuous category. This brunette was built…just right?

"Then what are you doing other than checking me out?"

He didn't fight the grin at her teasing tone. "Not much, I have to admit."

CHAPTER 3

*L**ana stepped into the* back room and froze. There was her dad and he was…she knew that posture. Enough boys had tried it on her on dates. That laid-back pose with the "I'm so cool" smile. They always thought they were so charming and handsome, and most of them were just jerks.

Her dad was like the handsomest guy on the planet, except maybe Francis the track team captain. But what was he doing?

She grabbed Tammy's arm. "Who's that? She your aunt or something?"

"Kinda. We're not related. Kari just looks like me or maybe I look like her. Seriously though, she's amazing."

Lana couldn't believe that Tammy had asked her to come be a model, because Tammy always had the most incredible wardrobe. Every guy watched her walk by, not that she was so beautiful—though she was awfully pretty. They watched because she dressed like she was gorgeous. A lot of girls hated her for it; others envied her. If Lana got Tammy's help, maybe Francis would look at her that way.

Lana had known Tammy since right after her mom died and they moved to Seattle four years ago. As friends, they now had Dad's divorce behind them and Tammy's new mom. Friends didn't get better than Tammy, but Lana still didn't like the way that Dad was looking at Kari.

"C'mon. You're like forever tall. I need to see how my clothes look on you."

Lana submitted, moving behind the screen to try on whatever Tammy had in mind. It felt weird changing with Dad in the room, but Tammy made it seem normal, so Lana did her best to calm her nerves. And peeked around the edge.

But her dad wasn't watching her.

Kari only had a distant look at the girl before she ducked behind the screen, but it was enough. The measurements that Tammy had given her had been good, these clothes should fit just fine. Rather than just leaving the fabric pinned, she dropped the dress she'd been working on under the sewing machine's foot and began running the seam.

"She's beautiful, Richard. She looks so much like you." His sleekly handsome and blond was transformed elegantly into her slender frame. She was a good choice for a model; a sharp contrast to Tammy's short, curvier frame and darker complexion.

"Scares the crap out of me every day," he rubbed at his face. "When she grows up I'm in so much trouble."

"Hello. Already grown."

He grimaced at her before slouching even lower in the chair and groaning. "I really didn't need to hear that."

"Oh," Kari did her best to sound contrite, "I mean she's such a cute toddler. Do the little boys follow her all over the pre-school grounds?"

"With their tongues hanging out. Have since she was about three. That's the problem," his chuckle acknowledged he was being ridiculous, which she liked about him.

"What's the problem?"

"I'm a guy. I know what they're thinking at their age and I can't believe they're thinking it about my daughter."

"Bad news first or good news?" Kari appreciated the way he talked about his daughter, as if she was precious and worth protecting. Her own father, well, he hadn't made her feel the least bit safe. He'd never groped her, but his big-screen sports drinking buddies hadn't been so hands off; she'd learned to be scarce come half-time or seventh inning stretches or even long commercial breaks.

Richard looked at her through blue eyes shaded darker by an assessing scowl.

"Good news?" he asked cautiously.

"I'd say she loves you a lot."

"How can you tell? Did you even notice her?"

"I know, because of how long she was glaring at you for talking to me."

At his "Huh?" she pointed up at the mirror leaning against the wall behind the sewing machine.

"It wasn't me she was glaring at or she'd have spotted me watching her in the mirror," it had offered a clear view of Lana and Tammy talking.

"Perfect. It's not as if I have a love life for her to guard against anyway."

Kari had just assumed he was married, but saw there was no ring. She kept her thoughts about handsome single dads to herself. But it was hard. Perrin had married one just a year ago, had adopted his two children, and would soon add a third to the family. Yeah right. And she'd known Richard for about five minutes. Stupid fantasies never did a girl any good.

"Okay, pretty lady. What's the bad news?"

"Sure you want to hear it?" *Pretty lady?* She rather liked that Richard was plain-spoken. Had he always done that, or learned it from his daughter? Teasing was fine, but she'd never liked games, and Richard didn't appear to be one to play them.

"No, but tell me anyway."

There was that straightforward thinking again. This time she waited until she finished her final seam and had clipped the thread.

She turned to face him fully for the first time. He was slouched low in the chair, but he was watching her face rather than her body. More reason to think he was decent.

"At her age…"

"Oh no!" Richard moaned and closed his eyes, wincing as if she'd just poked him with a sharp stick.

"…she's thinking along pretty much the same lines as the boys."

"Shit! I didn't need to know that either," he moaned.

CHAPTER 5

*L*ana *had kept an* eye out while Tammy went back and forth
bringing her different clothes. The first couple had looked
cool, especially the off-the-shoulder black-and-white zigzag
top, but Tammy had rejected every one. A lot of them she didn't even
get to try on; Tammy would just hold a killer blouse up in front of
Lana, sigh and take it away.

Each time Lana peeked, Dad was looking less and less comfortable
talking to the woman, which was good.

Tammy held up another, then took it away.

"Hey! That looked great!"

"Wrong color," Tammy insisted. "See?" She twisted Lana around to
face the small mirror behind the screen. First she held it up to her
own chest and it looked totally awesome. Then she held it up in front
of Lana. It was good; it was hot. Francis would definitely look at her
in it…but it didn't snap the way it did on Tammy.

"It's just because you're so different," Lana often envied Tammy
her gold-skinned beauty. Their high school was in Ballard, a Scandi-
navian neighborhood of Seattle, and a whole lot of people were
colored like Lana. And Tammy had developed real curves, Lana's body

487

was so flat that she was barely female—at least it felt that way sometimes.

"No," Tammy shook her head. "You'll see, once I find it."

"I want to knock Francis off his feet."

"Then try this." It was the woman, Kari. Up close she looked as if she really could be Tammy's mom. Way taller, but the same Italian gold skin and real shape, just way taller—almost as tall as her dad.

Lana started to turn for the mirror.

"Don't look," Kari turned her away from it. "Instead, put it on and step out to show it to your dad. Watch his reaction. That will tell you more than your own."

Lana squinted at her, but Tammy stood behind her nodding.

She took the clothes from over Kari's arm. It was a dress. "I don't wear dresses."

"Trust her," Kari nodded at Tammy. "She's an amazing designer."

"Then what's your job?"

"She," Tammy slipped an arm around the woman's waist, "is the most amazing seamstress on the planet. I can think it up; she can make it so that it hangs great and actually fits people."

Lana shrugged. She was half out of her clothes before she realized that Tammy and Kari weren't going anywhere. She wanted to shoo them out, but already they were helping her. No one had helped her dress since her Mom had forced her into a stupid formal dress for a birthday party when she was six—the only one not wearing jeans, she hadn't been able to play in a single game. She fought down against the bitter tears that apparently had no end. Stupid tears because Mom had only ever cared about how her daughter had made *her* look; they were so hard to stop.

Finally, she just closed her eyes against the pain and let them dress her in…whatever.

CHAPTER 6

*R*ichard *was so desperate* for a distraction that he picked up a teen fashion magazine. Lots of young women wearing far too little. Ratted jeans, crop tops, wide brim hats. Some looked okay, but then he hit the brilliant red dress with too many cutouts and barely enough material to cover the model's butt. On the next page a girl who looked like she was sixteen wore a black bit of cloth with cleavage practically down to her panty line.

No way in hell! Not his Lana!

He tossed aside the magazine, shoved to his feet, and made it one step in Lana's direction before he stumbled back into his chair which almost flipped him backward into the sewing machine.

There she was—it was his Lana. He knew it was. But he barely recognized her despite that.

The blond girl who looked so sharp in her black and white track outfit was gone. As was the sad girl, as devastated by her mother's abrupt departure as he'd been. In her place wasn't some under-clothed vixen. It was Lana, become herself. She'd blossomed into a version of herself he'd never imagined.

Her dress was the graffiti-laden fabric he'd watched Kari working with just moments before. It was purple, with pale-orange lettering

489

that looked hand painted. Quotes of great thinkers, silly faces, and words like: strength, passion, joy. It should have been garish—would have been if the shades and tones hadn't been so carefully selected—instead it was pure teen chic.

It hung loosely without hiding that she was lean and fit. Below a narrow belt that made a tight gather at the waist, it flowed to mid-thigh. No slutty tease of a neckline about to slide off her shoulder, the sleeves added a softness that belied the hard lines of her dead straight hair and tall figure.

Calf-high boots in a cobalt blue shouldn't have worked, but the tone matched the small purse slung low across her body on a thin strap and made her eyes shine. The only adornment, a thick copper bracelet tied her outfit together.

It wasn't sexy. It wasn't lurid.

But it also wasn't his little girl. It was a confident woman who was no longer afraid and no longer cowed by a mother's betrayal. Powerful in herself.

He staggered to his feet and went up to her, stopping half a step away.

"Daddy?" Lana asked him uncertainly. She hadn't called him that in a long time.

"You're magnificent." He didn't know what else to say to her. Didn't know how to say how proud he was of her, so grown and so strong. So he did the only thing he could think of, he folded her into his arms and held her as tightly as he used to hold a little girl afraid of the dark.

He mouthed a *thank you* to Tammy who was doing a little victory dance.

Then he looked at Kari. She had her back to him, but kept wiping at her eyes, her hand coming away wet.

CHAPTER 7

"*date?*" *Kari grabbed* Tammy by the shoulders and shook her. "What am I going to do? Richard wants to take me out on a date."

"Cool!"

"Don't *Cool!* me, girl."

"Why are you so wound up? Do you like him?"

Kari dropped onto a stool. It was evening, rain pattered against the darkened windows. The store and studio were empty, still echoing with Lana and Richard's most recent visit. She and Tammy were the last ones here, waiting for Perrin to get back from her doctor's checkup.

"Well?" Tammy stood in front of her with her fists planted on her hips like a school marm.

"Can you tell me one thing not to like?" She waved a hand helplessly. Over the last few weeks, father and daughter had come in several times. Kari had watched them closely. And it was as if he was rediscovering his daughter all over again. Tammy had made Lana look chic, smart, sassy, modest, and amazing in turn, without once hitting what Perrin called the "Slut Button."

Throughout the fittings, Richard kept revealing facets of how deeply he cared about his daughter's happiness. He hadn't cried when Lana tried on about the most amazing prom dress Kari had ever seen, but he'd come close.

Then he'd taken Tammy's hand and shook it with great respect. And when he'd taken Kari's hand, he'd asked her out on a date. She never even saw it coming.

"Well," Tamara finally answered her. "Dad likes him. Jasp and I have known him since forever. Jasp worships him."

"Leave your little brother out of this." Jasper Cullen was way too smart about people for a twelve-year-old boy.

"Richard is really nice to him. He's always teaching Jasp lighting design stuff or letting him run the control board or something. I thought you'd like him. And he's a real hunk for a grown up."

Kari eyed Tammy.

"You thought I'd like him?"

Tammy's jaw dropped, but she recovered it with a quick shrug and a sheepish grin, though not very sheepish, "Oops!"

"So this wasn't about Lana? You set me up?" Kari felt an anger rising, but not very strongly. It was hard to be angry after seeing father and daughter together. After the last fitting, Lana had given both she and Tammy a huge hug before walking out holding her dad's hand.

"I gotta help Lana with Francis. You see, if I do, then she promised to get Tony to ask me to—" Tammy clamped her mouth shut, slapped a hand over it, and blushed so fiercely that her golden skin went several shades darker.

Kari raised her eyebrows in question, torn between horror and laughter.

"You can't tell Perrin or Dad," Tammy mumbled through her hand. "She might be cool with it, but Dad would freak."

"I'll keep quiet under two conditions."

Tammy nodded carefully. She was just as much a matchmaker as Perrin. Kari had seen Perrin do it to others. Kari already had dodged a couple of Perrin's attempts. She didn't want to be set up, she just wanted to…meet the right guy. But she hadn't been watching out for

Perrin's daughter; even though not related by blood the imp was equally dangerous.

"First condition, if anything happens with Tony that you aren't comfortable going to Perrin with, you come to me. That's not optional."

Tammy nodded but didn't remove her hand from over her mouth.

"Second condition, I have no idea what to wear. You have to help me. Deal?"

"Total deal! I already picked it out. C'mon," Tammy grabbed her hand and dragged her toward the front of the store.

Yep. A complete and absolute setup.

CHAPTER 8

*"**hy here?" Kari felt* as if she was crouching under the umbrella in order to disappear rather than merely to stay out of the rain. And she never should have let Tammy talk her into heels; she had to clutch Richard's arm to not go down on the wet cobblestones of Pike Place Market. Or had that too been Tammy's plan.

Oh no!

"Wait, don't tell me. Your daughter said something like, 'Tammy told me about this amazing Italian restaurant named Angelo's'."

Richard's laugh was warm and welcoming, deep enough she could feel it rumbling about under the umbrella they crowded close to share. "I believe that's a direct quote. Why?"

Kari sighed and indicated for him to open the restaurant door, "It's a long story. I'll tell you over dinner."

They stepped in and Graziella greeted them, "*Ciao*, Kari. I didn't know you were coming."

Kari smiled back at the hostess. "Or you wouldn't have if Tammy hadn't already called you."

Graziella's smile didn't even flicker as she shrugged, "Oh, there might have been something about saving the nicest table, the one that sits close by the fireplace. But I wouldn't know anything about that." She took their coats, which raised a whole other issue.

"Oh my god!" Richard simply stared at her.

The dress Tammy had chosen from the rack had been a simple drape of dark blue with a copper-red trim that accented lines and curves. It suggested and implied without revealing. It wasn't blatantly sexy, because somehow Tammy knew she wouldn't be comfortable in anything that was. But it certainly showed her figure to its very best possible form. It was a dress that she'd sewn dozens of for Perrin's customers, but had never thought to try on for herself.

Graziella winked and escorted them in. Richard took her arm to escort her...after stumbling a bit, in a very satisfying manner.

"You look amazing," his breath was a warm whisper in her ear as he pulled out her seat.

"I'm guessing that's your one suit, but you look pretty amazing in it yourself." She wasn't sure she'd ever sat across from such a handsome man before.

"Lady's smart as well as gorgeous," Richard was studying her face intently.

Kari wanted to brush at her hair, but Tammy had insisted she should leave it loose over her bare shoulders.

"I'm guessing you've been here before."

Kari looked around at the cozy Tuscan elegance. The fire was already warming away Seattle's damp evening chill. She wanted to wrap herself up here and never leave. The air was scented with basil and citrus and red sauce. The music was a bright Italian dancing tune, lively but soft enough to be comforting.

"My first time. This is a little out of my range. But we get together for these amazing dinners every week at the owner's mother's apartment. Perrin is best friends with the owner's wife and his mother." It was one of the true tests of a man or woman entering the "circle," how they fit in at Mama Maria's dinners. Kari expected that Richard would be as hand to glove.

"So," Richard reached across the table and took her hand. The warmth that spread through her didn't only come from the fire.

"You were going to tell me a story about a conspiracy involving two teenage girls."

Kari smiled, "You're clever, Richard Nyberg. Figure it out and I'll tell you where you go off track."

CHAPTER 9

Richard didn't realize quite how smart he was.

Not that first night when they had eaten pappardelle and laughed and flirted.

Not the fifth night when they had tumbled into his bed and both wept with the wonder of discovery.

His introduction to the entire crowd at Maria's had been a huge shock and a wonderful one. Against his better judgment, he'd brought Lana as well—that was when he learned just how pointless it was to argue against a pair of fifteen-year-old girls with a plan. He'd been overwhelmed, but he'd watched Lana drink it in like a tonic. She needed family and friends—thrived on it.

By the time he took both gals—his daughter and his lover—back to Angelo's Tuscan Hearth Ristorante several months later, he thought maybe he was getting a little wiser. And maybe his daughter wasn't the only one who needed family. A whole family, with a woman who truly wanted to be there for them.

He'd watched the bond grow between Lana and Kari over Tammy's continuing fashion experiments. Richard had come to enjoy the sessions when he could get away to watch.

Tammy's eye was very good, but sometimes it just flat out missed.

Every now and then he'd be witness to his daughter the goof or the nerd—though Tammy thought that a few of the "failure" looks might work on another model. A couple of times the clothes had edged too far toward racy for his taste, but Kari had insisted these were safely conservative.

When he'd been dumb enough to argue, Kari had taken him to hang out by the parking lot a couple of times when high school let out —thankfully not his daughter's so he could retain some illusions. Then she took him to a Nickelback rock concert with the two girls— and two boys who he hadn't counted on but rather liked by the end— and even those few vague illusions had disappeared. He'd stopped arguing with Tammy's taste level after that.

Lana had also taken to using the sewing machine beside Kari. Her first efforts were…first efforts. But she learned. She didn't have Tammy's eye, but she learned to sew, to fit, and eventually to craft.

That was the unique thing that Kari brought to her work. She brought craft. That came from passion. And she had a passion that flowed through her work with Tammy, her patience with Lana, and the way she always shared so openly with him.

Tonight he had a beautiful woman on each arm as they arrived at Angelo's. The brightly lit ferry boats slid across Puget Sound looking like floating birthday cakes. He held the door and bowed for the women to proceed him.

Kari blushed and Lana giggled.

As he and Graziella took their coats, Richard could only marvel. Kari, who had revealed her casual side on most occasions, was once again dressed to kill. Instead of a classic simple black dress, it had been a simple, sleek red one—a dark dusky red that offset and warmed her skin. Open neck, sleeveless, and ending mid-thigh. A copper bangle on one wrist reminded him of that first dress; he'd wager it was a Tammy touch intended to do precisely that. In this dress, Kari wasn't merely gorgeous, she was also as warm and welcoming as the Tuscan ambiance.

Lana was dressed back in that first look that Tammy had made for her. She was wrapped again in words of strength, joy, and—across the top of either shoulder—passion. He'd questioned that word on his daughter's body the first time. He didn't any longer. Her wrist bangle matched Kari's. The two women looked incredible together.

They sat back at the fireside table; this time he had been the one to make the request. It was a table for two, but it didn't matter—he pulled a third chair up to the side with his daughter to his left and Kari to his right.

As close as family.

CHAPTER 10

Tonight was different. Kari could feel it, and it wasn't merely that they were at Angelo's or that they were together. The three of them had eaten together dozens of times: at Richard's house, at restaurants, or huddled backstage at the opera among lighting instruments and cables when Richard couldn't get away for more than a few minutes.

Kari had found her hopes and her dreams, but she couldn't ask for them to come true. Richard and Lana were the family unit—something far too precious, too fragile to risk. It was in such perfect balance that she only dared sit on the outside and dream of being inside.

Like her clothing designs that had never excelled. She could breathe life into Tammy's ideas, create an exciting collaboration, but she couldn't go off on her own and find success. She was meant to be a part of something else, something bigger. But she didn't know how to get there from where she was.

"Kari," Richard's voice was a warm caress. It reminded her of how it felt every single time he held her, or she held him. It was hard to tell holder from holdee anymore; had been since the beginning.

His voice was also rough as if he was having trouble speaking.

"Yes?" She tried to take strength from the moment, but just as when she'd sat with Perrin the moment before she'd been promoted to help create Tammy's design label, the nerves were winning.

Richard opened his mouth again, but no sound came out. He cleared his throat. Sipped some water.

Lana rolled her eyes at him.

Finally, it was Lana who reached across the table and took Kari's hands which were chilled with nerves she could no longer hide.

"Dad will recover soon enough. I think it's kind of fun that women can have that effect on boys, don't you?"

Kari nodded, unsure what they were talking about. Richard affected her the same way; speechless with the wonder of the man.

"I don't want a mom."

And now Kari knew. It was a death knell that rang inside her. Those foolish family dreams that had been fluttering about in her head a moment ago, sank leaden into her stomach.

"But I could really use a friend."

"What?" The word stumbled out. She was suddenly feeling stupid.

"Having a mom didn't work so well. But I think you're great and once Dad recovers, he'll tell you that he loves you."

"Lana!" He managed a protest.

Kari glanced at Richard. She knew that look on his face. It was the look of seeing his daughter truly herself for the first time, or the shock over the scantily clad teens at concerts; the look of total confusion.

Lana didn't look at her father, but her grin turned about as wicked as Tammy's.

"Frankly, I think you two should have another kid, just the way Perrin did. I'd probably think of her like more of a niece or something than as a sister, but I'd be cool with it if you decide. I just wanted you to know."

Lana let go of her hands with a final squeeze.

Kari was still trying to catch up.

And then she'd remembered Tammy's question when Kari had

agreed to help with her clothing line. One word that had covered a world of hope and joy.

She turned to Richard who still appeared to be stunned speechless by the daughter who had inherited her frankness directly from her father.

Taking confidence from Lana's encouraging nod, Kari was the one to reach out and take Richard's hand.

"Really?" she asked as loudly as she could manage, which was little more than a whisper.

He nodded.

"Say you love her, Dad," Lana prompted.

He nodded again.

Then he clamped down on Kari's hand as if to make sure she wouldn't leave before he recovered his power of speech.

Not a chance.

Now that she knew where she belonged, she wasn't going anywhere.

WHERE DREAMS ARE
WELL DONE

CHAPTER 1

"*What is wrong with* you? I needed that fish three minutes ago. Did you learn to cook in a cave?"

"You needed it twelve seconds ago," Sam shot back. And decided against telling Luisa Valenti that she wasn't going to get it for another thirty seconds. Besides, the kitchen's aboyeur was busy dressing the plate of pappardelle with wild boar ragù that he'd just handed across the line.

"Fine, then where's my trio of sea scallops and squid-ink pasta?" She didn't even stop for a breath. "Though why everyone at a table would order the same dish is beyond sad. Just keep cooking the way you are and maybe we'll never see such dweebs ever again."

"Open your pretty eyes, Luisa," he teased her as his sous chef Marlys slid the three matching plates onto the warmer shelf that separated his station from Luisa's.

She rolled those beautiful brown eyes at him, making it clear that she knew he was trying to distract her from the laggard glazed halibut.

A glance down the cook line either way told him that they were running a little rough, but okay. He dropped another two orders of orzo into a pot of boiling water to help out Valerie. He also passed a tray of stuffed and breaded squash blossoms from Tony to Valerie as she turned to the deep fryer, saving her three extra steps she didn't have time for. He dropped the next two pieces of fish into pans for Marlys and accepted the two plates of sea bass ready for saucing.

He'd never have dared talked to Luisa that way while he was still a prep chef. He'd noticed her of course, there were only a dozen staff at Angelo's Tuscan Hearth Ristorante, including the three waitstaff, but his duties had mainly been in the morning before the restaurant opened. Angelo or Manuel would do the shopping at daybreak, then all of the proteins and produce would arrive for him to prep. When Manuel had shifted to Angelo's new restaurant, Sam had been pulled into the lunch line.

Up until this morning he'd thought he was just being trained to fill in where needed. Tonight they'd dropped him instead of Marlys into the Executive Chef slot for dinner service because Angelo couldn't make it. If he had time, he'd be freaking out right now, but he didn't.

Over the last month he'd worked with Marlys the grillardin cooking the meats and Valerie at entremetier—the hot appetizers, soups, and pasta station, one of the keys to an Italian restaurant. He'd almost died at the sous chef position—keeping the saucier's eight pans always filled with whatever had to be sautéed to perfection, because Angelo accepted nothing less, which required being part magician, part juggler, and part octopus.

As a prep cook, the menu had been drilled into this head. Yes, it was always changing based on what was freshest in Seattle's Pike Place Market just out the back door, but there was a style, a flavor, a feel to Angelo's cooking that made sense once he understood it.

He'd even done some turns as the Executive Chef for lunch service. The lighter fare becoming second nature with practice.

That was when he first bumped heads with Luisa.

There was no way to miss Luisa's presence in the kitchen. It was the aboyeur's job to expedite service and did she ever. Luisa had every order in her head, never having to check a ticket twice. And she was very vocal about not getting everything in the exact order she'd called for it. Table Seven had a simple ragù, a pan-fried swordfish on a bed of angel hair pasta with one of Angelo's signature sauces that had to be made the moment before service, and a grilled lamb and baby asparagus with a Gorganzola cheese drizzle—and Luisa would throw a fit if they weren't all ready in the same five seconds even though they took drastically different amounts of time to cook. Actually, in the same three seconds.

But with Luisa in charge, there was never an undressed plate or a missed order. She was just as amazing as she looked. And as dangerous.

He slid across the missing halibut with a honey-rosemary-chestnut glaze and the accompanying bowl of the wild boar ragù.

"Finally!" she huffed at him.

Being the sole target for her ire was daunting. Everyone on this side of the cook line answered to him, but he answered to the fair Luisa.

He still didn't know how he'd landed in the Executive Chef slot through a dinner service. He'd entered the kitchen and Luisa had simply told him, "Angelo's busy tonight. It's your cook line." He'd taken his first breath about an hour into the meal, but hadn't had time yet to take a second one.

She finished dressing the plates with berry compote traced in an elegant line around the outline of the halibut. With immaculate timing, Graziella breezed in from the front of house, barely breaking stride as she gathered the completed dishes, and whisked back out.

It was a shock every single time to see them together. Two slender, beautiful Italian women with golden skin and lush dark hair that reached the middle of their backs. They could have been twins. Except Graziella was as gracious and patient as her name, unflappable under even the most dire circumstances. Luisa's heritage must be at least part Roman, as in Roman candle. Incendiary.

"What are you paying attention to, Chef?" she snapped at him.

Luisa hadn't looked up at him, but he'd been watching her and not his line and somehow she knew. A quick glance showed him that his momentary lapse to admire his aboyeur had just caused him more trouble.

"Fire three halibut and two sea bass, a lamb, a beef tenderloin, and two scallop."

Marlys grimaced, but hustled to get them all going.

It was too late, the next five tables were going to be all out of sync and he was going to catch hell for it.

CHAPTER 2

L uisa kept her head down to hide her smile.

She remembered her first day here, Angelo and Manuel purposely messing with her, testing her. Angelo would finish a fish and then sit on it for thirty seconds just to break her rhythm. When she'd chewed him out over the line, he'd merely smiled and handed it across.

Manuel had mixed up three different orders, just to see if she'd catch it, like she was that dense. She'd ripped him a new one and he'd told Angelo to hire her on the spot.

That had been a year ago and Angelo's Tuscan Hearth Ristorante was now a well-oiled machine, reproducing the chef's magic to the table with class and consistency.

And at last it was finally turnabout, her turn to be testing someone else to Angelo's stratospheric standards. Manuel had moved to run the new restaurant by the Seattle Center and Angelo wanted to focus on a third restaurant he was creating. She was the one who had suggested pulling Sam Walsh out of the prep role.

His prep had always been immaculate.

Then she'd spotted him making a quick lunch for himself and recognized the instinctual skill of his actions.

She'd spent three years in Italy studying restaurants, eking out every penny she could to continue doing so. Every three months she went to a new restaurant and volunteered to shadow and assist the aboyeur in exchange for food and a place to sleep. Many times she'd ultimately been offered a permanent job, but there'd been so much to learn, so many regional varieties of food, so many different chefs to study that she'd always refused. She'd worked her way from Rome down to Puglia, into Sicily and back up the west coast to Tuscany, Liguria, and the Piedmont before the money ran out.

She knew what a real chef looked like, even if Angelo and Manuel were too dense to notice what was in their midst.

When Sam had been momentarily called away, she'd snuck a forkful of his lunch and been stunned. No prep cook should be able to cook like that. Especially not a tall handsome one with auburn hair and such agile hands; he looked Irish not Italian for crying out loud. Of course Manuel was Mexican, but so were most of the sous chefs and line cooks in high-end restaurants throughout the U.S.

She'd stolen a second forkful, carried it over to Angelo, and fed it to him. His eyes had gone wide, then thoughtful when she pointed at Sam returning to his meal.

Sam spent some time looking for his fork, never spotting that she'd stolen it. It had been awfully cute.

But the fact that she'd been the one to discover him, meant that he had to perform even better than Manuel and Angelo did. If she had to hound him twice as hard to meet that standard, he'd just have to get used to it. And he had.

Until she'd distracted him.

She handed off the next order to one of Graziella's waiters and then did her best not to laugh at the cascading disaster his lapse had caused.

Luisa was used to men watching her. Hadn't thought much of it except when she wanted to take a likely candidate home with her. At least not until everyone started calling her Graziella's twin sister. When "evil twin sister" had slipped out of someone's mouth, she could only sigh in acknowledgment of the sad truth.

Grace and graciousness had never been in Luisa's genetic makeup; her "good twin" was elegantly second-generation Italian and Luisa was third-generation bitch. But that anyone thought she was that beautiful was still a surprise. And that Sam had noticed so much that he'd lost the thread of the meal…

"C'mon, Sam," she called out to distract herself. "It's your first dinner as Exec Chef. Don't drop the ball on me now."

He didn't snarl or glare at her. He didn't even frown. He simply turned to assist the suddenly overwhelmed Marlys trying to simultaneously fire nine dishes in eight pans.

Luisa moved down the line to chat with the patissier about a new dessert idea she'd had. She'd give Sam a little time to recover, but not too much.

CHAPTER 3

hen the last two-plate order had slid across to Luisa, Sam was ready to collapse.

Someone slapped him hard on the back and shoved a cold beer into his hand. A round of applause sounded down the line.

And across the cook line from him, even the bane of his existence was applauding with those elegantly fine hands of hers. He tipped his bottle to her in silent salute; they both knew he couldn't have done it without her help.

"So," Angelo and Manuel came in through the back door which had been left open to the warm September night, "Let's see how you did." He took up the two plates of the final order and handed one to Manuel. A test? Tonight had been a test?

For what?

The two chefs tasted, chewed, swallowed, and then tasted each other's dishes.

"He didn't follow your recipe," Manuel pointed at the smoked eggplant and shrimp ravioli.

"No, he didn't," Angelo closed his eyes for a moment. "Walnut, no. Chestnut." He opened one eye to glare at Sam. "How much?"

"A single light grating over the eggplant before I smoked it." He knew it was taking liberties, but it had seemed right. Now he was less sure.

"Seems odd to me," Manuel replied.

Angelo harrumphed in agreement.

Sam was starting to get really worried, he knew chefs who'd been fired for tinkering with the Head Chef's recipes. Then he spotted Luisa's expression. She winked at him. After all of the abuse she'd unloaded on him during the meal, she winked at him.

Greatly encouraged, he winked back, then waited for Angelo and Manuel to get to the point.

"Going to have to change the damned recipe now," Angelo grumbled, but Sam could finally tell that he was pleased.

Angelo waved him out from behind the cook line. When he reached them, Angelo shook his hand. Manuel gave one of his quiet nods that Sam had long since learned was his form of high praise. Graziella had joined them by that point and kissed him on both cheeks before tasting some of Manuel's dinner and sighing happily. She slid an arm around her husband's waist and he held the bowl so that she could take another mouthful.

Sam felt himself wilting a little every time he saw them. Manuel and Graziella were so sweet together. When would he ever find something like they had? Based on results to date, *never* was his best guess.

"Looks like you were right, Luisa," Angelo looked at the aboyeur.

"Told you," was her pert reply.

"Told him what?" Sam asked.

But she just kept grinning at him.

"Told you what?" he asked Angelo.

"I think you two are ready to run this restaurant. Interested?"

Sam looked at Luisa and saw the stunned look on her face, perfectly mirroring what he was feeling right at that moment. Well, something had finally put her in her place.

Angelo's Tuscan Hearth was top-rated as was the Piedmont Hearth which Manuel now ran across town. And not just top in the foodie Pacific Northwest, but nationally.

"We...*two?*" Luisa managed a bare whisper.

Her gaze slid to Angelo then back to him, her dark eyes gone wide. Not to do this for a single night, but every night?

He tipped his head in the slightest question to her. Angelo was right, he couldn't have done it alone. But to run such a restaurant had been his goal since forever.

"You game?" he managed, his own whisper no louder than hers had been.

The astonishment shifted through a hundred stages on her beautiful face through consideration, weighing factors, acceptance, and finally a blinding smile that stunned him right back on his heels. He'd known she could smile…but not like that.

"Hell yeah!" was her verdict.

They traded high fives and a quick hug as the rest of the crew cheered for them.

CHAPTER 4

*A**s far as Luisa*** knew, she and Sam had never actually touched, always separated by the width of the cook line. But his brief hug was warm and sincere. His big hands had wrapped briefly around her waist and she could still feel the impression of their easy strength. He'd smelled of the cook line; flavor and spice.

If she'd been seeing anyone, it might have had less impact on her thoughts. But she hadn't been. Not for several months even before she'd stolen that taste of Sam's lunch. Then Angelo had assigned her to lay out his training because he was too busy with his plans for the next restaurant, and that had preoccupied her thoughts.

So, she'd made sure that "Angelo's" official schedule rotated Sam through every position until he could do each as well as the station chef normally posted there.

And it had worked. Worked beyond her wildest imaginings actually.

"Run the restaurant?" she whispered to herself, but it couldn't be real.

She cleaned and prepped her station for the next day, tossed out the sauces and garnish that wouldn't survive overnight, stowed everything else where it belonged. The other chefs were tending to their own stations. She'd demanded end-to-end ownership, if you needed more pans or towels or a sharper knife in mid-shift and didn't have it, it was your own damn fault. Angelo himself had been the slowest to adopt the change, but now agreed it was the best way.

"Run the restaurant?" She'd been aboyeur for a year, the longest she'd ever stayed anywhere, but that was a long way from running a restaurant.

She was staring at her immaculate station when a hand landed against the small of her back—she knew it was Sam's by the feel alone —and swept her from the kitchen and out into the main room. It was dark, the last of the diners were gone. The shadowed room was spotless. The tables already set with the lunch service cloths and tableware.

Only one table remained candlelit, the one closest to the hearth that was the centerpiece of Angelo's. The fireplace was a simple affair of stone and brass that anchored the room and gave it a lush ambience.

The table contained a chef's meal: a cutting board of crackers and several varieties of cheese, and a bottle of wine uncorked to breathe. Two glasses.

"You trying to woo me, Sam Walsh?" she asked as he held out her chair for her.

"No!" He startled as if she'd just whacked him with a wooden spoon. "Trying to be nice; sort of to say thanks for getting me this chance and maybe try to figure out what's next. Is nice too foreign for you, Luisa Valenti?"

He teased her. He'd actually teased her, which was quite a step for Sam Walsh. She considered several acerbic replies as he settled into the chair opposite and began pouring the wine.

"Way too foreign," she sighed. "I don't think that *nice* runs very deep in my bones."

He snorted out a laugh, "Might have noticed. Pity. However, they're such very *nice* bones."

She squinted at him over her wine glass, he'd chosen an Oregon

Pinot Noir—her favorite Northwest wine. Luisa was starting to realize that Sam missed very little.

A part of her was offended by his easy agreement that she wasn't nice, even if most of her sadly agreed. But the compliment she hadn't been ready for.

"Now you're teasing me? Because I know that Sam Walsh never flirted with anyone." Which had stumped her at first. It was a standard part of her repertoire when trying to make male chefs behave. She'd had to find different buttons to push with Sam. And he was such a decent guy, she often fell back on simple cajoling. She didn't have a lot of experience with decent guys.

He slumped in his chair and rubbed at his face, "I'm so strung out that I must not know what I'm doing. Flirting with you doesn't sound like me, does it?"

"No, it doesn't. Why is that? Aren't I flirtable?"

Sam looked at the Mona Lisa beautiful woman across the table from him; right down to the enigmatic smile. The candlelight played across her dusky skin made it far too easy to imagine how *all* of her skin might look in such light.

He always felt oversized and awkward around her. And now? She was waiting for his explanation of…

He sipped at the wine. He'd noticed early on that when multiple American wines were circulating, this was the one Luisa always chose. He'd become partial to it himself. It had a fruity body and a low acidity that…had him thinking again about the sleek body and high acidity tongue that sat across the table from him.

"Well? Why haven't you flirted with me?" She did her best to sound offended, but she was also too busy looking pleased with their sudden change of circumstances to really pull it off.

And he was just tired enough to actually answer her question.

"I don't because I can remember every single thing about you since you walked in through that door."

"You what?"

"I was coming out of the cooler with a salmon almost as big around as you are. You breezed in looking like you already knew more about the restaurant than the guys running it. Turned out you did. Gorgeous, opinionated, and feisty as hell. Want me to tell you what you were wearing that day?"

She was looking at him with as much surprise as she'd shown at Angelo's announcement that the two of them were taking over the restaurant's operations.

"Forget it. Never mind. Let's talk about the restaurant," he took a large swallow of the wine. Should have kept his dumb mouth shut.

Luisa was continuing to eye him carefully. "No," she said it slowly, "let's talk about this."

Sam refreshed his glass, then set it aside because after everything else tonight, the alcohol was only going to make him even stupider.

"Talk to me, Sam." Luisa's voice sounded soft, uncertain—something he didn't even know she was capable of feeling until Angelo had blind-sided her with the offer.

Sam would rather—nothing came to mind. Climb the highest alligator? Wrestle the fiercest mountain? He was really exhausted.

"Sam," a flat, insistent tone.

"There's that tone," he acknowledged. "The utter surety of it. Woman who knows what she wants. Never thought you'd notice some lame prep cook."

"Of course I noticed you."

"Not really. I was just a lowly minion; not a chance that you'd actually see me. This was only supposed to be a damned temp job anyway."

"I—Wait!—What?"

"I was just back in Seattle for a few months. Spent a couple years in San Francisco at Acquerello. Then a year cooking for Batali in New York. Graziella got me the prep spot here while I figured out what I wanted to do next." Sam tried to think of some way to derail the story, but couldn't come up with a way now that it was rolling. *In the shitter now, boy!* was all he could think.

"But if you could do that, why did you stay here as a prep cook?"

"Yeah, good question. I eventually learned just how damn good Angelo was and realized this is where I was supposed to be. Watching that man build a sauce is a serious education; way beyond even my coursework at ICI in Calabria."

"You graduated from ICI?"

"Top of class," why was he bragging to her? Impressing Luisa wasn't something a guy was dumb enough to even try; she always knew what she wanted and just went for it.

"*Eventually,*" she drew the word out, "you were impressed with Angelo. But not at first?"

He shouldn't have said that either. He just shook his head and decided that the glass of wine would do more good inside him that it would sitting on the table.

"Because at first…" she was working it out.

Even shutting up wasn't going to do him any good. Luisa was too smart. He'd said too much. The moment he'd opened his mouth, he'd said too much.

"At first…" tasting it like a fine wine, half-lidded eyes, pursed lips. The way he'd always imagined she'd look in that half breath before a kiss.

"You sure it's not too late to talk about the restaurant instead?" But he knew it was.

Then he saw it click. Those stunning dark eyes zeroed in on him.

He shrugged, "Got me."

"You stayed because of me."

He nodded.

"Oh god. I really need a glass of wine."

"In your hand, Luisa."

She looked down at it in surprise, then knocked back a large swallow before returning her attention to him.

"It's not helping," she said as if it was his fault; which was probably true.

"Noticed that myself."

"Why didn't you say anything?"

CHAPTER 6

*L***uisa was trying desperately** to make head or tails of what Sam was saying. But it wasn't working.

"I saw the kind of men who waited for you after work. Slick, urban," Sam waved a hand at himself. He wore jeans, leather shoes battered and stained with too many hours in the kitchen, and a casual flannel shirt rolled up at the sleeves that had replaced his chef's jacket.

He was right; he didn't fit with what she'd always reached for. Looking the way she did, it was always easy to take almost any man she wanted off the shelf. She came from desperate poverty and kept picking some Mr. Rich-and-Successful. But they never seemed to fit when she tried them on.

"Did what I could to get over it. Then Angelo hooked me with his food," and again one of those easy shrugs of his powerful shoulders.

"And you told me tonight because you're—"

"Too exhausted to think before I speak." Then he glared at his half-empty wine glass. "I thought I was ready. Could handle whatever you…"

He cut himself off and looked up at her. She could see that the wine had nothing to do with what Sam was telling her.

"I wasn't ready for one thing," he continued.

"What was that?" She tried to guess. The hug had been nice, even promising. But if he was one of those guys who'd built a whole fantasy on such a brief contact, then he was in for a rude awakening. Life wasn't that easy.

"I've been cooking since I was six. Never wanted to do anything else. But I wasn't ready to find out that you believed in me. I still amazed that you're the one who saw…" he waved helplessly toward the kitchen.

Luisa knew she was in so much trouble. It wasn't the easy answer at all. Of course with Sam Walsh it couldn't be, could it? And once she'd seen him, and began tasting his food regularly…

"So I have a question," his voice was little more than a low rumble.

Was she ready for this? She wasn't going to just jump into bed with him because he'd…touched her with his answer. Of course, it hurt that he was right, she'd have brushed off a mere prep cook. But the way he'd cooked tonight? That man, she couldn't help but notice.

For once not trusting her voice, she nodded for him to continue.

"Now that I've been dumb enough to drop that fat in the fryer, are you still okay running this restaurant with me, executive chef and aboyeur?"

At her nod of assent—how could she not find a way to make such an opportunity work—he sighed with relief.

"Well that's something, anyway," he mumbled softly into his glass.

It was clear that he was speaking to himself, so she did her best to pretend she couldn't guess what else he was thinking.

or two months it was enough. A cool September turned into a cold November and they worked their asses off.

Their every waking thought was consumed by the restaurant. At first, Manuel or Angelo had joined Sam on the daily shopping expeditions in the middle of his night. The restaurant closed at ten, they were cleaned up and out the door by eleven, and except for a few fantasies about Luisa, he'd be asleep by one. Up at six in the chill, predawn darkness to get the pick of the market at Pike Place. Asleep from seven to ten, if he got back to sleep, and then into the restaurant.

Soon, he and Manuel had agreed to alternate mornings and do the shopping for both restaurants. But even on their off days, they were likely to bump into one another at the market, just seeing if there was anything particularly special that day.

Luisa showed up one morning, looking gloriously rumpled in sweatpants, a heavy sweater, and desperately clutching a large thermal mug of coffee. She was good, spotting some possibilities for the Daily Fresh menu that he'd missed. It was soon a routine to shop together and go out for breakfast afterward; watch the late sunrise and the early tourists while someone else cooked them breakfast. He slept less, but in those quiet mornings is when he grew to know his aboyeur.

At first they discussed Angelo's. But soon they were discussing travels, different chefs and their restaurants, eventually they even wandered into past lovers. At the restaurant it was all business, but for the few hours between the shopping and the start of lunch service, that was theirs alone.

Luisa worked with Graziella on the restaurant operations. He worked with the other chefs and his prep chef replacement. In the second month he started running dish variations by Angelo, who was often found experimenting with a new dish on a small side stove. The new restaurant was going to be Southern Italian, a broad departure from the Tuscan and Piedmont themes of the first two, and that needed a lot of prep. Soon they were collaborating and testing dishes together; Graziella and Luisa offering their own insightful palates to the process of turning dishes into a menu. Sam had never so enjoyed the simple craft of cooking as those moments with Angelo.

At the end of the second month, Angelo sat the two of them down and laid out a chart. He didn't need to say a thing. Rather than any dip in sales, there'd been a slow and steady increase. Angelo then laid down four new reviews that left no question he and Luisa were doing well as a team.

Angelo had shaken Sam's hand and kissed Luisa on top of the head before leaving them once again alone at the small table deep in the shadows of the closed restaurant. The silence stretched long after Angelo shut off the kitchen lights and left.

"I like that you still keep me on my toes on the cook line," Sam finally said to break the stillness. "Don't stop doing that."

"Deal," Luisa grinned at him. "Just don't stop blowing my mind with your new dishes." It was practically a caress that he felt right down to his heart. He loved that she loved his cooking.

After another overlong pause, it was Luisa who broke the silence.

"Do you think…" she trailed off.

"I don't know," he answered, fairly sure they were discussing the same topic. It had become like a live wire, or perhaps a tug of war across the cook line. The tension had built between them until he wasn't sleeping that much before the shopping trips either. They'd worked out such a deep cook line communication that it was, well, almost sexual. He couldn't think of any other way to describe it. It was sexual in every way…except the complete lack of sex.

But would that blow apart their working relationship? Since that one brief hug, they hadn't touched so much as a fingertip: not in the restaurant, not while shopping, and not over breakfast.

"All I can think…" All he could think was how she'd look at the moment of perfect ecstasy and just how much he'd like to be the one to help her find it.

"Yes?" her voice was practically pleading with him.

"We have to try. Because if we don't…"

"…we'll both go stark, raving mad," she finished for him.

Sam could only nod.

Again the long silence. His turn to break it.

"Not to sound crass, but…Your place or mine?"

Her smile quirked at that, "Mine is closer by about a block."

"All the difference in the world," he rose to his feet, and held out a hand to help her to her feet.

She looked at his hand, and then up into his eyes, studying him before she took it.

The shock was visceral, though not electric. Neither was it cooking fire hot. It was simply such a powerful feeling of rightness that he didn't stop there. With the slightest tug, he kept pulling her in until she lay against his chest, her head on his shoulder. He bent down to bury his face in her hair. Her slender form felt so perfect in his hands that he wrapped her tightly against him and simply held on.

"This had better be worth it, Sam Walsh."

"No guts, no glory, Luisa Valenti."

"I'm thinking…"

"…that your apartment is too far away."

A restaurant floor was no place to bed a woman for the first time. Then he remembered a luxurious sofa in the entryway for waiting patrons.

He swept her up in his arms and carried her there. The soft light of the fire reached just well enough that he was able to see that she looked as incredible under her clothes as even his wildest fantasies had thought.

Sam made love to her while the rain storm rattled the front doors.

*L**uisa felt thoroughly ravaged** and pleasantly trashy. They'd made it back to her studio apartment around three a.m. and passed out. The shopping alarm had gone off at five-thirty. They'd been half dressed by the time they remembered it was Monday and the restaurant was closed for the next two days. They hadn't gone back to sleep for a long while. The chill November rains gave them every reason to stay inside. So they did.

Now it was Tuesday mid-afternoon. Delivery pizza and Chinese cartons were scattered in among their discarded clothes. Damp towels from the most erotic shower of her life had been tossed on the floor as well. A shocking amount of protection was now in her garbage can hidden by a discrete Kleenex. And the most amazing chef and lover of her life lay draped across her like a man dead. They hadn't even gotten dressed—other than a quick robe for the food deliveries—in the last thirty-six hours.

Sam mumbled something unintelligible in her ear, rolled onto his side, then scooped her back against his chest and buried his face in her hair. He couldn't seem to get enough of that. He'd charmed her in so many ways that she could easily get lost in it.

She rubbed a hand along the back of his arm where it curled around her waist and held her tight. Her studio apartment had little going for it, other than a bed, a chair, and a dresser. It hadn't mattered to Sam. She idly wondered what his place was like. Did he have a masterful kitchen or did he care just as little for what lay beyond the restaurant as she did? No, Sam Walsh would have a one bedroom, maybe even a two. It would be messy around the edges, but the kitchen would be immaculate. He'd cook for her there.

Luisa didn't want to be charmed, not really. She wanted amazing sex and a challenging career. She had dreams, restaurant dreams. She knew how a restaurant should run—had learned an immense amount running Angelo's—and could easily imagine being aboyeur to a whole chain of them. But she couldn't imagine a chef-lover in that picture. Or at least she never had, which didn't make it any easier now.

Perhaps it didn't matter, her lovers never lasted long. They'd cross some line and she'd throw them out. Or they couldn't handle one of her caustic quips and they'd be gone.

Maybe that had already been dealt with. The blinders were definitely gone after what she and Sam had done to each other in the last day and a half.

"It's morning," she said even though the afternoon light—the first break from rain in days—was streaming in her west-facing window and warming the bed deliciously.

"Uh-huh," he grunted in her hair.

"So?"

"What?"

"So, do you still respect me?"

"I," he nuzzled the back of her neck. She could feel against her backside that other parts of him were impossibly waking up as well. "I respect your sexual prowess no end. If I live through the afternoon, I'll upgrade that from respect to worship."

It was hard to argue with that. Sam was a perfect blend of gentle, creative, and sheer stamina. His body was built to order by any woman, but what he could do with those strong chef's hands of his had to be classified as pure glory.

Even as she gave herself to his roving hands and carnal intentions, she couldn't help wondering how she'd be screwing this up.

She knew it would be her.

Sam was far too nice a guy to take care of that for her.

CHAPTER 9

"*You what?" Sam strangled* painfully on the last word and grabbed his throat to stop himself from grabbing Luisa's right across the cook line.

"I got a job offer," she repeated more calmly than she ever called out an order.

Sam looked up and down the line. Marlys was staring at Luisa while searing a piece of mahi-mahi for table fourteen. He pointed to get her attention back on the fish before it burned.

Valerie, Tony, Vic, even Marko the dishwasher had all ground to a halt.

He looked down at the empty plate in front of him and for the life of him couldn't remember what went on it. He looked back up at Luisa.

"And you tell me now?"

She shrugged as if his world wasn't falling apart. They were practically living together. For three months they had been together every night, usually at his place because he had a kitchen and a decent sofa.

"Where?"

"L.A. at first; maybe Vegas and overseas after that. Wolfgang Puck wants an experienced aboyeur to vet and enhance the operation of two of his high-end restaurants at the Bel-Air and the Ritz-Carlton. If that works out well, I'd expand into Spago and Cut."

It was the entire fine dining line with one of the leading restaurateurs in the country.

"It's just talk at this point," she finished prepping a plate and turned to hand it off.

But her timing was off; neither Graziella nor the other waiters were anywhere to be seen. It was his only clue that she was not nearly as calm or cool about this as she was pretending. Luisa never missed her cues, not once in the last three months since they'd become lovers had she eased up on pushing him for perfection in the kitchen. She'd also trained someone for Manuel and was helping Angelo do interviews for his Southern Italian Hearth over in Bellevue at the top of one of the towers.

"Just talk? You said you had an offer."

She shrugged negligently and he knew she was gone.

He wished to god he knew why.

He did his best to focus back on the service, managed to get the mahi-mahi with the right sauce and vegetables, even if it was on the wrong type of plate. He didn't change it and she didn't say a word before dressing it with a truffle oil finish.

All Sam knew was that there was small box in his pocket that had been burning a hole there for two days since he'd picked up the ring. And his plans to give it to her tonight, when they'd have the next two days off to celebrate, had just been burned past recognition.

CHAPTER 10

Luisa hadn't been prepared for her own pain when Sam had shut her out. Not that she could blame him; it had been one of her least smooth exits in history. But this wasn't working for her. He was too close, too real, too important. She'd sworn no man would ever get in the way of her dreams. The Old Boys Club of restaurant chefs would never limit her options. She'd prove—

But the scar that she'd just sliced across Sam's heart was so visible; she'd never imagined anything that bad.

He didn't say another word to her. Instead he returned to creating perfect food like an emotionless machine. She hadn't had the heart to offer a single prod or nudge—he didn't give her cause to, except that one plate. His part of the service was perfect. Machine perfect.

As the last plated dish crossed the line, he turned to Marlys, whispered something to her, and was gone out the back door before she could think what to say. Marlys began cleaning up his station without looking at her once.

No one else on the line was talking to her either.

Luisa cleaned up her station amidst the echoing silence and retreated as quickly as she could.

She entered her apartment too weary to turn on the light. She also couldn't bear seeing one of Sam's forgotten jackets over the back of a chair or the silly mobile he'd bought at the Pike Place Market and hung in her window, made entirely of twisted vintage forks and spoons.

Two days and nights later she was still sitting in the dark when an envelope was slid under her door. She'd hurried barefoot to the peephole, but there was nothing to see and she couldn't bear to open the door. She slid down until she sat beside the envelope with her back to the door.

Inside there was a check. It was two-week's severance pay, plus an extra month's pay for bonus. Signed by Angelo.

A post-it had been stuck to the front of the check.

Two words, no signature, but she'd recognize the handwriting anywhere.

"Good luck."

She caught the next flight to Los Angeles and wore sunglasses the whole way to hide her bloodshot eyes.

CHAPTER 11

*S**am finished the last** serving of the night and began cleaning up his station. He bantered a bit with Marlys; let the line see he was fine—after two months, he'd better be.

Graziella came up to him as he was finishing the cleanup on his station.

"I know," he told her. "I know. I'll put out an ad tomorrow for a new aboyeur. I just couldn't face doing it before. But I really want to thank you for covering, Graziella. You're amazing."

"I am amazing. Thank you for noticing."

He managed a smile. Her quick hug was surprising and kind.

She then nodded toward the front of house. "Someone waiting to see you." And she was gone.

Sam double-checked the kitchen. He was the last one, so he flipped off all except the safety night light and pushed out into restaurant.

The lights were out. The fire was still going and a single candle burned on the table for two close beside it. A lone woman sat at the table facing away from the kitchen.

For a moment he wondered how Graziella had circled around so fast, but then he knew. His stomach clenched so hard that he couldn't breathe and had to hold onto the door frame to remain upright. He considered moving back through the door, but Luisa sat so still. Even the sound of the swinging door behind him didn't cause her to turn, as if she'd shatter at the least movement.

He circled the long way around the fire so that he didn't approach her from behind. Her face was as frozen as the rest of her. She was normally so animated that she looked unnatural in her stillness.

Sam wanted to yell at her; spit out all of the hard hateful words that had rattled around inside him but never found any target. But the candle picked up the tracks of the silent tears that she made no effort to brush aside, if she was even aware of them. At a loss for what else to do, he sat down across from her.

He saw her swallow hard, several times, but he'd be damned if he'd be first to speak. If he was, he couldn't trust what would come out.

She nodded once, twice, as if trying to confirm something to herself, then began in a soft voice. Not quite looking at him, as if she didn't dare.

"My parents threw me out when I was fourteen. Boys and drugs and never going to school and crap like that was what they said. Maybe. But I know they also couldn't afford to feed me. I learned fast what cold and hungry were like. Got pretty desperate. Finally tried to hustle this chef coming out of a crappy restaurant. Offered to trade what I had to give for some food."

Sam wanted to close his eyes. Didn't want to see the hard memories that were crossing Luisa's lovely face, but he couldn't look away.

"Instead he fed me, helped me get a fake ID because I already looked like this, and gave me my first restaurant job. He paid me in food and a place to sleep on his floor. No money for the first six months because he didn't trust me to not buy drugs until I'd been clean a while."

Sam had heard stories like that. Except the offered payment was usually accepted. She'd gotten lucky.

"I don't have the palate to be a chef. But I'm smart. I earned my GED in two years even though I was missing four years of school. And I *saw* how restaurants worked; as clearly as a child's game. I cooked, cleaned, waitressed, did it all. But I was always fascinated by how it all worked. How things flowed."

Sam nodded. He couldn't quite bring himself to tell her just how good she'd been at her job.

"I always dreamed of running a chain. A big group of restaurants, making them function the way..." her voice stumbled and she took a deep gulping breath not far from a sob but continued. "...the way that we functioned. It was almost as good as sex. Better than, until I met you. Those months with you were the best of my life."

"Mine too," Sam managed his first words and she nodded rapidly in response.

"But I didn't understand about boys, men; about a man. About you. I didn't get that what we had wasn't like anything I'd ever had before. I did the job. I worked for Wolfgang in amazing restaurants. And people listened. I *was* good."

"Best I've ever seen," Sam finally admitted. He didn't tend to think ahead, but he found himself trying to second guess this conversation. He wasn't having much luck. There was a thin thread of hope, but it was blended with memory of a pain so intense that it was utterly blinding.

"I got that dream. The dream that a poor, desperate, cokehead girl had held up as a light to find her way out of the tunnel. But I missed the most important part."

"What's that?" Sam held himself very tightly. Even daring to hope hurt like a knife.

"You."

"Me? Just that simply. Me?"

She nodded again, her arms wrapped tightly around her as if she was freezing to death sitting right next to the fire.

"I'm just a dumb chef. You'd better explain it to me. Because last time I checked you're the one who—" He bit off the words. Clamped down on the recriminations that he wanted to spew all over her... because he didn't want to spew them any more.

For better or worse, he knew one truth absolutely.

He loved Luisa Valenti.

God help him.

He took a deep breath and spoke slowly so that he could choose his words carefully.

"We get back together and you're just going to wish you were back with Wolfgang's restaurants. And I don't want to leave Angelo's. He's perhaps the best Italian chef working today and he's given me his Number One restaurant to run. No way to solve that."

"There is. At least I hope there is."

"I'm listening," Sam hoped there was too. He'd never wanted anything in his life as much as he wanted Luisa, but giving up the restaurant dream would only make him bitter. Just as if she gave up hers.

"Oh god, Sam. You're the best man there ever was. I can't believe you're even listening to me. I didn't deserve you."

Sam waited for her to continue, unable to do more.

Impossibly she clenched her arms even tighter until her frame was shaking.

"I had the wrong dream."

"Say what?" That wasn't what he'd been expecting. He'd expected some plea for him to go with her. Or that she'd give up her own dreams, which he'd never allow. That's why he'd written the message he had even if he hadn't been able to bring himself to sign it.

"Angelo's was an amazing experience," he could hear the truth of it in her voice. "I never had so much fun. Angelo, Manuel, Marlys, Graziella, all of them. And that was before I noticed you. Then it just kept getting better. I asked to be busy, I asked to be challenged."

"And Wolfgang's organization does that for you."

"It did, past tense. He offered me consulting at Spago and Cut; flew in himself to do so. I thanked him and then I quit. I gave my two weeks' notice three weeks ago. I've been back for a week trying to find the bravery to come and see you."

"You quit?" Sam knew something was wrong here. "Because of me? No! That doesn't work. I won't let you—"

"It wasn't because of *you*, doofus. It was because of *me*," she shouted him down just as she so often did on the cook line.

"Because of you?" He still wasn't getting it.

"Because of me," she said more calmly and unwound her arms, finally resting her hands in her lap as if too weary to do more. "I was too young and stupid to understand the most important dream of all, even if you knew it from the very first day."

"I did?"

She smiled at him; that smile she gave right before she was going to unleash mayhem on his cook line just to tease him. That smile that also spilled forth when she'd woken in his arms to find him watching her.

"Yes," she continued. "I forgot to dream about being happy. I was happy with you, so god damn happy that I scared the shit out of myself and ran away. I'm hoping you'll give me a chance to try out that dream again."

"And I'm supposed to trust that?"

She nodded, but the fear was back and she hung her head to study her hands once more. Luisa wasn't afraid of anything.

"How? Please tell me how I can." Because Sam had no idea—no matter how much he wanted to.

And when she looked up at him, the tears had returned. "Because I learned something new by leaving you that I never would have learned while we were together."

"What was that?"

"How much I love you, Sam Walsh."

And there it was. How could he possibly deny such a statement, especially when it was so clear in his own heart? Had some part of him hoped that she'd be back? Was that why he'd never filled the aboyeur spot no matter how badly they needed it? Apparently so.

But he couldn't let her off the hook that easily no matter how much he was planning to.

Sam crossed his arms over his chest and struggled for a disdainful voice when he really wanted to scoop her into his arms and cry for joy.

"So, you think you can just come back, pick up where you left off at Angelo's. As if we'd take you."

Her face fell, so he went for a slightly lighter tone.

"Then you figure you can just slide back into my bed."

"Well," she was too sharp, and caught on from just that tiniest hint, "I did let go of my apartment, so I do kinda *need* a bed to slide into."

He kept his arms crossed, but backed it up with the smile he was feeling building deep inside him. "You're probably going to want the ring I had in my pocket that night."

She looked at him aghast, "You bought me a ring?"

"Uh-huh."

She covered her mouth in horror, "That same night? Oh god, I'm so sorry. I never thought anyone would ever do something like that for me."

"I did. *Doofus* that I am. And even worse?"

"What's worse than that?"

Sam rose and circled around the table, then knelt and took Luisa's hands.

She looked into his eyes and he knew he was lost. Happily lost.

"Even worse," he confirmed. "I love you so much that I can't imagine life without you."

The smile that broke out on her face was accompanied by a different type of tears. Then she giggled. A bright merry laugh that he'd missed more than anything about her.

"What?" he asked softly.

She leaned down and gave him a kiss seasoned with pure joy.

"I was just thinking, what with you being the best man I've ever met and all…"

"What?"

"I bet you kept the ring."

He had. He'd felt pathetic doing so, but now he knew why he hadn't returned it. Because some part of him had known that something so right could never be denied for long.

Sam lifted her hands to his lips and kissed her—right where he'd be slipping the ring on later tonight.

RETURN TO EAGLE COVE (EXCERPT)

A SMALL TOWN OREGON ROMANCE

"Almost home, sweetie."

"Oh joy," Jessica Baxter tried to clamp down on her sarcasm. It was a bad habit that worked fine in her social set back in Chicago, but sounded more petty with each mile they drove toward the Oregon Coast. She slumped down in the passenger seat of her mom's baby-blue Toyota hybrid. It still had that new car smell. As much as she'd dreamed of owning a hot sports car some day, she knew that she was enough her mother's daughter that this was probably the exact sort of eminently sensible car she would buy when her VW Beetle finally gave up the ghost.

Just like her mom.

Maybe she'd get it in red to be at least a *little* different.

Jessica sighed again, keeping it to herself so that she wasn't being overly offensive. Her mother was one of the many reasons that she'd gone as far away as possible for college and did her best to rarely return—she didn't want to turn into her mother and it was too easy to imagine doing so if she'd stayed in the small town of Eagle Cove, Oregon.

They were like twins separated by twenty-two years. The two of them had been able to trade clothes since Jessica hit puberty and had shot up to match her mother's slender five-foot-ten. Other than a very brief mistake of dying her hair black as part of a tenth-grade dare, which had turned her fair complexion past goth and into bloodless vampire, they were both light blond.

The one part of twin-dom that she couldn't seem to pull off even though she wanted to was Mom's casual-chic. Monica Baxter was always dressed one step above the world around her; not fancy, just really well put together. The closest Jessica ever managed was Bohemian-chic which wasn't really the same thing, but she'd learned to make it her own. Of course, Bohemian was easier on the budget and often available in consignment stores which had only reinforced her chosen style.

Jessica did her best to not regress as they drove up into the Coast Range that separated the beach towns from the rest of Oregon...and failed miserably at that as well. She felt as if she was rapidly descending back toward being a pouty, pre-pubescent twelve from her present urban and worldly thirty-two.

Why did crossing the Oregon state line always take twenty years off her intelligence?

Maybe it was only Coast County. Because of the landscape the Oregon Coast felt incredibly far from anywhere. The Coast Range topped out at a mere four thousand feet high, but only a half dozen passes made it through the three hundred mile range of rugged hills that separated the beaches from the broad farming and industrial realm of the Willamette Valley. The interior of the state might as well be in a whole other country for how little it had in common with where she'd grown up.

"It's so strange being back here," Jessica rolled down the window and sniffed at the air. The scents were so rich and varied that they tickled. Bright with pine. Musty with undergrowth. Damp. A first hint of the sea.

"Well, it has been four years, honey. That's bound to make it seem a bit odd. But I'm so glad that you came."

"Me too, Mom." Better. She managed to say it as if she meant it, however unlikely that might be. Chicago fit her like a...but it didn't.

The city was…something she was not going to give a single thought to for the next eight days. If she didn't fit there and she didn't want to fit in Eagle Cove, Oregon, then where did she belong?

Jessica breathed in deeply this time, trying to clear her thoughts with the fresh air of the Coast Range and nearly choked herself on how green everything smelled. The harsh slap of the mountains was almost an affront. The two-lane road dove and twisted along narrow corridors sliced through towering spruce and Douglas fir trees. The babies were sixty feet high along the shoulder as the car twisted up toward the pass; the mother trees behind them were much, much bigger.

And it wasn't just the trees that were lush. As they wound deeper into the Coast Range, each branch became covered with mosses and lichens. It soothed her eyes, so used to towering concrete and glass, with a living tapestry of greens, golds, and silvers. Beneath the trees grew an impenetrable tangle of salal and scrub alder. Old barns on the roadside didn't have shingle roofs, they had moss ones; some of them were covered inches thick. Many RVs, left unattended in front yards for too long, had a sheen of green growth on their north side.

"I really want to hate this," the Coast Range had three times the rainfall of Chicago, often surpassing a hundred inches a year. She expected to feel the weight of all that biomass crashing down on her shoulders, but instead she noticed the start of a disconcerting light-ness as if coming home was a good thing. Jessica did *not* like that encroachment of pending appreciation, perhaps even enjoyment, upon her *true* feelings. "But it smells so good. Like sunshine and new growth."

Her mother's laugh was amused as they twisted along the two-lane road slowly climbing up a narrow valley.

"I didn't mean to say that out loud."

"But you said it anyway."

"Not helping, Mom."

Thankfully her mother's laugh said that she had understood Jessica's response as a tease. Which it mostly was, partly.

Jessica didn't *want* to like coming back to the coast. She didn't have small-town dreams. That was the main reason she'd left Eagle Cove. She had big city dreams…which weren't exactly coming together for her despite her efforts over the last fourteen years. But scurrying home wasn't going to fix those. And the selection of men in such a tiny town was, to put it kindly, pitiful. Puffin High—

Why they hadn't called it Eagle High in Eagle Cove was a subject of heated debate by every single class.

Puffin High's problem was that she knew every male her age all too well. The only reason the town had its own high school was that it was too far away from everywhere else for busing to make sense. Her senior class had just thirty-four students. Grades seven through twelve numbered under two hundred. And she knew far too much about every single one of them.

Even more obnoxiously invasive on her sense of right and wrong, instead of dumping rain, it was a perfect day. The sun sparkled down revealing a thousand shades of green in the living walls that lined the road. The air coming through the open window was thick with pine sap and the gentle tang of rotting undergrowth. There was so much oxygen in the air that it made her feel a little giddy.

Yes, a perfect day, if she'd been alone…and still in Chicago.

"I could have rented a car and saved you the drive, Mom." Actually, her budget had been thrilled when her mother had offered to come and fetch her. Also, once in Eagle Cove there wasn't a lot of use for a car, except when the rain poured down. The whole town was only a few miles long and she could walk most places she'd want to go. As if there were any old haunts that she'd care to revisit. She'd made good her escape to Northwestern University's School of Journalism at eighteen but every now and then the town still sucked her back.

"Nonsense, honey. I'm always glad to drive up and get you. Besides, I needed a few things for the wedding."

"How many is this?" As if she didn't know. It took much of her journalistic skill to keep "that judgmental tone" out of her voice. Something her early teachers had dinged her on until she'd learned to eradicate it. But since she was regressing as they neared the coast, it was trying to make a comeback.

"Number four."

"Why, Mom?"

"Because I love the man." Her mother actually glanced away from the road to offer her a scowl. "I'd have thought that was obvious."

"It is. But you've divorced him three times."

"Because *your* father can drive a woman crazy without even trying." They giggled together because that was an absolute truth about Ralph Baxter.

"I meant, why marry him again? You're both legal age, your daughter lives in Chicago," and wouldn't complain if she lived on another planet entirely. "Just shack up together. Then you can lock the door whenever Daddy becomes too much like himself."

Ralph Baxter was always getting caught up in monster projects. Without a word of warning he would suddenly rip out the entire kitchen, once on the morning before a dinner party, because he'd thought of a better way to design it. Or he'd start building a new boat from scratch in the middle of the driveway, rather than in the generous side yard, which blocked parking near the house for months.

"Oh, honey. I'm too old fashioned a girl to 'just shack up'."

Which was almost believable, even in the twenty-first century. To hear Aunt Gina—who despite her name was as not-Italian as a pastrami sandwich—tell it, Monica Lamont had chosen Ralph Baxter as her sweet sixteen love. She'd never even shopped around. How 1950s was that for a woman who hadn't even been born then?

Jessica had shopped plenty, or at least window-shopped. She'd found only a few men worth the cost of trying on for size. Definitely not a one worth taking home to keep. She might look like her mom, all blond, tall, and waiflike—which she kind of hated though the men seemed to like it—but inside she wanted to be like Aunt Gina.

Luigina Lamont looked nothing like her twin sister...or Grandpop...or much like Grandma for that matter. She was a statuesque redhead, in every voluptuous sense of the word and completely lived up to her name: Luigina meant "Famous Warrior." Her merry laugh slapped up against you at the most unexpected moments and constantly poked at your ticklish spot until you were curled up on the couch begging her to stop. Unlike Mom and her serial marriages to the same man, Gina brought home plenty yet had only tried to keep one.

That "unholy disaster" (as the family tales described it) had produced Natalya Daphne Lamont—Jessica's three-hour-older (and Natalya never let her forget it) first cousin and best friend. Just like Gina, Natalya didn't look like either her mom or Gina's brief husband. Maybe that was hereditary on that side of the family to balance out how much Jessica resembled her own mom and their shared grandma. Jessica had a sudden flash of her own future daughter looking just like her...and felt the world spin just a little at thinking about children at all.

"If I hadn't seen her come out between my legs myself," Aunt Gina would announce loudly, "I'd have thought I adopted the kid. Maybe I signed up to be a surrogate then forgot all about it."

Mom blushed every time Aunt Gina let that one loose in public, without understanding that if she didn't, Aunt Gina would have stopped long ago.

"Such an exotic offspring deserves an exotic name. Natalya for the Russian Bond girl in *GoldenEye* and Daphne for du Maurier the romance writer, *not* the nymph who had to turn into a tree to escape that lusty jerk Apollo." The fact that *GoldenEye* hadn't come out until Natalya had already been in grade school hadn't changed Aunt Gina's story one bit.

Maybe Jessica's own child would be lucky and take after Cousin Natalya who was slender like Jessica, but had all of the curves Jessica had prayed for throughout her teenage years but never been granted. Natya was also dusky skinned like a permanent tan and leggy like some French model. Jessica's and her mom's fairy light hair and Aunt Gina's mass of red curls had been transformed to a smooth cascade of dark chestnut on her cousin. Yet she and Jessica felt like twins from different mothers: one light, one dark, but much the same on the inside.

Jessica smiled at the sign as they cleared Maxine Pass: eight-hundred and three feet according to the sign. The "three" always made her laugh. It was like Becky, her other best friend from Eagle Cove, firmly insisting that she as five-four "and a quarter" as if it made a difference.

Maxine Pass was technically Maxwell Pass. Or it had been until the day that Aunt Gina had declared it just wasn't right for all of the passes to have male names merely because men were the ones who drew the maps back in the 1800s.

For her sixteenth birthday Jessica hadn't received her first kiss— already happened a year before—or gotten laid—two more years until that event. Instead, she'd been recruited for a "Mission!" At two in the morning on their shared birthday, Aunt Gina drove her and Natalya up to repaint the Maxwell Pass highway sign to Maxine. It had become a tradition that every time the highway department changed it back to Maxwell, the three of them would have a two a.m. gals' outing and change the sign once again. The highway department had given up years ago. A few of the more recent road maps had even changed the name.

"Girl Power!" they'd shout after each time they finished repainting the sign, usually about three a.m. Then they'd break out the thermos of hot chocolate and drink it from a shared cup while they admired their handiwork by moonlight.

One time Martin, the town cop, had shown up while they were doing it. Jessica and Natalya had ducked, but Gina hadn't slowed down a single brush stroke.

"Thought it would be you," Martin had observed through his open car window, obviously talking to Gina.

"Out of your jurisdiction, Marty," had been Aunt Gina's awesomely calm reply. She had always been Jessica's hero, but that totally clinched it. The town limits had been left far behind.

He'd joined them for the hot chocolate and had a good laugh at the "Girl Power!" chant.

Today Jessica just waved hello to the sign as they crested the pass and began their descent.

"Didn't you ever bust out, Mom?" Jessica tried to imagine her doing so, but couldn't quite conjure it up in her mind.

"Bust out? You mean cheat on your father? Never!"

"But what about between times, when you were divorced? That wouldn't be cheating."

Monica Lamont's lips thinned as she tightened her jaw and finally shook her head in a sharp little snap. "I was only living in the other end of the house."

"What about with Dad? You and Dad could just…you know?" The thought of her parents having sex was uncomfortable enough that she couldn't quite say it aloud.

"Ralph says that if I feel so strongly about things that I have to divorce him, then I shouldn't be expecting any special concessions while we are divorced."

Jessica felt she had to side with Dad on that one. He'd become used to his wife's antics, but that meant he didn't get any either in the interims. No wandering for him—it had always been clear that Ralph Baxter was absolutely crazy about Monica Lamont. Jessica felt kind of sorry for him.

"Wait. You mean you haven't had sex in two years?" This latest was their longest divorce yet.

Again that little snap that made Jessica's neck ache in sympathy. Mom moved to the right as the road added a climbing lane to reach the six-hundred and thirty-four foot (not quite so much bragging) Rogue Pass. That name at least made perfect sense by Oregon standards…because it wasn't anywhere near either of the two separate Rogue Rivers in Oregon. A half dozen cars roared past. Mom always drove exactly at the speed limit instead of the nearly mandatory ten over that prevailed throughout the state.

"So you're waiting for the wedding night?"

This time her mom's nod was a little sad.

"I'm sure tomorrow will be a great night, Mom."

At that she smiled brilliantly. "If the past three are anything to judge by, yes, it will be. It's just too bad we had to delay it."

"Delay it? Wait! What?" Jessica bolted upright in the car seat and almost throttled herself with her seatbelt. The wedding was supposed to be *tomorrow*. She'd secretly planned on staying just one day past the wedding, and then catching the Airporter Express that wandered through the small coastal towns once a day. She'd already warned Natalya to expect her in Portland for the rest of the week until her flight back to the Windy City.

"Well, we were meeting with Judge Slater about the ceremony. As he performed the first three weddings…"

Jessica resisted pointing out that he'd done all three divorces as well. Maybe her Oregon civility was coming back. Yeah, like a toothache.

"…and he had all of the old records in a file; even had the new marriage license pre-filled out, the dear man. However, it turns out that the first time we were married was on July fourteenth, not July seventh as I had remembered. You know how your father loves the cycle of things. So we moved the wedding to next weekend to coincide properly with the original. I knew you already had your plane tickets, so I didn't see any point in telling you."

Didn't see any point? She'd have moved heaven and earth to— Actually, her mother was right because she'd purchased the cheapest non-refundable, non-changeable tickets she could find.

A week! She was going to be trapped in Eagle Cove from Friday morning until Sunday morning nine days later? Oh, that was so bad.

"I can't believe that we celebrated it wrong for all of those years," her mother continued, completely oblivious to the panic she'd just created. "The seventh was the date that had always stuck in my head for our anniversaries."

Mom's dropping voice spoke volumes. She'd always been terrible at keeping a secret.

"So why *did* the seventh stick in your head?" Jessica kept it as casual as she could, rather than rubbing it in that her mom always gave up whatever she was trying to hide. It must be the journalist in her coming out: ask the question and then wait patiently for a reply. Not pushing was another change between them. Jessica didn't feel as if she was mellowing with age, but perhaps she was. Being disillusioned at thirty-two was no more newsworthy than it had been at twelve or twenty-two; but a woman shouldn't mellow until...well, maybe a hundred-and-two.

On the back side of Rogue Pass, Mom concentrated on the winding descent. Jessica waved at a massive Roosevelt elk who grazed in a small clearing beside the road. Coming back to Eagle Cove might be only one step better than a nightmare, but it was a very scenic one. The road was soon joined by a stream rushing in a deep ravine on Jessica's side of the road; the problem was that they were both racing in the wrong direction—toward, not away from, her childhood home. The stream tumbled along almost as fast as they did down toward Eagle River which would eventually define the end of town where it opened into a broad bay before it reached the sea.

No one quite knew why the bay had been named a cove, but it showed that way on even the oldest maps. It gave the town an off-kilter personality to Jessica's mind, as if it was always seeking to find its true identity. No bridge crossed the Eagle to the wilderness area on the other bank. To reach that required either a boat or an hour drive back up to Highway 101, across the river, and then a long crawl back to the Coast over marginal logging roads.

"C'mon, Mom, give." Since not pushing at her mother had failed, Jessica went with regressing and shifted to the wheedling tone she'd perfected as a child. She might hate herself in the morning for slipping back into it, but it always worked. Sure enough, her mom gave in right on cue.

"July seventh was the one time we cheated. We didn't actually wait for our first wedding night," the blush on her mother's fair skin was almost bright enough to lighten the dark corridor between the towering trees. "Your father made it amazing. But that's also the day I became pregnant, though I didn't know it until after the wedding. All those years I was celebrating the wrong date. That's why we never fool around unless we're married."

"Sounds like you were celebrating *exactly* the right date, Mom." She tried to pin down the exact date of her own first time, but it hadn't been all that memorable. Good, but "earth-shattering" was just another one of those 1950s' myths that didn't happen in the twenty-first century. Except, apparently, for her own mother. How unfair was that.

"Maybe," her mom admitted, "but we're going to get married on the fourteenth anyway."

"So, I'm illegitimate?" Not that it bothered her, but she couldn't resist needling her mother about it. Maybe she hadn't matured all that much.

"Yes dear, but only by one week. I swear I didn't know." This time Jessica heard that her mom's confession was a sigh at Jessica's question rather than sounding contrite. Maybe it was time Jessica grew up a bit—even when in Eagle Cove.

"Does Aunt Gina know about all this?"

"No one does, except your father and now you. You only arrived three days early, which was actually four days late. No one gave it any thought."

Excellent! Forget being mature. Aunt Gina would love the extra dirt for teasing her sister and Jessica couldn't wait to be the one to tickle her aunt's funny bone.

\# \# \#

It had been another long morning of assisting the Judge—always with a capital J. Monday through Friday, six a.m. to ten, Greg Slater helped his father. At first it had been something that Greg did to help out, but he'd come to like the simple routines and structure to his mornings.

"Ready?" he called back to the kitchen as he did every day. There was no real need to ask. The big old clock hung high on the wall said it was exactly six a.m. and the Judge was a very punctual man.

But Greg looked for the solemn nod before moving out into the diner and flicking on the fluorescents, "The Puffin Diner" sign, and the porch lights. There wasn't much need for the last, sunrise was twenty minutes ago, but the sun itself wouldn't clear the Coast Range ridge until at least six-thirty. For now, Beach Way, the town's main street, was mostly cool shadows and darkened buildings.

The bell mounted on the back of the door rang almost right away as Cal Mason Jr. came in. Greg had already set a mug of coffee on the counter for him. Cal ran the Blackbird Bakery and was hours into his day. Five days a week he was as punctual as the Judge. Cal Sr. wouldn't be in for a few hours yet.

"Your standard, Cal?"

"Double," though Greg knew that was a joke. Cal was one of the few men in town big enough that he could have eaten two of the Judge's generous portions. Six-two and as powerful as a bulldozer; his hands dwarfed the coffee mug.

Because Cal sat at the six-stool wooden counter, the Judge was less than five feet away through the broad service window that connected the dining room with the kitchen, but he waited for Greg to fill out the order slip and clip it to the spinner.

It was Greg's own fault. The diner's service had been a bone of contention, or rather "lengthy negotiation" just as most things were with the Judge.

"They can pick up their own plates at the window. Coffee pot is right there behind the counter where anyone who wants a refill can get their own."

Greg had won that round by subterfuge. He'd numbered the tables and then only put the numbers on the order slips, making it impossible for the Judge to boom out with "Veronica, your order is up." Customers had slowly adapted to not having to leave their tables for every little thing.

At least Greg thought he'd won, until a full three weeks later his father had winked at him while sliding across a short stack with bacon and hash browns for Karen Thompson, "Like I don't know who orders what on a Thursday."

Now the Judge wouldn't cook a thing without a proper ticket. Well, he'd cook it, but he wouldn't serve it no matter how busy or harried Greg was.

Cal's plate came up less than thirty seconds after Greg hung the ticket just as it did every morning: western omelet, hash browns, farm sausage, and English muffin. The last was about the only kind of bread that Cal didn't bake.

"Gotta have something that I can order out for and enjoy without baking it myself."

Greg moved the plate across to the counter and refilled Cal's half-drained mug of coffee.

There wasn't much call for a judge in a town the size of Eagle Cove. Semi-retired for the last five years, he no longer spent three days a week in Newport to sit on the bench as he had throughout Greg's childhood. Instead he'd set up a small courtroom in town. He mainly handled family matters like marriages and estates, and fines for drunk and disorderly tourists who soon learned that Judge Slater was a fierce protector of the town. There was only the occasional speeding ticket—no matter how hard Martin the cop tried to catch someone. The town was perched against the Pacific Ocean at the dead end of a winding two-lane that had left the coastal highway a dozen miles back; it had enough "Sharp Curves Ahead" signs to quell even the most lead-footed of souls.

So, "for something to keep me busy," the Judge held office hours only in the afternoons because his weekday mornings were all spent working as a short-order cook. And ever since Greg's return to Eagle Cove three years ago, he'd been his father's front-of-house man: waiter, cashier, and busboy.

The Puffin Diner had been a near derelict before his dad had bought and reopened it. It was a classic small town place built to serve the early morning fishermen, especially those returning from a long night's work on the offshore shoals; it was little changed over the last ninety years.

The clapboard building stood high enough on a heavy stone foundation that even the Christmas storm flood of 1964 had crested two steps below the front entry. It was one of the only structures on the town's main street that didn't have a street-level entry. All of the other businesses that had existed then had high-water lines drawn halfway or more up their walls. The Grouse Hardware store, the lowest spot in town close beside the docks, had a small wooden plaque of a fish screwed in just above the main door lintel. It was bright yellow with "Dec 22, 1964" painted on it in tropical blue—it was generally considered to be a little boastful, but old man Jaspar refused to tone down the color scheme that he'd painted on that fish in his youth.

The interior of the diner was so retro that it would have been ironic-modern if it wasn't quite so authentic. The steel-edged tables of blue Formica were scuffed nearly colorless by the thousands of plates and silverware settings that had been slid across their surfaces over the years. The chairs' red leather was sun-faded and the old chrome had pitted with rust from the salt air, making them uncomfortable to the touch without quite being painful. The linoleum floor had been replaced...back in the 1980s when mauve and hunter green had been trendy colors. The six round stools bolted to the floor at the counter squealed every time someone spun on or off them. The kitchen was authentic right down to the large service window, the steel spinner rack for order slips dangling in one corner, and the big grill and burners in the back. The scents of eggs, hash browns, and frying bacon filled the main street each morning enticing all passersby to come and find comfort food.

Ralph Baxter and Manny McCall came in and took their usual spot by the corner window. They'd have tourists out fishing off their boats within the hour and were both after black coffee and tall stacks.

At first Greg had resented serving the Judge's fare—it was as invariable as his father. Scrambles, omelets, pancakes—no waffles because the iron had broken the same day Mom had died and he couldn't seem to fix it and wouldn't let Greg try. The pancakes were big and fluffy. The very crispy hash browns were not an option; they were on every single plate, even with the pancakes. Farm fresh sausage or bacon was the other staple on every plate—not that it was a choice. Everyone received whichever Carl Parker had delivered the day before along with the eggs.

All of Greg's efforts to vary the oatmeal recipe, served with bacon or sausage and hash browns of course, had been in vain. The Judge served only rolled oats—not steel cut—with sliced, not diced, dried apricots and diced, not sliced, fresh apple. Whether brown sugar or maple syrup was used to sweeten it was wholly up to the customer; local honey was also available.

Omelets were the Judge's real specialty and by six-thirty there were already a dozen slips up for them. Omelets were the only dish where variations were allowed. He offered them with cheese, mushrooms, or smoked salmon fillings. Never all three of course, because there were limits to what was proper.

The Puffin Diner mostly served coffee. Greg's sole triumph at adjusting the menu had been when he managed to switch from Dad's "fresh ground" granules purchased in large plastic tubs to fresh-ground French roast. Tea or hot chocolate were the only other options, but asking for marshmallows with the latter was frowned upon unless you were a kid—the whipped cream came out of a spray can.

They'd fought royally over the Judge's inflexibility, but of course fighting over things was a tradition in the Slater household. Not that voices were ever raised, because that would never do. The few times Greg had tried that tactic he'd been ruled "Out of Order" and banished from the dinner table: the sole forum for Slater "discussions." With Ma gone to cancer three years before—Greg's original reason for returning to Eagle Cove—he didn't have the heart to "force" the Judge into driving him from the table after that first time. When he'd been remanded to the kitchen two weeks after Mom's funeral, he'd made the mistake of glancing back as he'd moved off to finish his meal. His father had looked old, sad, and impossibly alone.

Greg hadn't been able to face living in the big old house out on the beach, so he'd moved into the guest house. Once he finally understood that no number of cogent debates were going to sway the Judge, Greg had let the menu go. It had been unchanged in either content or price in the last decade—other than the wavy black line of magic marker through the "Waffles (with blueberries when in season)."

Greg had been on the verge of leaving town when the Judge sat him down at the big house's dining room table. Ma Slater had been in the ground for a month. Greg knew he didn't really have anywhere to go, he'd learned all he was going to from the banquet chef at the Sorrento Hotel in Seattle and there weren't any top positions open for an untested executive chef wanting to make his mark. He didn't have the capital to make his own splash, not in the insanely competitive restaurant markets in the big cities. But he'd find something.

"Been watching you, son. Been tasting your food," the Judge had tapped a fork on his dinner plate. Greg had roasted a pair of fresh-caught trout in hazelnut butter with a dressing of spring greens and homemade basil vinegar. Though Greg had cooked half the meals since Ma's funeral—"fair is fair" the Judge had declared—it was the first time his father had spoken of it.

"Uh-huh," Greg had gone for a neutral acknowledgement. He knew the Judge hated such prevarications, but Greg didn't know where this was heading and went for caution.

"This is good. Real good."

Greg hadn't been able to offer even a neutral grunt over his surprise at the Judge's remark.

"Still needs some work, though."

Before Greg could snap at him about what did a man who scrambled eggs and ruled on law know about fine cuisine, the Judge continued.

"You need more seasoning," and he aimed a fork at Greg's chest, "and I'm not talking about salt. Your technique is the best I've ever seen, but I don't taste anything special. There's nothing here that isn't in any other fine restaurant. You need time to find your own voice, not some other chef's."

"My own voice?" But he didn't need to ask, he'd heard it a thousand times growing up.

The Judge looked down at the trout, one of the only times he'd ever said anything without looking at whoever he was addressing straight in the eye, "Your mother taught me that."

Ma had been a painter, a good one. Her seascapes had sold in galleries up and down the coast. Tillamook, Newport, Gold Beach, they all snapped up as much as she could produce and was willing to let go of—Grosbeak Gallery in town had always gotten first pick though. She'd often talked about finding your voice in your art so that it didn't look like everyone else's.

"So, here is the deal I'm offering you."

Greg knew that it wouldn't be open to negotiation; no one negotiated one of Judge Slater's "deals."

"The diner is mine on weekdays from six to ten every morning. I'd like you to stay as my assistant because you're good at it. That pays rent here at the house, a small salary, and we split the tips. What you do with the diner for the rest of the time, that's up to you."

And for three years, Greg had stayed in Eagle Cove and searched for his own voice. In the first year, he'd never cooked for anyone but himself and his father—who never again spoke about the food itself. Then one night Greg had invited a couple of buddies from high school who were still in town to the diner, as a test audience. Word got out about how good it was and folks had started asking when he'd do it again.

He'd eventually started "Irregular Friday Dinners at The Puffin." He only opened when he had a new meal to test. It was all *prix fixe,* fixed price—a twenty in the jar—and a set menu. After two years of those he felt almost ready to take his cooking out into the world; maybe spend a while as a pop-up restaurant—there and gone—rather than a full launch. He'd been saving his half of every morning tip and every cent for when he went back to the cities. At first he'd simply been trying to be better by the time he left Eagle Cove, but he'd become obsessed with finding and perfecting his "chef's voice." He wanted it to be so clear that it was undeniable. When he went back to Seattle, no one would label him the protégé of Charlene at Maximilien's or Angelo at The Tuscan Hearth. He'd be his own—

The old brass bell screwed into the top of the diner's front door rang like a small ship was coming into port. Morning service peaked as usual around eight and had now tapered off to just a few lingering diners.

Greg glanced at the big-face clock above the cash register—9:57—and suppressed a groan. Judge's rule was that if you were in the door by ten, you could take as long as you wanted. If it was ten sharp plus a second, you were turned away—"Fair is fair." Maybe they'd be quick; he'd had an idea for a savory roulade that he wanted to try out.

Greg turned back and had to blink, then blink again. The morning sunlight shone through the front window and silhouetted two dazzling blondes, their hair practically set afire by the sunlight streaming in from behind them.

Then his eyes adapted as they moved farther into the room.

Mrs. Baxter who was soon to be Mrs. Baxter once again.

And a woman he hadn't seen since the day she'd left for college, but he'd know anywhere.

Jessica matched his own five-ten and her hair, instead of being the waist-long waterfall he'd remembered, now floated about her shoulders in choppy wisps that framed a face of high cheekbones, full lips, and eyes that sparkled with mischief.

Halfway across the old linoleum floor, she stopped and looked at him.

"Greggie's gaping, Mom."

And he couldn't do a thing about it.

Available at fine retailers everywhere:
Eagle Cove

ABOUT THE AUTHOR

M.L. Buchman started the first of, what is now over 50 novels and as many short stories, while flying from South Korea to ride his bicycle across the Australian Outback. Part of a solo around the world trip that ultimately launched his writing career.

All three of his military romantic suspense series—The Night Stalkers, Firehawks, and Delta Force—have had a title named "Top 10 Romance of the Year" by the American Library Association's *Booklist.* NPR and Barnes & Noble have named other titles "Top 5 Romance of the Year." In 2016 he was a finalist for Romance Writers of America prestigious RITA award. He also writes: contemporary romance, thrillers, and fantasy.

Past lives include: years as a project manager, rebuilding and single-handing a fifty-foot sailboat, both flying and jumping out of airplanes, and he has designed and built two houses. He is now making his living as a full-time writer on the Oregon Coast with his beloved wife and is constantly amazed at what you can do with a degree in Geophysics. You may keep up with his writing and receive a free starter e-library by subscribing to his newsletter at: www.mlbuchman.com

Join the conversation:
www.mlbuchman.com

Other works by M. L. Buchman:

The Night Stalkers

MAIN FLIGHT

The Night Is Mine
I Own the Dawn
Wait Until Dark
Take Over at Midnight
Light Up the Night
Bring On the Dusk
By Break of Day

WHITE HOUSE HOLIDAY

Daniel's Christmas
Frank's Independence Day
Peter's Christmas
Zachary's Christmas
Roy's Independence Day
Damien's Christmas

AND THE NAVY

Christmas at Steel Beach
Christmas at Peleliu Cove

5E

Target of the Heart
Target Lock on Love
Target of Mine

Firehawks

MAIN FLIGHT

Pure Heat
Full Blaze
Hot Point
Flash of Fire
Wild Fire

SMOKEJUMPERS

Wildfire at Dawn
Wildfire at Larch Creek
Wildfire on the Skagit

Delta Force

Target Engaged
Heart Strike
Wild Justice

Where Dreams

Where Dreams are Born
Where Dreams Reside
Where Dreams Are of Christmas
Where Dreams Unfold
Where Dreams Are Written

Eagle Cove

Return to Eagle Cove
Recipe for Eagle Cove
Longing for Eagle Cove
Keepsake for Eagle Cove

Henderson's Ranch

Nathan's Big Sky

Love Abroad

Heart of the Cotswolds: England

Dead Chef Thrillers

Swap Out!
One Chef!
Two Chef!

Deities Anonymous

Cookbook from Hell: Reheated
Saviors 101

SF/F Titles

The Nara Reaction
Monk's Maze
the Me and Elsie Chronicles

Strategies for Success (NF)

Managing Your Inner Artist/Writer
Estate Planning for Authors

SIGN UP FOR M. L. BUCHMAN'S
NEWSLETTER TODAY

and receive:
Release News
Free Short Stories
a Free Starter Library

Do it today. Do it now.
www.mlbuchman.com/newsletter

www.ingramcontent.com/pod-product-compliance
Lightning Source LLC
Chambersburg PA
CBHW050559170726
48283CB00001B/27